Darksou

Anna Stephens has worked in a va...
years, the latest being in corporate communications for
an international law firm. She's currently living the
dream as a full-time writer and hopes never to have to
get a proper job again.

Anna loves all things speculative and horrifying, from
books to film to TV, and is a second Dan black belt in
Shotokan Karate, as well as a keen weightlifter and
beginner swordfighter.

You can follow her on:
Twitter @AnnaSmithWrites
or www.anna-stephens.com

By Anna Stephens

Godblind

DARKSOUL

ANNA STEPHENS

HARPER
Voyager

Harper*Voyager*
An imprint of HarperCollins*Publishers* Ltd
1 London Bridge Street
London SE1 9GF

www.harpercollins.co.uk

First published by HarperCollins*Publishers* 2018

This paperback edition 2019
1

A catalogue record for this book is available from the British Library

ISBN: 978-0-00-821597-2

Typeset in Sabon LT Std by Palimpsest Book Production Limited,
Falkirk, Stirlingshire

Printed and bound in the UK by
CPI Group (UK) Ltd, Croydon CR0 4YY

MIX
Paper from
responsible sources
FSC™ C007454

For Mum, Dad, and Sam.
Thanks for letting me grow up weird.

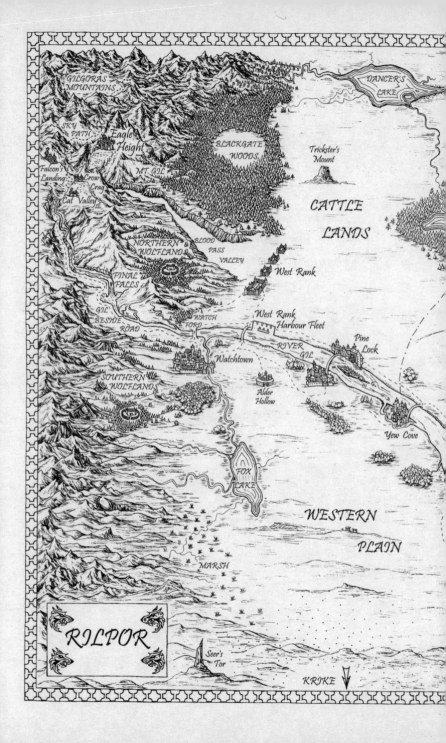

North
Rank

North Rank Harbour
Fleet

HORSE LANDS

N

W   E

S

Sailtown

THE TEARS

DEEP
FOREST

SILENT WATER

Three
Beeches

Maresfield

East Rank
Harbour
Fleet

East
Rank

GRAZING
LANDS

WHEAT
LANDS

North
Harbour

Shingle

Gate
House

Rilporin

LISTRE

King
Gate

DANCER'S
FINGERS

RIVER GIL

South
Rank Harbour
Fleet

South Harbour

South Rank

FOREST

DURDIL

The last length of yellowed, crusted bandage came away with a soft sucking sound, and the sickly-sweet, hideous scent of rot plumed into the air. Hallos's nose wrinkled; Durdil coughed hard and then snorted. It didn't clear the stink. On the opposite side of the bed, two of the priests faltered in their chanting, and then, halting, retching, caught up with the others.

Durdil peered over Hallos's shoulder. 'How . . .'

'How is he still alive? Gods only know,' Hallos grunted. He used a long silver spoon with a slim bowl to poke at the wound and Durdil was reminded, sickeningly, of eating a custard tart. He swallowed, tasting bile. 'The end's near though, Durdil. Very near.'

'And the enemy is clamouring at our gates,' Durdil fretted. 'I need to be on the wall. But . . . what if he wakes?'

Hallos jabbed the spoon against the neatly sutured, red and yellow, weeping flesh of Rastoth's chest. The dying man

1

moaned but did not stir. 'He's not waking up again, my friend,' he said softly. 'Not this side of the Light.'

He straightened and faced Durdil, and Durdil gritted his teeth against what he knew was coming. Again. 'He may be unconscious, but he's in unspeakable agony in there none-theless. It's time we eased his pain.'

'He's the king, Hallos. Ending his life would be regicide,' Durdil said, weariness taking the fervour from his words so they just came out defeated instead. The voice in the back of his head agreed with the physician, pointed out that if it was him, he'd be begging them to do it. He pushed it away and looked to the priests for aid, but the most senior, Erik, gave a slow nod of agreement even as he prayed. No help there.

Hallos's black eyebrows, flecked with grey these days, drew down and he touched Durdil's arm. 'It would be a mercy, Durdil. A mercy for your friend.' Durdil opened his mouth but Hallos held up a finger. 'Would you deny a soldier – an officer, even a prince – the grace on the field of battle? No. You'd end their agony and pray them into the Dancer's embrace. Rastoth was a soldier, campaigned for years to the south and the east. Fought the Krikites, fought the Listrans. Treat him as a soldier one last time. Do him that honour and let us gift him into the Light.'

At his words the priests shifted their chanting and Durdil recognised the song of mourning and of celebration of a life well lived. They were singing as though he was already dead and Durdil's last choice was taken from him.

His heart was breaking, had been breaking every hour of this endless, desperate siege. He was too tired to think clearly, too exhausted in body and mind to make any decision not immediately related to the preservation of the city for one more day. He had no idea what to do, why this decision had to fall to him. *I'm the Commander of the Ranks, not the arbiter of life and death for kings. Not my king, anyway. Not Rastoth.*

The king's face was ashen, except for the hectic spots of red caused by the fever. Black lines ran from the neat tear in his chest and the lips of the wound were red, angry, puckered, straining at their stitches as they swelled. Monstrous and on the point of bursting. Obscene, over-ripe fruit that wanted only a touch, a breath, to split and spill its horror.

Durdil had chewed his lip to ribbons since the siege began and winced as he bit at it now. He scrubbed a hand across the back of his head and down his neck. Erik nodded again when he looked to him for aid. Hallos was waiting, the plea clear on his lips and in his eyes. *Give him what he can't ask for himself. Help him, as you've helped him all your life. Serve him.*

'I'll tell the council he succumbed to his wound,' Durdil said eventually. 'They know it's inevitable, so we'll let them think it was a natural end. Otherwise, our noble Lords Lorca and Silais are likely stupid enough to accuse us of treason in the midst of this . . . mess.'

Each of the priests nodded and their voices swelled louder, urging Rastoth's spirit to begin breaking its anchors to his dying, rotting flesh.

'Opium?' Hallos murmured, selecting a small jar with a hand that didn't – and Durdil felt should – shake.

'You'll never get him to swallow it. Will you?'

Hallos's smile was weary and sad. 'There are things you will never know of my art, my old friend. Don't worry. Just . . . say your goodbyes, yes? We should do it quickly, now the decision has been made. We should spare him any more of this . . . this sham of life.'

Hallos stepped out of his way and Durdil looked again

at his king, his decades-long friend, lying still and pale against the pillows. Rastoth's breath came in tiny pants, clammy sweat glistening in the gloom. His hands were claws. From the open window came the sound of a dog-boy playing with a litter of puppies, uncaring of the dying king or besieged city.

Durdil fell to one knee by the bed, his armour clattering about his shoulders. 'Sire, forgive me,' he whispered, 'I should have protected you, kept you safe . . .' The man might be old and mad, but he was Durdil's king and Durdil's friend.

'I will save Rilporin, Rastoth. I will save our country and our gods, our people. All of it. I swear on my hope of reaching the Light. When we meet again, I . . .' He choked back a sob.

Hallos squeezed past him and an involuntary denial sprang to Durdil's lips, a hand reaching to stop the cup on its way to Rastoth's lips.

Erik rounded the bed and pulled him gently to his feet. 'Your last act for your king, Commander, should be the one that brings him peace,' he murmured. 'Don't interfere now. Pray.'

Durdil's lips began moving in prayer as the priests sang, as Hallos raised Rastoth's head with pillows and tipped small, patient sips of wine and opium into his mouth, massaging his throat until he swallowed. Rastoth's breathing slowed as the drug stole his pain, as it relaxed his limbs, as it took his mind far, far away from the ruin of his body and the ashes of his reign.

Durdil crowded close, found Rastoth's leg beneath the covers and rested his hand there. 'Marisa's waiting,' he said hoarsely. 'Marisa and Janis both. In the Light. Waiting for you. Tell her I said hello and . . . and ask her to forgive me. I failed you, all three of you. I'm sorry. I'm so sorry.'

4

Something that might have been a smile, or just the last twitch of dying muscles, crossed his face, and then Rastoth the Kind, Rastoth the Mad, exhaled a last, bubbling breath and died.

Durdil stared in silence at the council gathered in the war room, his fingers steepled before his lips. His eyes were red with fatigue and grief, and he'd delivered the news of Rastoth's death into a silence that was thick with alliances and churning with calculation. As expected, both Lords Lorca and Silais were clearly vying to win the majority of the council and be the next power in Rilporin. Perhaps even to sit on the throne.

'My lords, as grievous as this news is, I will not be releasing it to the populace or the Rank. Nor will we be flying the scarlet or declaring a week of official mourning, as is customary. We are at war, my lords, and as of now martial law is in effect. Those of us who live to see the siege's conclusion can carry out the funeral rites with all pomp and ceremony at that point. For now, we concern ourselves only with the fight.'

'This is preposterous; you have not the authority,' Lord Lorca began, his silver tongue momentarily losing its sheen. 'King Rastoth must be—'

'King Rastoth is dead. We the living have more important things to worry about than feasting his memory or arguing about interim governments. The state of the wall, for instance. The enemy's trebuchets have been loosing at it for days now. The Stonemasons' Guild is inspecting it daily for weaknesses. I've asked them to—'

'You do not ask the stonemasons anything,' Silais muttered, 'not if you want them to actually do anything. You order them. Order, I say.'

'Thank you for your opinion, Lord Silais, but they're working ceaselessly and providing regular reports,' Durdil said. 'There is little more I, or they, can do than that. I have also spoken with the pigeon-master, and it appears that while he was in the city, Prince Rivil—'

'King Rivil, surely,' a voice said. Durdil glanced at Questrel Chamberlain. The man simpered and smoothed down his oiled hair. 'By right and blood, my lords, Commander, the prince is now our king. Surely we should address him as such.'

A babble rose among the nobles, ermine flying as they gesticulated, the volume increasing, the tone becoming angry, strident. Durdil steepled his hands again and leant back in his chair, waiting, the sound of arguing noblemen washing over him.

It got louder before it got quieter, but eventually more and more councillors noticed Durdil was taking no part in the debate. They loathed him to a man, but he was Commander of the Ranks and led the defence. The decision, ultimately, was his. Either he opened the gates to Rivil, proclaiming him king . . . or he didn't, proclaiming them all traitors to the throne.

A fine choice. I cannot wait to make it.

Durdil waited until there was silence, and then he waited a few moments longer until they were squirming.

'My lords, Prince Rivil attempted regicide. Before that he was implicated in his own mother's murder and converted to the bloodthirsty faith of our ancient enemies by way of killing his brother, the rightful heir to the throne. There is no man more unfit to rule our great country than he. As I began to say, the pigeon-master confirms that all birds trained to fly to Highcrop in Listre, the home of the only surviving – and distant – member of the line of succession, were killed by Rivil or the Lord Galtas Morellis. We cannot inform Lord

Tresh that Rastoth has fallen, that Rivil is cast out of the succession. Once this siege is lifted, however, I will send an emissary to his lordship with all haste, informing him that he is now our king.'

'Tresh? Never heard of 'im,' a voice muttered.

'Not even a full blood,' another whispered. 'More Listran than Rilporian. Listran, I ask you!'

'Tresh is a bastard, isn't he?'

'King Tresh,' Durdil snapped, his temper wearing ever thinner, 'is by all accounts a studious man and astute judge of character. He will make a fine king, especially with a council such as this to advise him.'

To hinder him, to kiss his arse and bleed him dry and blind him to all but their wants, their needs, their desires. If only the gods would allow me to put every last bloody one of them in the catapult baskets and send them out to meet their foes.

Durdil bit down on a smile as he imagined the long, drawn-out wail of outrage Lorca would make as he flew skyward. *Please, Dancer, just one.*

'Until then, my lords, we remain at war. And martial law is the order of the day.'

'I support your proposal,' Lorca said, though they both knew it was no such thing. 'Take steps to curb the unruly peasantry even now hoarding food from their betters and breathe new strength into our men. A good thing, too. Some of them flag already.'

Already? They've been defending this city for over a fort-night. They've done more for Rilporin and its people in that time than you have in your entire life. They spend their lives like coppers, without thought, and they do it for the city and the king. They do it, gods love them, for me. And I have to order them to . . . calm, Durdil. Calm.

7

Durdil found that his grief and his fatigue combined to make a heady, dangerous, short-tempered brew. He raised his fist to his mouth and bit the knuckle hard, focusing on the pain as the muttering swelled anew.

'If that is all, my lords, I have a wall to defend,' he barked, screeching his chair back over the flagstones and cutting the conversation dead.

The council rose and paused; normally this was when they'd bow to the king. A couple dipped their heads in an awkward half-salute. Lorca's pale eyes studied Durdil for a moment too long, and then he swept from the war room with his cronies hurrying after him.

Silais remained seated, inspecting his perfect fingernails until Lorca had cleared the doorway. It just wouldn't do for him to be held up by the man. Durdil resisted the urge to spit on the table and stalked from the room, Hallos trailing miserably behind him and Major Vaunt bringing up the rear. In the days since the siege had begun, the hour in the war room was the only time most of his officers got away from the wall or the barracks or the hospital. Durdil had taken to rotating the privilege between them so that each of them had the excuse for a bath and a change of clothes every few days.

And aren't they already seeing it as a luxury, he thought. *How quickly the unbearable becomes normal. And now I have to tell my officers that Rastoth is dead and to keep it secret.*

And there's still no word from the North Rank. Where the bloody fuck are my reinforcements?

GALTAS

'The siege progresses as expected, Sire.' Galtas handed him the distance-viewer and waited while he scanned the wall, the men scurrying across its top and around its base like ants. 'We are making good progress.'

'Are we?' Rivil turned a sour look on him, slapping the viewer in the palm of his hand and no doubt shaking the lenses out of alignment. 'Are we really? Does it feel like that to you? Because it feels to me like we've been sitting on our arses for three weeks while our men attempt the wall and fail. Over and shitting over again.'

'The siege towers are making a difference now,' Galtas began, 'and the trebuchets are definitely having an effect. You can see the defacement of the wall to our left of the gatehouse.'

'Having an effect. *Defacement*,' Rivil sneered. 'You realise we're destroying my fucking city in order to conquer it, don't you? Or at least, we're attempting to.' He threw up his hands. 'Why did I ever let you talk me into this mad scheme?'

9

Because you didn't have a plan and your military mind consists of how many wagonloads of luxuries you can take on campaign rather than soldiers or weapons. Because you're a spoilt little shit who's never done a day's work in your life and couldn't plan a siege if your life depended on it. Oh wait, it does.

So does mine.

'General Skerris approaches,' Galtas said instead of voicing any of the thoughts hurtling around his brain.

The fat general of the East Rank wobbled to attention and saluted. 'Prince Rivil, Lord Galtas,' Skerris wheezed, 'we're about ready for another push, if you'd like to give the order? The Mireces are readying their new tower after the . . . mishap with the first. Trebuchets will keep up the bombardment until the troops are within range, then cease fire to avoid casualties. Our target is Second Last—' he pointed a fat finger at Second Tower and Last Bastion, the section of wall to their left of the gatehouse. 'The Mireces will assault Double First.' He indicated First Bastion and First Tower to their right.

Skerris's words conjured a vivid image of the Mireces' first siege tower bright with flame as the defenders' fire arrows lodged in the unprotected wood. It'd burnt fast and hard, killing several of the Raiders inside it. *A fucking shambles.*

'Defenders'll have to split their forces again. If we can establish a decent bridgehead this time . . .' Skerris trailed off as Rivil's scowl returned.

'How many men have we lost so far?' he snapped.

'Some hundreds, Sire.'

'It's too slow, Skerris. All of this is too slow. We might have destroyed the West and North Ranks, but that incompetence at the harbour two weeks ago allowed fucking thousands of South Rankers into the city to reinforce the defenders. What if they've sent for the rest?'

'Sire, we are doing all that we can. Progress is steady. Yesterday we held a bridgehead for the better part of three hours,' Skerris added.

'What do you want, a fucking medal?' Rivil shouted. 'We're running out of artillery for the trebs and a bridgehead is not a bridgehead unless it accomplishes something other than the deaths of our men.'

'Standard divide and conquer, Sire, and the same tactics will apply if the remainder of the South Rank does come. It may not look like it, but we're doing well. We're winning.'

It was probably the worst thing Skerris could have said. Rivil's face purpled and saliva flew. 'Winning? Does this look like fucking winning to you, fat man? We're living in tents and shitting in fields while they live off the provisions of an entire city. They have *months* of supplies in there, hospitals, armouries, inns and cooks and clean clothes . . .'

Rivil stopped talking, and neither Galtas nor Skerris moved to fill the silence. Rivil's temper had been shortening by the hour this last week. He faced the city again just as the lead trebuchet unloaded its stone at the wall. The ground in front was littered with spent boulders and giant slabs of rock that had been cracked off the outer face, all of which further hindered the ladder teams and siege towers.

'Skerris, send the men, ours and the Mireces. Full assault. Galtas, you're going with them.'

Galtas sputtered a laugh. Go into the city? As part of a ladder assault? 'Sire, I'm not Rank-trained. I'll be too slow up the ladder. I could better serve—'

'The gods will watch over you,' Rivil interrupted. 'So you need not be afraid. If the Mireces have the balls for it, I'm sure you do too. I want you in Rilporin and I want definitive proof that my father is dead. These bastards are too motivated for my liking; the king clinging to life might be enough

11

for them. Then I want you to do something to get us in, either frontal assault or a quiet infiltration. Either will suit.'

'Do something?' Galtas echoed. 'Such as?'

Rivil snarled at him: 'Improvise.'

Galtas's face was wooden, unresponsive, but he managed a bow and plastered an insincere smile across his mouth. 'As you command, Sire,' he said stiffly. 'I'll see to the orders immediately. General, shall we?'

He stalked across the field towards the half of the Third Thousand whose turn it was to die today, his ears straining behind him for Rivil's voice telling him he was joking. It didn't come. Galtas would be running up the inside of a siege tower and out across a gangplank on to the wall while archers loosed shaft after shaft at him, or he'd be scaling a ladder along with the Rankers, up into enemy territory with arrows, rocks and boiling oil being poured down on his head, to roll on to the allure and face a thousand defenders.

Galtas was going to die.

'His Highness is getting a little fractious, eh, milord?' Skerris said as they marched towards the assault teams. On his right, Galtas could see a swarming mass of blue-clad Mireces readying themselves, their second siege tower, this one covered in fire-proof animal skins, already rumbling towards the wall.

'Fractious?' Galtas said, and then bit down on his response and chose other, less volatile, words. 'He chafes at the delay. He is of course too valuable to risk at the wall, and so there is little he can do until we have forced an entry. He wishes to fight alongside his men, to lead them in battle.'

Galtas suspected Rivil wanted no such bloody thing, but he couldn't exactly put forward his theory that Rivil just wanted the big chair and the shiny crown and someone else to do all the actual governing for him.

'If it is the Lady's will, he will get that chance,' Skerris rumbled. 'As for you, what's your preference? Tower or ladder?'

'I suppose a quiet way in through a gate is out of the question?' Galtas quipped and Skerris laughed, slapped him on the back and knocked him off balance. 'I would value your opinion on this one. Which is more likely to get me killed? And of course, there's the matter of my disguise for once I'm in the city.'

'Disguise?'

Galtas tapped his arm, the blue of his shirt visible between the half-sleeve of his mail and the thick leather vambrace. 'Not sure I'll get access to the king's quarters or anywhere else dressed like this.'

'What did you have in mind?'

'I'll need the shirt off one of your corpses,' Galtas said. 'Clean, preferably.'

Skerris nodded slowly. 'I understand. As for the way in, if you're quick and the gods love you, the ladder's your friend.'

I suspect the ladder's my death, Galtas thought sourly. *Still. The Lady's will.*

THE BLESSED ONE

There was a crackle to the air, and the fine hairs on the nape of Lanta's neck and along her forearms stood erect. The gods were so close now, ever-present, like the scent of a lover on skin. She didn't need to be in a sacred space to hear Them now; Their voices were everywhere and Their commands were simple: take the city, slaughter the inhabitants, burn the temples. Kill or convert, but leave no one alive who held the Dancer and the Fox God in their hearts.

Commands that filled Lanta with joy and holy fire. There would be thousands for sacrifice once the city fell, thousands whose blood would wet earth dedicated to the Dark Lady and Gosfath, God of Blood.

'Your will, Red Ones. All this to your glory, all this in your names. Rilporin will fall and your children will rise in its place. Gilgoras will be yours.' Lanta knelt in the grass of a spring morning, surrounded by the stink of thousands of warriors waiting their turn to fight and die.

No cave-temple rock walls lit with fire watched her prayers, no cold stone dug into her knees, witness to her ritual pain. Lanta knelt in the light of the world and the gods were there with her, in a country from which They'd been forced a millennium before. A shiver ran across her skin. They were under the same sun as her, no longer separated by an impenetrable veil but merely its tattered remnants. Gilgoras trembled beneath Their presence and Their vengeance would be terrible and beautiful in its glory.

She waited, but the Dark Lady did not summon her. Lanta's disappointment was keen but she could understand the gods' delight in being back in Gilgoras, free to roam Rilpor, Listre and Krike and visit those pockets of true believers that Lanta was convinced must still exist. The gods would speak when They needed to. They came when They chose, not when Lanta wished it. A lesson hard learned many years before. Until then, the children of the Dark Path knew what they had to do.

The Blessed One finished praying and eased herself to her feet, the sun warm on her scalp and the breeze gentle across her cheek. The gods may not have spoken, but still They hovered close, Their bloody wings outstretched across the army, shrouding it in divine right. Victory was promised, and Lanta would pay any price to ensure it was so. Pay it gladly, gleefully, secure in her righteousness.

She gazed at the city, and then around the vast expanse of the Wheat Lands. They called this place the bread basket of Rilpor, and this year those crops that hadn't been trampled into the mud would feed Mireces bellies. More wheat than she'd ever seen. More crops, more grass, more flat farming land than Lanta had believed existed stretched around them and the city nestled in the embrace of Rilpor's mighty rivers. All theirs soon enough.

'As the gods will.' Lanta sighed and looked back at the city again, grey walls looming over the plain like a storm front, scarred and battered and still imperious, intact and mocking their efforts. She brushed grass and flakes of dirt from her skirt. Of all she had expected of the holy war, the possibility that the siege would be boring hadn't occurred to her. But the days had stretched, one into another, with no significant gains and more than a few losses.

Lanta's thoughts strayed to Eagle Height and the women and children waiting in the snow and rock of the mountains. The snowmelt would be flooding down the narrow channels carved into the rock now, taking the unwary, driving carcasses, branches and stones before it, leaving the land behind cleansed. The slaves would be planting their own poor crops now, carrots and turnips in the hard ground, coaxing them to life with goat manure and prayers. Pask would sacrifice a man for their victory, and a woman that the crops would not fail, that there would be no late storms.

Eagle Height – home. She sighed, staring around the camp filled with the chatter of Mireces. It would be good to summon the women, children and priests after they had secured victory, to send them into the towns and villages like a sacred flood, driving all before them who would not live beneath their rule. Rilpor would become Mireces, and Rilporians would become their slaves. Once the city fell and the Flower-Whore and Her bastard Trickster son were dead, there was nothing they could not do.

Once the city fell. Lanta's smile was grim. So much work still to do, even once all Rilpor was theirs.

'What did you learn?'

The words startled her and Lanta returned to her surroundings. She faced Gilda and sneered. 'Many things,' she said, 'things you would not understand, lost in your petty delusion that life is anything other than brutal and full of pain. You fail to see how, in accepting those things to honour our gods, that we become stronger.'

Gilda folded her hands over her stomach and gazed into the sky for a while. 'You're right,' she said eventually, her eyes twinkling as they met Lanta's, 'there's little I understand about your religion, about why you would choose a life of fear and an eternity of pain over a world of life and light and beauty and an afterlife of joy and oneness. Because life is hard, aye, but it isn't brutal. Brutal's what we do to each other. Hard is what the seasons do to us. But I meant, did you learn anything about the siege? Been going a while now, hasn't it?'

'I would not tell you if I did,' Lanta snapped. 'That is between the king, Rivil, myself and the gods.'

Gilda's mouth quirked. 'Oh,' she said quietly, 'you said "if I did". So you didn't, then. Learn anything. Gods not chatty today?'

Lanta's fists clenched. 'Don't push me, old woman,' she snapped, gathering up the chain attached to Gilda's slave collar and jerking her forward. 'There's little reason for me to keep you around any more. Your sacrifice may speed along the siege and bring our victory that much sooner.'

Gilda grabbed her chain and tugged in turn, pulling Lanta a step closer to her. Lanta's free hand dropped to her knife. 'Then why don't you?' Gilda hissed. 'Instead of the endless threats? Why don't you just do it? I tire of your company, and frankly this camp stinks of shit. Do you people have no idea how to dig a latrine pit?'

Lanta pulled her knife. 'Do you want those to be your last words?' she snarled, pressing the knife to Gilda's stomach.

Gilda laughed, loud and genuine. 'Latrine pit,' she repeated and broke into fresh giggles. 'Why not? It'll be something to tell my family when I see them in the Light.'

Lanta dug the tip of the knife in hard and Gilda's amusement vanished like tears in a lake. 'When you're sacrificed, old woman, it won't be the Light you go to, oh no. Sacrifice sends you somewhere very different. Sends you to the Afterworld, to the Red Gods and all Their faithful children. And when they learn what you are there, they'll spend eternity tearing you to pieces. And you'll feel it. You'll feel everything. You'll die a thousand times a day, every day, forever.'

There was sweat on Gilda's forehead and she pulled hard on the chain to make some space between them. 'That doesn't sound like fun,' she managed, but the fire was gone from her voice. 'But that's where you'll go too, isn't it? Why would you condemn yourself to that?'

Lanta scoffed and, letting her step back, sheathed her knife. 'That's not my fate. I will sit with the other Blessed Ones and enjoy the company of my gods. I will watch while the dead are given everything they were promised the Afterworld would provide – endless food, endless scores to settle, endless enemies to kill. They will run and kill and die and fuck in the bloody grass of the Afterworld for eternity. And you will be their favourite toy.'

Gilda licked her lips. 'I see. Well, when you do get around to killing me, remind me to change my last words, will you? I think "Fuck you, cunt" has a better ring to it and, by all accounts, I'll get to shout it at you on a daily basis forevermore. Wonder how many centuries it'll take before it drives you mad.' That insufferable grin returned. 'I look forward to ruining your afterlife.'

Lanta's lips drew back from her teeth, but before she could respond they were interrupted. Skerris, Corvus and Rivil walked along the invisible line that marked safe distance from the small catapults poking out at them from the four towers and the top of the gatehouse interrupting Rilporin's great western wall.

'You said the North Rank had been dealt with,' Corvus said, a scowl marring his brow. Lanta moved closer, Gilda clanking along behind her like a reluctant puppy on a rope.

'We acted to neutralise the North before leaving the forts to come here, yes,' Skerris said. 'I've faith in the scheme, Sire, but we've had no confirmation as yet that it was successful, though every day they don't march over the horizon strengthens my conviction we dealt them a fatal blow. It's possible the rest of the South Rank may come, and if so, combined with the defenders, they'll very nearly match us in number. We propose that in such an event we would face the South on the field while your warriors ensured the city stays locked tighter than a miser's purse. Keep the forces separate, crush them separately.'

'If that day comes, General, we will do as you suggest,' Corvus said. 'But I hope to end this before then. I've men ready for the day's push.'

'As do I,' Rivil said. 'Shall we do as before? You take Double First and we'll assault Second Last? My man Galtas will be going with them this time. He's orders to infiltrate the palace and see what intelligence he can gather. He will attempt to sabotage one of the harbour gates.' He gestured to either end of the wall. 'You've seen that they're secured behind the stump walls that stick out from the towers all the way to the water, but if he gets one open, wet feet or arrow volleys won't stop us. We're days away from victory; I can feel it.'

'The Lady's will,' Lanta said and the men bobbed their heads. 'Victory will come when the gods decide. Continue to play your parts in Their honour, and that victory may be soon. I will pray the assault is successful.'

Corvus came to a halt and faced the Rilporians. 'Say we did take Rilporin before reinforcements arrive. What then? We end up being the ones besieged. Trapped inside a city we at least don't know while its citizens and any surviving Palace Rankers use every building and alley as an ambush site to pick us off while the South Rank assaults the walls. You weren't in Watchtown, Rivil, you don't know how they used the very streets against us. We'd be massacred. Why not face them on the field, destroy them out here? I say we march out of Rilporin when the South is sighted, face them in open battle.'

Lanta understood his caution and shared his concern. The Rilporians were supremely confident in their forces, while the Mireces didn't know the city and were far slower on the scaling ladders. The firing of their siege tower was an embarrassment and the second, while built, was lighter and less sturdy. Who knew what damage a direct strike from one of the tower catapults would cause. *Though at least this one is fire-proof.*

Corvus looked around the group, his face thoughtful. 'The more I think about this, the more I wonder if we need to take it? Is conquering Rilporin our only option?'

'What other choices are there?' Rivil asked, spreading his hands in confusion. 'What do you propose, that we destroy it?'

He laughed; Corvus didn't and Lanta saw the path of his thinking stretching before them. *We burnt Watchtown and killed the survivors. The gods have told us to cleanse the country of heathens. Why should we bother to take this city if we can achieve our ends with its destruction?*

Excitement flared in her belly and Gilda's chain rattled as she squeezed it. Skerris and Rivil were staring at them both with identical expressions of horrified disbelief.

'Wait, you can't be serious?' Rivil demanded, his voice strident. 'That's my city, my fucking capital city and my home, the seat of my kingship. I won't have you burn it to the ground and slaughter its inhabitants just because the cock-up at Watchtown has made you cowards—'

'Prince Rivil,' Lanta snapped in a tone as smooth as ice and just as chilly, faster even than Corvus's hand went to his knife hilt, 'we Mireces fear only the gods, as is right and proper. Your countrymen are nothing to us but meat to be ground under our heels. Moreover, we have been fighting, killing and dying for centuries in the names of the gods and we will do anything, anything They command to see Them return to Gilgoras as They deserve. You, meanwhile, have been a convert for a mere handful of years, your soldiers for a matter of weeks. Do not dare speak to us of cowardice, or of not doing all the gods require. You have done nothing but make demands of Them since you first stepped on to the Path. You should be wary lest the Dark Lady's patience expire.'

Rivil flushed an angry red, but Skerris's stony glare warned him to mind his tongue. 'You are as wise as you are lovely, and I apologise for my hasty words,' Rivil responded with clear effort. 'It . . . galls me to think that Rilporin may have to be sacrificed for the glory of the gods.'

'Nothing that is to the gods' glory should be galling,' Corvus put in. Behind her, Lanta heard Gilda snort and mutter something beneath her breath.

'It is King Corvus you should apologise to,' Lanta said and Rivil's lip twitched. 'It is his courage you have doubted, despite the fact that he himself fought in Watchtown while, so far, you have yet to set foot on the field.'

Rivil's flush this time was even more pronounced, and Lanta took a brief pleasure in it, though she knew she played a dangerous game. It was not wise to taunt their allies; and, despite her words, victory was far from assured. If Rivil turned on them, or abstained from battle, they could still lose all.

'King Corvus, my apologies,' the prince grated. 'The slowness of the siege wears upon me. But I will not see Rilporin razed to the ground unless there is no other possible route to victory. I will explore all those routes before I agree to such a scheme. Rilporin is mine, the throne is mine, and the gods will see me take my place upon it before long.'

Lanta bit the tip of her tongue to prevent her lips curling in disgust. *You are a mewling boy spouting words you cannot understand. I was born into the gods' bloody embrace, my soul wedded to the Dark Path before you first soiled your linens. And yet you presume to know Their will, Their desires for you? You have no humility, Prince, and you will be shown no mercy in consequence, in this world and the next.*

'If we did destroy Rilporin,' Skerris said, to Rivil's clear disgust, 'then it would leave us without options if the South Rank comes. Capturing the city gives us power to negotiate, walls to shield our wounded, our holy.' He gestured at Lanta. 'Without Rilporin, we must fight, must win, on the very day the enemy arrives.'

'We talk in circles,' Corvus said, waving his hand and dismissing Skerris's words, 'and about things we cannot yet control. I have a third of the men from Cat Valley ready to assault the wall, with more held in reserve should the first wave be successful. The sun is not yet high; we have a whole day's killing still to come. Let's get on with it.'

Rivil opened his mouth but Skerris cut in, smooth and oblivious as though he didn't know his prince was about to speak. 'At once, Your Majesty. Sire, the Third Thousand is ready, as is Lord Morellis. With your permission?'

'Yes, yes, send them in. Let's hope they make a bloody dent in the enemy this time, eh?' Rivil folded his arms and stood beside Corvus, affecting boredom as though the outcome meant nothing to him, while the two forces reacted to flag and drum and began to move, siege towers rumbling across the plain, assault teams carrying long, flexible scaling ladders scurrying behind them, trying to keep under cover as long as possible.

They picked up speed, only slowing as they wended their way through the debris at the base of the wall, until finally they splashed against the stone and began to climb.

'My feet are on the Path,' Lanta murmured. At her side, Gilda let out a noisy yawn and scuffed a foot in the grass.

'What's for lunch?' she asked. Lanta gritted her teeth.

DURDIL

He had three thousand men of the Palace Rank and the two Thousands he'd summoned from the South Rank, who'd arrived five days after the siege began and fought their way into the city from the River Gil. Five fucking thousand, or at least that's what the numbers on the books said. Hundreds fewer now, and more wounded every day. Five thousand soldiers and more than double that in frantic civilians, a hundredth in hysterical nobles of every stripe, and a fifth in City Watch whose only skill was clubbing drunks and collecting taxes.

Durdil liked numbers to be neat and easily divisible, but right now he'd have settled for any number that had several zeros at the end of it and every one of them friendly, well armed and fucking lethal.

His face was neutral as he stood on the roof of the gatehouse with his hands resting on the waist-high wall. They'd forced back the latest assault after hours of close, bloody

24

fighting, the Easterners and Mireces establishing multiple bridgeheads around their siege towers and ladders. Durdil's arms and shoulders ached from wielding sword and knife, spear and shield. His voice was little more than a croak these days, and he was drinking honeyed water to try and restore its vigour.

Three weeks of frontal assaults, of ladders and siege towers and those godsdamned never-ending trebuchets sending rocks against the wall.

Three weeks and still no North Rank.

Perhaps there's unrest on the border. Perhaps word's reached Listre of our situation and the Dead Legion's pushing into our lands, using our distraction against us. If the Legion can summon enough numbers, General Tariq won't risk leaving the northern border open . . .

We're on our own.

Durdil watched two men help a third into the stairwell, no doubt headed to the nearest hospital. It sparked a memory and he sighed, added checking on the numbers of wounded to the bottomless list of things he needed to do today. So many demands on his time, from appointing a new major into dead Wheeler's position to combating the food hoarding, managing the production of replacement arms, and navigating the bloody council of bloody nobles and their endless, bloody stupid demands.

A figure erupted out of the stairwell leading down into the gatehouse and shouldered men aside, clouds of dust drifting from his beard and his enormous shoulders. Renik and Vaunt, Durdil's surviving majors, spun to face him, hands on sword hilts, squinting up at the giant.

'Commander Koridam, sir? Commander, it's me, Merle Stonemason,' the huge man said, in case anyone could mistake him for someone who didn't haul blocks of stone around all day. 'You got a problem, Commander. So we've all got a problem.'

'Merle Stonemason, what news then?' Durdil asked heavily. 'I do hope it's not a big problem. We've already got rather a lot of those.' Flippancy didn't work on Merle, or on Durdil for that matter, and a cold weight settled into his stomach as the honest brow of the stonemason crinkled.

'Me and a couple of the lads checked the wall this morning as per your orders, sir, like we done every morning. She's been taking more of a pounding than a two-copper whore since this siege began and . . .'

Durdil bit hard on the inside of his cheek. 'And?' he asked, straining for calm. He could feel sweat gathering at his hairline.

Merle stroked his beard, loosing a small drift of dust and stone chips to patter down his shirt. He brushed them away and shifted, uneasy. 'And like said lady of easy affections, the wall's well and truly fucked, Commander.'

Durdil went very still, blood tingling in every limb as something screamed at him to run, run anywhere, just away. 'Wall's what?' he croaked, resisting the urge to press a hand to the slowly tightening band around his chest. Now was really not the time for another heart twinge.

'We done some digging around, Commander, on the wall and in the guildhouse. Those repairs you ordered three years ago?' He pointed to Second Last, the end that the East Rank had been bombarding ever since they'd arrived. Durdil nodded, dumb.

'Didn't happen. Oh, they did some superficial work down past Second Tower just to make it look like everything was going to plan, but it's a veneer of good stone over rotten stone that should've been chipped out and replaced. You weaken that wall enough, it's coming down, sir. Ain't nothing there to stop it. And . . .' He paused, awkward, and Durdil's chest tightened a little more, 'far as we can tell from the paperwork, well, the order to make good rather than mend come from the palace, sir.'

Durdil inhaled through his nostrils with a squeak. His majors were silent statues of denial. It was testament to Durdil's desperation that he got hold of Merle with one hand and dragged him to the outer edge of the wall, the huge man bobbing along behind him like a cork on a stream. Durdil leant between two merlons and jerked a finger across and downwards.

'You telling me this wall will crumble? When? How long can it stand?'

Merle didn't protest being manhandled, probably too surprised someone had managed it to take umbrage. 'Gatehouse is always the weakest point, Commander, on account of the huge fucking tunnel cut through it. But having walked the length of this wall this morning, and done what tests I can without alerting suspicion, I can tell you the section between Second Tower and Last Bastion is just as weak, where the repairs were supposed to get done and weren't. She ain't cracking yet, but when she does . . .'

'They knew this,' Durdil hissed, pointing at the trebuchets and the army behind them. 'Rivil and that one-eyed shit Galtas knew those repairs hadn't been made. Have they really been planning this for three years?'

'Couldn't say, Commander,' Merle said as though the question hadn't been rhetorical. Together they watched as one of the trebuchets unwound and unleashed a rock the size of a carthorse. It tumbled end over end towards the wall between Second Tower and Last Bastion, smashing into the stone with a jarring impact they could feel from the gatehouse. Merle leant dangerously far out over the wall and squinted along its length, as though he could see the damage from here.

Then he stood back and rubbed his palms hissing together. He smelt of smashed rock and sweat. 'If they're not stopped, Commander, and emergency repairs aren't made, I reckon they could get through there in a few more weeks. Same with the gatehouse, if they put their minds to it.'

'I'm not liking this conversation, Merle,' Durdil said, amazed at the steadiness of his voice. Bile coated his teeth.

'Me neither, sir,' the big man said, 'but them's the facts.'

Major Renik was pale as snow and clutching at the healing wound in his side as though Merle's words had reopened it. Major Vaunt had turned to a pair of runners and sent them for Durdil's colonels, Yarrow and Edris.

Three weeks to full breach and no reinforcements. Nothing from Mace and the West Rank, nothing from Tariq in the north.

Three weeks until there're Mireces and heathens killing door to door and raping anything that moves.

Durdil bit down on the surge of nausea, sucked in air and tried to think. Merle was watching him with much the same expression as an ox facing the poleaxe. Durdil wanted to punch the merlons but knew it'd not only hurt his knuckles but, if Merle was to be believed, might actually bring the bloody wall down.

'How many good masons do you have, Merle?' he asked, working hard at maintaining a neutral tone.

'Eight.'

'Is that enough?'

'For what I think you're suggesting? No. But I can muster a dozen skilled apprentices for the carrying and the labour once we've chipped out the worst stone. O'course, we're weakening the wall further by doing that. You need to get those trebuchets off us for a day at the least. Mortar'll take time to set. Day and night'd be preferable, two days and a night ideal.'

'Impossible,' Vaunt murmured, 'not unless we send a suicide mission out there in the middle of the night to disable the engines.'

'Right now, there isn't an idea I'm not prepared to consider, suicide missions included,' Durdil snapped.

Colonels Edris and Yarrow appeared on the top of the gatehouse and Renik moved towards them, speaking quickly and quietly, giving them the latest. Both men swore and then crowded close to Durdil to listen.

'Get your masons and get on it. I want the stone ready and waiting to be put in as soon as the old stuff is removed. But I don't want you doing that until you hear from me.' Durdil glanced past Merle at his officers. They nodded, grim-faced. 'I can guarantee each one of the masons a lordship and ten gold kings to the apprentices if the wall holds,' Durdil added, wondering if he could.

Merle looked affronted. 'I don't want so much as a copper knight, let alone a gold king or a lordship, Commander,' he protested, waving hands like hams in the air between them. 'You can have my skill and my time and my sweat for nothing more than food and drink to keep me working. And I can say the same for maybe half my men. The rest, well, best keep that coin to hand. I won't mention the lordships and my advice is you don't either. We've seen enough poor nobles lurking around the palace that a title don't hold as much enchantment as gold. For me, though, my promise is good. Feed me and keep me in water and weak ale and I'll see you well reimbursed.'

Durdil did a mental adjustment of the man before him and swallowed the sudden lump in his throat. *Greatest city in the world, they say,* he thought as he resisted the urge to throw his arms around the massive mason.

'Forgive me, Stonemason, I didn't mean to impugn your honour. These are . . . trying times. For now, send me numbers of how many men you need to cut, dress or transport stone, and what help the Watch and the citizenry can be in this matter. I'm afraid we won't be able to spare you any soldiers.'

'Send them to me,' Yarrow interrupted, 'Second Last is my command. I'll see it done, sir.'

Durdil nodded and felt the smallest easing of tension. Someone else to share the burden. Thank the gods he'd invested so much time in training his subordinates, in insisting that the best men be stationed in the city to guard the king.

Not that that had saved him.

Merle clapped his hands. 'Strong backs and uncomplaining natures would be most welcome. At least three score to get us moving at speed.'

'I'll get them to the guildhouse by dusk, Stonemason,' Yarrow said, saluted and disappeared.

'And the gatehouse?' Durdil asked as Merle began to edge towards the stairs after him. 'What can we do with that?'

'Bar and prop the gates, pile rubble against the inside face of the wall that can be shovelled into the tunnel to seal it. They look like they're getting through the portcullis at that end, you do seal it. And then pray.'

'Thank you, Merle. We'll all be doing that, I think,' Durdil said. 'I'll be here or at the palace until this siege is defeated. You'll always be able to find me.'

Merle nodded and squeezed back into the stairwell. There was distant thunder as three trebuchets unwound and, seconds later, the whine of stone moving at great speed and the triple shattering boom of impact. Durdil clutched at the wall, not sure if he could feel it swaying or whether his panicked imagination had taken over his senses. Didn't appear to be any casualties along Second Last, though, and he breathed a quick prayer of thanks.

'Sir, should we cut the rope to the portcullis? Don't want them pushing the gate up and engaging the mechanism. It'll lift straight up and let them into the tunnel and at the door.'

'No, or not yet anyway. Despite everything, I haven't given up hope that the North Rank is coming, despite the lack of communication. Perhaps even my son and the West. If they are, we'll need to support them on the field. That means exiting through the gatehouse at the double to help crush these bastards. So no cutting ropes or sealing tunnels for now.'

'I hope you're right, sir,' Vaunt said a little unsteadily and Durdil realised how young he was.

He slapped him on the back. 'This siege is going to be bloody, and it may be protracted, but we'll get there, Major. We have to.'

Colonel Edris forced a reassuring grin he clearly didn't feel. 'Damn right we will,' he added. There was a commotion on Double First and he saluted and then hurried back into the stairwell and along to his command.

'Commander Koridam?' a red-faced palace messenger panted to a stop before them.

An endless parade of bloody messengers, each with news direr than the last, he thought.

'Yes?'

'The council of nobles requests your presence, and that of your colonels, to discuss matters of state.'

Durdil blinked. 'Matters of state? You mean the war?'

'I was not privy to that information, sir,' the messenger said. 'If you could proceed with all urgency to the palace?'

'No. If this is not a military matter, I trust them to resolve it themselves. The only "matter of state" with which I am concerned is the survival of this city and victory. If they wish to discuss the progress of the siege, I will make time for them.'

'My orders were very specific, sir,' the man said, and now the flush was embarrassment and worry. 'You have been summoned specifically by Lord Silais and Lord Lorca.'

Ah yes, the sycophant and the snake. 'Unfortunately for the noble lords, my authority outweighs theirs in time of war,' Durdil said. 'Don't worry, you can say you did everything possible to force me to attend. Off you go. Vaunt, I'll be at the hospitals checking the wounded. Send a runner if they try another assault, will you? I want us reconvening on the first floor of the gatehouse at dusk.

'Are you still here?' he snapped to the messenger, who looked as unlucky as it was possible to get. Durdil didn't care. If Lorca and Silais weren't offering their immediate support for the siege – and he knew they wouldn't be – there was nothing they could be discussing that would possibly interest him.

Durdil's step was heavy as he descended the stairs, leaving the man open-mouthed behind him.

GALTAS

Fourth moon, afternoon, day twenty-two of the siege
Second Last, western wall, Rilporin, Wheat Lands

Galtas would never presume that he had the favour of the gods, as that was a sure way to have it removed, but the fact remained that he was at the base of the wall, alive and unhurt, while dozens of highly trained soldiers were screeching their way to becoming food for the crows.

He'd let the first three assaults proceed without him, and he'd watched them fail, the men annihilated for no gain, but there was only so long he could delay the inevitable and the fourth wave carried him along, helpless but for the paltry protection of his shield.

Skerris had given him the quick version of scaling a wall – be quick. Galtas needed to be up the ladder as fast as the man in front of him, or he'd not only hold up those below, but he'd create a gap in the line of shields hanging from each man's back and expose himself. As long as he stayed close, the shield of the man ahead of him would offer some protection from the arrows being loosed down the ladders.

If they stick with arrows. What if they use pitch and fire? Or boiling oil? Or fucking great rocks? What if they turn the stingers on us? Galtas wiped sweat from his eyebrows and sucked in a lungful of air, trying not to think about the portable catapults that shot arrows the size of horses. One of those down a ladder would skewer half a dozen men like a rabbit on a spit.

'The Lady's will,' he said, loud and firm. It steadied him as he crouched beneath his shield among the rubble, waiting his turn to sling it on his back and begin the climb. A few others echoed his words, but Galtas recognised them as true believers. None of the forced converts uttered a word – the Dancer wasn't listening any more and they refused to ask the Red Gods for aid. Bereft in the midst of a fucking battle-field while death rained from the sky. Galtas shivered, glad that his faith was strong.

Behind him on the sward, East Rank archers crouched and loosed from the paltry protection of moveable wicker barricades, aiming at the men at the top of the wall. Galtas didn't look up, not wanting to see how many arrows were low, bouncing off the wall around the ladders, as much a danger to their comrades as the enemy was.

The line was moving fast. Galtas glanced behind him and by the time he looked back, a dozen men were on the ladder and there was a gap opening in front of him.

'Shit,' he grunted, stood and slung his shield on to his back, leapt forward and on to the first rung of the ladder. He climbed fast, hands slipping on rungs muddy from the boots of those who'd already ascended. A man fell screaming past him and Galtas fought the urge to freeze and cling to the ladder, forced his hands and legs to keep moving, keep climbing, the man in front of him getting further away with every second.

Galtas's boot skidded on the rung and he stumbled, his foot flailing and catching the shoulder of the man below. The soldier grunted and swore at him, told him to hurry the fuck up or they were all dead, and an arrow whined past Galtas's nose to emphasise his point. Galtas yelped and started climbing again, as fast as he could, breath whistling in his lungs and thighs burning. The noise of fighting and shouting got louder the higher he climbed, and then the ladder shuddered and slipped sideways, halted, and then slipped again. He chanced a look up – there was no one on the ladder above him, and there was no one defending its head. Four men in Palace Rank uniforms strained to push it away from the wall.

The men below him were still climbing, pushing at him, threatening to tip him off if he didn't move. *Everyone who went up here before me is dead. They're just waiting for my head to rise over the parapet and they'll cut it off. This is stupid.*

Galtas looked down. 'Stop,' he yelled, 'stop climbing. Retreat.'

'Climb, you fucking coward,' the soldier below him yelled. The man shoved at his leg, punched his calf. 'Move or die, cunt.' Galtas moved, starting the climb again. There was nothing else he could do, and the gods would protect him or call him to Their side if it was his time to die.

Please don't let it be my time to die.

The ladder lurched again and Galtas saw himself falling, screaming, to the base of the wall, already littered with corpses and rocks and spent arrows. And then he was at the top of the ladder and he dropped his left shoulder fast so the shield swung from his back on to his arm. Galtas's fingers fumbled the straps and he nearly lost it, caught the rim and jabbed it in the face of the nearest soldier, poked him back spitting teeth and leapt through a crenel on to the allure, dragging at his sword. Less than a second later another soldier joined him, then another and another as the East Rank poured on to the wallwalk and fanned out into a bridgehead.

'Still alive,' he breathed as a knot of soldiers charged him. Galtas laughed and waded into the fight, sword silver on the down swing and red on the way back up. 'Still alive!' he screamed.

The ladder to his right was less successful; Palace Rankers shoved it away with long hooked poles. Men clung yelling to it as it swung in a slow, elegant arc away from the wall and past the vertical. A man at the top of the ladder flung himself desperately at the wall; he missed the top by a stride's length, slammed into the stone and slid all the way down.

The ladder picked up speed as it began its inevitable descent to the earth, and the screams of the soldiers faded with distance and were cut off on impact. But more men were climbing Galtas's ladder, flooding into the space behind him and pushing the front rank further in both directions along the wall. They were spreading, taking more wall, killing the defenders. They were fucking winning.

Galtas fought alongside the Rankers, no time to look up and out and across to see how the Mireces fared, no breath in him to care one way or the other. It'd be the Rank that won this; everyone knew it. The Mireces were little more than bodies to throw on to metal, the sheer weight of numbers rather than skill securing any victory they might win.

He was closer to Second Tower than he was to the gate-house, which suited him well. Without seeming to, he allowed small gaps to form that the Easterners hurried into, no doubt thinking him some untrained idiot for threatening their tenuous hold on the wall. Slowly they drove for the tower and Galtas fell back into their midst. He'd need to be well protected in the seconds it'd take him to effect his disguise. Though of course, once he had, he was at as much risk of being killed by his own side as he was by the defenders.

The Lady's will, he told himself again. A defender over-reached himself, bursting through the East Rank's front line into the space behind where Galtas loitered. Galtas grinned at the flailing defender, punched him in the teeth, swept his arm low and under the man's knee, and hoisted. He went over the wall with a whooping shriek more of shock than fear, and then he was gone.

An arrow buzzed past Galtas on his blind side; it looked to have come from further down the allure. It reminded him to take off his eye patch; the first part of his disguise lay in removing the thing he was most well known for. He ripped it off his head and dropped it over the wall, ducked a slash and let the man next to him riposte, skipped behind a third's shield and stabbed over his comrade's head into their attacker's neck where it met the collarbone, sword angled down so half its length vanished into the man's body, cleaving lung and liver, maybe stomach. The man puked blood and Galtas ripped his sword free, scooped up a fallen shield and inched and killed his way towards the tower.

Still alive.

GILDA

Fourth moon, afternoon, day twenty-five of the siege
East Rank encampment, outside Rilporin, Wheat Lands

She was under guard, of course, and had been for what felt like months. *That's because it has been months. There's a comforting thought.* But despite her gaoler Scell's omnipresence at the other end of the chain and collar she'd worn all that time, the East Rank healers were too busy making her work to care that she was a slave.

I'm not a slave, she corrected herself. *I'm a prisoner. There's a difference.*

And there was. Today was the first time they'd put her to work, whereas their slaves worked from the day they were captured until the day they died. *More of a guest, really,* she told herself. *They like me so much they can't bear for me to leave.* She clanked the chain against her collar and snorted faint amusement.

Today though, the healers had finally admitted that the number of casualties from both armies had become too great for them to cope on their own. Decades as high priestess of the Dancer and the Fox God had given Gilda ample opportunity to hone her skills in healing, birthing, and easing men into the Light. She didn't expect to have much cause to employ the middle skill, but healing and the grace were in high demand.

Scell's curiosity had faded hours before and now he was the one trailing after her at the end of the chain as she strode between the rows of men lying in the hospital tents, lending what aid she could. The low roar of battle still drifted across the grass between the city and the East Rank's precise, square, tidy encampment, so unlike the ragged, broken-down, stinking mess of a camp the Mireces inhabited. There, the latrine pits had begun to overflow, and Gilda knew disease would rip through the men like wildfire if they weren't careful. She didn't bother worrying she might contract something; death by fever was likely the easiest end she was going to suffer.

All her amulets had been taken from her, but as she knelt next to a man missing his left leg above the knee, she found the words coming anyway, so low Scell couldn't hear. 'Dancer's grace be with you, lad, and the Fox God grant you His favour.'

The man's eyes were wide with pain but they widened even further, so much that Gilda could see the red-starred whites all around. 'You mustn't,' he breathed. 'It's forbidden.' There wasn't much fire in his voice, though. He groaned against a stab of pain, clutching at his foreshortened leg, cords standing out in his neck. 'It hurts,' he gasped. 'Help me, it hurts so much.'

Both of them looked at Scell, but the Mireces was too busy poking at a fresh corpse, disgusted fascination lining his face, to pay much attention.

'I will do what I can, soldier, however little that may be. I can pray with you and for you.'

'It's forbidden,' he repeated, but there was no defiance in his tone now, just a desperate hope. The bandages around the stump were soaked and leaking blood on to the cot and through the thin straw mattress. Gilda could hear it pattering on the mud below.

You poor bastard. She tapped a fingernail against her collar and tipped him a wink. 'Not much more they can do to me, soldier. Burnt my home to the ground and slaughtered everyone I've ever known and loved. Kill me too, soon enough.' She leant very close, so the man went cross-eyed trying to focus on her. 'Doesn't mean I should give up my faith, does it? Doesn't mean I shouldn't help where I can, offer comfort. Offer . . . absolution.'

His mouth twisted with shame and tears spilt from the corners of his eyes. 'I gave up my faith,' he muttered, 'for something as pointless as gold. Gave it up without a thought.'

'Turning to the Red Gods and being tricked into doing so are two different things. Repent, do you?' Gilda whispered, her hand on his chest, glancing again in Scell's direction. 'Embrace the Light, yes?'

'I can't,' the man sobbed. 'They said I couldn't, said once I'd sworn that I was bound. Bound to Her, the Dark Lady.'

'Horseshit,' Gilda snorted, wondering if it was. 'Your soul belongs to no one but you. If you want to give it to the Red Gods, be my guest. If you want to give it to the Dancer, then all you need to do is pray. Here, now, with me.'

Hope and shame and fear warred across his pasty features. 'Who are you?' he hissed.

She tucked her hair back behind one ear. 'Gilda, high priestess of Watchtown and member of the council of priests – if such a thing still exists. Now, lad, would you pray? Would you reclaim your soul from Blood and consecrate it again in the Light?' The soldier nodded feverishly. 'I cannot offer you a cleansing – there's no godpool here – so we'll do the best we can. The Great Trickster is always pleased to see our inventiveness, is He not?'

'Will . . . will the Dancer want me back?' the man whispered, his hope breaking.

Gilda took the soldier's waterskin and shook it, smiling at the sloshing from within. She unstoppered it and bent her head. 'Of course. Of that I have no doubt. Now hush a moment.' She closed her eyes and expanded her soul to encompass the man, draw him close and still within her embrace. She could feel the Dancer; despite everything, beneath the hate and fear and blood and shit, She was watching. Waiting, Her arms open.

'Holy Dancer, Lady clothed in sunlight, I ask that you hear me now and bless this water with all the holiness of your sacred pools. Fox God, lord of cunning and resourcefulness, bless these our efforts to bring this man—'

'Nils.'

'This man Nils out of the darkness and into your sacred Light.' Another swift glance about, and Gilda dribbled water over Nils's face and neck, into his mouth. 'Bathe in this water and be cleansed, from the outside in. Drink of this water and be cleansed, from the inside out. Reject the darkness, reject hate and pain and shame and fear. Embrace Light and love and comradeship. Open your heart and your soul to the Light, my friend. Let it in. Let it heal your soul and cleanse your mind, to bear you up against the waters of evil, to hold you close in love.'

Nils's face was ecstatic as he closed his eyes and stretched his head back into his pillow. 'I feel Her,' he whispered. 'I think She's coming. The Dancer's coming.'

'I know.' Gilda said, wanting to hush him, knowing she couldn't. There was a feather-light brush across her mind, a warm breeze of laughter and overwhelming love. Peace came into Nils's eyes even as it flooded Gilda's heart. 'Child of Light, let go. Of pain and fear and shame. Let it all go.'

'Thank you, priestess,' he murmured, breath thready, shallowing. 'I'm ready.'

'Thank you, Nils, for your faith and strength,' Gilda replied. She bent down and kissed him softly on the forehead. 'Go in grace, go in peace, and rest now in the Light,' she added, and Nils turned his face away from her so she had the right angle to punch her slender-bladed knife through his temple into his brain. He died without a twitch and with a smile.

'What are you doing?'

Gilda jumped and looked up into the face of Brevis, the East Rank's chief physician. The man's red-blotched face spoke of too much wine and too little sleep, but his hands were steady and Gilda had seen him wield the bone saw with skill.

She stood. 'Nils was bleeding to death and in agony. There was no saving him. He begged the grace; I gave it to him.' She sheathed the knife she'd stolen from his operating tent earlier.

Brevis scowled. 'You have no right to make those decisions. The man might still have been of use.'

Gilda pointed to the stump, to the pool of blood still accreting beneath the cot. Scell wandered over, curiosity piqued by the raising voices and, no doubt, the sight of another new corpse. The man was a maggot, with a maggot's lust for dead flesh.

'Would you have me leave him alive in agony to do nothing but beg you for opium and curse you when you refused?' Gilda asked.

Brevis looked at Scell, at the knife and sword he wore.

'The grace is,' he began. 'The grace is . . .' He trailed off, unable to repeat the dogma that had been forced upon him.

'The grace is a heathen practice outlawed in the East Rank as it is among the Mireces,' a new voice said.

Gilda looked past Brevis and bobbed a curtsey. 'General Skerris,' she acknowledged, 'I find it odd you would outlaw such a thing. The grace is, after all, one of the only things your soldiers can be sure of – that if they are mortally wounded they will be ended quickly, with as little pain as possible. Surely you risk rebellion if you take it from them?'

'They fight for a higher purpose now,' Skerris rumbled. 'Their pain glorifies the gods and brings Them closer, therefore we should not see it ended prematurely.'

Gilda glanced at the beds closest to her; wounded soldiers stared at them in disbelief, or hunched on their sides as far from Skerris as they could get, shoulders shaking as they wept. *No swift end if infection takes them, no painless drifting away from a world filled with agony. No blink from life to death as a blade enters your brain. Instead, a protracted, lingering, pointless death that will fill them with despair and their fellows with horror.*

'Idiots,' she snapped, careless of to whom she spoke. 'You are making a grave mistake. These men are professional soldiers. They have pledged to fight for you, to obey your commands, and have given their souls to your filthy gods. You have already taken everything they have to give. They should at least be allowed to die in dignity, if death be their fate. You cannot take that from them. You must not.'

'Mind your tongue,' Scell snapped, jerking the chain as though Gilda was a snarling dog. She staggered, grunting as the collar reopened the scabs where the metal had chafed her neck raw.

'You have no idea what the men in this hospital do and

do not deserve or how they should spend their last hours,' Skerris said calmly, as if lecturing a new recruit. 'They are no longer mired in the delusions of your faith. They belong to Blood now, and if they must die steeped in it, they will do so to further the aims of our gods, the true gods. Treat them and do all you can to save them, but if they are dying, you will leave them to do so in their own time and not go near them again. It will purify their souls ready for the Afterworld. Do you understand?'

Gilda clicked her tongue against her teeth and scanned the closest beds; everyone was listening and she knew without doubt the news would spread to every soldier in the hospital and then to the entire Rank before dusk tinged the sky. Whether it would be enough to begin a rebellion, she'd no idea.

I hope so. Those who rise up against tyranny and the gods they've been forced to pledge themselves to will be welcome back in the Light when their time comes. If they've the strength to deny the pull of Blood with their final breaths, as Nils did.

Brevis held out his hand for the knife, and Gilda drew it and slapped it into his palm. He gasped, thinking she'd cut him, but she'd reversed the blade at the last second and his skin remained intact. His lip curled at her and she smiled back, the picture of elderly innocence. *Where can I get another knife? Do I dare?*

The thought was almost enough to make her laugh aloud; she dared, of course she did. Gilda had no illusions about her fate; her only plan now was to save the souls of as many of the East Rankers as she could before they killed her. Even if they were, officially, the enemy.

'I will do as you ask,' she said to Skerris, turning his order into a request. Skerris didn't rise to it the way Corvus or

Rivil would, or even Lanta; instead he nodded once and crooked a finger at Brevis to follow as he made his way up the aisle between the beds.

'Don't let her kill anyone,' Brevis snapped at Scell as he hurried after the general.

Gilda turned a smile on Scell. 'You heard the Rilporian, Scell. Don't let me kill anyone, will you?' She laughed. 'Anyone would think I was the mass murderer, not your priestess. Come on then, let's see who's next. All right, mate, what's your name? Captain, are you? Acquitted yourself well?'

She sat down on the next bed before Scell could answer and pulled the man's blanket back, began to examine the bandages. 'Did you hear me with Nils?' she breathed. The man nodded, frightened. 'You're not dying, I can see that, but I can still pray with you if you want? If you'd like to try?'

His eyes wobbled in their sockets as he eyed the tent, Scell, Gilda herself. His mouth opened and closed like a fish a few times; then he nodded.

Gilda smiled.

DOM

*Fourth moon, eighteenth year of the reign of King Rastoth
Road to Rilporin, Wheat Lands*

She'd told him to cross at the West Rank's harbour, and he
had. She'd told him to walk southeast, and he had. She'd
told him not to stop unless he must. He hadn't. Now he
was a week's walk, maybe less, from Rilporin, from where
he needed to be.

Dom's feet were blistered and the muscles in his legs kept
twitching even after he'd sat down, but he was close now.
Close to them. Close to Her. His left hand was healing well
from the knife the God of Blood had rammed through it,
and although the fingers remained stiff and slow to close, it
wouldn't stop him when it came to a fight. He could always
tie his hand to his sword if necessary, as long as he remembered not to scratch his arse with it afterwards. Or his throat.
He snorted.

The fields were quiet, the winter wheat golden-brown and
growing, but few people were working the land this close
to Rilporin and the enemy. Dom wasn't sure whether they'd

fled or merely cowered in their homes, but their absence had encouraged the wildlife, and rabbits and hares hopped among the stems, nibbling the sweetest. Dom sat ten paces outside the edge of the field on a hard-packed track, waiting for something to jump into his snare. He had a few sticks ready for a fire and a ragged, soot-stinking blanket from Watchtown. A waterskin. His weapons. And the gods.

Watchtown. Home of Wolves and of Watchers. Heathens. Traitors. Murderers. Dom crammed his right wrist into his mouth and chewed, gnawing away at the itch, gnawing away the scars of his blood oath. Despite the divergence of their paths in the last months, Dom had lived with the Watchers his entire life, and so he'd done what he could to lay out the dead before She had commanded him to leave. He could still feel their skin, crispy from the fire, crumbling in his hands, sliding away in the grease to reveal pink flesh, flesh that peeled in slabs from charred bone. It was still on his hands even now, fat melted into the bandage on his left, the stink still in his hair, his clothes. There was a good chance he'd never wash it off, no matter how many baths he took.

A squeal and kick brought him back to the fields and he hurried over to his snare and killed the rabbit, ripped it from the thin cord and reset the trap. Food that wasn't his own arm. Dom giggled. *Need my strength, don't I, my love? You said I will and look, here I am, ready for rabbit.*

He unbandaged his left hand while the rabbit roasted in the top flames and poked at the sealed wound, sniffed it for signs of the rot, then splashed it with water and let the sun dry it. The smoke from his cookfire attracted attention, and he could see figures peering in his direction, armed with sticks and pitchforks, a few scythes that should be in storage until the harvest came in. So they were still there, then, watching their crop be destroyed.

Dom unbuckled his sword belt and made a show of putting it on the ground on the far side of his fire. Then he sat with his back to them. They wouldn't hurt him; She'd said so.

He hummed as he prodded the meat with his knife, his stomach growling in counterpoint. Too long since he'd eaten enough to fill him, and too long since anything other than meat had passed his lips. What he wouldn't give for a hearty leek and cabbage stew. His hum descended into a groan at the thought. Still, he'd be there soon, and they'd have supplies to share.

'Travelling to Rilporin, stranger?' The voice came from behind, gruff but with the tightness of fear beneath it.

Dom gestured, not turning. 'You need to tend these fields; rabbits are making a right mess of your crop. Work the land so that when the war's over you've got food to eat and sell. You'll be dead otherwise.'

The man came around to face him, and Dom knew there were others at his back. The stranger was tall and broad, a lifetime in the fields honing his arms and shoulders and back. He planted his feet either side of Dom's sword; Dom's eyes flickered towards it and away.

'We're like to be dead soon anyway, those Raider scum come this way again. They've taken everything we've had put by; you're not the only one living off rabbits.'

'Ah. Is that the problem?' Dom asked. 'You want my rabbit?'

'What? No. Man's going to fight the Mireces, he's welcome to a rabbit off my lands. Just wondering if you'd any news, brought any messages or anything. You've come from the west – is the Rank on its way? Reinforcements? They've been hammering at the wall for days now, sending men up there on ladders, cutting down our woods to build siege towers. I'm no soldier, but it looks pretty desperate from the glimpses we've had and the news we've heard.'

Dom licked his lips. 'Going to fight the Mireces?' he asked. 'Why'd you think that?'

The farmer laughed. 'Why else would you head towards the city? You're a scout, a messenger or a warrior. Mind you, I've little idea how you expect to get past the Mireces and into the city without taking an arrow between the eyes. Still, you know best, I'm sure.'

Dom rubbed his face and paused as long as he dared, but Her instructions were quite clear. He rose to his feet and looked up at the farmer, still a head taller than him. He glanced behind: three more. 'Rilpor's doomed, my friend, and so is Rilporin. The Gods of Light are failing. There's only the Blood now, blood spilt and blood sacrificed and blood in Her name. I go to join the Mireces, to pledge them my sword, my life, my everything. You'd be wise to do the same; it might spare your families when the time comes. Spare you sacrifice, or slavery. Gift them half your crops and they might let you live your lives without a collar around your neck.'

The farmer's mouth was hanging open, his face red with disbelief and growing anger. There were curses from behind, muttered prayers for protection, a half-choked threat. The farmer strode around the fire and grabbed Dom by his rusty chainmail, jerking him forward on to his toes. 'You fucking coward,' he snarled. 'You treacherous, weasely, snivelling little shit. How can you say that? You're a— Look at you, you're dressed like a warrior. Gods alive, you're one of them Wolf-folk, ain't you? Sworn enemy of the fucking Raiders!'

'Guilty as charged.' Dom grinned. 'Though my feet are on the Path and it is dark and bloody and glorious.'

'Get out of my fucking fields, you scum,' the farmer roared. 'I should kill you here and now. I should—'

Dom's knife took him under the chin, punching through

his tongue and into the base of his brain with a wet crack. He fell without a sound and Dom ripped the knife free, his fingers clumsy from the wound, and spun to face the others. 'My feet are on the Path,' he bellowed, waving the red knife. 'Come, come and stop me. Come and try.' Part of it was a plea, but the rest was ravening bloodlust, rage and hate. He'd kill the world if She asked him to. He'd kill them all.

The three men clustered together exchanged identical, terrified looks and then fled, tools falling from their hands. They didn't look back. Dom spat on the corpse and snatched up his sword. The rabbit was burnt on one side, raw on the other, but he took up the spit and wrapped it in a fold of his blanket. He stared into the flames for a long moment, in case anything looked back, but the Dancer was silent. She had nothing to say about the murder, nothing to say to him at all these days. Just as he liked it. He hawked and spat into the fire, set his back to the farmhouse and marched towards Rilporin.

'My love,' the Dark Lady purred in his ear, sending shivers down his spine. 'My good, strong love. How pleased I am.'

It was the same dream he'd had every night since leaving Watchtown. Those Wolves too broken to carry the fight further, who'd elected to stay in the ruins and lay out the dead, corralled between the God of Blood and the Dark Lady, Dom forming the third point of the triangle imprisoning them. Wolves for Gosfath to play with. Dying in the god's bloody embrace. Rotting from the outside in. Screaming from the inside out.

'Stop,' Dom screamed in his turn, as loud as he could, fists balled at his side. 'Stop it. I'll do it. I'll do what you want. I'll do everything you want.' His heart thudded slowly in his chest, as though his blood was thick as tree sap. 'Please, Lady. My feet . . .' He paused and swallowed hard as another died writhing, blackening, melting. 'My feet are on the Path.' A broken whisper from a broken soul.

The Dark Lady raised one finger and Gosfath paused in his selection of further victims. At His feet eight men and women curled in on themselves in fetid death, their organs turning to mush and pus inside them even as they rattled their final breaths, outlines sloughing and melting into each other, a pool of decay. A pool of people.

'What did you say?' She asked in a voice of honey.

Dom stared at the surviving Wolves huddled together, hope warring with terror on their faces, then back at Her. *Do it. Say it. It's true anyway, has been true for months. And it might save the rest of them.*

'My feet are on the Path,' he said, knowing the disgust and terror on the faces of the Wolves – his kin – would haunt him forever.

'Yes,' She whispered, 'they are. So you should ask yourself what you owe these people, the enemies of the true faith. Ask yourself why you care what happens to them, the men and women who've spent centuries killing those whose feet walk the Path. People like you, my love.'

'Nothing,' he said, suddenly understanding, seeing the hate in their eyes for what it was. 'I owe them nothing.' It was like light dawning after the blackest of nights. All his final doubts, all his lingering care, washed away in the red-tinged light of Her, the promise of Her redemption. He looked at the Wolves again, at their dying hope. It tingled over his skin like feathers. 'You need me to go to Rilporin, my love. I will go. Now.'

The Dark Lady put a hand on his shoulder. 'And these?' She asked.

Dom bit the raw flesh of his right wrist as he studied the half-dozen surviving Wolves. Her glory was a fire that burnt and he exalted in the pain. He lifted a shoulder in a shrug. 'They're yours.'

The Dark Lady's smile was radiant and warmed Dom's belly. 'There he is,' She whispered. 'There's my true believer. My calestar. My Godblind.' Dom bowed to Her and to Holy Gosfath, and he walked away.

Behind him, the screams began again.

He woke with a jolt, as he always did at that part of the dream – *don't lie, it's a memory, not a dream* – and the sky was still black, glittering with stars like the hangman's eyes through his hood. The screams rang at the edge of his hearing: his people dying.

Not my people. Nothing to do with me. Past is dead. Past doesn't matter. My life is Hers, my love is Hers. All else is ruin. There is only the Path, and Her at the end of it. I will not walk that Path.

I will run it.

'I'm coming, my love,' he said and the endless, burrowing, worming itching in his arm faded and he was left with just the pain of it, the slow-flowing blood and the great scabby holes he'd chewed in his flesh in a desperate attempt to find the source of the itch. He grinned, waited, and then laughed. It was gone.

Dom leapt to his feet, abandoning the half-cooked rabbit carcass, and snatched up his blanket. 'My feet are on the Path,' he crowed, capering in the dark, 'and my arm doesn't bloody itch!'

The Dark Lady's laughter drifted on the breeze, teasing, taunting him with flashes of different images this time, of Wolves drowning, dying in the dark. Rillirin was one of them, the slave destined to save or destroy them all. She was wrapped in another man's arms as the water flooded over their faces. He could see her screaming.

He laughed again, rolled the blanket, and broke into a steady run. Rilporin was close now. So close. And so was She.

DURDIL

A muscle flexed in Durdil's jaw. Lorca and Silais had acted behind his back and called a series of emergency councils, and now they presented him with their decision at a meeting he'd expected to be routine. A decision signed, sealed, and utterly fucking ridiculous.

Maybe I should've met them when they insisted on it. I might have been able to stave this off for a while longer.

He stared at the paper in front of him until his eyes watered, letting the thunderous silence build until it felt like the pressure in the room would blow out the expensive windows. The councillors, who had been sitting in smug, self-satisfied silence around the table, began to fidget, then to exchange glances, then gulp at their wine. In the corner, Questrel Chamberlain simpered, oblivious to Durdil's towering rage, or perhaps just untroubled by it.

'Gentlemen, Rilporin stands firm and the walls are yet intact. While the loss of the king is a huge blow, it is one

we can – we are – surviving. Besides which, the enemy will
have eyes on the King Gate, as they are watching all the
city's exits; any attempt to evacuate the populace will be
seen and countered swiftly. It is far too dangerous to move
thousands of people; they'll be slaughtered on the road.
Rilporin is the safest place for them.'

Someone coughed to cover a laugh. 'You misunderstand,'
Lord Lorca said, his tone affable and amused. 'The people
will stay, of course. There is nowhere else for them to go,
after all and, as you say, no doubt your soldiers will triumph.
But the, ah, the essence of Rilpor, the values and culture that
makes our country what it is, that resides in its upper classes.
We propose simply that those of appropriate position who
wish it be allowed to leave Rilporin for less dangerous climes.
I, for example, though my heart desires to stay and support
the city, am prepared to undertake the dangerous journey
to Listre and inform Tresh that he is now our king. I pledge
to see him safe until such time as you have secured the
country for his arrival.'

I bet you bloody do, Durdil thought bitterly. *Set yourself
up as his chief adviser, orchestrate the fall of your enemies
within the council, and bag yourself a nice big stack of gold,
eh? All under the guise of advising him, and all while sitting
safe in another country!*

'I, too, will visit Tresh,' Silais said, as Durdil had known
he would. 'Our new king must be protected. Must be . . .
apprised of the state of his kingdom.'

'You want to run away with your families and all your
money while the rest of us fight,' Durdil said in a voice
devoid of all expression. 'Fine, go. I'll not stop you.' *A few
hundred fewer weak-chinned idiots roaming the city can
only be a help. And despite the identity of the messengers,
Tresh does need to know he's king.*

Lorca's smile was small and pained and he gave off an air of weary resignation at Durdil's words. 'We are pleased to hear it,' he said. 'Those who wish to go will assemble at East Tower tomorrow. Your force will be ready then, I presume?'

Durdil pursed his lips. 'Force, my lord? What force would that be?' His tone was polite – for now. He had a horrible feeling he knew what was coming next.

Lorca spread his hands and exchanged an amused glance with Silais. Hardoc of Pine Lock wore an expression he no doubt thought was stoic, when in reality he looked consti-pated. He'd ventured a small tut at Lorca's suggestion they leave Rilporin. He was also wearing full armour. Ceremonial, naturally. No need to be silly and lug around real armour, but it did make him look so much more martial than the rest.

Durdil coughed into his hand to hide his smile. The Haddock had decided he was a warrior, despite the over-whelming evidence to the contrary. Durdil couldn't wait to see the expression on his face when he invited him up on to the wall to repel an assault. Still, at least he wouldn't be fleeing the city, which meant Durdil could commandeer his household guards if he needed—

'The Thousand to escort us in safety to Listre's border, Commander,' Lorca said, pulling Durdil's attention back. 'We cannot be expected to ride in state without sufficient protec-tion.' He exchanged another amused glance with Silais, their interests for once aligned. 'There is a war on, after all.'

Durdil stared at Lorca in silence for a moment, trying to work out whether he was being mocked, and then he roared with laughter. He slapped the table and laughed until tears ran down his cheeks.

Lorca's face reddened and his eyes narrowed until he

snapped, 'Enough, Commander. You will explain the meaning of this outburst.'

Durdil looked around the table at the affronted, pompous faces and the last dregs of his mirth drained away, along with the last reserves of that day's energy. 'You're serious?' he asked. 'You think the city is going to fall and so you want to run away and save yourselves under guise of meeting Tresh – all right, I understand that. It's a natural reaction. You want to take your families for the same reason; again, I understand. But you also want me to send a fifth of my defenders with you, further weakening the city's defences and leaving the people staying behind without adequate protection?'

Durdil waited for a denial or a protest that he had misunderstood their request; none came. 'No. No, my lords, there will be no armed force accompanying you. If you wish to go, then go; your household guard will have the job of keeping you alive, though by rights every one of them should be mine to aid in the defence. Not a single man of the Palace or South Ranks, or the City Watch, will accompany you. Their charge is the safety of this city, and the thousands of citizens within it. They will discharge that duty and no other.'

Lorca opened his mouth and Durdil held up his palm. 'Let me be very clear,' he said. 'Without a king, heir or any single member of the royal family in residence in Rilporin, defence of this city, the country and the faith falls to me. You all agreed to suspend the ordinary governance of this city in return for martial law. You placed me in power, my lords, and I plan on discharging that duty to its fullest. And my duty is to preserve the lives of as many of our citizens as possible.'

Lorca made to interrupt again and so Durdil slammed his palm down on the table, the flat crack making them all jump.

'No, *my lords*. If you would go, then do so and may the gods preserve you, but you will be going alone. If you elect to stay, then war-room discussions will be confined to military matters only. Now, if none of you have anything serious or pertinent to the defence of Rilporin to discuss, I have a wall to defend.' He pushed up from the table.

Posturing, sycophantic, arrogant, pompous little—

The door burst open. 'Commander, there's a bridgehead on the allure between the gatehouse and Second Tower. Fierce fighting, sir; they're pushing hard and throwing more men at the ladders. Easterners and Mireces both. Colonel Yarrow requests more men.'

'On my way,' Durdil bellowed and bolted for the door, ignoring the shouted questions from the councillors and Hardoc's tentative offer of aid, made quietly enough that it was unlikely Durdil would hear it and accept. Even the thought of a breach wasn't enough to dampen his enthusiasm at being out of that room.

He found a little spike of fresh energy from somewhere and hurried for the assembly place and his waiting horse, flung it into a gallop down the King's Way, racing towards war and away from the much messier, harder to understand, knife-in-the-back infighting that was politics.

CORVUS

Fourth moon, evening, day thirty of the siege
Mireces encampment, outside Rilporin, Wheat Lands

Corvus watched through narrowed eyes as the East Rank established a new bridgehead on the wall and the Mireces did their best to emulate them on their section. His men were slower and clumsy compared with the Easterners, but lethal if they reached the top. *If they reached the top.* Even as he watched, small figures fell, arms and legs flailing against the air until they disappeared into the shadows at the base of the wall.

A fucking month we've been here and still we're no better on the ladders. Still there is no progress.

There had been only minimal defenders on the wall when the attack began, but that'd changed soon enough and now the battle was hand-to-hand and fierce all along the northern end, what Rivil and Skerris referred to as Second Last. His men had Double First, and while they didn't have the same skill on the ladders, they'd established a fragile bridgehead around the siege tower.

The Blessed One had vanished hours before to pray for their victory, and Corvus paced the grass out of catapult range, chewing a fingernail and flicking his gaze between his men and Rivil's. It didn't matter who established the first serious breach, didn't matter who took their section of wall first. What mattered was victory. Corvus told himself he believed that.

'What?' he snarled, rounding on whoever was tugging at his sleeve.

His eyes widened and he fumbled for a knife as Valan yelled in shock and barrelled past him. The stranger was thin and ragged, his cheeks straggly with black beard, but his eyes were those of a man touched by madness or the sun.

'The fuck are you?' Corvus demanded as Valan wrestled the stranger away. 'I said, who the fuck are you?' he asked again, his heart hammering. He glared at his guards. 'Why didn't you see him, stop him? Man gets close enough to put a knife in my ribs and you stand there stroking your cocks? I should load you into the trebs and send you face first into the fucking wall.'

The men shook their heads, unable to answer, knives and spears pointing at the figure now kneeling patiently in the grass. Valan retreated to Corvus's side, his sword drawn. The stranger watched Corvus with dull brown eyes, blank with indifference, burning with madness. It was as though he'd simply appeared in their midst. More wraith than man. Corvus fought a shiver.

'Who am I?' the man said at last and giggled, clapping his hands. 'Don't you recognise me, war chief? I am your Godblind, and I laid out my dead and then killed some others and I walked away from Watchtown's ruins and then I walked the long road here, Madoc of Dancer's Lake, Corvus,

King of the Mireces, chosen of death. I walk with gods, while you walk with fear. And my feet are on the Path.'

He raised a finger as Corvus bristled and opened his mouth to order the fucker's death. Corvus found himself silenced. *He called me Madoc. Only Rillirin and Gilda know that used to be my name. Has he met my sister?*

Hope flooded through him, and then another thought struck him to the core and his breath tangled in his throat until he coughed. *He named himself Godblind, as the Blessed One foretold. Gosfath's balls, could this really be him, the calestar of the Wolves?*

'The Blessed One wants me, but she can't have me, oh no.' The Godblind giggled again at the shock on Corvus's face, so closely did the words mirror his thoughts. 'You and I have a path to tread, Madoc. A bloody one with no clear end in sight. Will you walk it with me, the bloody path and the Dark Path both? Walk with me as far as we can go?'

'Who are you?' Corvus asked again, kneeling in the grass opposite the man and uncaring of the bemused expressions on the faces of his guards. 'Tell me your name.'

The man put his head on one side and winked. 'My name is Godblind. I have others, but they're not yours to call me, oh no. What name should I give you? Corvus? Madoc? King? Slave?'

He cackled as Corvus backhanded him and he fell into the grass, laughing as though the blow had merely tickled. He pushed himself back to his knees, making no move for the weapons he carried and that Valan had somehow neglected to take from him. It was as though he'd cast a spell over them all, but Corvus knew the man wouldn't use them, not even now, when they were close enough to touch. To stab.

Maybe the spell was on him too, to take such a risk.

'Corvus then, to save my teeth from your knuckles. Sire, even,' he added as Corvus narrowed his eyes. 'Though there is only so much reverence I can give to one who walks this earth on mortal feet. Our Lady and Her Bloody Brother require my attention, my . . . devotion. You can have what is left, if you want.'

'You say you walk the Dark Path?' Corvus asked. The Godblind shoved his bloody, mangled arm in Corvus's face and he recoiled, grimacing. The man prodded at something with his other hand, and reluctantly Corvus leant closer. Then he saw it, mostly obliterated now but still standing proud in his flesh, unmistakable. His eyes widened. 'Scars of a blood oath? You are bound?'

The Godblind pulled his arm back and clutched it to his chest. 'Bound,' he whispered, rocking on his knees as Valan, standing above him with a knife, gaped. 'Bound to serve. Bound to kill. Bound to die. Anything She asks. My feet are on the Path.'

'As are mine,' Corvus found himself saying, and frowned at the tendril of pity that curled through his gut as he studied the maddened, dying idiot before him. There was little doubt he was not long for this world. All he knew of becoming godblind was that it was a temporary and very terminal condition, and this Wolf, this calestar Lanta had told him of, had obviously been suffering for some time.

'Your place is here, isn't it? Here with us?'

'Yes, Sire,' the Godblind said. His shoulders slumped and tears trickled from the corners of his eyes. He raised a weary hand to his face. 'Here where I shouldn't be is exactly where I belong. She said so.' Then he brightened and sat up like a child with a secret. 'But She took away the itching. In here, the itching in here. She took it away.'

'Sire,' Valan muttered, 'Prince Rivil and Skerris approach.'

Corvus ignored him and the Rilporians, intent on the ravaged face, the eyes that met his own for just a second before drifting to something only he could see. Corvus couldn't find a shred of doubt inside himself – this was the Godblind. Soul in torment, mind shattered by the blessed visits of the Dark Lady, the man was incapable of falsehood, unable to dissemble. Everything he said would be true. He saw more even than the Blessed One.

'That's the Godblind?' Rivil asked when Valan had outlined what was happening. 'A filthy, stinking Wolf?'

'Skerris, will you fetch the Blessed One for me?' Corvus said. 'She must meet this man and verify what he says before we do anything else. Hurry.'

Skerris glanced at Rivil and then nodded. 'As you wish,' he said.

The Godblind laughed again and his eyes were clear and lucid, dancing with amusement. 'Lanta Costinioff, Blessed One and Voice of the Gods. She won't like me being here, no matter what tales she spins you. And she will, she'll pretend my presence brings her joy.' He coughed, harsh as a raven calling. 'She'll lie, and you have to decide what to do about that. She may well try and kill me, and you'll have to decide what to do about that, too. My death will secure her power over you and your people, over Rilpor. She'll want that. But then, we don't get everything we want in life, do we, Sire?'

Corvus and Rivil exchanged glances. Rivil shrugged, still clearly amused – or at least, trying hard to pretend that he was amused, that all this was beneath him and their victory beyond doubt. An act that was wearing fucking thin these days.

You still think your desires and expectations carry weight in this war, don't you, Prince? Corvus thought sourly. *The Godblind is the blade that tore the Dancer's veil and let the*

Red Gods return, not you. You know this, but still you don't understand it. I think now that you can't.

And yet Rivil had brought an army bigger than Corvus's. An army better equipped and better suited to this tedious sort of warfare. They needed each other; Corvus just hoped Rivil hated it as much as he did.

He rose to his feet and turned his back on the Godblind. Rivil's eyes sharpened, perhaps hoping the man would lunge for him, but of course the Godblind did nothing. 'Strip his weapons and put a slave collar and chain on him. I want him close and under control at all times. Even when he's quiet, even when he's broken, I want him collared and chained. And bring a scribe: whatever he says, no matter how insane it sounds, I want it written down. Everything.'

'Your will, Sire,' a guard said and snapped his fingers. Two men ran for their supply cache as Valan stripped the Godblind's weapons from him, muttering in disgust at the grime coating him, his emaciation, his smell.

'And give him a bath and some food,' Corvus added, scratching unconsciously at his scalp. 'Bastard's probably got lice.'

Corvus stared hard at the city, his eyes roaming the length of grey stone, forcing himself to focus on the recurrent problem of accessing it rather than the tantalising puzzle of the godblind Wolf.

The problem is I have too many problems.

What were the chances of them taking the wall and finding an empty city behind it, the citizens all fled through the so-called King Gate hidden from view at the rear? What would happen then? *We'll be fighting pockets of resistance for years, or skirmishes, or full-scale battles. We need to take this city and crush its defenders at the same time.*

But the Godblind. And Lanta. And Rivil. He slapped his

thigh irritably; there were too many things happening at once.

The Godblind looked up with a ghastly smile. 'If you had more siege weapons you could bring down those stump walls leading to the rivers and shatter the bridges behind them. Well, the two closest, anyway. You'd never get an engine over the river to take out the eastern bridge from the King Gate, but if you've demolished the other two then you just need to station men at the end of the eastern bridge and they'd be trapped inside.'

Corvus staggered back a step, his sword in his hand. Valan reacted to Corvus's movement, grabbing the Godblind by the hair and placing his blade against the skinny throat.

'You read minds?' Corvus croaked. 'You see my very fucking thoughts?'

The man wheezed another laugh. 'You were staring from the trebuchets to the city. It wasn't hard to guess. And no, I don't read minds. I speak the words of the Dark Lady.' He laughed again. 'But those ones before, they were mine, not Hers.'

'What is happening here?'

Lanta's face was hard with interrogation as she strode into their midst, her eyes fixing on the kneeling man, judging, weighing. She stared for so long that even Corvus squirmed. The Godblind knelt in the grass, looking up with the patience of a blind man, seeming unaffected by her gaze.

'This man claims to be the Godblind you told us of. He has just been suggesting a way we could more quickly gain entry to the city.'

Lanta's eyebrows rose and her lips parted, an expression of genuine surprise quickly masked. 'You betray your country? Your people?' she demanded.

'My feet are on the Path. I do as my Lady commands.' Another bloom of shock, swiftly hidden.

There was another interminable silence as they all waited for Lanta's verdict. It didn't come.

'He's right,' Corvus said eventually. She twitched. 'About the stump walls and the gates. The more we can engage at multiple sites, the quicker we can force an end to this siege. We mustn't forget the six soldiers we caught yesterday escaping the city to try and find aid. For all we know, more may have slipped past us. They could be raising a mercenary army in Listre within a week.'

'Reinforcements, yes. Almost three thousand of them,' the Godblind muttered, nodding. 'Not mercenaries though.'

Corvus stilled, his eyes locked on Valan, and together they swivelled to face the kneeling man. A guard was fixing the slave collar on him and he blanched when their twin gazes settled on him. He locked the collar and stepped back, not wanting to be under those eyes.

'How many did you say?' Corvus asked, dropping to one knee in the grass. The others crowded forward. 'Who?'

'Just under three thousand. The survivors of the West Rank and the Wolves. Your ploy in the tunnels didn't kill them, not all of them anyway. Not enough of them. They're about three days away. The North isn't coming, of course,' he added and pointed at Skerris, 'because he killed them all, didn't you, Skerris? Poisoned blankets. Clever, but unkind. Men should be given the chance to die fighting.'

Valan was crouching beside him, and Corvus realised he was gripping his second's forearm hard. Lanta knelt on his other side, blue eyes like chips of ice nailed to the Godblind's face.

'How do you know this?' she asked, her voice hoarse.

The Godblind frowned and looked up from the ruin of his arm. He tapped his temple with a finger. 'The gods, of course. That's who I am, remember, the vessel? You may style yourself Voice of the Gods, but I'm Their mouthpiece. Where you interpret images, I hear the actual words of our Bloody Mother. The Dark Lady sees the armies moving; She sees what's coming. She tells me; I tell you.' He shrugged. 'It's not complicated.'

The Blessed One flushed pink and Corvus saw her hand go to her belt and the knife and hammer it carried. Her fingertips flirted with the weapons, and then fell away.

'You have yet to learn humility, Godblind,' she said in a soft tone. 'The Dark Lady may be pleased to teach you before too long.'

'Forgive me, Blessed One,' he said, looking anything but chastened. 'You and I should be allies. We both serve a greater purpose than ourselves.'

The air seemed to ignite as their stares met and Corvus found he was holding his breath. Though, of course, you could always count on a Rilporian to break the tension.

Rivil spat on the grass. 'Five thousand in the city and nearly three thousand on their way. We still outnumber them.' He shrugged even as the Godblind blinked and used the interruption to look away. Corvus wasn't sure if that meant the Blessed One had won. Or what the stakes might be. 'Why not send a force to kill them before they make Rilporin's harbour?'

'And so finally, Sire, you will get to face your ancient enemy,' the Godblind said, staring into Corvus's eyes, 'and on a field of your choosing.'

'You offer up your own people to us?' the Blessed One demanded again. 'Why?'

The Godblind's lips curved in a gentle smile that sent shivers worming down Corvus's spine. 'What are they to me now, when I have the gods in my heart and my head and my eyes?'

His serenity, the unshakeable faith that armoured him so effectively, was to Lanta a slap in the face, an insult she could not tolerate.

'Yes, and isn't it convenient,' she snapped. There was a shrill tone to her voice now. 'You appear out of nowhere to tell us everything we need to know. And yet we have no way of verifying your words. What's to stop you lying? What's to say this isn't some last desperate ploy by our enemies?'

'I am Dom Templeson, Calestar of the Wolves and chosen of the Dark Lady. Called Godblind by Her and by you. You foretold my coming to these very men on this very field on the first day of the siege. I felt you tell them. Felt your power,' he added with a diplomacy Corvus thought he'd had to force. 'Ask and know the truth of my answer. Ask anything.'

Lanta pressed her lips together and put her head on one side. 'A children's game,' she said dismissively, as though it was of little matter. 'The time will come when your truth or lies are laid bare.'

'That time will come to us all,' the Godblind agreed. 'As for me, believe me, I have no wish to incur the Dark Lady's wrath or punishments again. I will not – I cannot – lie. My feet are on the Path.'

'So you say,' Lanta hissed, jerking the chain attached to the collar so the Godblind lurched closer, 'and I say we will find out soon enough.'

The Godblind pushed back up on to his knees and wagged his finger in her face. 'You doubt the gods?'

Corvus went cold. *She'll kill him for that. She's killed men for far less than doubting her faith. For laughing at her.* He knew he couldn't let her, and he knew he couldn't stop her either, not unless he was prepared to lay a hand on her. The King of the Mireces found that he was not.

'I doubt *you*,' Lanta hissed. They were nose to nose, will to will, and although Corvus would have wagered everything he owned that the Godblind would back down, the opposite happened. Lanta let the links of the chain slide through her fingers one by one, releasing the tension so the Godblind could sit back. She waved a hand in dismissal, as though nothing of much importance had occurred.

'I will commune with the gods.' She rose to her feet and stared down at the men kneeling around her. 'Do what you must to win this war. I will seek knowledge of our enemies. Remember whose voice it is that has guided you thus far.' She stalked away through the grass, and the guards scattered from her path like sparrows from a cat.

'Fuck me,' Valan breathed once she was out of earshot. The Godblind cackled, and then they were all grinning foolishly at one another.

'I'll get the trebuchets moved,' Skerris grunted, hauling himself to his feet.

Corvus nodded. 'Agreed. Let's get those stump walls down and that weak spot exploited in the time we have before the fucking West Rank arrives. I want those inside the city too busy to sally in support when they arrive. We fight on as many fronts as necessary.'

Corvus stood and held his hand out to Rivil, who clasped his wrist. 'We know the timeframe, if this one is to be trusted,' he added, though there was no doubt in his mind. Not even a shred. The Blessed One's communion would confirm it. 'What say you we get busy taking the city?'

'Agreed,' Rivil said. 'And there's to be no let-up, day or night, until it's ours.'

Corvus glanced at his guards. 'Bathe the Godblind and find him some fresh clothes. Put him in something blue. I think the colour will suit him.'

MACE

'You've got that look again.'

Mace started and focused on Dalli. 'What? What look?'

'Like someone just kicked your puppy,' she said, and then put a conciliatory hand on his thigh. 'At the risk of repeating myself – because I am repeating myself – it wasn't your fault and we'll get there in time. We were out of choices at Yew Cove and it's not like you ordered us into those tunnels. You didn't do this, Mace. Look, your Da knows how to defend a city. Gods, he'll probably have won it single-handed before we arrive. And wouldn't that be bloody nice?' she added under her breath.

Mace's smile felt false even to himself, and judging from Dalli's expression it looked even worse, but it was still the best he could do. 'We lost days in those bastard tunnels and recovering afterwards. The city might have fallen by now.'

Dalli puffed out her cheeks. 'We couldn't have moved any faster than we did. Not with our numbers of wounded. If

70

we hadn't rested, there'd just be corpses crewing these ships down to Rilporin. You know that.'

He stared back out across the harbour at the approaching dusk. When they'd come up out of those tunnels in the aftermath, the pitiful, shattered remains of his proud Rank, there'd been no thought of continuing the march. Too heart-sore at the scale of their losses, at the sheer callous deliberation on the part of the Mireces to drown them, in the tight, choking black beneath the ground.

Easy to blame the villagers who'd been forced into the deception. Easier to blame himself. The semblance of order he'd managed had lasted until Lim Broadsword, chief of the decimated Wolves, had climbed out of the tunnels with his wife's corpse in his arms. A hundred folk of Yew Cove had died under Wolf blades – Wolf and Rank blades – before Mace and Dalli had been able to calm them.

We turned on our own to try and stop the hurting. Took innocent lives.

What is this war turning us into?

Mace didn't have an answer. Mace had just one overriding imperative now – to reach Rilporin, aid his father and the defence, and take his vengeance on the Mireces. *Justice,* his mind insisted. *Vengeance,* his gut replied.

Whichever one his Rank was after, once they'd rested – the first genuine rest since the battle of the Blood Pass Valley – they'd marched with him, and the Wolves too. None of them had anything to go home to, after all. They'd all given everything for their country, and it had chewed them up and spat them out. They were the broken remnants of war's ravenous appetite, and they were going back for more.

The South Rank's fleet had been mostly destroyed, no doubt Corvus's work, but it looked as though there were enough ships, just, for his troops and the Wolves to set sail for Rilporin and the siege.

There was splashing as someone waded into the river towards a drifting bow line and Mace shuddered and looked away. He remembered the water taking his legs from under him as he and his Rank charged through the smugglers' tunnels towards the surface. Too slow, too far to run, the water a screaming animal behind, around, above and then in front of them and no air left, no air to breathe, water battering them against tunnel floor and roof and walls, smashing them into each other, men in plate armour tossed like straw dolls to twist and flail and sink and die.

'Mace? Mace, love, easy now. Breathe, that's it, just breathe.' Dalli's voice was firm and strong and he clung to it as though he was drowning again.

He came back to the sunlight and the warmth and the wide-open skies, his palms clammy and his chest heaving for air. Dalli's normally short hair was growing out, he suddenly noticed, beginning to curl down on to her forehead. He focused on those curls and focused on breathing, and after a long minute she put her hand over his and prised his fingers out of the flesh of her elbow.

'Ouch.' She smiled. 'Better?' He nodded and straightened as the panic receded, made himself look at the river again. Think. Function.

'Good.' She pressed a kiss to his cheek. 'I'm looking forward to taking those bastards by surprise; no doubt they think we're all dead. Can't wait to ram my spear up a few arses and prove them wrong.'

Mace snorted, thankful she didn't acknowledge his moment of panic. Of weakness. 'It's your way with words I love the most about you,' he said as a surge of anger filled his chest. Dalli wasn't the only one with a score to settle.

'There're a lot of things you love about me, General Koridam.' She laughed, sticking out her almost flat chest and squeezing her elbows together to give the cleavage some help. Mace stuck his face in her shirt and she laughed again, batting him away. 'I'm going to check on Rillirin and Seth; don't leave without us, all right?'

'Believe it,' Mace said and meant it. 'Send Lim to me, would you? And insist this time. We can't – mustn't – have a repeat of what happened back at the Cove.'

Dalli's face twisted and she nodded, getting to her feet with a wince. 'I'll try.' She patted his shoulder and limped away and Mace couldn't help but watch her arse until his view was blocked by a decidedly less attractive form.

'Colonel Dorcas, how fares the eye?' he asked, and then forced himself to listen as Dorcas related, for what was possibly the tenth time that day, the story of how, while heroically defending his men in a side tunnel, a Mireces had skewered Dorcas in the face and taken his eye as a trophy.

Mace was a little hazy on the practicalities of trophy eyes. Ears, fingers, teeth, hands he could understand, but not eyes. Just squishy balls, weren't they? Couldn't string them around your neck without them bursting, couldn't dry them into leathery sticks to keep in a jar to frighten children, couldn't . . .

'Astonishing,' he murmured when the flow of words ceased. 'And yet you march on without complaint.' Dorcas preened, oblivious of the irony. 'Oh, but if you would excuse me, Chief Lim approaches. I need to speak with him in private.' Dorcas saluted and wandered off to find someone else to regale. 'If you could ensure as many boats as possible are ready to set out tomorrow, Colonel,' Mace called after him. 'Every able-bodied soldier to be put to work.'

Mace eased himself to his feet and waited for the Wolf chief to reach him. Lim's face was closed, locked tight on emotions Mace couldn't begin to comprehend. His right hand rested on his knife hilt; his left carried a charm. Mace forced himself not to look at it.

'Lim, my friend. Thank you for coming.'

'What do you want, General?' Lim's voice was as closed as his face.

'How are your people, Chief?' Mace asked, switching to the formal title Lim seemed to prefer. *Putting as much distance between us as he can. Telling me we're allies, not friends. Not any more. Not after everything that's happened.*

'As expected. The strength they'd begun to recover is being wasted. Wounds are reopening, stitches ripping under the rigours of the march. And you're forcing them back towards danger.'

'With respect, they made that decision for themselves. As did you . . . Chief, what happened in Yew Cove, afterwards, that can never happen again. Never. Every one of us is here because we swore an oath to protect the citizens of Rilpor from her enemies. The slaughter of innocents cannot be countenanced. And I will not allow it to be repeated.'

Lim's eyes blazed challenge. 'I saw a few of your own wielding blades, General. You're not so fucking pure, and neither are your men. And we're not under your godsdamn command.'

Mace bit back an unwise retort and took a breath. 'Lim, I know you're hurting—'

'Don't,' Lim interrupted, his eyes brown granite. 'Don't say we've all lost people, don't mention her name. Not to me, not to anyone.' He stepped so close Mace could feel the tickle of his breath on his cheek. 'Not ever. Or I take my people and leave. Clear?'

'Clear,' Mace said. 'But if you're staying, I need to know you can control your people. And yourself.'

The punch nearly took his jaw from his face and Mace was flat in the grass, his ears ringing and white lights sparking in his head. Lim straddled him and sat on his stomach, knees in Mace's shoulders, fist in his shirt and jerking him up off the ground. 'You don't,' punch, 'give me,' punch, 'orders,' punch, '*General*.'

Mace bucked his hips and twisted to the side, just enough to throw Lim off balance. He wriggled his arm free and shoved Lim off him. They both came up on to their feet, fists raised. 'I said control,' Mace spat and saw renewed fury in Lim's face.

'Fuck you,' Lim screamed and swung.

'She's dead,' Mace shouted as he spat blood and ducked. Lim roared. 'Sarilla's dead, my friend, and this won't bring her back.'

He parried a flurry of blows, skipping sideways, slipping the straights, blocking the hooks, not fighting back. 'You dishonour her!' he bellowed when Lim showed no signs of stopping.

The Wolf froze mid-swing. 'What?'

'Sarilla Archer, finest shot I ever saw, scariest woman I ever met. What do you think she'd say if she could see us scrapping like a pair of boys because you're hurting?' Lim's fists slowly came down. 'That wasn't rhetorical, Lim,' Mace said, spitting another mouthful of blood and a fragment of tooth. He blinked away the lights in his head and his own anger, yammering on the end of a fraying rope. 'What would she say?'

Lim's left fist unclenched and the charm was still in it – a thick plait of long ginger hair, bound with a bowstring. He stared at it without moving. 'She'd tell me to put the hurt away until I had time for it,' he whispered. 'Until I could use it.'

'Well, it's certainly fuelling your punches, but is now that time?' Mace's voice was soft, with steel beneath. 'Is it?'

Mute, Lim shook his head, and then his shoulders shook and he dropped to both knees in the grass. Behind him Major Tara Carter and a couple of Wolves looked on, wary, hands on weapons. Mace waved them away and knelt opposite, put his arms around Lim and drew him close as he sobbed.

'Scariest woman?' Lim croaked after a while.

'Gods, yes,' Mace murmured and Lim hiccupped, managed a chuckle. 'And the best.'

'And the best,' Lim echoed. 'I miss her, Mace. In here.' He rubbed his chest. 'It hurts.'

'I know, my friend,' Mace said, his voice rough. 'I know.'

Lim jerked away so hard Mace thought he was going to get punched again. 'You have my apologies, General. Mace. The Wolves are yours, as always, and we hunt at your command,' he said, and for now at least, the pain had scabbed over, leaving cold rage burning in its place. 'Your father better have left us some Mireces to kill.'

Mace hoisted him to his feet; the Wolf Ash slung an arm around him and led him away and he watched them go, regrets thick as shadows in his heart.

War makes savages of us all, and none of us will ever be the same.

I hope it'll be worth it.

DURDIL

Fourth moon, dawn, day thirty-one of the siege
Gatehouse, western wall, Rilporin, Wheat Lands

The sky was bruised with the coming of day, the defenders bruised from the previous night. The assaults had continued well after the sun had set, wave after wave, allowing those on the allure no respite. The bridgehead had formed, broken, been washed away, formed again further along, broken there, formed again, a bloody river carving its own path through the landscape.

Durdil had spent the night on the wall, lit garish red and yellow with a myriad torches, as men fought and killed and died in the guttering light, the uniforms hard to tell apart in the gloom, men killing friends and comrades by mistake. The worst fucking sort of fighting, but eventually they'd pushed them back and secured the allure in the darkest part of the night.

Hallos had, hours before, given up waiting for the wounded to be brought to the hospitals in Second Circle and climbed up on to the wallwalk with a dozen other healers, moving from First to Last Bastion and treating everyone he could, using his scalpel on those of the enemy who came too close.

As the sky finally lightened, Durdil could hear the shouts and screams of the day's first assault echoing brassy and blood-red across the city. The three trebuchets loosed, one each at the north and south stump walls, the third still – always – at the weak spot between Second Tower and Last Bastion. So far the stump walls were holding, but as they were more a deterrent to easy access than a formal defence, Durdil knew they'd be down soon enough. After that the enemy would be knocking at the harbour gates and things would be even more interesting.

'They're early,' he muttered as the clamour rose louder and Hallos grunted, mired in blood from his boots to the crown of his shaven head, like something out of nightmare. Durdil didn't think he looked much better.

'Take a few hours off,' Durdil said, 'and preferably take a bath. You look worse than my soldiers.'

'I'll rest soon enough,' Hallos grated and tipped a ladle of water from the butt over his head, gasping at the chill. He scrubbed his face and head. 'Better?'

'Not really, no,' Durdil said. 'Possibly worse.'

They stood at the base of the wall with Major Renik, wincing at every scream. They'd held it through the night with Vaunt, and now Yarrow and Edris had the command. Supposedly, the night watch could stand down until dusk.

'I should just—' Durdil started as the clash of arms grew suddenly louder.

Hallos and Renik both put hands on his shoulders. 'Not a chance, Commander,' Hallos rasped. 'Eat, bathe, sleep. Physician's orders.'

He nodded and moved north, towards Second Tower and the distant Last Bastion, where Merle and his masons were arriving ready to prop the wall. They'd tried everything they could to force the trebuchets off the wall, to no avail. Now that there was only one loosing at the weak spot, Durdil and Merle had decided to risk the repairs.

There weren't any bodies down here, but whoever had taken them away had left the bloodstains behind. Men thrown to their deaths from the wallwalk above. Men who'd fallen accidentally. Men who'd been wounded or skewered through and then vanished over the guard wall into the depths below.

He scuffed a rusty stain and eyed Merle's huge outline; the mason had taken to lurking at the wall almost constantly, as though his presence alone could prevent a collapse.

'Losses?' Durdil asked Renik, and sipped at the cup a soldier had given him as he'd finally exited the gatehouse. Watered wine. Nectar.

'Four hundred in the night, as of an hour ago. We estimate the enemy lost at least three times that, but they show no signs of slowing. Something's stirred them up and they've got the numbers to rotate in so that there's no let-up for us.'

'Right, and what are we running out of?' Merle had a lot of masons with him today; the sight of the big men wound his nerves a notch or two tighter.

'Arrows. Bandages. Opium. Stones for the catapults, bolts for the stingers. Men. Hope.'

'All right, Renik, that's enough, go and get some sleep.' Durdil held his eyes, no need to say anything. Renik blushed and then saluted, staggered away towards the slaughter district and its gate into Second Circle. The north barracks was just inside and Renik could be in a cot and asleep within five minutes. Durdil envied him.

'Merle, my good man, give me good news,' Durdil said, forcing cheer into his voice. *Please, gods, give me good news.*

Merle looked like he'd been asked to tell lies in front of the temple godpool. 'Well, we're ready to go when you are, Commander. Have been for a week now. Stone's here, chisels and men are here, mortar's ready to be mixed. Just that trebuchet that's the worry now. Any chance?'

I can't stop that trebuchet loosing for an hour, let alone the time you need, and if you think I can then you're madder than a stoat down a fat man's trousers.

'Out of interest, if you completed the repairs while the treb kept loosing, what would happen?' Durdil asked.

Merle's dusty eyebrows rose high. 'Depends how far the bad stone stretches. If we have to chip deep into the wall, then it'll be so weak she won't withstand more than a few hours' bombardment. Half a day at the most. And that's with only the one engine loosing at it instead of all three.'

'That bad? All right, and we need to make the repairs soon, do we?'

Merle folded his massive arms. 'You're already gambling more than you've got to bet with, Commander. Them moving the two other trebs definitely bought us time, but that's gone now. If we don't make these repairs today there's no point in us making them.'

Durdil puffed out his cheeks and flapped his hands around. 'How about if we prop the wall on the inside and do the works like that?'

Merle coughed a laugh. 'Prop the wall? Sir, it's three times the height of a man. Prop it with what?'

'Masts from the boats in the harbour,' Hallos said when neither of them seemed to have an answer.

Merle frowned up at the wall looming over them. 'It's a possibility, Commander, but I wouldn't want to stake my reputation on them holding.'

Just your life then. And all of ours too.

'All right, we're out of options,' Durdil said heavily. 'The fact is we can't reach that siege engine and stop it. I'll send five Hundreds to the harbour to protect the dockworkers unstepping the masts. Start work chipping out the stone now and prop it when they arrive. The treb will loose until night-fall, so pray the masts hold it up until then. Get the new stone in as soon as you can, before dark if possible. If you can, work through the night and with luck and the Dancer's grace, the mortar will have dried by dawn.'

Merle scratched his scalp. 'You're putting a lot of faith in those masts, Commander, and in the drying properties of good mortar. It's my lads who'll be inside the wall if she comes down.'

'And it's my lads who'll be on the top of it, fighting and dying all day and all night, too. We're under siege, Merle; every single one of us is risking death now. Can you do it?'

Merle stared at the faces of his masons and their appren-tices, at the mounds of dressed stone, the tubs of sand and limestone waiting to be mixed. Then he clapped his huge hands once. 'Work'll go slower in the dark, sir, so we'll need plenty of torchlight to see by, and if you've got men up there fighting, well' – he pointed to a bloodstain – 'not sure my lads want to be killed by a hundredweight of soldier and armour dropping on their heads. Still, we'll give it our best and leave the rest up to the Dancer.'

Durdil stepped forward and looked up into Merle's honest, dusty face. 'I don't think we can leave this one to the gods, Merle. If you don't manage this, we all die.'

Merle's chest inflated so much he nearly pushed Durdil back a step. 'Aye, Commander. We understand. We won't let you down, will we, boys?' There was a chorus of grim affir-mation and the masons turned away from Durdil, stepped up the wall and the indecipherable markings scratched in chalk and, without another word, began to chisel.

'You're a credit to your trade and to Rilpor. I have no doubts you'll succeed. Anything you need today, Colonel Yarrow up above will see you get it. Once night falls, come to me.'

Merle bobbed his head, and Durdil nodded again and headed for Last Bastion and the North Gate. The harbour nestled behind the stump wall had been probed but not assaulted; the boats remained intact, their masts the only thing between Rilporin and defeat.

Durdil had been asleep for approximately three and a half seconds when someone burst into his room and yelled him awake.

'What?' he grunted, knuckling grit from his eyes and letting out a long, protracted groan as his muscles sparked into rebellious, agonised life.

'I said, they've built a sow and it's heading for the gatehouse. Looks like they're going to try rope and tackle to bring down the portcullis. If they manage it, they'll slap pitch against the gates at this end of the tunnel and set the whole thing on fire.' Vaunt's voice was calm as ice, but there were hectic spots of colour in his cheeks.

'The room above the tunnel's manned, correct? They're opening the murder holes?' Durdil asked as he staggered upright and squinted as Vaunt flung open the shutters. He looked out – mid-afternoon, apparently. Still not enough sleep.

Durdil shrugged into chainmail and jammed a helmet on, ignoring Vaunt's protest that he should be in plate armour. 'No time,' he snapped, buckling on his sword and snatching up vambraces and gauntlets.

He strode to the door and out into an eerie, silent Second Circle and then jogged heavily towards the gate into First Circle. Vaunt caught him up, slung him a waterskin and then a heel of bread with butter spread as thick as his little finger was round. Durdil's eyelids sagged and he groaned at the taste, mumbled thanks as Vaunt reclaimed the waterskin and replaced it with a thick pink wedge of what turned out to be lamb.

Gods, food. His stomach reminded him that as welcome as the meal was, it was nowhere near enough and that he'd forgotten to eat before tumbling into his cot – and that, actually, there were a few more points his body would like to raise now that he was awake, such as the unexpected rigours of battle, the bone-deep bruises from swords and axes trying to hammer through his armour, the general lack of food, water, sleep and a spare minute to take a godsdamned piss, if you please.

Durdil bit down on the meat, turned to face the closest wall, hefted his chainmail and let loose a stream of golden urine that glinted magnificently in the sun. He groaned again.

'Are you all right, sir?' Vaunt asked worriedly. 'Blood in your piss, sir? I can get Hallos and—'

Durdil grunted around the chunk of meat in his mouth and then shook his head, finished up and stuffed himself back in his trousers, remembering to wipe his hand on his sleeve before taking the meat out of his mouth.

'I'm fine, let's go,' he said and forced himself into a run again, pounding through the killing field beneath the curtain wall, where an enemy would be trapped between the walls and so vulnerable to arrow shot from above – *gods, don't let it come to that* – on towards the gatehouse on legs that really shouldn't shake this much and in through the door and up and up and up the stairs to the level of the wallwalk, where Edris and Yarrow had the command.

And Renik, too, apparently, though the man was supposed to be sleeping. *I'm supposed to be sleeping. So's Vaunt.*

'Show me.'

Renik gestured to an arrow slit and Durdil pressed his face to the stone and looked down, still chewing the fatty lamb and trying not to drool. The sow was an upturned cart with plates of metal and animal hides nailed to its bottom, the legs of a dozen men visible underneath as they carried it as protection above their heads and made their way towards the gate.

He could see the ropes unfurling behind them and knew they'd be attached to grappling hooks that they'd latch on to the portcullis. As soon as they'd hooked on, the squad on the other end of the rope would start cranking, hoping to pull the portcullis free of its housing before the defenders could sprint the length of the tunnel and unhook them.

Standard manoeuvre, one we know how to counter . . . Durdil's eyes tracked the long ropes trailing from behind the sow. Looked as though they stretched back to the trebuchet, now facing away from the city as though it was going to hurl rocks into its own army.

'Fuck the gods,' Durdil breathed and grabbed Renik by the shoulder, pulled him to the arrow slit. 'What happens if they connect the ropes from the portcullis to the treb's throwing arm?' he hissed. 'Could it work?'

Renik paled and swallowed. 'Dangerous,' he said. 'Either it flips the treb, shatters it, snaps the ropes or rips free the portcullis. Three of those will be lethal to the men around it. The fourth could well be lethal for Rilporin.'

Durdil spun from the window and shoved Vaunt towards the stairs. 'Get those fucking hooks off the portcullis right fucking now.'

Vaunt didn't hesitate, didn't protest a major shouldn't be

doing something like this, didn't mention the arrow shot he'd be under from the men in the sow the second he got close to the hooks. He just dodged a knot of soldiers and threw himself down the spiral staircase.

'Help him,' Durdil shouted, and the men gaped for a second and then followed. 'Renik, get a Hundred and muster this side of the gates. If they get that portcullis open, hold them there until I can get you reinforcements.'

'Sir,' Renik said and bolted for the same staircase that had swallowed Vaunt.

'Edris, Yarrow, whose command is under the least pressure?'

'Mine,' Edris said, 'we've had them pinned back for a good few hours now.'

'Right, fifty men. Fetch both the stingers stationed outside the gate into Second Circle. Vaunt's going to stop the sow tearing open the portcullis if he can, but if not I want those stingers rolled into the tunnel and loosing at any advance. Renik's your support. *Do not* let them through that tunnel. Understand?'

'Yes, Commander,' Edris said and saluted. Durdil returned the gesture. 'It's been an honour, sir.'

'Shut up, Edris. I'm not sending you out to die,' Durdil said, and they both knew he was probably lying. 'Dancer's grace. Go.'

Durdil was almost at the stairwell in the back wall when half a dozen blue-clad men slammed through the door from Double First's wallwalk. The first hurled a dagger. *So much for this wall being under control.*

Durdil threw himself out of its path and dragged his sword from its sheath. He snatched up a shield from the pile stacked inside the doorway and charged. Yarrow was a second behind him, despite his command being Second Last.

The Mireces Durdil faced was covered in blood from the flap of scalp hanging in his eye. He feinted left and then right, attacked left and Durdil whipped the shield laterally across his body, turning side-on behind it. The sword clattered off the shield boss and struck sparks from the stone floor. Three more Mireces circled behind him, grinning, two engaging Yarrow, the other looking to stab Durdil in the back.

Durdil parried a flurry of attacks, backing slowly across the room, but then reinforcements from somewhere arrived and together they drove the Mireces back through the door on to the allure. Durdil followed with his shield up. The wallwalk was a chaos of men in Mireces blue – too many – and Palace Rank green struggling and screeching in mad dances across the stone. Splashes of red that were the Personal Guard here and there, but for every defender there seemed to be three attackers poking up over the wall from the ladders.

Durdil cut through a gap between two of his men, shoved a Mireces hard in the back so he impaled himself on a Ranker's sword, punched his mailed fist into the face of another and sent him back-flipping off the wall in a spray of teeth and blood, and then he was in the thick, his blood singing and his feet sure. His fifty-six summers fell from his shoulders like an unneeded cloak and he killed his way towards the siege tower and the Mireces around it.

Durdil put his weight behind his sword and forced the tip through a man's ribs from behind; he'd been too busy sidestepping out of the bridgehead to notice Durdil's approach. He screamed and then stopped as the blade stole his breath, the sound strangled, pathetic, a consumptive child's last whimper. He fell to his knees and Durdil put his boot on his shoulder and wrenched his sword free. It grated against ribs, slid soft and silky through lung, and emerged with its length dull and black with blood.

Yarrow was at his side now and Durdil slashed past him and took the nose and cheek from a Raider. The man screamed blood and pain and Yarrow finished him with a graceless shove over the wall into the attackers waiting below.

A swift glance showed him the sow was almost at the portcullis; he needed to be down there. 'Can you hold?' He grabbed Yarrow's arm. 'Colonel, can you hold?'

'I – yes, Commander. On my honour we'll hold.'

'Good. I'll station a runner in the gatehouse; you need further reinforcements, let me know. Though I don't expect you will.' His meaning was clear and he saw Yarrow take it. The colonel swallowed, nodded again. 'This is the biggest push we've seen from them. I'd say don't be a fucking hero, Colonel, but I need you to be.'

'Understood, sir.' Yarrow wiped sweat from his face and managed a grin that was more a grimace. 'Been a while since . . .' His words trailed off as he stared up and over Durdil's shoulder, and Durdil turned to engage, sweeping his blade in a wide diagonal to cover as much space as possible, the rest of him tucked tight behind his shield. His blade thunked into the wooden haft of a two-handed axe wielded by a giant wearing a blue tent over his chest and shoulders, bracers on his arms that might have been adapted from horse armour.

Durdil ducked under the swing and the giant let the momentum spin him in a circle, Palace Rankers, Personals and Mireces alike scurrying out of range and falling into each other to avoid the whining blade. Durdil came back up in time to meet the Mireces face to face, hacking his sword upwards to slice into a thigh, skitter out and across chainmail and graze the man's armpit. The giant howled and swung again, the blade smashing into the stone where

Durdil's foot had been and sending shrapnel hissing into the crowd. A fragment caught him on the pauldron and bounced up into his face, stinging his lip.

Durdil danced backwards, sword and shield raised, adrenaline sharpening his sight and tempering the poisons of worry and fatigue with just a little more sweetness.

He leapt in again, screaming and slashing and then skipping out of range – or what he thought was out of range. The giant grinned and the axe hummed in a flat arc towards him, inexorable as time. Durdil reversed fast, but his heels hit a body and he slammed on to his arse, tailbone smashing into stone, the agony blinding him with tears. The Mireces arced his axe upwards, spun once more, and sliced it down towards Durdil's face.

He knew the impact would shatter his sword before his head but he swung anyway, a desperate parry to buy himself one more instant of life. Durdil's sword met only air and he opened eyes he didn't realise he'd shut to find the giant standing slack, axe hanging loose, an expression of puzzled incomprehension on his bearded face. He jerked, jerked again, and Durdil heard the sound of metal cleaving flesh. The giant went to one knee and behind him Durdil saw Yarrow, a Mireces axe in his hands, chopping at the stump that was a man like he was felling winter firewood. Blood juddered into the air, scarlet droplets hanging against the sun for an endless instant before raining on them all.

And still he didn't die. Instead he twisted, throwing an arm over his shoulder and grabbing for Yarrow. His hand closed on the colonel's sleeve and tugged him forward; Yarrow crashed into his back and the giant grabbed again, harder, and tried to pull him over his shoulder and on to the stone in front of him. The colonel bleated and Durdil realised it was up to him to do something.

He lurched upright, tailbone creaking protest, and punched the Mireces in the teeth, his gauntlet mashing the man's lips to pulp and shattering enamel. The man blinked and focused glazed eyes on him. Durdil punched him again and Yarrow pulled away, leaving a vambrace, a sleeve and a fair amount of hair and skin in the giant's possession. Durdil punched a third time as Yarrow stepped into space and pirouetted, the axe leading, trailing a gleam of sunlight from its edge and slamming into the side of the kneeling Mireces' neck.

Durdil heard a triple scream, one from the Mireces, one from Yarrow of triumph, and one that must have been his own, his throat suddenly raw and echoing. The Mireces' head sagged to one side, the neck partially cut through, and he could see the dull shine of bone in the meat and gristle and spurting, fountaining blood. Yarrow didn't bother with a second blow. The giant fell and they left him to bleed to death, bubbling breath and shrieks and life into the air.

'Thanks,' Durdil gasped.

Yarrow raised a finger in acknowledgment, too busy sucking in air to answer straight away. He hacked a harsh, dry cough and attempted to spit over the wall.

Durdil rubbed his arse and winced. *That's going to be a bastard of a bruise.* He glanced along the wall; the bridgehead was contracting, pressed on all sides back towards the ladders. 'Hold,' he said one more time, and then started eeling through the press around the bridgehead, making for the nearest tower and set of stairs.

The trebuchet released and there was the scream of rope under immense tension; the entire gatehouse shuddered, dust exploding into the sky as the enemy attempted to rip the portcullis free.

'Shit.'

CORVUS

Fourth moon, afternoon, day thirty-one of the siege
East Rank encampment, outside Rilporin, Wheat Lands

'Did it work?' Corvus asked. He stood by Lanta, Rivil and Skerris, Valan and the Godblind a few paces behind.

The noise from the gatehouse had been like distant stone and metal beasts tearing into each other, and all was obscured by dust. Rivil was silent as he stared through the distance-viewer at the gatehouse, Corvus twitching with the desire to snatch it from his grip and look for himself. The trebuchet they'd used to rip out the grate was a twisted wreck littered with corpses and splashed with blood; one of the ropes from the portcullis to the throwing arm had snapped under the force and scythed through the warriors under the sow, cutting them in half before whipping into a squad of Rankers standing fifty paces distant. Not distant enough, it seemed. The Lady's will.

The throwing arm was cracked and one of the giant axles had snapped under the awful force. The engine was useless. The question, though, was whether the portcullis was still down or whether they'd effected a breach that the defenders couldn't plug. The best scenario was that the entire grate had been ripped free. Rivil and Corvus had two thousand men each standing ready to flood into the tunnel if it had worked.

'No,' Rivil said eventually, and passed Corvus the distance-viewer so he could see for himself.

Motherfucker.

Lanta rose on to her toes, hand on Corvus's shoulder to steady herself, and squinted towards the city. 'Is it burning?'

'Just dust,' Corvus said. 'It's hard to tell, but it seems damaged, wouldn't you say, Rivil? Could be it's jammed in place, trapping them inside. If we've at least prevented them from marching out in support of the West Rank when it arrives, then the loss of the treb is surely worth it.' He glanced at the Godblind.

'Soon,' the man said. 'The West Rank will be here very soon.'

'But we can't get in, either,' Lanta pointed out, and that Corvus couldn't deny. He squinted again as the dust half concealed, half revealed the gatehouse. Why hadn't it torn free? Why hadn't the gatehouse cracked, slumped, fallen? Why were they still on the outside?

'Skerris, send five Hundreds at the wall between the gate-house and Second Tower. Let's not give them time to recover.' Rivil had reclaimed the distance-viewer. 'We haven't got through either of the stump walls, but now this treb is useless, we can't pound that weak spot further down. Let's move one back on to it, especially after this – surely we shook the wall to its very foundations. We could be one good throw away from dropping the wall.'

'Tell us, Godblind,' Corvus said and felt the anger rise like heat from the Blessed One. He should have asked her.

She fears the loss of her power.

Corvus took her gently by the hand. 'Blessed One,' he said

softly, 'please know that your wisdom and insight can never be surpassed by this drooling madman.' Lanta looked as if she was about to scoff, to deny his words or take umbrage. 'But please also know that a gift such as the Godblind cannot be ignored. The gods have given him to us; we must seize every advantage and his link to the gods is strong. Better we break him than you.'

He leant close so no one else could hear. 'I do not think he lies, and you and I must present a united front to our allies. If you have doubts about his words, tell me afterwards, not in front of the others. And please, Blessed One, as I have had to share power with Rivil, do not dismiss the Godblind's words out of hand. Together we will triumph; alone we may yet fall.'

The Blessed One's inhalation was sharp with fury and her eyes blazed blue ice at him. Very deliberately she pulled her hand from his and took a pace back. 'I act only in the interests of the gods,' she said. 'Even your desires are second to Theirs, and I would do nothing – *nothing* – to jeopardise Their triumph. All is as the Lady wills it, even your failure here.'

Corvus bowed his head to her, seething at her choice of words. 'The reminder is timely for us all, Blessed One,' he said.

'Remember that you are bound to tell the truth,' Lanta said to the Godblind before Corvus could speak. 'Do not lie to us – about the siege, the war or anything else. Will you die for the Red Gods?'

'I will die, I will kill, I will live, I will murder. All that They command I must do. I cannot do otherwise.' The Godblind's eyes were owlish and empty, blinking slowly in the sun.

'Good,' Corvus began but Lanta held up her hand, cutting him off again.

'And do you worship with a full heart, or because you are afraid to do otherwise?'

The Godblind was silent for so long that Corvus felt a lurch of unease.

Shadows flocked across the man's face so his features were hard to make out. They all stood in shadow, Corvus suddenly realised, though the sun shone undimmed in the sky.

'You were told of the Godblind's coming, you were told his identity, and still you doubt,' he snarled suddenly, and there was a harmony in his voice that Corvus had never heard before, a timbre that vibrated his bones and set dread in his bowels. And it was a higher-pitched, more feminine voice. He sounded like a woman.

The Godblind pointed at them each in turn, his eyes golden despite the shadow, seeming taller than he had. Wisps of black curled around him, obscuring, revealing. 'Show humility when your goddess speaks to you. Lanta Costinioff, daughter of a tenth-rate warrior and a poxed bed-slave, you rose to prominence as my instrument. Madoc Fisher, slave of Dancer's Lake, your ascension fulfils my desires, not your own.'

Corvus felt the blood drain from his face and fell on to his knees, pressing his forehead into the grass. *It's Her. It's Her inside him.*

The Godblind's head moved like a snake's, sinuous and full of menace as the others knelt in awed terror. 'Prince Rivil Evendoom, your father is dead and the council has elected Tresh to be the new king. You have been overlooked, as you were your entire life. Only in me have you found purpose. Only I have seen your worth.'

The Godblind brought his hands together hard and the sound was as loud as a thunderclap. Lanta cried out and Corvus was flattened as Valan threw himself over him in instinctive protection. 'I am served by the lowest of slaves, whom I raised to prominence to do my will, *and yet you question me? Question my chosen vessel, my Godblind? Think to raise yourselves above him? Above me?*'

Corvus could just see him out of the corner of one eye. The Godblind's shape shifted so that sometimes he was himself, other times something . . . else. He pulsed and fluttered, shape changing man to woman, man to woman to snake to horror to woman, and he pointed at them one by one in much the same way Lanta chose sacrifices. Corvus felt his bladder twitch. He squeezed hard.

'If it were not for the time it would take, I would find replacements for you all. As it is, know that I am displeased. Move the northern trebuchet off the stump wall and back on to the weakness. There is to be no let-up of men or siege engines. And do not ever question the Godblind's devotion again.'

The presence drained away and the Godblind's back arched and he rose on to his toes, arms flung at the sky, before collapsing. One flailing arm caught Skerris in the face, knocking him backwards. Corvus shoved Valan off him and knelt up, staring at the Godblind in awe and fear. *She was in him. She was here in the world, in him. She is everywhere and everything. I will never doubt again.*

'Skerris,' Rivil said in a shaky voice, 'get the trebuchet moved immediately and get those men up the fucking wall.'

'Your will, Majesty,' Skerris said, lumbering to his feet and hurrying away with much haste and little dignity.

'Valan, send the men at the wall. Go now.' Valan too vanished and Corvus exchanged a long look with the Blessed One; she was grey, pupils dilated. Her fingers shook.

'Our feet are on the Path,' she whispered.

Corvus heard sobbing and reached out; he put a gentle hand on the Godblind's back. 'Come on, man, let's get you somewhere comfortable. You'll have much to do before this is all over.'

TARA

Fourth moon, eighteenth year of the reign of King Rastoth
South Rank harbour, River Gil, Western Plain

'You keep poking at it and it'll fall off.'

Tara snatched her hand away, but seconds later it was back, prodding, teasing at the stitches holding the bottom half of her ear to the rest. The bandages had come off that morning and everything still seemed to be attached, but gods it stung, and the accompanying row of stitches just below her cheekbone still made it difficult to open her mouth wide. Yawning was bloody agony. Still, all things considered, a knife to the head could have had a much more terminal outcome.

'Seriously though, Ash,' she said, both her hands pressed to her chest, 'am I still pretty?' She batted her eyelids and smiled, the stitches pulling at the muscle so her lip turned down instead of up.

Ash grimaced. 'You were never pretty, Carter. Face like the arse-end of an arse.' Tara threw a punch and he ducked. 'All right, let's have a look. Gods, it's fucking ugly,' he said, squinting at it. 'Are you sure it's even your ear? Could be anyone's, or just a bit of gristle they picked up off the floor and stitched on. Might not even be a fucking ear.'

He put his head on one side and poked at it himself. Tara hissed and jerked away. 'You know, I don't think it is. Looks a bit like foreskin, just hanging there all shrivelled and useless. Best not get too excited, woman, you might get an erection.'

Tara shoved him in the chest and he staggered backwards, laughing. 'And there was me thinking the only useless thing attached to a cock was a man,' she said and Ash laughed again, gave her an approving round of applause. 'But come on, Bowman, I think we both know that if I had a cock I'd be the bloody King of Rilpor.'

'Now that, Major, I do not doubt for a second,' Ash said and together they hauled at the planks that had once been the boathouse and dragged them towards the growing pile of timber. Those ships that hadn't burnt to the waterline in the blaze set by the Mireces needed patching.

'Don't suppose you're a master carpenter among your other manifold abilities?' he asked.

'I can bang a nail in straight, and that's about it,' Tara said.

'Can you stop talking about cocks for one minute,' Ash complained and she sniggered.

'And there was me thinking that you of all people would enjoy that kind of talk.'

'Oi,' Ash snapped and she stopped in surprise. 'You want to get me executed?' he hissed, shushing her. 'We're in the middle of a bloody Rank, woman, and what I am would get me killed if anyone knew, so keep your shitting voice down.'

Tara blushed. 'I'm sorry, Ash, truly. I just . . . feel like I've got someone to talk to for the first time. Someone who knows what it's like to be different.'

'Having tits doesn't make you less of a soldier,' Ash said, shrugging, 'and me liking men doesn't make me less of one. But it's the rest of the world we need to convince, eh?'

Tara sucked a splinter out of the palm of her hand and spat it as they moved back to the ruins of the boathouse. 'True enough. So then, when I become King of Rilpor, I'll change two laws – women in the military isn't odd and . . . same-sex love is legal. How's that?'

Ash shook his head, but he was grinning. 'Tara, love, if you grew the necessary bits to make you king, changing the law would be the last thing you'd be worrying about.'

'Good point. Guess we're both still fucked then, eh?'

'Guess so. We should probably sort this timber out now, aye?' They picked up the next load of planks. 'And for what it's worth, even without a cock, you've got bigger balls than most men I know.'

'Oh Ash,' Tara sighed, batting her eyelashes again, 'you say the nicest things.'

Tara stared at the drifting galleys in frustrated anger. 'Godsdamn bastard shits,' she bellowed across the water, startling waterfowl and soldiers in equal measure. A flight of ducks burst into the air, honking away from her.

'What happened?' Major Crys Tailorson asked.

'Bloody rope snapped; it was singed through, but the boats themselves look intact. We could've really used those boats,' she added.

'Ships,' Crys amended and began pulling at his boots. 'Pass some good rope, will you?' he asked.

Tara frowned at him, then at the water. 'You're going in there?'

'Why not?'

There were several reasons why not, and every one of

them had to do with the thousands of Rankers and Wolves who'd died screaming in the Yew Cove tunnels. Tara swallowed nausea. 'Are you sure?'

Crys frowned. 'Of course I'm sure. I can swim.'

'So could every man in the West Rank,' Tara mumbled. 'Didn't stop them drowning.'

Crys unbuckled his sword belt and pulled his jerkin and shirt off. His upper back and ribs were patterned with bruising and it looked as though every knob of bone had had the skin scraped off it, exposing patches of raw flesh. 'Rope,' he said, holding out his hand, and Tara threw him the end of a line. Crys tied a loop and threw it over his head and arm, slid down the bank into the water, waded out to his thighs and began to swim.

All activity along the bank ceased and men and women lined the river, watching Crys swim hard after the boats drifting on the current. 'Is he bloody daft?' Ash muttered, coming to stand at Tara's side. 'Gods, he's an idiot. What's he doing?'

'Fetching the boats, or ships, or whatever,' Tara said. 'How can he just do that? Just get in there like it's nothing? Like what happened didn't happen?'

'He went back down the tunnels to search for survivors once we were out, remember,' Ash said. 'Twice. I thought it was just adrenaline at the time; now I can see its lunacy.' Ash's knuckles were white where he was gripping the haft of his hand axe. 'You've got hold of the other end of that rope, yes? So we can pull him in?'

Tara looked at the end of the line slowly inching towards the water and stamped down on it. Blushing, she snatched it up and then began following Crys along the bank as he swam, closing the distance to the unmanned boats. He reached the stern of the closest and reached up, pulled himself high enough to loop the rope over the tiller, then hauled himself in and checked the line connecting it to the others was secure.

He turned to Tara and seemed surprised at the crowd on the bank. 'All right, pull us in,' he called and circled his arm above his head. Tara and Ash began dragging at the rope with the help of half a dozen others, and the small fleet came to a stop and then, slowly, made its way back to the battered dock.

'What?' Crys asked as he jumped out. 'Were you worried, love?' he asked Ash and winked at Tara.

Tara let go of the rope and stared at them. 'Love? What are . . . are you two . . . what?' she spluttered.

Crys laughed and slung his arms around them both. 'Come on, we need to get to Rilporin.' He jogged over to the pile of clothes and boots he'd left on the grass. Men were smiling at him, congratulating him.

'How does he do that?' Tara muttered. 'Just get men to like him so easily?'

'I have no idea,' Ash said. 'And no, don't ask. What you don't know can't hurt you. Or me. Or him.'

'Well, I'm pleased for you,' she said, stamping down on the twinge of envy curling through her chest.

Crys glanced back at them and grinned, beckoned them over, and as the low sun threw his face into shadow, his eyes glowed yellow. 'More to the point,' Ash said in a worried voice, 'how does he do that?'

'Yeah,' Tara said. 'That's . . . weird.'

'And it's happening more and more,' Ash fretted. 'What is it?'

'If we get a shift on we can set sail this evening,' Crys interrupted as they approached. He had a twitchy, manic energy about him, as if he was gripped by a fever, but with the exception of that eye shine, he was healthy enough. *Healthier than most of the rest of us. No major wound from any of the fighting he's done, or if there was, it's healed. Which is impossible.*

'Sounds good,' Tara said with an effort. 'I'll inform Colonel Dorcas and the general that we'll be ready to leave in a couple of hours. We'll be in Rilporin in the morning.'

That soured the mood some, but it was the truth and they all knew what they were here for. After what had happened in Yew Cove, Tara'd been convinced they'd have a mutiny on their hands when Mace announced his intention to raise the siege at Rilporin, but the Rank knew its duty. Tara stared at the weary faces around them, heart swelling with pride. *Not out of the fight yet.*

She noted the way they watched Crys when he wasn't looking, as though his presence was a charm or a comfort. She'd felt the same herself, a time or two.

Harness this and there could be no stopping us, no matter what the Mireces try. They'll die for him if he asks, and he doesn't even know it.

She waved them on and walked away, her gait slow and her face thoughtful as she poked at the stitched-on earlobe. The men weren't the only ones who'd die for him, she realised. She was drawn to him, as though he was north and she was a lodestone. There was a burst of laughter from behind, something she hadn't heard in weeks, and she knew who'd caused it.

Who are you, Crys Tailorson? What are you?

GILDA

They still hadn't let her see him, not to speak with. He trailed around behind Corvus or Lanta while another warrior trailed him, writing down his words as though they were holy.

He'd ignored her completely when he arrived, shambling past towards the tent, still wet from his dunk in the river and shivering beneath the blue of a Mireces shirt a little too big for the skin and bones he was now. As though he didn't recognise her any more.

It's just a ploy. He doesn't want them to know how close we are, that's all.

Gilda didn't believe her own lies, not this time. She sat outside Lanta's tent as darkness fell, chained to a spike driven deep into the hard earth, an empty cup and bowl at her side. They'd cut her rations again, and her stomach growled its protest. After the work she was doing now at the field hospital, a meal was the least they owed her. Unless they

102

found out how many Rankers she'd guided back to the Light, of course.

She pulled her blanket tighter around her shoulders and tried to listen, but she couldn't hear words, just voices, the rise and fall of questions and answers and more questions, on and on as, in the distance, Rilporin's curtain wall was lit bright with torches, the better to see who they were killing and who was killing them. Something Dom had said had made them elect to fight through the night and there'd been no let-up in assaults since the afternoon.

That's it, then; he's told them there are reinforcements coming. Sweet Dancer, let it be the truth, even if they have lost the element of surprise. Let it be the Wolves, Cam and Lim and Sarilla and all the others. Let it be thousands of soldiers, overwhelming numbers to crush these bastards into the dirt.

She knew nothing about the fate of the Wolves who'd marched to the Blood Pass Valley to aid the West Rank, nothing but the reports she'd overheard from Corvus, that some had survived the battle there and were following them, so Corvus had left men behind to stage an ambush in Yew Cove's tunnels. That had been weeks ago and there'd been no word since, but now Dom was in there and he'd have news, have information about everything that had happened in the last weeks. And she couldn't hear him. It was maddening.

'Who's dead?' she muttered to herself. 'Which of my family are gone to the Light? How can I mourn them if I don't know who they are?'

She prayed into the echoing silence of her skull, prayed for all of them, alive and dead. It didn't feel enough. For the first time in decades, Gilda's prayers faltered and all the terrors and imaginings that came with being a warrior's wife, a warrior's mother, flooded in upon a black wave that even the strength of a priestess couldn't stand against.

She wept, and when she was done, she dried her face and put her mask back on and dared any Mireces to try and break her. She was Gilda Priestess, child of Light, and they could do their worst, because it would never be as bad as her own dark fears.

'Blacked her eye,' she whispered to herself, 'knocked the Blessed One right on her arse. Do it again, too, she messes with Dom. That and more.'

The words buoyed her and stirred her courage again, steeled her will and stiffened her spine. Dom being here gave her something to focus on, a goal to aim for: get out, and take him with her. It was clear that he was the Godblind of which Lanta had spoken.

Gilda had never heard the term before, but there was no denying Dom was the thing they spoke of with such awe and trepidation. That his knowings had increased to such an extent that he could see the future. And the past. And everything in between, maybe.

And that they were destroying him.

Then we put a stop to it, get him into a temple where the Dark Lady can't reach him, where he can't spill secrets in the wrong ears, and keep him there until this is over.

Easy. Slip my chain, get him away from Lanta and Corvus, sneak to the edge of the camp before dawn and just walk away.

Easy.

Somehow, she'd slept, and now the night was deep and chill, noisy with thousands of men sleeping, crying, grunting through pain and, in the distance, fighting, killing and dying. There was no murmur of conversation from the Blessed

One's tent now, and aside from the misty orange glow of a single torch, it was dark and quiet inside.

Where would Dom be? With Lanta or with Corvus? 'Lanta,' Gilda breathed. 'She's got a new pet and she won't let him go. I've been replaced.' Her smile was grim as she clambered to her feet.

She tugged experimentally at the chain, then wrapped it around both fists, planted her feet and hauled, teeth gritted. For long seconds nothing happened except that her upper spine crackled and popped from the exertion, and then, slowly at first but gathering speed, the spike slid from the earth.

Gilda glanced around longer this time, but the Mireces were resting while they could and anyway, no one would dare skulk around outside the Blessed One's tent in the middle of the night, not if they wanted to keep their eyes.

Gathering up the links of chain and muffling them in her ragged skirt, Gilda gripped the spike in her hand, the cool slickness of earth squelching between her fingers, and ducked into Lanta's huge tent with her breath held. It was a combination temple and bedchamber, lit with a single torch, the ground scattered with blankets against the damp. Lanta was sitting on an ornate stool, her back to the tent flap and her hands weaving a complex charm over a set of armour.

Well, shit. You're supposed to be asleep.

Dom was curled on a tangle of blankets like a sick hound, shivering in his sleep, his right arm cradled to his chest, eyes moving beneath the lids as he dreamed horrors. Gilda's heart lurched in her chest when she saw him again. They'd shaved him and washed his hair, tied it back from his face and she could see the lines of his skull beneath his papery skin, all sharp cheekbones and jawline, sunken eyes and chewed lips. *Oh, son, what have you done to yourself? I've seen corpses with more life in them. Nils looked better than you do, before and after I drove a knife into his head.*

Gilda weighed the spike in her hand, its length dull with earth, unable to catch the light. She drifted closer, studying the line of Lanta's neck where it met the shoulder, the back of her head. One solid blow. She advanced another step. Her hands didn't tremble.

Have I really come in here to kill? Is that what these people have reduced me to? No, of course not. But I do need her to be . . . sleeping. She hefted the spike.

'Scell's going to be flogged for letting you escape so easily,' Lanta said affably as she finished the charm on the armour – Corvus's, most likely. Her voice was low and honeyed, the harsh Mireces accent rolling smooth from her tongue. She didn't bother to look up.

Gilda moved around to face her and sat on the stool opposite. Lanta's smile was reptilian. 'Scell's more interested in poking around in dead bodies than watching me,' she said, dropping the spike to the ground by her foot. 'Dread to think what he's poking into one tonight. And besides, I'm an old woman weighed down with collar and chain. Not a threat, so no one watches me.'

'And yet here you are in my tent, unaccompanied, and arguably armed. Some people would find that threatening.'

'But not you? Because we're past all that, aren't we, Blessed One?' *Though the memory of punching you in the face still warms my heart.* She gazed around the tent with open admiration. 'Nice place you've got. None of the hardships of siege for you, eh? And a friend to warm you in the night, too.' She indicated Dom, and saw the muscles around Lanta's eyes tighten. 'Oh, not to your liking?'

'The Godblind is very much to my liking, just not in the way you infer.'

'What's a Godblind?' Gilda asked, playing the daft-old-lady card that neither of them believed in any more. Lanta just smiled, and Gilda looked at Dom again, sensing his scrutiny. She caught the glint of eyes in the gloom, but gave no sign to either of them that she'd noticed. *Well, you're awake at least. That's a start if we're going to get out of here.*

'Dom Templeson, Wolf, Calestar and your adopted son,' Lanta said and Gilda's attention snapped back to the woman seated opposite. Lanta's chuckle was undiluted malice. 'Did you think he was still yours, old woman? Did you think you could save him?' She affected surprise. 'Is that why you're here? You were going to kill me and steal away with your boy, return to the wilds with him and wait for this to all be over?'

'Something like that,' Gilda said with a shrug. 'Though I'm not a killer. But you haven't answered my question.'

'Godblind,' Lanta said with forced patience. 'Blind to everything but what the gods show him. Your gods, my gods, whoever wishes it. Though he says he hasn't heard from the Dancer and the Fox God in weeks. It's funny, isn't it, that now, when he's a still pool just waiting for the Dancer to write Her words across his surface, that She doesn't have anything to say? Why do you think that is?'

'Because he's doing what She needs him to do,' Gilda said, her voice calm. 'He's not here for you, Blessed One, or because the Dark Lady has commanded it. He's here because the Dancer needs him to be here. And She'll reveal Her purpose to us all soon enough.'

That rattled her. 'You have no idea what you're talking about,' Lanta said. Gilda just lifted a shoulder in reply and watched the other woman twitch with annoyance. Then she poured a cup of wine and passed it to Gilda, smiling warm enough to melt a glacier. Gilda took the cup on reflex and then sniffed. Lanta smiled.

'He's been more than a little forthcoming, your boy there. Told us so many things. So many interesting, useful things. Godblind, I'm sure Gilda would like to know who of her family – and yours, I suppose – has been slaughtered. Would you tell her?'

'No,' Gilda said, holding up her palm. She gulped wine too fast, coughed. 'No, thank you. Dom doesn't need to parade his gift for me. I have been with him through dozens of knowings over the years, I know what they're like.' Her heart was hammering and a voice in her head was screaming, *Yes, tell me, tell me who lives. Cam? Lim? Sarilla? Tell me!*

'You're sure?' Lanta asked as Dom sat up. He was watching the exchange with a manic energy, a glee verging on hysteria, that Gilda had never seen in him before. There wasn't the man she knew or the boy she remembered in that gaze.

'May I?' Gilda said, standing. 'Dom, love—'

'You may not,' Lanta said, and if her smile had been hot, her voice now was wintry. 'Sit down and drink. We're not done here yet.'

Gilda sat and sipped her wine. 'Did you always want to be a priestess?' she asked after a pause. Dom was still kneeling close by, his gaze flicking between them, waiting for orders, perhaps. 'Is the priesthood the only way to power other than climbing into bed after bed until you reach someone with a scrap of authority?'

Lanta snorted. 'Being a consort to a warrior, even a war chief, was never to be my fate, just as being a farmer's wife was never to be yours. Women like us control the worlds in which we live. We mould the world to shape our wills; we are not moulded by it. I wanted to serve the gods. In turn,

They have honoured me with position and a voice in the king's council.'

'So you mould your world to your will, or that of the gods?'

Lanta's smile was full of pity. 'I am Their instrument – my will and Theirs move as one.' She drank and Gilda watched the pale column of her throat as she swallowed, wondering how it would feel to wrap the chain around it and pull.

'How lucky you are, to feel so at one with your gods, to know no doubt,' Gilda said, her eyes straying to Dom again. 'Sleep, son. There's nothing for you to do here.' Dom bobbed his head and lay down. Lanta's brow furrowed. Gilda smelt the mud in the lines of her hand – loamy, tangy, a hint of metals – as she watched Lanta's face and eyes. 'Look, I'm not going anywhere; I think we both know that. Dom can't come with me until he's fulfilled his purpose, and now that he's here, I'm not going to leave him. He's as good as a chain for me, and that being so, is there any chance you'd take this collar off me? It chafes something awful.'

'Don't push me, old woman. We are not friends and we are not allies.'

Gilda puffed out her cheeks. 'Why am I still here, Lanta?' she asked, noting how the Blessed One's lips turned white at use of her name. 'What's the point? We've dissected each other's religions, holy workings and practices. You've destroyed my town, my temple and my people and you're well on your way to winning this war. What use have I been in any of that?'

'You want me to kill you?' Lanta asked.

Gilda chuckled. 'No, I want you to take off my collar and let me stay by my son, to soothe him as best I can. When this is all over, then you can let me – let us both – go. That's what I want. What do you want?'

Lanta was silent.

'Other than to be queen, of course,' Gilda continued. She smelt the earth on her hand again while Lanta's expression solidified. 'I never realised it before, but you're lonely. That's why you won't let me go or have me executed. I'm not a Mireces, so you can talk to me without worry that I'll tell anyone else – I mean, who'd believe me?' She reached out on instinct, took Lanta's unresponsive hand. 'You're utterly alone in a camp of thousands. It must be awful.'

Lanta stiffened and pulled her hand away. 'I am never alone; my gods walk with me.'

Gilda raised both her hands and sat up a little straighter. 'I'm not asking for your confession, lady, but a conversation. Friendship. I mean, why not? What have you got to lose?'

Very deliberately, Lanta wiped her hand on her skirts, her meaning plain. 'I have no need of friends, or of conversation. I live only to serve my gods, to bring Their holy words to my people, to assist my king in his duties. It is balm enough for my soul. I need nothing else.'

Gilda scratched under the collar at the raw skin, hissing at the sting of parted flesh. 'But what if this goes wrong? What if you do lose? You'll need a friend then, someone to vouch for you.'

'We won't lose,' Lanta said, as Gilda had expected. 'My gods will not allow it.'

'All right, then what about love? You were . . . close to your King Liris, I understand, and Rillirin told me he was hideous. But none can deny Corvus's attractions.' She laughed at Lanta's expression, though she marked Dom's twitch at mention of Rillirin's name; she was his love, his hope of redemption. If anything could get through to him, surely it was memories of her.

'I'm old, I'm not dead,' Gilda continued before Lanta

noticed her preoccupation with Dom. 'I can appreciate a pretty man as much as you can. So what's stopping you? Or do you prefer Prince Rivil? The King's second, Valan, perhaps?'

Lanta blinked.

Ooh, was that a flash of something there? Valan? As King's second, he'd rule if Corvus died without issue. Of course, you'd need to secure Corvus's death and that of any bairns he might have, but then I don't think you'd have much difficulty with that, would you, Lady Lanta?

'I tire of your babble,' Lanta snapped, and the heat in her voice and cheeks convinced Gilda she was on the right path. 'The gods are my succour and They are all I need. Liris required . . . instruction in the proper forms of worship, nothing more.'

Gilda arched an eyebrow and coughed a laugh. 'Really? From what I heard, Liris was a fat old goat, and I've seen that Skerris chap, and he's a big sweaty bastard – and an anointed priest to boot. Maybe you could invite him in one evening.' She tapped the side of her nose. 'You're too wound up, Lanta, too stiff. I reckon an energetic seeing-to will do you the world of good.'

Lanta surged to her feet on a tidal wave of outrage and blue skirts. 'You disgust me,' she snarled, bending low into Gilda's face, her breath washing across the other woman's cheek.

Gilda laughed and stood too, forcing Lanta back. 'Look, if you like Valan, take him. He's King's second, so if Corvus dies without issue – and this is a war, after all – Valan'll be king and you're only one step away from being queen and having everything you've ever dreamt of.'

'I don't . . . Shut up, just fucking shut up,' Lanta shouted, the shell of her calm cracking. 'I don't know what you think you know, but you don't. You don't know anything.'

Gilda put her head on one side. 'I know you want to be queen. I know you'll do anything to see that happen, kill anyone you have to, marry anyone you have to. Maybe you think Valan would be a more . . . malleable king, and a very grateful husband. I mean, no doubt you'd kill him after a couple of years and rule alone. Blessed One and queen both. It has a certain ring to it, I'll give you that.'

Lanta stepped forward like a predator, her mood shifting from outrage to danger in a heartbeat. 'Or maybe I'll take your son into my bed,' she hissed, 'bind him to me and to the Dark Path forever. Maybe I'll show him delights he's only ever dreamt of as we commune with the Red Gods even as I let him take me. Think he'll do what your Dancer commands then? Care to test the strength of his faith?'

'I know Dom,' Gilda said as steadily as she could, but her palms were slick with sudden sweat. She wasn't one to underestimate her enemies, but she had done so here, and badly. 'His love is for Rillirin, King Corvus's sister. He'd never betray her.' Again the twitch. 'And the Dancer doesn't command.'

I do know Dom, and I know he wouldn't let himself be used. I know he's fighting this, fighting the Dark Lady with everything he's got. And I know he'll win.

I know it.

'You think so?' Lanta asked, sly and abruptly amused. 'Because I think you'd be surprised how little you really understand him. Come here, Godblind,' she added and Dom stood and moved to Lanta's side. 'Who do you love?' she purred, one hand on his back, a knife somehow in the other, though it was pointing in Gilda's direction.

Gilda took a careful step back. 'All right, all right, I apologise,' she said, raising her palms. 'I'll just go and chain myself back up outside, shall I, and we'll forget all about this?'

'Stay where you are; you should see what the boy raised

in your temple became when he embraced his truth. Godblind, answer the question. Who do you love?'

Dom's smile was on the far side of madness. 'My feet are on the Path, and my love, my only love, is our Bloody Mother. All others are dead to me. She is water to me, She is blood, and I will bathe in Her and be reborn.'

'Oh, gods,' Gilda breathed. 'Dom, listen to me. Listen to your—'

'Shut up, old woman. I'm finished with you, with your clever words and your clever little insults. You're quite right, I do need a friend, and Dom here is going to be it, aren't you, Dom? You and me and the Dark Lady and Holy Gosfath and the subjugation of Gilgoras.'

'Yes,' he whispered, 'my life to serve. There is nothing but the Path, nothing but Her.'

'She spoke through him, you know,' Lanta said casually. 'She entered his body and entered this world and spoke to us – to me – through him. I could see Her inside him. The Godblind is a living sacrifice now, a permanent link to the gods. His every breath is a torment to him and a tribute to Them. That is who your boy is now.'

Gilda felt the refutation spring to her lips, and then she looked at Dom with the clear, objective gaze of her calling, and she was silent. Racked with pain, but silent.

Lanta was ugly with triumph. 'And Rillirin? Do you still love her?' she asked, caressing Dom's shoulder as though he was a heifer she was considering purchasing.

Dom blinked once. 'Even though she carries my seed in her belly, even though her child could be born in Light or in Blood and seal the fate of the world either way, even though her past is my future and the destruction of Gilgoras itself may rest in her womb, she is nothing to me. My Lady, my love, is Dark and Bloody and beautiful.'

Gilda rocked back on her heels and the shocked look she turned on Lanta showed an equal disbelief. Rillirin pregnant with Dom's child?

Born in Light or in Blood? The destruction of Gilgoras itself? What madness does he speak? How? When?

'Who else knows this?' Lanta snapped, the knife beneath Dom's ribs now and all her smug superiority fled.

'No one. Even she does not yet know. We can tell her when she gets here tomorrow. When we bring her home.'

'Dom!' Gilda shouted, grabbing for him, 'what are you doing? Stop saying these things. This is Rillirin; this is your babe. You mustn't—'

Lanta pressed her knife into Dom's hand. 'No one else can know about this, Godblind. Kill her.'

Gilda's heart stopped. *No. Holy Dancer, Lady clothed in sunlight, don't make him do this. Not my boy.* 'Dom, just wait a—'

'I said kill her. Now.'

Dom stepped forward, madness gleaming in his face and along the edge of the blade.

CRYS

*Fourth moon, eighteenth year of the reign of King Rastoth
Approach to the south harbour, River Gil, outside
Rilporin, Western Plain*

Rilporin was taking a bastard of a battering.

A trebuchet was eating away at the stump wall that extended out from the side of First Bastion and down to the river to prevent overland access to the gate into the city. Throw by throw, stone by stone, the stump wall was eroding. *And exactly how do the Mireces have a trebuchet anyway?*

They were too far away still for the shouts to reach them, but Crys saw the flurry of activity around the siege engine and figures sprinting from the shabby ditch and mound fortifications sprawling across the fields towards the river. They'd been spotted already. Damn.

Rilporin itself still stood, proud and tall and scarred. There was scarlet flying from the palace towers and the sound of battle had a desperate edge to it, like they were tired. *Like they're losing.*

'All right, lads, this is going to be bad, but we're used to

115

that, and the Palace Rank needs us, so keep your heads down and your shields up. Those at the oars, start rowing. We need to dock and unload at speed, make space for the ships behind.'

'That's a Rank-made trebuchet, Captain,' Tara said slowly. 'Where did they get one of our trebs? And they're flying scarlet.'

'I know; Rastoth must be dead,' Crys said, his voice low. 'They wouldn't fly it for anyone else. As for the treb, Durdil would've sent for reinforcements; maybe they brought them but had to abandon them?'

'Hmm,' Tara said, as unconvinced as he was. 'Even if they'd managed to haul them all the way here, they'd have destroyed them rather than allow them to fall into Mireces hands. As for Rastoth, if he is dead, where does that leave us? Rivil's the heir. If we stand against him it's treason.'

Crys frowned. 'Then we've been committing that for a while now: Rivil's a traitor who needs to die. He's allied with the Mireces and, look, there's another force over there, a large one. Must've brought mercenaries in – maybe they built the trebs? Doesn't change our orders. We still have a war to win.'

'No king to win it for, though.'

'No king is better than no victory.'

Tara looked as though she was going to argue, but then Mace was bellowing across the water from the lead galley and they hustled to the prow to listen.

'All right, West Rank, pay attention,' Mace shouted, hands around his mouth. Wolves and soldiers crowded the rails. 'They've got a trebuchet on the stump wall, which is bad, and they've spotted us, which is worse. There're Mireces making for the bank and they'll have archers, so we'll be under sustained volleys for at least the final mile to the city and probably artillery shot as well. I don't need to tell you what a direct hit from that treb will do.

'There's no landing site between here and the city, so we sail straight into the south harbour, then cross the bridge to the gate into the city. We can expect supporting artillery and volleys from First Bastion and South Tower One, but even so, that bridge is wide and open for a reason – we'll be sitting targets on it, so I want you moving fast. Understood? Pass the word back. Rowers, stand by for full speed, and for the Dancer's sake, get your heads down.'

He paused a second longer. 'Good luck.'

'Bollocks,' Tara muttered, 'he never says good luck. Now I know we're dead.'

'Have you got this?' Crys asked. He gestured at the galley on their starboard. 'I'll head over to this lot if you have, lend them a hand. The Wolves are good sailors, but we'll need to tie up and disembark in a hurry. They might need my help.'

'Go, go,' Tara said and Crys grinned, saluted and ran for the side, pushed off the rail and threw himself at the Wolf ship. The water was far colder than he'd expected, his chainmail far heavier, but he only needed to swim a few strokes before Ash threw him a rope.

'Are you bloody mad?' he hissed as Crys hauled himself over the rail and collapsed in a puddle on the deck. 'You could've drowned.'

Crys waved away the comment. 'What can I say?' He lowered his voice. 'I missed you.'

Ash ran a hand through his curly hair and shook his head. 'Crazy idiot,' he complained, but there was a smile at the corner of his mouth. He indicated the haphazard pile of kit stowed around the mast. 'There's a spare shirt and jerkin over there. You may as well die dry.'

'Ever the optimist,' Crys said as he dragged the chainmail over his head, wincing as it pulled his hair. He jerked his head at Lim. 'How's the chief?'

'Looking forward to bloodying his sword and probably reckless enough to get himself killed doing it.' Ash sat on the rail with the ease of a born sailor and watched with open admiration as Crys shrugged out of his jerkin and shirt. Crys was blushing, but he still took a few extra seconds to wring out his wet shirt and use it to scrub away at his hair. When he pulled the material away from his face, Ash's smile was even bigger and Crys's mouth twitched at the appreciation.

'Captain Tailorson, get your bloody armour back on before you get shot in that rather unimpressive chest,' Tara called, generating a burst of laughter and jeers from her galley and his, a relieved breaking of the smothering tension, and Crys hurried into the fresh clothes and let Ash dump the wet mail back over his head and arms.

'Enough,' Mace yelled before Crys could respond, and there was little humour in his tone. 'Rowers, full speed. Rest of you, protect yourselves. There's Mireces on the northern bank; we're about to have incoming.'

The mood soured faster than it had sweetened, and Crys adjusted his mail and then unsheathed his sword and dagger, wiped the worst of the wet off them. He made his way to the fore. 'Here to assist with the docking, Chief Lim,' he said. 'And anything else you need.'

Lim didn't acknowledge him; they'd had words after Sarilla's death, words bitter and accusing from Lim, mostly uncomprehending from Crys. Words that recalled the first time they'd met and Dom's foretelling and how the calestar had labelled Crys something other, something more. Apparently, during their time down in the tunnels as they fought and died and, eventually, drowned or lived, Lim had convinced himself that Dom's knowing meant that Crys should've been able to save them all. Or at least save Sarilla, because when you've lost so much, when you've lost everything, you cling to the one thing that hurts the most and clutch it tight, so tight it makes you bleed.

They watched in silence as the banks slid by, as the Mireces loomed closer, as the trebuchet wound back for another shot. Lim wouldn't speak to him, so Crys moved back to the middle of the deck, checked the rowers had shields between them and the Mireces. One man slumped, weeping silently as the bandages around his chest darkened with red, fresh blood over dried, his face a ghastly grey.

Crys dragged him out of the way and took his place. 'Have a bit of a rest, and then take over for me when you can, all right?' he said with a smile, spat on his hands and got in a rhythm with the other rowers on his side.

'Stand by for fire arrows,' he heard someone shout alongside the stroke call.

'Don't panic! Panic gets you killed quicker'n anything,' he shouted as a couple of rowers lost the rhythm, too busy staring at the bank blooming yellow and orange with flame.

'Quicker than a blazing arrow in the face?' someone muttered.

'Quicker even than that,' Crys said solemnly. 'If you can't row, shoot. If you can't shoot or row, keep your bloody heads down.'

'Watch your rhythm, rowers,' Ash called and Crys looked up to see him on the yard at the top of the mast, quiver on his back, bow in hand. The first volley whickered across the water, thuds as bodkin arrowheads drove into wood, into shields. Screams as they drove into flesh. Crys flinched and rowed, the palms of his hands slippery with sweat and sore already.

The muscles of his back were protesting as the helmsman called for a yet faster stroke. Crys gritted his teeth and hummed a marching song to keep the rhythm. He contemplated singing aloud and rejected it. *There's only so much horror these people can take.* He swallowed the urge to giggle.

The second volley was luckier – if you were a Mireces – with scores of arrows finding homes in soldiers and Wolves. More screams, drowned out suddenly in the thunderous smash of a stone impacting the stump wall ahead. A huge chunk of masonry tumbled in a slow parabola into the river.

'Shit,' he breathed, his humming stuttering into silence. Something about that crumbling wall stole the music from him. There was no clear water ahead, the river jammed with ships and oars clashing as the fleet funnelled closer together, those nearest the northern bank steering a course towards the southern, desperate to get out of range. Ragged flights of arrows arced into the sky and then down, from them to the Mireces this time, and Crys grinned savagely when screams that weren't theirs pealed into the air.

An arrow buzzed past his nose like a giant, bad-tempered hornet and Crys yelped, nearly dropping the oar. 'Uh, anyone available to hold an extra shield?' he asked the crew, and then kicked the unconscious man at his side. He didn't move. 'Fucking brilliant.'

The trebuchet loosed again, all eyes drawn inexorably to the wall as more of it cracked and tumbled into the river. Even the Mireces paused, hoping no doubt that the whole thing would come down and they could storm the southern gate, cut off the West Rank from the city, strand them on the wrong side of the river with no cover.

The stump wall held this time, but Crys's sigh of relief didn't last. Fire arrows thumped into the ships, some up in the sails, others on to the decks or into men and women. Four stood proud in the wood near where he sat. More screams, and shouts of alarm this time too, and panicked rushing as people ran to smother the flames. Smoke began rising and warriors and soldiers started to cough, rowers to falter as they choked. Ships began to slow.

Rilporin's shadow fell over him and Crys felt hope rise. 'I said not to panic,' he bellowed, 'so don't. It's not much further. Smother the flames and keep going, fire's not bad enough to sink us.' There was no response, just the sound of archers loosing and Ash cursing from above, oars threshing the water, and men groaning or shrieking as arrows found them. The front galleys were turning into the harbour now, the stump wall protecting them from further assault, but there were scores more behind, wide open to attack.

'Too slow,' he muttered, 'too bastard slow.' Crys's back and shoulders were liquid agony but there was no thought of slowing down now. Any delay here and the ships behind would never survive the volume of shafts, aflame or not.

Arrows were flickering out from First Bastion, and they were shifting the catapult too. It couldn't reach the treb, but it could reach the Mireces on the bank. Give them something else to think about. The southern gate opened and men sprinted out, across the road and on to the bridge, laying down protective volleys to cover the fleet.

Others were gesturing wildly to the galleys to hurry up, and then the hull scraped the side of the dock at the furthest end of the harbour and Crys was up, dragging at the unconscious man and getting his shoulder into his armpit, a Wolf on his other side lifting him.

They shoved the man up on to the quay and Crys sprinted

the length of the deck, snatched up the bow line and leapt on to the dock, looping the rope three times around a cleat and hauling it taut. No time for a stern line and anyway, the current would twist the galley arse-out, leaving more space for the next. Didn't really matter if they smashed themselves to kindling right now. It was the people that mattered.

Crys reached out a hand and Lim took it, jumped the gap to dry land and between them they pulled the Wolves to safety. Ash was the last off, sliding down the mast and jumping the last few feet to avoid the flames. He scrambled on to shore. 'Whole harbour will go up if we don't put these out,' he said.

Crys looked the length of the dock; more ships were coming in under full sail, full speed, more than half of them alight. 'This harbour's fucked anyway. We'd never put all these out. Let's get into the city and get orders. If Durdil or Mace want the flames fought, I'll see what we can do.'

'Ever the fucking hero,' Lim snarled, but then he loped for the bridge without waiting for an answer.

Crys waved the comment away and shoved Ash to get him moving. They ran together up the slope of the bridge and out on to its wide, open roadway. An arrow punched through a man's chest and he fell in front of them, slamming into the stone. The Palace Rankers on the bridge had wicker shields to crouch behind, but the runners were big, obvious targets and not enough had grabbed their shields as they disembarked. They hurdled the body and kept running.

Crys chanced a last look back, just as the trebuchet unwound and smashed a ship into kindling, screaming voices cut off in an instant. There were still dozens of vessels out there, some fully engulfed in flame, their sails gold and crimson with flags of fire crowning the masts, others with rowers dead or oars lost, floundering in the water, ramming other boats, tangling rigging and holing keels. His advice about not panicking was as dead as the corpses floating in the water, burnt, crushed and arrow-peppered.

'We should—' he began and Ash grabbed his hand as he began to slow and dragged him down the other side of the bridge, across the sward and in through the southern gate, hundreds of soldiers and Wolves piling in behind them while hundreds more died on the water.

RILLIRIN

Fourth moon, eighteenth year of the reign of King Rastoth River Gil, outside Rilporin, Wheat Lands

It was the blue shirts that did it.

Seeing those flashes of forbidden colour under their armour was like a flame to the moth of her courage. Rillirin shrivelled, nausea surging in her chest and throat. Courage in the heat of battle was one thing; watching as you sailed towards them was another.

'Rillirin! Rillirin, I need you.' Dalli was sitting at the side, heaving at a long oar, and an arrow stood out from the rail a finger's breadth from her head. There was another in the deck, and the back of Dalli's neck glinted red with fresh blood.

'Shield,' she screamed, still pulling furiously, and Rillirin saw that the shield she'd been hiding behind had slipped, exposing her to the archers on the bank. Another volley and Dalli ducked, cursed badly enough that Rillirin blushed at it, and then uttered a wordless yell in her direction.

Rillirin sucked in a breath and tensed as though sheer

force of will would cause any arrows to bounce off her, then she fumbled up a spare shield and ran to Dalli's side, pressed against her back with the shield just about covering them both. It was massive and rectangular, Rank-made, and its weight dragged at her arm, its face wobbling about within seconds and clattering into the rail and the deck as she fought to keep it steady. Her muscles trembled and the stitches in her back burnt like hot wire. She groaned and pressed her face into Dalli's straining back.

'Nearly there,' Dalli gasped. Rillirin looked; they weren't nearly there at all, there was clear water between them and the turning into the harbour. Still in arrow range, still in artillery range.

'Liar,' Rillirin grunted and then patted Dalli to show she didn't mean it.

There was a shrill cry of alarm, a shouted 'Look out!' and then the galley shuddered and jolted as another rammed into it. Rillirin knelt higher, trying to see over Dalli's head as the Wolf cursed and fought the oar. The ship that had rammed them was well ablaze, sail burning merrily, the deck on fire. The men piloting it threw themselves off the deck towards them, desperate to escape the flames.

Wolves tried to push the other galley away with oars but it was already beginning to list. Rillirin got one hand on Dalli's shoulder, ready to pull her away if the flames came too close, but then the rigging tangled, there was a whump of flame as fire raced into their sail and the deck shuddered. Rillirin skidded sideways with the impact, smacking her head into the rail, and then the weight of the shield dragged her through the gap and into the Gil.

The shield was heavy, banded with metal, and Rillirin scrabbled with her free hand at the strap as it began to sink, carrying her deeper into the cold.

The current was swift and she had lost all sense of up and down by the time she finally freed her arm. The last of the stale air in her lungs carried her towards the surface and when her face broke into the air she sucked it in, three deep breaths before she even opened her eyes.

The river was nearly a mile across and the current powerful, unbeatable as it dragged her along, and it was all she could do to keep her head above water, kicking hard. She breathed in water and choked; she heard someone calling her name, her mind thrown back to the time she'd fallen out of her Da's boat on the lake. Or had Madoc pushed her? She couldn't remember.

She was in the centre of the river now, far from the harbour, and Rilporin was looming large above her, its shadow lying chill in the water. Rillirin struck out for the city, fighting the drag of her boots and jerkin and desperate to get out of the path of the oncoming ships.

There was another grinding crash and shouts, screams from behind. She looked over her shoulder and saw two more ships collide, men and women thrown overboard with the impact, flames dancing on the river.

She concentrated on swimming, not fighting across the current but going diagonally with it, the city looming closer until, after what felt like hours, her feet scraped the riverbed and she struggled towards the shallows, her back a stiff board of agony and the chill settling deep in her bones.

Sobbing for breath, Rillirin fell on to her face with the water still lapping at her legs and then rolled on to her side and stared up. The wall loomed huge and grey and implacable above her. She was on the wrong side of the river, and only the steepness of the bank hid her from the Mireces a few hundred strides away.

Rillirin lay in the shadow of the city, teeth chattering and trying to summon the nerve to raise her head. She was about a hundred strides out from the stump wall, the end of which had once jutted right to the water's edge, protecting the bridge and the gate behind it, but now was a twisted, tumbled pile of rubble.

All right then, climb over the rubble and head inside with the others. I can do that. She squinted at the far bank, pulling wet hair from her face. Boats were being smashed to splinters by the trebuchet, others were fully engulfed in flames, and the last stragglers, limping and alight, were heading into the harbour. Smoke drifted along the surface of the river like autumn mist, hiding the city from her, and her from the city.

Go. Now, before they close the gate. Go.

She'd got her legs under her when the pounding of feet and shouted curses, pleas for mercy, thudding of flesh on flesh wrenched her head around on her neck. A dozen men and women had made it to shore from a capsized ship and were in a desperate fight against the Mireces. The odds were insurmountable, and the Raiders weren't slaughtering them where they stood either. They were clubbing them on to their knees and tying their hands. Taking them prisoner.

Rillirin's breath stopped in her throat. Sacrifices. For one mad second she thought about trying to rescue them, but then a Mireces was looking along the bank towards her and she flattened herself to the sandy mud. He came forward a few steps, and then his gaze slid on.

As soon as he looked away, Rillirin pushed herself slowly back down into the water until only her head and shoulders were on the bank. Face turned to the Mireces, she half closed her eyes and let herself go limp. There were enough corpses drifting on the river and bumping along the shore that if she stayed still for long enough, she'd be safe.

What she'd do after that was another matter. Gritting her

teeth to stop them chattering, she focused on the rise and fall of her legs in the current and tried not to flinch as the trebuchet launched a rock towards the stump wall. It whined overhead and smashed into the dressed stone. Rillirin wondered how long the engineers would stay with the engine. She couldn't move until they left. If they left.

And then what? Walk up to the gate and ask to be let in? I'll get an arrow in the eye.

The chill was more than just the water and the city's shadow now. Rilporin's defenders wouldn't let her in; she was a nobody to them and, even worse, she sounded Mireces. She was trapped outside the city with only enemies around her. She swallowed a surge of nausea.

Rillirin was on her own.

MACE

When the last of the survivors were in and it was just the Palace Rank archers on the bridge providing support, Mace hurried through the South Gate and into the merchants' quarter of First Circle, deserted but for his men and the Wolves standing, sitting and lying on the road. The city was bright with noise, the shouts of Rankers and the thrum of bowstrings from above, the irregular thump and scream of the catapult and the reply of the trebuchet. And a distant roar that must be the western wall.

Mace sank on to his haunches and contemplated the dust and his battered, ruined boots. His stomach was pinched with tension and hunger and he dry heaved a few times, waiting for the shakes to dissipate.

Thousands dead. But thousands more alive, remember that. No one could've done more than we did.

Yes, they could've. I could've.

'Mace? Mace, Rillirin fell overboard. I want to go and—'

129

Mace stood and cut off Dalli's words with a hug that squeezed the breath from her. 'No,' he said fiercely. 'Not a shitting chance. You are not setting foot outside these walls. Hundreds went overboard. She'll either have been swept past the city by now, or taken by the Mireces. I'm sorry, she's lost.'

'You don't know that,' Dalli said, her voice rough and fists clenched on his chest plate. 'She was helping me . . .' She looked dazed, like she'd taken a blow to the head.

'She's gone, love. I'm so sorry.'

A hundred of the king's Personal Guards clattered around a bend in the road and Mace choked on a sob when he saw Durdil at their head; he staggered forward into his father's arms with the desperate abandon of a small boy who'd thought himself lost.

'You're alive,' Durdil whispered fiercely as he hugged his son, tears in his eyes. 'I knew it. I knew you wouldn't be dead. Too bastard stubborn for a start, too good a soldier for a second.'

Mace could've stayed in that embrace for the rest of the day, but he had a Rank to see to. Reluctantly he pulled away, scrubbing his filthy sleeve over his grimy face. He found a smile.

'Thanks for the assist at the gate,' he said. 'It was getting a little hot out there and not just because we set fire to your harbour.'

'Would've been a lot hotter if we hadn't cleared out the Mireces camp they'd set up out of bowshot to try and bottle us up in here.' Durdil grinned wolfishly.

'Commander, the Mireces have renewed their assault on Double First, and Second Last is still under sustained artillery fire. You shouldn't be this close to the action.'

'I'm at the other side of the city,' Durdil grumbled and

then ignored the speaker. 'Rastoth is dead. I'd thought to keep it from the city to sustain morale, but the godsdamned council stabbed me in the back and flew the scarlet against my express orders. I fear they're deliberately trying to undermine me.'

Mace tapped his fingertips to his heart. 'Poor Rastoth. Still, at least he's in the Light now. I have to say I'm glad for it. He'd suffered too long.'

'He suffered a lot more when Rivil stabbed him in the chest as he fled the city,' Durdil growled, and Mace nearly choked on his own tongue. 'I'll tell you everything later. It's done, and, predictably, the city's a tinderbox now the news is out. But get everyone to the hospitals – I've put them on alert to expect you – and get some rest and food. You're to be barracked in the palace; we've no room anywhere else. Take what you need from the armoury, but not yet. Hospital, then the palace. Healing, food and a brief rest. I need to know how many men you have. Get your junior officers to keep them moving and if you have any that are able to fight immediately, direct them to Colonel Edris. He has command of Double First.' He pointed down the road. 'But I need you and as many of your senior command as you can find with me, now. We'll have a good enough view from First Bastion and you can rest afterwards.'

'Of course.' Mace looked around. 'Dorcas, Carter, Tailorson. Chief Broadsword, Dalli. With me please. Is Captain Salter here? Salter, you've served here before, know your way around. Direct any able bodies to Edris and then lead the wounded to the hospitals. We'll meet you there soon. Dismissed.'

The officers signalled and the ragged army snapped to attention, saluted, and then marched for the gate into Second Circle and the hospitals, the Wolves trailing after, too exhausted to pay much attention to their surroundings.

Durdil led Mace to the base of First Bastion, then up and around the spiral stairs to the allure, Mace's knees twinging and exhaustion gnawing deep at his bones. He shoved it aside. For Durdil to need them immediately, the situation had to be worse than it'd looked from outside.

And it looked pretty fucking dire from where I was standing.

The Personals pushed respectfully past and cleared the door before they allowed Durdil and, Mace realised, himself, out into danger.

'Where did the Mireces get a trebuchet?' he asked, the question having niggled ever since they'd spotted it from the river. He'd a growing feeling he wouldn't like the answer.

This part of the wall was clear of the enemy, so Durdil stood between two merlons and gestured. 'That should answer your question.'

Mace squinted down at the field, and then squinted some more. His stomach dropped at the sight. 'Is that . . .?'

'The East Rank, yes,' Durdil said in a blank voice. 'Converted to the last man, allied with Rivil and the Mireces. Five thousand highly trained soldiers with ladders and siege engines. Nearly ten thousand probing our walls all told. Or were at the start of the siege, anyway. Another reason we're glad to have you.'

Mace could feel the exhausted disbelief battering against him from the men and women assembled behind. To have faced everything they had, only to discover their own were against them. 'We have twenty-one hundred Rankers and, Chief, your Wolves?' Lim was silent, his knuckles white on the stone as he gazed down at the Mireces and the East Rank. 'Lim, how many Wolves are left?'

'Six hundred and thirty-two,' Dalli said when Lim didn't so much as blink. 'Another hundred or so we left behind in the ruins of Watchtown, half that at Yew Cove who were too badly injured to make the journey here. Not that the ones we left behind matter to you.' Her voice was suddenly bitter.

'Thank you, Dalli,' Mace said. 'Every life matters, to all of us.' He leant back on the wall before she could say anything more. 'Just under three thousand in total then. And yours?'

'General Hadir of the South sent two Thousands, plus the Palace Rank and Personal Guards. All told, there're probably four thousand of us left still able to fight. And there's still no word from the North. Whatever's happened there, we're no longer counting on their aid.'

'Surely the South Rank can spare us more than two Thousands?' Mace demanded. 'We fucking brought everyone who can still stand.'

'I could order them here, but as it stands the rest of the South Rank is the only fighting force we have left. They're it, they're all we have, and we must keep them in reserve. I won't lie,' Durdil said, looking them each in the eye in turn, 'it's desperate. But you've done more than bolster our numbers. You've boosted our morale. You survived to come all the way here and fight with us, for us. The Rankers and citizenry will take heart from it. You should too.'

He grinned and a score of years lifted from his face and Mace remembered why men fought and died for Durdil Koridam. He felt the same lifting of his spirits they did, saw it reflected on the faces of his officers; even Lim's expression lightened a little.

'We wear them down, winnow away at their numbers – they must be running out of food because gods know we are – and then when they're desperate and filthy and starving, when disease is rife among them, we march out and slaughter them. For now, you'll be used to plug gaps in the line, starting at midnight the day after tomorrow. I can't give you any more time than that, I'm afraid, though anyone who finds themselves at a loose end before that will be more than welcome on the defences or as a runner. The wall by Last Bastion is weak and Rivil knows it – he's been throwing rocks at it ever since the East arrived. Latest report is they'll have the southern stump wall down in the next couple of days, so we can expect a strong push there as well.'

'And the Red Gods?' a voice asked and Mace looked at Crys. 'Dom told us that if we killed too many Mireces, we would tear the veil and the gods would return. Has it happened? How do we find out?'

Durdil sidled closer to Mace. 'Dom? Veil?'

Mace closed his eyes for a second. 'It appears the Wolves' calestar, the chief's adopted brother Dom and a fine warrior, has foreseen that if enough blood is shed, it will allow the Red Gods back into Gilgoras. I know, I know' – he held up his hand before Durdil could say anything – 'but Dom . . . saw Watchtown's destruction. By the time we got there, it had happened. He knew Corvus wasn't really heading for the West Forts. I don't know how, but he did. We acted on that information and it was correct.'

Durdil found a smile for them. 'I'm afraid we cannot prosecute a war without spilling blood, and we certainly cannot successfully defend this city without doing so. I will speak with the high priests in the temple district and ask them to pray for the veil.' He waved a hand vaguely. 'But we cannot develop a sound strategy that is based on the possibility that what we do may or may not result in a mystical visitation of the gods.'

'With the number of lives that have already been lost,' Mace said when Crys and Dalli both looked as though they were about to argue, 'I can't believe the veil isn't already torn. And if it is, then winning this war is even more important. And while we've been through the Red Gods' own hell these last few weeks, we're not done yet. We came here to do our duty and aid our brothers in arms; let's focus on that. Even if we knew the veil was about to tear, would we surrender to try and prevent it?'

Heads were shaken; fists tightened on weapons.

'Then let's concentrate on winning.'

There were grudging acknowledgments as he looked them over one last time. Carter was bloody and sagging, absolutely spent and too proud to admit it, but she gave him a nod when he met her eyes, and something that might have been a smile. Dorcas's single eye blazed with a righteous fury that Mace had never seen before. Lim didn't glance his way, but Crys gave him a half-shrug of acceptance.

Dalli's eyes were red-rimmed and her fists clenched at her chest, fierce as a wildcat, more buoyed by his words than she had any right to be. Whatever room she was assigned to later, he planned on finding it. No energy for anything but sleep, but he'd a feeling he'd do it better wrapped around that hard little body than he would alone.

He dismissed them, returning their salutes, and stared back out over the wall again, watching the flight of a stone from the trebuchet to his right. Once they were alone except for the Personals, Mace fumbled at his belt and unbuckled the scabbard. He dropped to one knee and held the sword out, willing his arms not to tremble.

'Commander, this is the heir's sword. It needs a clean and I'm afraid I've had to use it, but you should have it until a new king can be found.'

Durdil snorted and clapped him on the back, 'I can't think of anyone who deserves to wear it – and use it – more than you. When this is over, you can take it to King Tresh at Highcrop. He'll decide what's done with it. Until then, if it has served you well, then I trust it will continue to do so.' He winked. 'Of course, should Tresh decline the throne, I can't think of anyone better to take it on than you. Your Major Carter wanted me to have it at one point. I turned her down, of course, but you? Yes, I think you'd fit that chair very well.'

Mace stayed on one knee, his mind a fizzing blank of incredulity. 'Wha'?' he managed.

Durdil chuckled, a weary, disbelieving bubble of noise. 'Large ideas for another day, son. Don't worry on them now. Besides, we could all be dead by dusk.'

Mace wobbled to his feet and buckled on the sword with numb fingers. 'Sounds better than being king,' he muttered, reaching for his scattered thoughts among the hot fuzzy blanket of fatigue.

Durdil sighed. 'Now I know you're my son. Only good thing to come of Rastoth's death was that I got control of the Personal Guards and threw them straight into the defence. Though, of course, now I've got a bunch of the clattering idiots following me around. In the absence of a king, they've decided I'm their new priority, and apparently if I fall, so does the city. Sheer nonsense, of course.'

One of the clattering idiots stepped forward and saluted. 'General, my name is Cobbler, sir. Please, please can you convince your father that he mustn't put himself in harm's way? If we were to lose him so soon after King Rastoth, it would be a crushing blow to morale.'

Mace and Durdil exchanged glances.

'This is Commander Durdil Koridam of His Majesty's Ranks, soldier. Tell me, have you ever known your Commander to do anything but put himself in harm's way for the greater good?' Mace patted a steel-clad shoulder as Cobbler's face fell. 'That's what my father does, it's who he is, and I have no doubt morale is the greater for seeing him fight alongside his men. However, I agree that it would be a catastrophe to lose him, so it's up to you to keep him safe, all right? On the wall and off it. If you don't, we're all fucked.

'And now, I'm going to hospital and then to bed. Wake me up if they make it over the wall. Anything else, I don't even want to know.'

RILLIRIN

*Fourth moon, eighteenth year of the reign of King Rastoth
River Gil, outside Rilporin, Wheat Lands*

After nine years in the mountains, Rillirin had thought herself
used to the cold, but the river's slow sucking at her legs in
the shadow of the city as the sun rose, crested and tumbled
away the day proved her wrong.

As the hours slipped by with the water, she eased herself
further up the bank until only one foot rested in the shallows,
and then she lay in her wet clothes, sprawled out like a
corpse when she wanted to curl for warmth, and she waited.
And shivered, mind drifting on the cold tides of her breath,
hazy half-dreams wispy as gossamer, soft as sunlight. She
sucked water from her sodden sleeve to ease her thirst, and
she waited.

The trebuchet didn't stop, but at least the Mireces lining
the bank had retreated after the last of the ships passed
around the stump wall – or what was left of it. Rillirin knew
that as soon as they'd smashed away enough of it, more
Mireces would come, charging along the bank right past her

to try and take the exposed gate. As long as the trebuchet was working, she was safe from that. But as long as the trebuchet was working, she couldn't move and risk being seen by the engineers.

Rillirin woke from a frozen half-doze as the sun tumbled below the horizon; something wasn't right. She waited, stiff with cold and half convinced she was already dead, and listened. Nothing.

Nothing? What about the trebuchet?

It had been as regular as time all day, and the absence of it now was a wrongness worrying at her ears. They'd stopped. The wall must be down. Shit, they'd be coming. She'd lain all day with her head turned up towards the lip of the bank to watch for approaching Mireces, and now her neck muscles creaked painful protest as she shifted and twisted, squinting from the corner of her eye at the city. It loomed black and crowned with fire – hundreds of torches leavening the onrushing night. The stump wall was a black and jagged tooth, silhouetted with more fire. Rillirin could see past its jumble of debris towards the gate.

She wanted to run towards it, screaming her name – as though anyone would know it or care, would open up and let her in. Instead she looked ahead, along the long, curving line of the bank and the suck and shush of dark water to her left. Slowly she drew in her limbs, a spider curling into death, and even more slowly, breath quiet and muscles shuddering with cold and tension, she began to crawl. Along the edge of the river, knee and elbow sprawling into thick mud and shallow water, the bank rising above her and cutting off her view of the enemy – and their view of her.

She had a knife strapped to her forearm under her sleeve; if they found her, she'd kill herself rather than go back to the Mireces and the untender mercies of the Blessed One.

The pad of feet through the grass, the jingle of chainmail and creak of leather. Rillirin collapsed and let her eyes unfocus, half-shut, mouth open, fear stilling her shivers.

'Check the water's edge.'

Relax. Just lie still. Look dead.

Closer, and closer still until she could see legs in her periphery. Silence. Eyes on her, calculating. Rillirin breathed slow and shallow, high in her chest, imagining jumping up and ripping the knife free, the surprise enough to take the first, a low gutting slash from below. And then run from however many others there were.

'Just the dead; come on.' The legs moved away and so did the voices, leaving her in the gathering gloom, only slightly more alive than the corpses below her.

Rillirin lay there a while longer, disbelieving. Then she breathed a prayer of thanks to the Trickster and slowly, painfully, she began again to crawl.

The sounds of fighting had faded with distance. Night cloaked the river when Rillirin finally stopped. She estimated she'd crawled, and then walked, several miles away from the city, following the river as it curled in a wide, lazy loop. Now when she stopped and turned around, she couldn't see so much as the glow of the city in the distance. Just the faint light of a half-moon on the river as a guide.

She had no idea where to go. The Dancer's Fingers, the long range of hills around which the river curved, were ahead in the dark, but after that? Rillirin had tied her fate to that of the Wolves and now she was cast adrift, alone in a country being torn apart with no destination and no allies to help her.

Her knees and elbows were raw with crawling, sleeves and trouser legs and boots and feet soaked from repeated slides into the shallows, hunger rivalling sickness in her belly and the wound in her back throbbing, the only thing about her that was hot. And that probably wasn't a good sign. She walked another hour along the narrow track by the side of the river, the bank looming up on her right, arms wrapped around herself for warmth. There were sticks dotting the shore, and she collected an armful, throwing back the wet ones, keeping the dry. Her fingertips were numb, toes too, her thoughts muddled and slow. Cold.

Rillirin's boot went into the mud up to the ankle and she stared at it stupidly, then around her in the hazy moonlight. The river had broadened and slowed into a marsh, rifted with runnels of water and peppered with young shoots. Reedmace. She threw the driftwood up the bank and dug feverishly into the mud around the nearest plant, dragging the whole thing out, root and all, and bit into it, ignoring the cold slimy tang of the mud as she ate the fresh young growth and then gnawed at the thick tuberous root.

She ate another five and then collected her firewood before making her cautious ascent of the bank. Surely she'd come far enough not to be spotted? The going was easier and faster on the flat, and she used the scent and sound of the river to keep her on course as the movement brought some warmth back to her limbs and made her damp clothes just a little more bearable.

The sun was rising when Rillirin made it to the Fingers, her feet blistered and everything a weary blur in the first pale kiss of dawn. She wended between the first of the hills and clambered around to the back of one, putting its bulk between her and the city. Surely now, finally, she could risk a fire and get herself warm, decide what to do next? A croaking challenge and Rillirin dropped the firewood and yanked out her knife before she recognised the figure slumped in the narrow dell between the two hills.

'Gilda?'

The old woman looked up, brandishing a wicked-looking spike in a trembling hand. She squinted. 'Who's there?'

'Gilda? It's me, Rillirin. Gods, Gilda, you're alive!' Rillirin rushed to her as Gilda sagged back against the slope of the hill, her breathing harsh and rattling. 'What happened?' she asked as she threw herself on to her knees at Gilda's side. One sleeve of the priestess's gown was torn and stiff with dried blood, and through the rent Rillirin could see a nasty, swollen wound, a slice that looked as if it went down to the bone and up into the shoulder.

'When did this happen? How, where?'

'Few days, I think,' Gilda croaked. She shrugged her good shoulder. 'In truth, I don't know. Bit blurry.'

'They left you here?' Rillirin asked, ripping the material further. The wound was red and angry, swollen and hard to the touch. Infected.

'Escaped,' Gilda said. 'Thirsty.'

'I'm sorry, I don't have anything to carry water in. We'll have to walk. Come on, up you get.' She helped Gilda to stand, scared by the heat that came off her skin, the lightness of her frame as she leant on Rillirin's shoulder. Together they staggered around another hill and found a small pool. Rillirin breathed a swift prayer of thanks; she didn't think the old priestess would have made it as far as the river.

She scooped water to Gilda's mouth and then made her comfortable where the ground was drier. 'I'm going to start a fire and then take a look at your arm,' she said. 'You just rest. When was the last time you ate?'

'The Dancer Herself put me in your path, Rillirin, so that you could save me. Or at least learn the truth before I die.'

'You're not going to die,' Rillirin said, her voice harsh with worry. 'Stop talking such shit, woman.'

Gilda's mouth curved in a faint smile. 'You found your voice since I've been gone, I see,' she mumbled. 'Go on, make a fire, then look for bog moss to pack in my arm. It'll help fight the infection.'

Rillirin did as she was told and managed to find some edible greens as well. It was a meagre meal, and she made Gilda eat it all, ignoring the growling of her own stomach. Gilda passed out when Rillirin packed the wound – even nastier now that she'd cut away the material to inspect it – with bog moss and bandaged it with the remains of the sleeve.

The light was fading when Gilda woke, and Rillirin had foraged a little more food and firewood. Gilda watched her with eyes that seemed to penetrate her skin and see right inside her.

'There are things you should know,' she said eventually. 'And I need to tell you now in case . . . Dom is with the Mireces. He's working with them. No, don't interrupt. He's a Darksoul now, like your brother. Converted. Ejected the Light from inside himself and filled his soul with Blood.'

Rillirin's head was spinning with the abruptness of the revelation and its utter impossibility. 'No. He wouldn't. He couldn't, not Dom. Not my Dom.' Her stomach lurched and she dry heaved, cramping with hunger and nausea both, and spat into the grass by her side, throat raw with bile and horror. Goosebumps broke out across her back and arms, her head pounding with sudden pain. 'It's the wound. You're misunderstanding things, that's all; the fever's confused you. He wouldn't do something like that. The gods are everything to him.'

'I'm sorry, but it's true. My arm . . . he tried to kill me, Rillirin, on Lanta's orders. He didn't even hesitate.' She gestured to the long spike still attached to the collar around her neck by a chain. 'I protected myself with this, fled while Lanta was screaming for her guards. If it helps at all, I don't think he converted willingly. I think the Dark Lady . . . broke him.'

'He tried to kill you?' The words came out in a harsh croak unlike any sound she'd ever made before. It was preposterous, insane. It was the fever. But Gilda's eyes were clear enough and filled with a sorrow that made Rillirin wince and wrap her arms around herself. 'Did you kill him?' she whispered, her skin icy with dread.

Gilda held herself very still. 'I don't know,' she said. 'I hurt him, badly I think, but . . . I hope not.'

Rillirin slumped with relief despite herself. She of all people had cause to hate the Mireces. Dom allying with them should make her sick, but all she cared about was that he might still be alive. *Maybe it's not as bad as she thinks. Maybe there was some sort of mistake.*

'There's more,' Gilda said, relentless; Rillirin thought she'd never be able to understand it all. 'You're pregnant by him.'

'What?' Rillirin felt herself blush, ridiculous as that was. *Pregnant? That's impossible.* It had only been one night, with Dom damn near gutted by a Mireces blade after the Blood Pass Valley battle and both of them grieving for Cam's death. Just one night, Rillirin tense and afraid despite his gentleness, both wanting and fearing his touch, desperate to be a woman for him and not the broken thing she knew herself to be. And for a short while, there in the dark, she had been. For a while she'd understood him and been understood in a way she hadn't even known was possible. Even so, though. *Pregnant?*

But the words spoke to something inside her, a deep well of knowing that embraced the knowledge, accepted it, confirmed its truth. 'I'm pregnant?' she whispered.

Gilda's smile was gentle despite the sweat gathering on her face. 'You are, lass. Did you not suspect?'

Rillirin blinked, her hand going to her belly. It was flat. 'No. I've never had a steady cycle; never been strong or well fed enough to bleed regularly.' She managed a wan smile. 'Then with the fighting, and the tunnels, and coming here, I thought the sickness was wound-fever or fear. You're sure?' she clarified, even though now that she knew, she could feel the rightness of it, the tiny seed of new life – hers and Dom's, created in love amid pain and horror – sleeping warm inside her. A connection between her and Dom that could never be broken.

This. I can use this to bring him back, to save him. Our child can make him see what's real, where he belongs. I can do this. I will do it.

'I have to go back to Rilporin,' she said. 'If he's . . . fallen, then this pregnancy, our child, might be the thing to restore him. I can bring him back to the Light, Gilda. I know I can.'

Gilda bit her lip. 'You can't go there, not now, not while the Mireces are there,' she said, her voice strong despite her pain, adamant.

Rillirin felt the newborn joy crystallise and then shatter. Instinctively, she wrapped her arms around herself. 'Why not?'

'Because Lanta knows. And I have no doubt she's going to want you – and your bairn.'

GALTAS

Fourth moon, afternoon, day thirty-three of the siege
The heir's wing, the palace, Rilporin, Wheat Lands

He was wearing the uniform of the Personal Guards to the royal family. It secured him unparalleled and – more importantly – unquestioned access to the palace, but the Personals were a small, close-knit unit. Any one of them would know instantly he was an imposter.

Best just stay out of their way then.

But that, of course, was easier said than done. He'd chosen the meeting place because he knew Rivil's quarters as well as he knew his own. He hadn't reckoned on the fucking West Rank turning up and taking over every spare room and common space. Fortunately, even Durdil wasn't stupid enough to throw open the royal apartments to defeated soldiers, but slipping through the palace had been more fraught than he'd expected. Next time – if there was a next time – they'd meet somewhere less full of soldiers who wanted him dead.

Still, his palms were clammy and cold sweat made its

miserable way down his back into the crack of his arse as he waited in a shadowed corner of Rivil's audience chamber. His guests were to meet him in the bedchamber, meaning they'd pass him by on the way through the suite and he could ensure they were those he was waiting for, and that they hadn't brought unexpected friends. Still, the risk was enormous, and doubly so now the palace was heaving with stinking, exhausted soldiers and lice-ridden Wolves. How they'd survived to make it this far, any of them . . .

Focus. If this meeting goes to plan, I'm not only free of the city, but firmly back in Rivil's favour. And why wouldn't it go to plan? They were happy enough to fly the scarlet at my suggestion. No, I just need to keep them dangling a little longer . . .

Footsteps. Galtas tensed and drew his knives, checked his approaches, his line of sight and ease of movement. Could be those he was here to see, could be Personals, could be West Rankers. Someone knocked at the door – what the fuck? Did they think he was going to stroll up and open it, welcome them in with a smile and a glass of wine? Galtas breathed quietly. There was a pause, and then the click of the antechamber door opening.

More footsteps, slow and hesitant. Galtas flexed his fingers on the knife hilts. Someone coughed. 'Hello?' Another voice hushed him, there was frenzied whispering, and then the men came through into the audience chamber and crossed it, making their way to the bedchamber. They didn't even glance around. Galtas watched them go, his ears straining back into the antechamber for hidden guards or assassins. Nothing.

The men came back out of the bedchamber, alarm plain on their faces at his absence. Galtas melted from the shadows, his knives glinting. 'My lords,' he said and they jumped, squeaked in fear, but didn't call for aid and he relaxed a fraction. 'I've been waiting.'

'Forgive us, Lord Morellis. We wanted to ensure we were not being followed. There are so many soldiers here now, it was . . . not easy.'

Galtas suspected it had been impossible. These fools couldn't lose a blind tail on a dark night in a labyrinth. Only their rank and arrogance would have allowed them to move through the palace without suspicion. Still, better to keep the meeting brief and get the fuck out while he still could.

'How circumspect,' he said drily. 'Would you take a seat?' He gestured and rounded the desk to sit in Rivil's chair. It put him in a corner, but it also put the desk between them. They perched on the edges of their seats like wild birds. 'The latest intelligence, if you please.'

The men exchanged a look. 'We require assurances first,' the first said cautiously, tugging repetitively and unconsciously at the lace of his cuff. 'That all you promised is in hand.'

Galtas sighed. He sheathed one of the daggers, used the other to clean beneath his fingernails. He didn't bother looking up as he spoke.

'As agreed, King Rivil will see you richly rewarded for your . . .' He gestured with the knife and both men leant away from it. '. . . aid in bringing this siege to a swift conclusion. After all, none of us want to be killing our countrymen, and if Rastoth had done the decent thing and died years ago, then none of this would have been necessary. King Rivil sent me into the city to procure such help as you are able to provide. In return for the information you gather at the war council each day, I will secure you safe passage out of the city. You will not be harmed, and you may take as much wealth as you can carry. Your women and children will of course accompany you, and once peace is restored, you may return to your estates here to find them untouched. I have no doubt that the king will welcome you back on to his council.'

'And what is it you intend to do with the information we provide?'

Galtas did look up at that. 'How easy do you think it will be for me to get you out of the city?' he demanded, leaning forward and thumping the knife point-first into the polished table. They jumped again. 'The best – the only – time I can get you safely away is when all the action is focused on a breach of the walls or one of the gates. You tell me which section of the defence Durdil thinks is likely to fall first. I relay that message – don't ask me how, I won't tell you. We then assault that very section and ensure a breach. When all eyes are focused there, I spirit you away through a different exit.'

The men before him eyed one another. 'Many soldiers will die,' the second ventured, though only the mildest concern touched his face at the thought.

'Then it is a good thing that is what they are paid for!' Galtas snapped, working the knife out of the table and sheathing it. 'Neither of you have territory in the Western Plain, so if it's the Mireces you are concerned with, you don't need to be. They will settle the scrublands once the city surrenders and you will hear nothing more from them.'

'And the rumours of Prince Rivil's—' Galtas raised a finger. 'Forgive me, King Rivil's, ah, religious beliefs?'

'Are rumours, my lord.' Galtas spread his hands. 'King Rivil did what was necessary to bring this city from under the heel of a mad tyrant. An alliance with the Mireces was unfortunate but necessary and, of course, the foolish and the deranged will spread rumours in consequence. You've seen he has the East Rank fighting for his cause – do you actually believe all five thousand of them could have converted to the Red Gods?'

He laughed and they joined in, albeit tentatively. 'No, my lords, there is nothing to fear from King Rivil, and much to be gained. Yes?'

The men exchanged another look, a small nod. 'Yes. Very well, let us continue. We have a written report here—'

'Verbal please,' Galtas interrupted, holding up a hand. 'And I'd suggest you burn that. We don't need any evidence pointing back to you fine gentlemen, do we?'

They blanched and acquiesced so quickly that Galtas wondered, not for the first time, if he wasn't dealing with drooling idiots. Still, a man took his allies where he found them, especially in times such as these.

He leant back in Rivil's chair and put his boots on the table. Across from him, as he had known they would, Lords Lorca and Silais began spilling their guts.

CRYS

It was weird to be back in the quarters he'd stayed in when he'd brought word to Durdil of Rivil's betrayal and Janis's murder, and what was even weirder was that he was now sharing them – and the bed – with Ash Bowman.

It was just the two of them, and they weren't due at the wall until midnight. Alone for two perfect, heady days. Crys had decided as soon as they got in there that he wasn't leaving the room for anything, and neither was Ash, whether he wanted to or not. So far they hadn't.

'Left eye.' Crys closed his left eye. 'Right eye.' He closed his right eye, opening the left. 'Left eye.' Ash paused and then grinned. 'Amazing. Blue eye, brown eye, it's like being in bed with two different men.'

Crys arched his eyebrows even as he blushed. *Why am I still blushing after yesterday, and last night, and this morning, twice?* Just the memory of it heated his skin and made him want to kiss Ash, but even now he didn't know

151

how to make the first move. Which was more than stupid.

Ash solved the dilemma for him, though, seeing the want in Crys's face and burning kisses along his throat to his mouth. Crys's stomach did a lazy somersault and his hand tightened on Ash's waist. 'Let's never leave this bed,' he murmured when Ash let him up for air.

'If wishes were horses, lover, I'd ride you all night.' Ash laughed and stroked his thumb across Crys's cheekbone. 'I love that you still blush, love. And I love the feel of you next to me.' He kissed Crys's jaw. 'On me.' His mouth. 'In me.'

Crys's stomach flipped harder this time. 'It's settled then. There's food and wine and water. A bed. A fire. A locked door. We're never leaving.'

Ash chuckled and licked the lobe of his ear. 'There are all those things, yes. And outside that locked door is the palace of Rilporin. We're in the very heart of Rilpor, the seat of government where they make all those laws that says this' – he splayed his hand on Crys's chest – 'is wrong. Illegal.'

'This isn't wrong,' Crys protested, pulling Ash tighter against him. 'It isn't,' he insisted and kissed him, their tongues twining together, Ash's sweat on Crys's skin, salty-hot.

Ash groaned and broke the kiss. 'You don't have to convince me, love. But the fact remains we're already courting disaster by not having opened that door for a day and a half. If anyone finds us, you'll be court-martialled and hanged and I'll be beheaded with the common criminals. And it's not very easy to pledge undying devotion to you when I'm dead, is it?'

Crys barely heard him over the hammering of his heart. He looked up, a little bleary, as the words cut through the fog of lust. 'Undying devotion?'

Now it was Ash's turn to blush. 'Sorry, I've always had a thing for men in uniform. Forget I said it.'

Crys shook his head. 'Not a chance.' His mischievous grin was suddenly back and he felt more at ease tangled in Ash's arms and legs, enjoying the play of sunlight over their skins, Crys's pale to Ash's dark. 'Say it again,' he whispered and kissed Ash's chest, licked the sweat from the hollow in his throat.

Ash laughed low in his throat. 'Devotion,' he whispered, 'utter, uncontrollable, endless devotion. I could spend the rest of my life with my hands on your arse – and not just my hands, either.' Crys blushed yet again but the thought set his heart racing and cock yearning.

'You're my hearth in winter,' Ash said, his voice suddenly serious and Crys looked up, met his eyes with his heart leaping like a salmon. *He's not saying that. Not those words . . . He wouldn't . . .*

'My hope in war, my ship in a storm, my—' Ash continued. *He is. He's saying them.* 'My heart in your chest,' Crys finished for him. They stared at each other in silence for a few moments. 'Those are serious words for someone you've only spent a few weeks with, Ash. Words like that can hurt if they're not meant.'

'I'm a simple man,' Ash whispered as he rolled on top of Crys, mindful of his broken ribs. 'I say what I mean, when I mean it. I rarely lie, and never in bed. I've never met anyone like you, and I am . . . smitten. I am, if you will have me, heart-bound.'

Tears gathered in Crys's eyes and a muffled sob made its way out of his chest as Ash jerked up. 'Gods, your ribs, sorry,' he began and Crys dragged him back down, heedless of the pain, fingers tight in Ash's curls.

'Kiss me, you idiot,' he whispered, suddenly fierce. 'My heart-bound, beautiful idiot.' There was a tightness in his chest that had nothing to do with broken ribs or Ash's weight pressing down on him and although it was hard to breathe, he had no intentions of letting Ash up or letting him leave. Not ever. 'I will have you, Ash Bowman,' he said after the kiss. 'And I give you mine, both heart and hearth, if you will have me.'

Ash's smile was wide, his eyes alive with love. 'Then it is done,' he said.

Heart-bound. To a man. To Ash. I'm heart-bound to Ash. Crys found he was laughing and wincing at the same time and he found Ash's cock had swelled and Ash's fingers were tracing tingling lines of fire across the back of his thigh and—

There was a knock at the door. 'Captain Tailorson,' called a voice that sounded suspiciously like Major Renik and Crys yelped, flung Ash off him and leapt out of bed, his cock shrivelling rapidly and all his hurts overtaking the lust in one great crashing wave so that he staggered, groaning, and nearly fell, only undiluted panic keeping him upright.

'What do we do?' he hissed as Ash stretched in the bed and pulled the covers back up, looking anything but concerned.

Ash chuckled. 'Put your clothes at the bottom of the other bed and get in it, you sex-crazed maniac,' he said, as though it was obvious. Which it was.

Crys followed his advice just as a second knock, this time brash and imperious, shattered the quiet of the room. 'Just a moment,' Crys said in his best just-woken-up voice and Ash pressed his face to the pillow to stifle his giggles as Crys leapt into his trousers and opened the door. He snapped to attention and saluted. 'Major Renik.' Renik peered into the room and Ash closed his eyes. Crys held a finger to his lips and gestured to the corridor, grabbed a shirt and followed Renik out, closing the door behind him.

'Is there a problem, sir? The enemy?' *Gods, I smell of sex.*

Stink of it. Can I say it was Dalli? He coughed over a laugh. *Only if I want her to cut my lungs out.*

Crys did up his shirt with unsteady fingers and snapped into parade rest as he tried not to ooze sex. He swallowed another giggle.

'General Mace Koridam has apprised his father, Commander Durdil Koridam, of your conduct over the last weeks,' Renik began and Crys's manic laughter dried up as the noose of his impending execution tightened around his throat.

'Major, whatever you may have heard—'

Renik spoke over him. 'He's aware, of course, of your earlier efforts to bring us news of Rivil's treachery and to save the Prince Janis. You are henceforth promoted into Major Wheeler's position, with all the rights and responsibilities that entails. Congratulations.'

Crys gaped at him and Renik took his unresisting hand and shook it, then clasped his forearm in the warrior's grip. 'You're allowed to say thank you, Tailorson,' he added.

'I thought I was being arrested,' he said and Renik frowned. 'Thank you, sir,' Crys managed, not sure how he felt about stepping into Wheeler's boots on account of having killed the man who'd previously worn them. 'When should I report for duty?'

'Dusk, I'm afraid, not midnight like the Commander originally promised. We're sorely pressed for officers, so you'll have to do.' He managed a tired smile. 'You'll have command of the southern wall, operating out of South Tower One. The trebuchet's nearly through the stump wall and then they'll be on that gate like crows on a dead dog. There is to be no breach, do you understand?'

'Yes, sir,' Crys said.

Renik slapped him on the arm. 'Just Renik now, Tailorson. We're equals.'

'Yes, sir, Renik,' Crys said and saluted.

'Probably don't need to do that either.' Renik laughed. 'Just out of interest, what did you think I was arresting you for?' he added, a quizzical twist to his eyebrows.

Crys's mind fizzed hot blankness. 'Men . . . do things in war, sir. Renik,' he managed.

Renik sobered and gave him a slow nod. 'That they do, but we answer for those to the gods and our own consciences, not to each other.' He brightened. 'Go on, get back to bed, Major. Dusk, South Tower One. Don't be late. I remember you had a problem with timekeeping back when you were a captain.'

'Dusk, of course. I'll be early,' Crys added as Renik waved and walked away, his chuckles echoing back from the stone. Crys leant against the door as his heartbeat slowed down from its frantic, squirrel-fast hammering.

'Devoted and promoted in the same hour,' he muttered, shaking his head as he went back into the room. 'Godsdamnit, I'm actually going to need to get some sleep now.'

'How's it looking?' Crys asked when he reached the top of the tower ostentatiously early. Leaving Ash asleep in his bed – *our bed* – had been both difficult and weirdly wonderful. He hadn't managed quite as much sleep as he'd needed, though. Ash hadn't been lying when he'd said he had a thing for men in uniform – particularly newly promoted majors, as it turned out. Particularly when they weren't actually in said uniform.

Crys touched the ranking symbol on his sleeve and over his heart. Though he came from a family of tailors and could've done a much better job, he'd let Ash sew them on for him, crooked, with huge looping stitches and a droplet of his blood from a needle-stuck finger.

It was perfect.

'Most of the stump wall's down, Major,' a soldier said. 'First Bastion'll cut 'em to pieces when they do start to breach, but I reckon enough'll make it that we'll have some action.'

Crys watched, a light wind picking away at his hair beneath his helmet. From South Tower One he couldn't see much past the bulk of First Bastion obstructing the view of the field, but he did have a clear line of sight to the stump wall, and it wasn't pleasant looking. It was still up, though, and that was what mattered.

'All right, what's your name and who're the officers I need to know?'

'You're the only major for South One and Two and East Tower as well, sir,' the man said, as though Crys should have known this. He probably should have. 'Whole length of the wall along the Gil. Normally you'd be in South Two to have sight up and down, but as we know they're coming through up here, we were told to expect you up here. Of course, if you'd rather move to South Two . . .'

Crys recognised the hope in the voice and general demeanour of the man in front of him. 'I'll stay here, thanks. You still haven't given me your name.'

'Lieutenant Oiler, sir.'

'All right Oiler, you don't know me and I don't know you. You probably think I'm some prick from a rich family who bought his commission and doesn't know his arse from the hole in the ground he's supposed to shit in, but let me tell you: I worked my way up through the ranks like any decent commoner and I came in with the West Rank, and fought two major battles in which thousands of my lads died. I'm not in the mood for pussies and cowards. Which one are you?'

'Neither, sir,' Oiler said with an alacrity that told Crys all he needed to know.

'Who are my captains?'

'Only Captain Lark, sir. Captain Norris was killed yesterday on the bridge when you arrived. And there's Kennett, who's just gone off watch.'

'Kennett I know, and I'm sorry to hear about Norris,' Crys said, having no idea who Norris was, 'but he died a hero saving a lot of lives. Fetch me Lark, will you? I'll be on the catapult level. When they do start clambering over the rubble they'll be easy targets. I want us to make the most of that. And get some pitch torches dropped behind the stump wall as well, give us some light to kill them by.'

'Aye, sir,' Oiler said and vanished into the torchlit gloom.

'It's going to be bloody,' Crys muttered to himself, gusting a sigh at the thought of Ash, a bed, some wine. He cleared his thoughts and focused on the coming of night, the coming of the Mireces. 'But then these days, when is it ever anything else?'

GALTAS

'Need any help?'

Galtas leapt to his feet and spun, drawing his sword as he did. It wasn't one of the Personals, wasn't anyone he recognised. His heart pounded; he'd been in this city far too fucking long. He was losing his nerve.

Just a couple more days.

'Whoa, whoa, not a threat.' The stranger laughed, his hands up away from his weapons. 'Gods, you jumped like I was a bloody Mireces.'

Galtas slid his blade away and eyed the otherwise empty courtyard. The East Tower defenders were locked up tight at the top, keeping a watch for flankers trying for the King Gate.

'What are you doing here?' he asked and the man's smile faltered.

'I'm manning the south wall in a few hours, but for now I'm just trying to work the stiffness out of my legs. I could

159

barely fucking move when I woke up.' He glanced past Galtas at the locked gate securing the mouth of a tunnel. 'Where's that go?'

'All the way under the walls to the palace. Royal family's emergency escape.' The man whistled. 'Look, I really have to get on,' Galtas added, praying the idiot in front of him didn't pay too much attention to the gate itself.

'Oh, sure, sure. Mind if I walk with you? Name's Ash, by the way. Like I said, I'll be on the wall later, so anything to take my mind off that is perfect. I was here once before, you know, start of the year, with a Rank officer. Didn't get much time for sightseeing then.'

'Now isn't time for it, either,' Galtas said, frustrated, as he hurried through the livestock district. Lorca had sent word the Mireces were through the southern stump wall and massing for an assault on the gate; if he could get a message to them, his half-formed plan would fall into place.

'Suppose not,' Ash said, though he craned his neck and peered into every alley and shop front they passed, long legs easily keeping pace. 'So how long have you served the king? Ah, sorry, didn't catch your name.'

'Didn't give it,' Galtas grunted. 'Simon. Name's Simon. And three years.'

'Bet you've seen more action in the last weeks than all those three years, eh? Same for me, for all of us. Mace called and we answered, but we didn't expect . . . this. Few border skirmishes, few dead on each side, that we know, we understand, but this? This is like nothing I've ever seen.'

'You're a Wolf,' Galtas said and the man nodded. 'Only heard rumours what happened to you and the West. Hasn't really been much time for swapping news, if you know what I mean.' They reached the district gate and Galtas's uniform got them through into the temple district.

'Well, we won at the Blood Pass Valley, that much you must know,' Ash said, his voice low as the sound of chanted prayers rose from the holy places around them, 'but the fuckers had a second army – the one outside – and they used it to slaughter everyone in Watchtown, everyone in Pine Lock, everyone in Shingle. The people of Yew Cove survived by betraying us, tricking us down into their smugglers' tunnels. Then the Mireces in charge of the townsfolk smashed the dam and did their best to drown us all. Those that made it out, well, let's just say it's personal now. We spent a couple of weeks resting, healing as best we could, then made our way here. We came as soon as we could, whatever you might have heard to the contrary.'

Galtas nodded. 'Sounds bad.'

Ash snorted. 'Understatement.'

'And the last time you were here?' he asked. Not that he cared, but the Wolf gave a little more credence to his disguise as a Personal.

Ash grinned and Galtas saw something else, something more than respect, light his face for a second. 'Came in with a Ranker named Crys Tailorson. He'd seen what that traitorous bastard Rivil had done to his brother. He faked his own death and came here to warn Durdil and Rastoth. Turns out Rivil and his man Galtas were here, and we got in and out under their very noses.'

Galtas halted, and Ash stopped and turned as well. 'Crys Tailorson was here?'

'Aye, and he's here again now. Promoted to major too, by Durdil himself no less.'

Galtas grunted and raised one hand to stroke the hole where his eye used to be. Crys would recognise him in an instant if they met, eye patch or no.

Good. About fucking time I ended that cunt.

'Oh,' Ash suddenly breathed, and Galtas saw the precise moment when it clicked, when he made the connection between the name and the man standing before him. They were in the middle of the temple quarter, far from either district gate and their attendant guards.

Ash slid his left foot back a little, casual but only a breath away from a fighting stance. He glanced back up the street. 'Why did you say you were checking that gate to the palace . . . Simon?'

Galtas shrugged, his own left foot moving. 'I didn't. Something on your mind?'

'I heard a lot about Rivil and his assassin from Crys,' Ash said, hand drifting to the axe on his belt. 'Crys was pissed, see, about what they'd done to Janis. I got more detail than I cared for, every encounter, every moment of their time together. Of course, in all that, I got a good impression of what they looked like as well.'

The axe came out of his belt and Galtas's sword slid free of its scabbard. 'You thought taking off your eye patch would be enough, Lord Morellis?' Ash asked, a long knife in his other hand. His knees flexed and he dropped into stance, moonlight limning the wicked head of the axe.

Galtas laughed. 'I've been in this city nearly three weeks and no one's recognised me. You've never even met me. How did you do it?'

'Arrogant, missing one eye, other one green, black hair, breath stinks like shit. But mostly, it was the look of absolute hate that crossed your face when I mentioned Crys, and the anger that he'd been here and you missed him. You shouldn't let your emotions get the better of you, Milord Galtas. Dangerous in a fight.'

'I shall have to learn to mask my feelings better,' Galtas said, and lunged. Ash blocked with the haft of his axe and thrust with the knife, aiming for the armpit. He was tall, his reach long, and the point was raking cloth before Galtas slid away. He didn't have a shield, so he pulled out one of his knives to even the odds.

They circled in the temple square, the night silent but for the prayers drifting on the wind and the clash of steel, stamp and slide of feet, grunts of effort. The Wolf was good, using the axe head to hook Galtas's knife when it came for him and jerking it wide, slipping by the sword so close it skirled across the back of his armoured shoulder. His knife punched into Galtas's gut, was turned by the stolen breastplate, and slid off. Before he could recover, Galtas flicked his wrist and the sword sliced into Ash's left elbow. Ash grunted and skipped back on his left foot, axe and knife both chopping down, knife to deflect the sword, axe to take Galtas's hand off at the wrist.

It was faster than he could blink, but Galtas moved without thought, dropping his right hand to avoid the axe, the left curving up and then down, punching the knife in the man's back just above his shoulder. He caught the edge of the chainmail, but then the tip bit deep. Very deep.

Ash roared, but the axe was still moving. Having met no resistance when Galtas lowered his hand, the arc continued through until the blade slammed home. Galtas screamed as white-hot lightning earthed itself in his right knee. Ash ripped the axe free as Galtas pulled his knife from the Wolf's back and they separated, staggering, bleeding, spitting curses. In a city constant with the sounds of battle, no one marked their duel among the temples.

'You cunt-fuck little bastard!' Galtas howled, his right leg shuddering beneath him, threatening to dump him in the street. Pain pulsed, sending waves of nausea through his gut and chest. 'I'll suck your fucking eyes out for that.'

Ash grinned, but it was a rictus of agony and his right arm hung by his side, the axe slack in his fingers from whatever damage Galtas's knife in his back had dealt. He beckoned with a bloody hand. 'Come on, then.'

He held his ground, and Galtas knew he'd have to go to him if he wanted to end it. He'd never outrun him, not with a shattered kneecap. Part of him was surprised he was even still standing. 'My feet are on the Path,' he muttered, and hobbled forward, gasping each time his right foot took his weight.

Ash tapped his fingertips to his heart and readied his knife. The axe came up slow, the head wobbling about in a trembling hand, and the old scar on his face stood out purple against the pallor of pain and blood loss.

Galtas lunged on the cross-step, when his weight was on his strong left leg. The Wolf batted it down with the axe and then jabbed the flat of the head into Galtas's face; his knife deflected it and even as Ash's own knife clattered into the sword and knocked it down again, Galtas stepped through, screaming, on his right leg and brought the knife around back-handed to shear into his jaw.

Ash's weapons fell from nerveless fingers and he went over backwards, making no effort to save himself as he crumpled, head bouncing from the road, blood spurting from the ruin of his face. He bubbled something that sounded like 'Crys', jerked a couple of times, and then his eyes rolled back and he stilled.

'Cunt,' Galtas muttered again. He spat on the body and poked at it, checking for life. 'Think Crys will avenge you? Let's see, shall we? It's about time he got what he deserves.'

Using his sword as a crutch, he grabbed Ash by the back of his collar and began to drag him, a wide smear of blood stretching out from the body. South. Towards Crys's command.

THE BLESSED ONE

Fourth moon, night, day forty of the siege
Mireces encampment, outside Rilporin, Wheat Lands

Lanta paced before the men kneeling in her tent, her hammer dangling from one hand. The temptation to kill them all, the Godblind included, rose strong inside her. She fought it back.

Corvus hadn't allowed her any men to search for Gilda, forcing Lanta to send her own guards out in pursuit. And here they were, returned empty-handed and penitent as children caught stealing.

'Forgive us, Blessed One,' Scell said, 'we cannot find her. The witch has vanished.'

Lanta ignored him and stopped in front of the Godblind. His right arm was in a sling and he stared at her out of a swollen, ripped face. The spike attached to Gilda's chain had gone into his shoulder even as his knife had ripped open her arm, and her second strike had, without doubt, been aimed at his eye. She'd missed though, the Godblind's own attack foiling hers, and the unexpectedness of the violence

165

– *I underestimated the bitch* – had allowed her precious seconds to slip through the tent flap and sprint into the night while Lanta screamed for her guards.

Her fingers twitched on the haft of the hammer. The Mireces fell to their faces before her, grovelling. The Godblind didn't move.

'Forgive you?' she said softly. 'I think not. Godblind, pick him up.'

The Wolf stood and lifted Scell on to his knees with his one good arm, fist tight in the back of his shirt. 'Stand,' he grated.

'P-please, Blessed One, please,' Scell tried. 'We'll keep looking; the search isn't over yet. There's still time.'

'No, there isn't,' the Godblind said. 'Gilda has met Rillirin. She knows; soon she'll know everything. The future has changed already.'

'And where are they?' Lanta demanded, excitement flaring in her belly. 'Tell me and we can send men out to retrieve them.' The haft was warm in her fist, a comforting reminder of the gods, of her duty. Her privilege.

'They flee together.' She watched as his face writhed, right eyelid flickering. A low whine like a beaten dog's shoved its way out of his throat and his back arched, though he didn't let go of Scell. 'They . . . ah! They flee south. Let them go, let them go and focus on the siege. On Rivil and the breach – breach soon. Treachery.'

Lanta put her head on one side. 'You would see them escape?'

The Godblind curled in on himself so hard and fast he dropped to one knee behind Scell. He whined again and the Mireces shied away from him. 'She carries my seed; I'll always be able to find her. When we have the city we can bring her in. The babe is months away; victory is not.'

Lanta pursed her lips. 'Stand, Godblind. Hold him.'

Shaking from the knowing, fresh blood darkening the bandages on his shoulder, he complied. Scell babbled something frantic and pointless, and Lanta didn't wait for him to finish. Failure could never be ignored. She stepped forward and swung, hard and around, the hammer crunching into his temple. He fell, boneless, blood and brain oozing through shattered skull and torn skin.

The remaining Mireces looked at the twitching corpse and prayed, readying themselves with more grace than Scell had managed. 'Next,' Lanta said, pointing with the gory head of the hammer. The Godblind raised the man on to his knees and held him tight. She swung.

When it was done and more Mireces had dragged the bodies away, Lanta called for the prisoners they'd taken on the river. Corvus's interrogators had been to work on them, but so far none had said anything of any use.

She beckoned the Godblind to her. 'Every time I think I can trust you, you do something like this, tell me to turn from my chosen path.'

Bloodshot brown eyes stared into hers. 'Rillirin and Gilda have crossed the Gil and are heading south. Gilda has told Rillirin that she's pregnant. She's told her about . . . me. What I am now. Rillirin . . . grieves for me.' He put his left hand on Lanta's cheek and she jerked away. 'You can go and get them now if you want, but the wall's coming down and they're nearly through at the South Gate and Rivil will never let you win and all the world hangs in the balance.'

She stepped back and licked her lips.

'I will always be able to find them,' he repeated softly.

The tent flap opened and Corvus strode in ahead of the prisoners, heavy chains weighing them down.

'We are so close, Blessed One, so close to a breach now.' He gestured to the prisoners. 'Sacrifices?'

'A test,' she replied shortly. She eyed the prisoners and then the Godblind. 'Start with the Wolves,' she said. 'Make me trust you again.'

'They have nothing else to tell us,' he said. 'Nothing of import.'

Lanta licked her teeth. 'And why should that matter?' She studied him intently as he looked over the prisoners.

The Godblind bowed his head. 'Your will, honoured.' He gestured. 'Bring me that one. Seth Lightfoot, tracker, the little cousin of little Dalli Shortspear. An unrequited love for Rillirin. Thinks because he saved her life she should love him. Jumped into the river to save her after she fell in. Failed.'

The young Wolf's head was hanging, his face swollen beyond recognition with bruises. 'Dom?' he slurred. 'Gods, Dom, what are you doing here? Help us!'

The Godblind slid his arm out of his sling and flexed it, grunting at the pain. Then he hauled Seth to the water barrel set in the centre of the tent. Next to it was a table covered with knives and other things. 'Convert or die,' he said.

'What?' Seth managed before Dom shoved his head into the barrel and held him while he thrashed. The other Wolves shouted and struggled, and their guards clubbed them on to their knees, more bruises to add to the multitude. Lanta folded her arms and watched Dom. The prisoners didn't interest her.

'Is everything all right, Blessed One?' Corvus murmured.

Lanta waited while Dom roared the question in Seth's face again before shoving him once more into the water. 'Your sister let the Godblind put his seed in her belly,' she said and saw Corvus's mouth tighten in disgust.

'I had thought to make her my queen,' he said in a low

voice, 'as the Mireces kings of old did, marrying their sisters to honour the Dark Lady and the God of Blood. This . . . changes things. Still, a pennyroyal tea when we have her in our grasp will end that.'

'No,' Lanta said quietly, 'the babe is not to be harmed. It may be . . . useful,' she added, unwilling to say too much even to him. 'Its mother, though. Well, you may do whatever you please with the whore once she's spawned. But for now, let her think herself free of us. He assures me he can find her wherever she goes. These will die to reassure me he tells the truth.'

Corvus sucked his teeth and then shrugged. 'As you say, Blessed One, so shall it be.' He pointed with his chin at the scene across the tent. 'How long do you think until that one breaks?'

Lanta frowned. 'He's a Wolf. He won't break.'

'We might have said that about the Godblind once.'

'Oh no, I think the Godblind was always going to break. When a man sees as much as he, his grasp on himself is never very secure. But these?' She gestured at the prisoners and then dismissed them. 'I think these will go screaming into death before forsaking the Flower-Whore. It amuses me to see the Godblind send them there.'

Even as she spoke, Seth's thrashing lessened to twitches and gentle flailing. His feet kicked, kicked again, and he was still. The Godblind pulled him out of the water and let him thump to the ground. He beckoned to the next.

'Blessed One,' he said as he punched the woman in the face and pushed her into the barrel. 'Everything comes to its climax, and yet everything is in flux. Rivil is a threat.'

Lanta felt Corvus tense at her side. 'And why is that?'

'Ambitious, petty, blinded by greed. Allied with you only to use your army, expected you to be defeated by the West

Rank. You won, and now he doesn't know what to do with you. You're all supposed to be dead, you see. Expect treachery.'

'Of course we expect treachery,' Lanta snapped. 'I said make me trust you, not tell me what I already know.'

'Rivil may encourage you to spend your strength on the siege and then attack you, or he may allow you to take up residence on the Western Plain like he promised and then order the South Rank's remaining Thousands to annihilate you. There are many possibilities, but there is one path we can take now to eliminate them.'

'What path?' Corvus asked.

'Me.'

'Explain,' the king snapped, but Lanta could sense his interest. The issue of the Rilporian prince was a constant irritation.

'Years ago, when I swore the blood oath, it was for vengeance on the killers of my wife and unborn child. Rivil and Galtas are those killers. They disguised themselves as Mireces and killed her, hoping to provoke a war. Let me fulfil my oath to the Red Gods. With Rivil dead, Skerris and the East Rank will be yours. Skerris's faith is pure; he will put you on the throne rather than see all we have accomplished come to nothing. Rilpor will belong to Blood again and my Hazel will finally have justice.'

Interesting.

'Is this what everything has been for?' one of the chained Wolves shouted. 'Everything you've done, everyone you've betrayed, has been for Hazel? You think she'd want all this?'

'She was my wife,' the Godblind said as he dragged the woman out of the water again and casually stabbed her in the belly, threw her down on Seth's corpse. 'I swore to bring her peace. I did not say what limit I would put on my efforts.'

'Yes,' Corvus breathed at Lanta. 'This is perfect.'

She gave a tiny nod. 'I will consult the gods. We are done here, Godblind. You should rest and eat if you truly wish to take this road. You, we have no need for these.'

She snapped her fingers and the guards' knives glinted in the firelight. It was over in seconds, a quicker death than they deserved, but Lanta had no time to waste on such as them.

'Hoth-Nagarre,' Dom confirmed, wiping his hands. 'Single combat in sight of the gods. No quarter and no retreat; the gods as witness. And my feet are on the Path.'

DURDIL

Fourth moon, night, day forty of the siege
Double First, western wall, Rilporin, Wheat Lands

Durdil blinked gritty eyes and gave Edris his most wolfish grin. 'Well, Colonel, looks like your end of the wall is going to see some action.'

Edris dragged his grimy hands over his sweaty face. 'How marvellous,' he murmured. 'It's been all of twenty minutes, after all.'

Durdil beckoned to his runners. 'I want status reports from every tower while we've got a bit of breathing space. We might've broken their second siege tower, and I still can't believe we withstood the attack on the portcullis, but whatever our recent successes, they're regrouping and they will come again. I want to know what's happening everywhere else.' The runners saluted and hared off along the allure in opposite directions, calling for men to get out of the way.

When was the last time I had enough energy to run like that? he mused, but he knew the answer. It was about three hours ago when that bridgehead had threatened to spread to a third ladder and secure the stretch of wall between the gatehouse and Second Tower. He'd run like a hare then, hadn't he?

Durdil tapped his teeth with a fingernail and then touched Edris's elbow, drew him away from the closest knot of men and lowered his voice. 'Colonel, I need to ask a favour of you.'

Edris's eyebrows rose. 'Anything, sir.'

'My son, Mace. He's a fine man and an outstanding general. A born warrior. He's the only thing that'll keep this army and these people together if I fall. I shouldn't ask this, but I am. If you can, protect him, see he stays alive. Am I clear?'

Edris's face was anguished. 'I'm sorry, sir, but your son made me swear a similar oath the first day he arrived, that I would save you over him. I couldn't refuse.'

Durdil bit the inside of his cheek hard. 'That little bastard,' he muttered. 'Gods, Edris, he's only thirty-five. What's he doing throwing his life away?'

'I don't actually intend to die, you know, Father,' Mace said from behind him and Durdil jumped. 'I just wanted to make sure you didn't do anything stupidly heroic because we're fighting in the same battle. I remember what you did when we fought the Dead Legion together twelve years ago.'

Durdil felt his cheeks grow warm. 'Well, you were young and particularly idiotic that day. Someone had to save your arse.'

'Maybe. But it shouldn't have been the general of the North Rank. You yourself taught me our most inviolable order: don't jeopardise the battle for the sake of one man. Not even an officer. Not even a general. Not even a son.' Mace slung his arm around Durdil's shoulders, his vambrace clattering on Durdil's pauldron. 'It's done, the oaths sworn. Besides, it's not like they took much convincing. You're revered by your men, did you know? I'm a nobody in this city. You're a hero. And you deserve that title.'

Durdil's blush was more pronounced this time. He cleared his throat noisily. 'Don't be ridiculous. Mostly they're just glad I keep Hallos and his endless experiments away from them. Speaking of which, he told me you were exhausted and needed to rest. Why are you up here?'

'That was yesterday. I've slept since then.'

Durdil squinted at him, at the glint in his eye and the small smile at odds with their situation. 'Well, you've done something in a bed since then,' he said and now it was Mace's turn to blush.

Durdil was just winding up to thoroughly humiliating the boy and enjoying every moment of it when Last Bastion's catapult loosed, followed a few seconds later by North Tower One's. Durdil spun to his right to peer north along the length of the allure. The men on the wall stilled, straining their ears for the sounds of attack. The East Rank's trebuchet unwound in reply, hurling a stone screaming through the air to impact, yet again, on the patched and repaired weak spot.

'Gods, they're like a dog on a rat with—' Durdil began.

The door to First Bastion slammed back on its hinges and Merle Stonemason emerged as though conjured from the depths of a particularly dusty hell. Yarrow was following him, face as white as the flowers of his namesake. 'Commander? Commander, she ain't gonna hold, sir. You need to clear the wall. Right fucking now.'

Durdil stared at Merle and the noise surrounding them fell away behind a blanket of buzzing. His vision narrowed down to Merle's honest, grimy, panic-stricken face. 'Say that again?' he croaked.

'Stone set crooked, mortar got squeezed out when it was still wet so there's nothing to hold the blocks in place. We've been propping it, mortaring over the cracks, but the wall's starting to bulge where we did the work, sir. Stone's being pushed out with every impact. She's going.' He grabbed Durdil by the breastplate. 'Get everyone off the wall.'

'Here they come,' Edris shouted and there was an explosion of noise and shouting as ladder tops appeared along the battlement.

'Make ready,' Mace roared.

'Get off the fucking wall,' Merle boomed in a voice that nearly ruptured their eardrums. Men came to a shocked standstill all around them until Mace yelled again and Edris did likewise and they began to move, jerky, like puppets dancing to the tune of a drunkard, preparing to fight, wanting to flee.

Durdil found his fist in Merle's leather apron and the big man's face close to his. 'Will the entire wall collapse or just the part above the repair? Answer me!'

'With luck, just that section, sir.'

'Thank you, mason, then we defend Double First,' Durdil said and released him. Around him chaos raged as soldiers shoved away ladders and hacked at the men climbing them, men in blue, slow but lethal.

'Yarrow, clear the wall between Second Tower and Last Bastion. East can have it. Fill those towers with men, barricade the doors. They can have the wall in between but not the towers. Understand?' Yarrow nodded, mystified but trusting Durdil to know what he was doing. Durdil hoped that he did.

'Once that section of wall is overrun, tower catapults are to loose on it. Fucker's coming down anyway, may as well fall when we want it to, not them, eh?' Yarrow blinked rapidly and raised a finger. 'Say "yes, sir",' Durdil snapped.

'Yes, sir,' Yarrow said automatically. He puffed out his

cheeks, shook his head once, but then a dazed grin split his face. 'Every enemy on that wall will be killed.'

'See it done.'

'And me, sir?' Merle asked as Yarrow ducked away and began shouting orders.

Durdil shook his head and stumbled as Mace shoved him away, yelling incoherently. They ran into First Tower and slammed the door on the noise. 'You've done enough, Merle, you and all your boys. Get into Second Circle. Once that section of the wall comes down, the enemy'll be up and over the rubble like goats. It'll be hand to hand in the streets down there. You don't want to be part of that.'

Merle stroked his beard and then slapped Durdil on the arm, knocking him sideways. 'This is Sweetie,' he said, drawing an enormous hammer from his belt. 'Me and Sweetie like hitting things. I'm guessing Raider heads are softer than granite. Maybe I'll hang around a while.'

Durdil found the breath to laugh. 'You stand in the breach once it's made,' he said, marvelling, 'and there's no fucker who'll try and cross it. Welcome to the Palace Rank, Merle. Not sure we've a uniform big enough for you.'

'Don't need no uniform,' Merle protested. 'Man's got to fight for his home when it's threatened, don't he? Don't need a fancy jacket for that.'

Before Durdil could reply, the mason squeezed across the room and followed Yarrow on to the allure.

CRYS

Fourth moon, dawn, day forty-one of the siege
South Tower One, southern wall, Rilporin, Wheat Lands

'Are they coming?' Crys demanded, shoving an archer away from an arrow slit and peering out. 'Course they're coming. Bastards.'

And they were, hundreds of them, running full pelt around the shattered end of the stump wall and charging for the gate. At their centre a dozen running in formation, an iron-tipped tree-trunk battering ram held between them.

Crys patted the archer's shoulder and jogged down the stairs and out on to the southern wall's allure. He hopped up on to the guard wall, balancing over the dizzy drop into the city below and waved his arms until he had everyone's attention.

'All right lads,' he shouted, 'they're coming and they've got a battering ram, so I won't lie: the situation's as sticky as a bad shit, but we're up on the wall shooting them, and they're banging a twig against the gate. I know you're tired, we all are, but we've got arrows aplenty and we've got light

177

to kill them by. I know you all: you're loyal, you're professional, and you're killers. I need all three, and so do you. Do your jobs, and we live.'

'Nearly at the gate, sir,' Lieutenant Weaverson called.

'Right, I'm going down to take a look and speak to the men down there. Roger, get them loosing as soon as they're—'

'Loose!' Weaverson howled.

'—in range,' Crys finished and headed for the stairs.

The merchants' quarter was silent and shuttered, no lights in the windows when he exited the tower. 'All right, Tailorson, looking good,' he muttered to himself as he scanned the area. 'Streets are empty, clear lines of sight. You're tucked up safe here, they can't . . . get . . . in.'

He came to halt and peered into the recessed shadows cast by the fortifications around the gate. Furtive movement, the soft slide of cloth on stone, the harsh squeak of metal on metal, like the sound of bolts being drawn.

Crys broke into a run, drawing his sword on instinct, eyes fixed on the gate and the faint blush of dawn showing through. It was open.

'Sweet Dancer,' he breathed. 'Some bastard's betrayed us.'

The light touched the bodies slumped around the gate, the soldiers he was here to check on. Now the wide, open courtyard used by the merchants to unload wagons was empty except for Crys and a small boy with very big, very round eyes. *So first, who opened the gate and second, where's he gone and third, oh gods, I can hear the Mireces coming.*

'Are you a soldier?' the boy piped and pointed. 'Those men all fell over. It was very funny.' Crys followed the little finger to the gate. 'Thump thump,' the boy said and laughed. 'All fall down.'

'Go home, lad,' Crys said as a cold finger prickled down his back. 'Right now.'

The boy wandered over to him and tried to take his hand; Crys snatched it away. 'Will you fall down too?' he asked, unperturbed.

Another cold shiver wormed beneath Crys's armour. 'It's looking increasingly likely,' he muttered. 'Go home,' he hissed with a bit more vehemence. 'Right now.' There was movement along the base of the wall. 'Run,' he yelled into the boy's face.

The boy froze, his lower lip wobbled, and then he burst into tears. 'I hate you,' he sobbed.

'Get in line,' Crys snapped, 'now just fuck off, will you? There's a battle on.'

The war cries of the Mireces went up a notch, triumph in their screams.

'Weaverson,' Crys roared, 'South Gate breach, South Gate *fucking breach*.'

There were shouts of alarm from above and Crys grinned; then he shoved the boy hard sideways so that he sprawled on the cobbles and jumped forward to engage the three men sprinting through the gate, howling their victory. The boy was wailing about a skinned knee and Crys had a fraction of a second to wish that was all the pain he would ever suffer, and then there was a notched and angry sword arcing at his face.

Crys jinked left, parried the blade with his own and loosed a sloppy punch with his left fist as the man stumbled past, a glancing blow to his ear that did nothing but piss him off. He roared and stumbled again, tripped over something. His sword flashed. There was a high-pitched squeal that stopped Crys's heart, and when the man attacked him again the point of his sword was smeared red.

The boy. He killed the boy.

Crys's lips peeled back from his teeth and he drew a knife

with his free hand, used it to block the second attacker's overhead lunge and dragged it quick as lightning down the man's face, through the eyeball and cheek, ripping open the lips. His scream was almost as high-pitched as the boy's had been and he dropped like a stone, sword forgotten, fight abandoned, hands pressed to his face.

An arrow flashed past him and took the third man in the throat; another skewered the first through the calf.

'Mine,' Crys yelled, savage now, and no more arrows flew. He stalked his victim as the man limped away. Crys knew it was stupid to follow, knew the man was leading him towards the gate and the others now openly pouring through it, followed anyway. 'P-please,' the Raider stuttered, 'p-please.'

'Fuck you,' Crys snarled, jumping forward and punching his sword into the man's neck. 'You killed a child. A boy. There are no pleases left in the world for scum like you.' He sensed movement, glanced over his shoulder.

'Need a hand?' Dalli asked, hundreds of Wolves at her back, grim-eyed and grim-faced and swathed in dirty bandages all.

The corner of Crys's mouth turned up. 'Fresh as daisies, are you?'

'Fresh enough.'

'That'll do.' He pointed with his sword. 'We need to seal this gate; I don't know who opened it, but I intend to find them and feed them their own intestines.' He looked around. 'Where's Ash?'

Dalli frowned. 'Isn't he with you? I saw him around dusk; he said he was going to come to you.'

Crys went cold. 'What?' He looked around as though Ash would suddenly appear. 'He never got here . . .'

Lim shoved past them, knocking Crys off balance. 'Aren't you two lucky you still have someone to worry about in all this? Let's hope your lovers live forever, eh? Seeing as they're so important.'

He raised his sword over his head. 'Sarilla!' he roared. 'For the dead!' The Wolves howled with him and charged, flowing around Dalli and Crys like smoke.

Crys watched them go, twitching with the need to find Ash, his stomach full of hot lead. He couldn't go; he knew he couldn't, but gods he wanted to. Needed it. Horror like he'd never felt crawled into his throat, cutting off speech.

He looked at Dalli as though for permission. She narrowed her eyes and jerked her head. 'Let's seal this gate, Major,' she growled and then her face softened. 'And then we'll go and find him together.'

Crys managed a nod and then leapt into the fray; the sooner this lot were dead, the sooner he could look for Ash.

DURDIL

Fourth moon, dawn, day forty-one of the siege
Double First, western wall, Rilporin, Wheat Lands

Yarrow was dead. Word had come along the allure, through the gatehouse and into Durdil's ear, and he'd responded without thought, running back the way the messenger had come, roaring men out of his path.

'Multiple assaults,' Durdil muttered as he jinked and dodged around the soldiers on the wall. 'Gods preserve us from multiple breaches.' He was almost at Second Tower and shoving a soldier out of his path when the trebuchet's next strike impacted and nearly shook him off his feet. He made a wild grab for the wall and clung on as the whole thing rocked.

'Imagining things,' he gasped and reeled across the allure to the guard wall, peered down into the killing field. A mess of rubble and a clear and horrifying bulge in the wall's surface told him he was imagining nothing. The masts propping the wall had tumbled like kindling and masons were hard at work shoving them back into place, their shouts strident with alarm. Durdil was astonished they were still there, risking their lives.

The wall rumbled, shivered and then settled.

'Full breach between Second Tower and Last Bastion,' came the shout he'd been waiting for and Durdil turned away from the killing field and charged on, feeling as if he was running downhill, as if the wall had tilted . . .

He skidded again to a halt, stood still and stared at the wallwalk in the pink light of dawn, then turned and examined the other end. Then he lay flat on the stone and stared along it, ignoring the men hacking away at the ladders and the soldiers climbing them. It was crooked. The allure was definitely sloping. His gaze was snagged by a snaking crack up the guard wall.

This part of the wall's supposed to be safe. The towers are supposed to . . . That tower's leaning. Bugger me with a bargepole, the tower's leaning!

Durdil sprinted for Second Tower and crashed inside. 'Merle Stonemason,' he roared, 'Merle Stonemason, where are you?' He grabbed Vaunt. 'Where?'

Vaunt pointed. 'Outside, sir, got cut off when we pulled back.'

'How long?'

'Just now.'

'Come with me,' he snapped. 'We need that man alive.'

Vaunt pressed his lips together on whatever protest – whatever eminently sensible and perfectly justified refusal – he was about to utter. He hefted a shield and snatched up a spear, handed them to Durdil and took the same for himself.

Durdil strode to the opposite door. 'On my mark. Three. Two. One.' The door was wrenched free and Durdil lunged, slamming his shield out in front and jabbing with the spear. There was an arm's length of space around Merle as the huge man swung Sweetie with economical force as though he was working stone. The hammer had already killed a dozen by the look of the corpses. But his face was purple with strain and his other arm was missing from the elbow and there was a lot – a *lot* – of blood pooling around his feet.

Vaunt and Durdil killed their way to him, and then a score of Palace Rankers flooded out around them, forming a shield wall against their brethren from the East. They retreated as a unit, a bristling hedgehog shambling backwards, men being picked off one by one until they reached the tower.

Four Easterners tried to follow them in and died on the threshold before Vaunt managed to slam the door and the rest piled barrels and tables against it.

'Can you walk? Can you walk, man?' Durdil shouted at Merle. The big ox gave a slow nod, Sweetie falling from his fingers and landing on Vaunt's foot. Vaunt's mouth opened in a silent howl of pain, but he handed Durdil a tourniquet without a word. Durdil tied it around the stump of Merle's arm and led him to the stairs. 'This tower's leaning. Will it fall?'

'Tower should be safe,' Merle said, blood draining from his face as fast as his arm now. 'Strong.'

'It's leaning,' Durdil repeated.

Merle blinked owlishly. 'See it from outside,' he mumbled.

'Shit. Right, Vaunt, hold this tower only until the collapse, then get the fuck out that way. Towards the gatehouse, not downstairs. That way. No one stays inside.'

'Yes, sir. But you shouldn't—'

Durdil grabbed him. 'Stop those catapults,' he hissed. 'I told them to loose on the wall, to bring down just the weak section, but something's not right. It might all go.'

He pushed Merle into the stairwell and they began the dizzying descent, Durdil going first and hoping the mason didn't lose consciousness and crush him to death. The trebuchet sent another, possibly the final, stone into the wall and the entire tower lurched to the side. A crack appeared in the wall to his right and Durdil made a noise part horror, part defiance. 'Don't you fucking dare,' he yelled, as though his words were mortar in the cracks.

Merle came to a halt and ran his hand over the fault, his brow furrowed. ''S not right.'

'No it isn't,' Durdil said. 'So let's hurry.'

Durdil scurried on, dragging Merle by the sleeve, turn after turn, breath whistling in his throat and that damned tightness back in his chest worse than ever. A slight greying of his vision around the edges, his pulse outracing his feet. 'No,' he panted, 'not now. Not . . . now.'

The sun had gilded the sky by the time they came out of Second Tower's door and into the killing field. The other masons had fled. Durdil squinted against the brightness and dragged Merle thirty paces out from the wall, then turned the big man around and pointed.

There were more cracks down here, a lot more, all of them jagging out of the rebuilt section of wall. 'Merle, look. I'm right, the towers are leaning. You said just the wall would go, not the towers. Are my men safe?'

Merle didn't say anything. Instead he stood swaying, eyes unfocused, and then he folded up and slid on to his knees, his side, and then his back. He was paler than stone dust, and one look at him and Durdil knew he was dying.

He knelt down. 'Merle, you're going to listen to me and listen good. You're a big bastard and I'm an old fuck, so you're going to have to help me, all right? No way I can lift your flabby arse without help. So, count of three and

you're going to stand, and it's going to hurt like the Red
Gods are buggering you, but you're going to do it because
that's the only way I can get you to hospital. Ready? One,
two . . .'

'Stop,' Merle whispered. 'Get up there, evacuate all the
way to the gatehouse. Towers're wilting like a poxed cock.'

There was yet another impact even as they sat there and
a crack exploded in the wall in front of them with the sound
of thunder splitting the sky. The wall *rippled*.

'Fuck,' Durdil squawked. He got his shoulder into Merle's
armpit and screamed him up to standing, the pair of them
tottering towards Second Circle's wall and the right-hand
bend into the slaughter district. There was a gate there; they
could get through to safety.

Merle made a sound like a cow giving birth and went to
his knees again. The stump of his arm wasn't bleeding much
any more, but from the look of him it was because he didn't
have any blood left. 'Come on,' Durdil shouted at him,
dragging frantically at his remaining arm. 'Come on!'

'Sorry.' Merle toppled sideways and lay still, his visible
eye fixed on the wall. They were a hundred paces from the
corner. Durdil saw a flag waving frantically from Second
Tower – cease fire. His brow wrinkled and then he looked
right just as Last Bastion's catapult released straight into the
faltering wall.

'Godsdamnit,' he whispered.

The impact shattered the top of the wall, tossing East
Rankers about like straw dolls. There were screams from
high up, thin and distant, and a stream of defenders fled
Second Tower for the gatehouse, staggering as the wall rocked
beneath their feet.

'Run!' Durdil screamed at them, his fists clenched at his
sides. The rumbling grew into a screaming stone beast and

suddenly, with a plume of dust like a woman's skirts, the wall between Second Tower and Last Bastion swayed, rocked some more, and began to slump.

Durdil looked up at the wave of stone breaking over his head. He puffed out his cheeks and barked a single, mirthless laugh, tapped his fingertips to his heart.

He didn't run.

CORVUS

'That's it. It's down. Send everyone.' Corvus was nearly dancing with excitement; he took Lanta's hand and kissed it, laughing.

'Fost comes,' Valan said, pointing, and Corvus raised his arm. Fost broke into a run. 'Sire, are you sure you want to send everyone? A rearguard to protect you and the Blessed One . . .' Valan fretted.

'Sire, a breach!' Fost yelled.

Corvus laughed. 'Well, yes,' he shouted back. 'Did you think we hadn't noticed?'

Fost waved his arms. 'No, South Gate. We've breached the South Gate.'

Corvus slapped his fist into his palm. 'Two? Now we've got them. Now we'll have victory, eh, Prince Rivil?' He looked at the Rilporian's stony face. 'Sorry, King Rivil now, isn't it? Anyway, a day or two, bloody and protracted and street by street no doubt, but they're nearly done.'

188

Fost arrived and stumbled to a halt, hands on his knees. 'And word from . . . the Lord Galtas,' he gasped.

'He still lives?' Rivil demanded, shouldering past Corvus. 'Where? What word? What did he say?' Fost held up a scrap of paper and Rivil snatched it from his hand. 'King Gate, midnight tomorrow.' A grin spread across his face. 'If two breaches weren't enough, Galtas is going to give us three. Did you see him? He's well?'

Fost straightened and glanced to Corvus before answering. 'None of us saw him. When we charged the South Gate it was already open, half a dozen guards dead around it. The note was nailed to the gate, where only someone coming in from outside could see it.'

'Godblind?' Corvus said.

Dom swayed on his feet, his arms outstretched, finger joints popping, head thrown back on his shoulders. He grunted, spraying drool, and then slumped, head hanging to his chest. Slowly he nodded. 'The note speaks true. The King Gate will be opened from inside at midnight tomorrow. It will lead on to a courtyard and the entrance to a tunnel. The tunnel goes all the way to the palace, the heart of the city.'

'That's where the council will be, with Durdil and the officers. They'll command from the palace, using distance-viewers and runners to relay their orders. If we take the palace, take the high command, we take the city. The army won't fight if we've got Durdil.' Rivil was gleeful now.

'Once again your inside knowledge of Rilpor and its customs aids us,' Lanta said. 'We are grateful.' She turned to Corvus. 'But do we need three breaches?'

'Yes,' he said immediately. 'The more ways in, the better. The South Gate is open now, but they'll throw everything they've got at it to close it. A way in from the rear of the city will divide precious resources, stretch them so thin they break. This is it; the city's death throes.'

Rivil's sneer was plain. 'And who has accomplished that? Us. We told you of the weak point in the wall. Galtas opened the South Gate. Now he will open the King Gate.' He narrowed his eyes at Corvus. 'In fact, tell me again why we allied with you?'

The Godblind stepped forward before Corvus could move. 'Because there are many deaths yet to come, King. Many deaths to come, many to atone for.'

Rivil backhanded the man hard across the face. The Godblind screeched and reeled back, the swollen cut in his cheek weeping fresh blood.

'Do not speak to your betters,' Rivil snarled.

'Enough!' Lanta barked. 'The slave is not yours to punish.'

'The Godblind is arguably more important than you or me, Rivil,' Corvus warned him. 'Do not touch him again without permission.'

Rivil flicked his fingers in dismissal before wiping Dom's blood from his knuckles. 'Enjoy your toy,' he said. 'I will have no need of him when I sit on my throne.'

Corvus exchanged a meaningful glance with Lanta. 'We waste time,' he said. 'Rivil, I will send a third of my men at the South Gate now, and tomorrow at dusk lead another third over the river with a view to taking this King Gate. The rest we hold in reserve, to protect the Blessed One and the Godblind.'

'I will send two-thirds of the Rank against the main wall breach today,' Rivil said, 'and keep up the pressure through the night and all of tomorrow, draw them off the East Tower if possible. Perhaps we shall meet in the middle and share wine over a conquered city.'

'Perhaps we shall,' Corvus said.

'The gods will be pleased to see you fight, Your Majesty,'

Lanta said sweetly, as though that was what Rivil had meant. 'You have commanded an excellent siege, but the gods always like to see a man risk his skin in Their name. You will be much envied by your officers when you climb the breach yourself. Will you go today, or tomorrow?'

Rivil's face paled a little, but he summoned his customary sneer with an effort. 'At the point when I can do most good, of course. Corvus, you will enter the city through the King Gate?'

Corvus nodded; he had no such qualms about fighting, had been itching to get involved for days.

'Good. I will judge the best moment to engage as the siege progresses.' Rivil's smile was wooden. 'Blessed One.' He inclined his head and spun on his heel, hurrying back to his own camp with his guards scampering to keep up.

'He'll do no such thing,' Valan muttered and spat. 'He'll get within bowshot and then find something more important to do. Like empty his linens of fear-shit.'

'Be careful, Sire,' the Godblind said suddenly. He dabbed at the cut on his cheek with the cuff of his shirt. 'Something in the city stirs. Something wakes.'

'Something wakes?' Lanta asked. 'What does that mean?'

Dom pursed his lips and winced as the cut stretched. 'I'm not sure yet. Something hidden.' He spread his hands. 'More dangerous than running into an enemy city. When the hidden is revealed, the weak become strong. There is no more, not yet. Perhaps with time but . . . even the gods cannot penetrate this shadow. That is all there is to know.'

Corvus licked his teeth and then spat into the grass. 'I'll be careful,' he said. 'For now, let's get on to that bastard South Gate and force entrance. I want this city on its knees.'

'Your will, honoured,' Valan said and Fost echoed him.

The Godblind was silent, staring at the city with haunted eyes. 'It wakes,' he muttered.

TARA

Tara led her squad along the allure from North Tower One towards the giant dust cloud occluding the western wall.

Last Bastion was standing, but slumped like a drunk, tilted down towards the haze over Second Last. Even as she watched, there was a whump, tiles fell from the roof, and then an orange glow began on the tower's crooked catapult platform.

Shit. Something's caught light in there, and the fire barrels are in the storeroom below. If that fire eats through the catapult platform and reaches those barrels, the whole tower's going to go up like a Bel-fire. It'll be carnage.

She sped up, no idea what she was going to do but determined to do it anyway. Her men pounded along behind her. Just another day in the glorious West Rank.

The dust was drifting on the breeze now, dancing and swirling in the killing field and around the tower like morning mist, brightening and then obscuring the flags of flame. 'This

192

is a bad idea,' Tara gasped as she slammed open the tower door and began pelting up the stairs to the catapult level.

The smoke was drifting down the stairwell already, thick and stinging. Tara put her nose and mouth in the crook of her elbow and carried on. It was getting hotter. The catapult platform was the very top level of the tower, with moveable partitions that could open one wall in turn from which to loose. Three were closed and one of those was well alight as Tara stepped through the door and the heat slapped her in the face. A strong breeze blew in through the open wall, whipping at the flames and driving them ever higher. The platform was floored in wood to absorb impact from the catapult, and her best guess was that the wall collapse had knocked over the brazier used to light the fire barrels.

Fire barrels. Tara could see barrels in the far corner. Her heart leapt like a fish. *They brought up the barrels from storage!*

'Douse those barrels now or we all die,' Tara yelled over the crackle of flame. The men who'd followed her up each had a pail of water from the cistern at the base of the tower. Three threw their buckets, making about as much difference as a piss in a rainstorm, and as the soldier closest to her made to do the same she heaved on his arm.

'No! There, throw it there. There, fucker,' she yelled, pointing and coughing. He threw the water and doused a section of floor. It was just enough. Tara tapped her finger-tips to her heart, held her breath and sprinted through that tiny avenue between walls of fire.

Crouching, scorching, her hair beginning to smoulder, she grabbed the boot she'd spotted and the foot it contained and began pulling back the way she'd come. Back through an ever-narrowing corridor of safety.

The fire roared across the gap ahead of her, cutting off

her escape route. The air was empty of oxygen and searing her lungs, so Tara stopped breathing, stopped looking, took another grip on the leg and heaved again, but he was armoured, and he was heavy. Her knee hit the blackening wood and she felt the skin blister through her trousers. Wool wasn't the best defence against fire, it seemed.

A noise and she turned her face up, eyes slitted against the fire, and caught a bucketful of sweet, cold water right in the face. Hands grabbed her, grabbed the body behind her, and dragged them clear.

Someone was slapping her repeatedly around the head, and she was about to punch them in the balls when she realised her hair was on fire. Another bucket was poured right over her head and shoulders: cold bliss.

Someone carried her clear of the fire, and they were halfway down the stairs to wall level when the barrels went up and took the whole fucking roof with it.

'Protect the general,' a voice yelled over the roaring, rumbling, crackling as the stairs shuddered and, she'd swear, tilted.

General? Tara smiled. 'I'm a major.'

The man didn't reply, stumbling sideways into the wall and bouncing her skull off it. He cursed, slipped down a step, yelled over a twisted ankle, nearly dropped her, and then ran heedless down the stairs as the rumbling from above increased. Tara tucked her head into his chest as her feet and ankles cracked into the wall with every turn.

They reached the allure leading to North One and the soldier threw her on to it, turned back into the stairwell, grabbed the body of the man she'd saved from those carrying him and slung him directly at Tara with a screamed 'Catch!'

Tara was on her arse but she held out her arms on instinct and the figure slammed into them, his pauldron splitting open her chin he hit her so hard. They crashed on to the wallwalk and she just got her head up in time to see Last Bastion sway, cracks like veins jagging through the walls, and then the tower's top level folded in on itself like a flower and it tumbled into the killing ground below. The soldiers, the burning catapult, and most of the corner wall went with it.

All movement ceased except for the swirl of smoke and dust and fire. The figure next to her groaned and raised a reddened, blistered face. Tara recognised Mace.

'Why were you in there?' she yelled, suddenly furious.

Mace watched her mouth moving with little comprehension. 'Downstairs when the fire started. Men burning. Tried to . . .' He gave up and coughed, great gobbets of black phlegm splatting on the stone beside Tara's head. Black snot ran from his nose and he emitted a long, drawn-out groan as he slumped to one side.

The tower was still settling, blocks of stone bigger than her head bouncing and skating across the allure. 'Time to move,' Tara croaked and rolled on to her belly, struggled to her hands and knees, and paused to cough. Perhaps a score of soldiers had made it out on to the allure with them, in various states of smoking ruin, and they'd got the same idea, dragging themselves and each other towards the dubious and distant safety of North One.

'Up you get, General,' she said, though she couldn't seem to get past hands and knees herself. 'And make it quick. We're not safe yet.'

'Excellent,' Mace groaned, and started to crawl. Most of his hair was gone, the side of his face red and blistered, burns running down his throat and disappearing under his dented, smoke-stained armour. Cords stood out in his neck as the pain began to register.

'Gods alive,' she muttered, stomach sinking into her feet. 'How hurt are you?'

Mace coughed; he didn't look at her. 'I need to get across to the gatehouse and organise some sort of defence before those bastards start climbing the debris. Hallos can shout at me if I'm still alive by dusk.' His voice was a strangled wheeze, as though he was being throttled, and something that looked like steam wisped up from inside his armour.

Tara smelt meat cooking and bile rose in her throat. 'You should—'

'We might all be dead in an hour,' he interrupted, his voice jagged. 'I'll get treated later.' He saw her expression. 'I promise.'

When they were far enough from the splintered end of the allure, Tara forced herself to stand and dragged Mace's unburnt arm to help him up. She hooked her shoulder under his arm and together they staggered towards North One, and eventually made their painful way down the steps and into First Circle.

The gatehouse seemed miles away. Tara coughed and coughed, the shakes setting in hard now, and then put her hands on her knees and threw up while Mace wobbled, unsupported. She decided not to do anything like that again ever. Her head was spinning, the ground heaving slowly like the swell on a lake.

'All right, Major?' Mace asked, and there was a strain in his voice she hadn't heard before, not even after everything they'd been through in the last months. *Pain.*

She turned to look up at him, caught him unguarded with his jaw clenched so tight she could almost hear the enamel squeaking. She straightened. 'Absolutely fine, sir,' she said, suppressing another cough. 'But you're not. The gate to Second Circle and the hospital isn't too far—'

'Gatehouse. Now. The enemy isn't shitting around with hospitals. Neither am I.'

'The enemy wasn't just cooked in his own armour,' Tara snapped, but it set off another coughing fit and ruined her point somewhat. Mace joined her and hawked up some more black filth. But then he started moving again, and not towards the gate. Towards the killing field – or what was left of it with the wall's shattered remains filling most of the space up to Second Circle's wall.

Tara swore, spat, and then limped after him. Together they moved towards the gatehouse.

A runner was loping towards them. 'South Gate breach,' he gasped. 'South Gate breach.'

'Bloody bastard shits,' Tara snarled. 'Sir, there're Rankers milling around down there. I'll take a hundred of them, bolster the southern defence. The rest can help hold the breach. General, with your permission?'

Mace focused on her and then nodded. 'Do it.'

Tara stepped close and dropped her voice. 'Gatehouse then hospital. Sir.' Mace waved her away and she knew he wouldn't go, knew she couldn't make him, either.

She forced her aching legs, her burning lungs, her pounding heart, into yet another run towards the soldiers staring in shock at the shattered wall, the broken defence. Beyond it, there were Mireces in the city.

CRYS

He was too busy trying to stay alive to pay much attention to the screaming, roiling, grating of stone breaking, but he knew what it had to mean. The fuckers had finally made it through the western wall.

If there's no one there to stop them, they'll be running up our arses in minutes. We'll be caught between two forces, like the fucking Blood Pass Valley all over again. Need to shut this gate.

The Mireces were piling through the breach, driven by the scent of victory and outnumbering the Rankers and Wolves opposing them. Crys ducked an axe and chopped his sword into the man's ankle. He went down howling and Crys finished him with a hurried, graceless stab and rip to the belly.

A soldier went down to his left, screaming, pleading, 'No, don't, *don't*!' but the Raider's spear tip took him under the chin, nailing his tongue to the roof of his mouth and punching through into his brain. Quick death, anyway. He didn't see his killer killed, or Roger Weaverson, for all his youth and spots and inability to grow a beard, performing a lethal dance in between three attackers and ending them all.

'We can't hold, sir,' Captain Lark gasped, grabbing Crys's shoulder. 'For every one we kill, three more pour through the gate. We can't hold.'

'Course we can,' he said, tone cheerful despite the situation and the hot swelling of anxiety for Ash and the breach at their backs. 'We're going to drive these bastards back into the Gil and drown them. That's what we're going to do, because we don't have any other choice.'

'A controlled retreat—' Lark began, breaking off to sidestep a spear thrust and punch the man wielding it in the face. Crys followed the punch with a lunge, sheathing his sword in the man's groin and twisting as he ripped it back out.

'You ever heard of a controlled retreat being a success, man?' he snapped, eyes roving the battlefield. 'Get in line. We hold.'

A howl rose up behind them and the attacking Mireces faltered. Somehow the Wolves had extricated themselves from the fight and formed up into two columns blocking the roads to either side of the square. Mireces weren't getting any deeper into the city, at least. They had a chance now.

'To the gate,' Crys roared. 'Palace Rank, wedge formation.' The surviving Rankers, their number dwindling every minute, fought their way into a wedge aimed at the gate. Crys was the point, head down, scavenged shield on his arm. 'On the double, ad-vance!' he screamed and set off, driving through the Mireces. Right now it didn't matter if they sealed a hundred Raiders in here with them, as long as they sealed the gate.

The Mireces understood what they were about and

charged, the men on the outside of the wedge flinging up shields and poking out swords, anything to hold them off long enough to reach the opening.

'Drive,' Crys yelled, putting his shoulder into the shield, 'drive on, bastards, or we all die.' They responded, locking shields on the outside, the inner ranks linking arms to stiffen the spine of the wedge. They slowed but they didn't stop, blows raining on shields and helmets, wounded men held up by their mates and still pushing, those on the outside falling and being replaced by the next man in. The Wolves split in two again, leaving only a thin line cutting off access to the city while others flanked the Mireces, distracting them from the wedge, giving the Rankers time and space.

They reached the gate and threw themselves at it. It shifted in a few feet and they yelled, straining, pushing harder. It closed a little more and then there were dozens of Wolves surrounding them, hacking down the Mireces with a savagery Crys had rarely seen.

There were more Rankers, more Wolves, falling to the blue-clad fuckers. They were all slowing, the days of attrition, the nights of fighting, combining so that the battle was more a lurching melee with edged weapons.

The gate slammed and was immediately jolted as those outside threw themselves against it. Bolts were hammered across and the wedge sagged for a few seconds, just breathing, but then the Mireces trapped inside lunged for them, knowing they'd never get out alive and determined to take as many defenders with them as they could.

Crys got into step with the soldiers to either side and set out to stop them.

There was still a score of Mireces fighting back to back to the death when another force came charging around the corner and Crys thought they were all dead. Then he recognised Major Carter through the smoke and soot and tears streaking her face.

She slowed out of her laboured, wheezing run and lowered her shield. 'Heard there was a breach,' she croaked.

Crys waved behind them. 'Sealed, just finishing these last.'

Tara nodded approval.

'Look, have you seen Ash? No one's seen him for hours and—' But Tara wasn't looking at him, too busy staring past his shoulder away from the trapped Mireces' last stand. Crys felt awareness crawl up his spine, the back of his neck and across his scalp. He turned, slow as sunset. Someone stood in a shadowed doorway and Dalli was leaning against the wall next to it, puking.

The awareness crawled on, down his face so that his eyes stung and his lips pulled away from his teeth in a feral snarl. The shield fell from his hand and he walked across the square, ignoring the fighting only strides away. Tara yelled something; he ignored her.

Dalli put her hand on his arm and tried to stop him. He pushed her gently away and stepped up to the door. It was Ash, as he'd known it would be.

Ash, whose face was a mangled ruin.

Ash, who'd been nailed to the door with a spear through his chest.

Ash.

The blood was rust-brown, puddled and smeared below him and streaked across the cobblestones of the square; he'd been dragged here, put up on display for Crys to find him. Part of him knew who must have done this, but the knowledge was distant, unimportant.

'No.' His voice was a whisper.

The curly hair was matted with blood, plastered to the skull.

'No!' Crys threw himself at the figure, wrestling with the spear. Ash's face was gone, teeth visible through the flap of flesh hanging from his cheek and jaw. His eyes were open, staring up at the sky just past the lintel, unblinking.

'*No!*' Crys screamed, every muscle rigid with grief. Something shifted inside him. In his mind, in his body. Silence fell across the square behind him as he wrenched the spear free and pulled Ash into his arms, lowering him on to the stone, hands finding a second wound, deep and ragged, in his back, a third inside his left elbow.

Crys rocked back on to his heels and roared at the sky and the thing inside him roared as well, fury and pain and loss and a terrifying triumph that made no sense.

The scream shattered every window in the merchants' district.

Glass blew out and fell, razor sharp, winking as the early sun caught it spinning in the air so that it fell like a splintered rainbow. Crys got his arm beneath Ash's knees and rose to his feet, legs trembling. Clouds boiled overhead and the thing inside shifted again, flowing into every limb until Ash's limp weight was easy to hold and Crys stood straight as an arrow and just as deadly.

He walked away from the shade of the building into the centre of the square, to the small patch of sun just peeking over the rim of the wall. Rankers melted from his path, hauling their injured and the Mireces dead out of his way; Crys had no eyes for them.

'*Don't you fucking dare!*' he screamed at the sky when the sunlight was on them both, its rays too weak to warm the pale dough of dead flesh. '*Dancer! Help him!*'

Crys sucked in air and sobbed it out, his heart on fire, sucked in another breath and pressed his mouth to Ash's slack, mangled lips, and exhaled into him. 'Come back to us, love. Come back, heart-bound. We've got you; we're here. Come back.'

Nothing.

A hand touched his back and then fled when Crys roared again and cracks zigzagged across the square from beneath his feet, the thing within shifting, growing until it pressed against his skin from the inside. He let it come, embraced it, pulled it close.

'Save him. Save him and I'm yours. The godlight will lead them, to death and beyond. I swear I'll do it, I'll be it, whatever it is. Please. Just save him.'

Crys bent his head, tears falling on to dead flesh and gaping ruin, and he kissed Ash again. Kissed him and felt something, a stir, a movement, the bird-fragile beat of a heart, delicate as a wren's wing. He slumped to his knees amid the cracking flagstones, right hand on the devastation of Ash's face, left pressed to the hole in his back. Silver light flared around them, so bright against his eyelids as he breathed into Ash's mouth.

A twitch.

A ripple.

Breath.

All around them in a wave of movement, men and women fell to their knees, wondering. Some touched fingertips to hearts, others made the sign against evil, but all watched, all bore witness.

Ash opened his eyes, blinked.

'Welcome back,' said the Fox God. He smiled, and His eyes flared yellow.

MACE

'Stop your bloody fussing, Hallos. You've said I'll live, so let me up.' The words would've carried more weight if they hadn't been wheezed through an airway that tasted of soot and cooked meat and hurt more than the rest of his wounds combined.

Hallos's eyebrows bristled and a hand the size of a ham pushed on Mace's chest, sliding him effortlessly back on to the bed. 'No. You need to rest. You have extensive, though superficial, burns.'

'It's funny you should say that, Hallos,' Mace croaked, 'as I can feel each and every one of them.' In truth, the burns were a hot, burrowing madness tickling constantly at the edges of Mace's mind, flaring with every movement, impossible to ignore. It was taking all he had not to let his officers see the pain he was in.

'Then take the opium,' Hallos snapped back, echoing the little voice in Mace's head that was pleading for pain relief.

204

Mace clenched a fist. 'Opium? Are you insane? My men have been holding that fucking breach for three hours now without my aid, we're losing more to fatigue than wounds and my father is still missing. I don't have time for opium. I don't have time to be injured.' He made another effort to get up, the skin on his arm and chest and belly crimping and screaming as it shifted and rubbed. Hallos shoved him down harder this time.

'And yet you are injured,' Hallos retorted, 'and I thank Major Renik for alerting me to that fact, as you clearly had no intention of seeking treatment. You cannot help the men defending the breach or scouring the wall for your father. He is no doubt in one of the towers, bleeding from a minor wound and hiding there so he doesn't have to face me. You, however, do, and that means you will do as I say, general or not.'

Mace was silent and mutinous and so, so tired and the shameful weakling part of him gloried in Hallos's order. 'Hallos, step back from this bed or, so help me, I will make you step back,' he said quietly.

Hallos stared intently at him for an uncomfortably long time, and then he threw up his hands. 'Fine,' he bellowed, 'go and die somewhere in some futile, heroic gesture that does nothing but leave us without yet another officer.'

The door burst open and cut him off, much to Mace's relief. Major Tailorson with a body in his arms.

'Please, you have to save him. You have to,' he said desperately. Mace slid off the table and Crys placed the body down with exaggerated care. The Wolf. Ash.

Hallos made soothing noises and bent over the table, a wet cloth rubbing gently at the blood. He grunted and moved on, peeling off Ash's chainmail and then his shirt, rolling him this way and that, cleaning at the blood. So much blood.

Mace watched Crys watching the physician, noting the pinched expression on his face. Tara appeared on his other side. 'We really, really need to talk,' she murmured. 'Really.' Mace nodded but Hallos spoke before he could gesture her to the exit.

'There's nothing to do,' he said and Crys let out a strangled groan. He lunged for Hallos, a knife pressed beneath the physician's beard and into the soft skin of his neck.

'Save him or join him,' he growled. Mace and Tara yelled and reached for him, but Crys pressed the knife tighter and cursed them away.

'You don't understand,' Hallos tried.

'No, it's you who doesn't understand. You will save him, you will save Ash or I will kill you and every last man in here. All of you.'

'I can't save him—' Hallos tried and Crys's growl deepened, an animal threat that would've made the hairs on Mace's neck rise if they hadn't been burnt away. The knife cut deeper, parting skin, and Hallos's voice went up an octave. 'I can't save him because there's nothing wrong with him!'

Crys paused; they all did, eyes swivelling to the body on the table. 'What?'

'He has no visible wounds. Several newly healed, but nothing that needs treating. Look at him. He's breathing, man.'

'What?' Crys whispered again. The knife came away from Hallos's throat and the physician stepped hurriedly away as Tara twisted the blade – not unkindly – out of Crys's hand and palmed it to Mace.

Crys ignored them, drifting towards the table. 'If this is a trick . . .'

Mace took a step closer. Ash lay half-naked and still, eyes closed, chest moving slowly. His face bore a thick purple scar through the jawbone and up across the cheek; his jaw was dented, but there was no wound, just rusty stains where Hallos had wiped away the blood. There was another purple wound, healed, in the middle of his chest.

'But he was – there was blood everywhere. He was dead. He was dead.'

'Did you find him like this? Unconscious, I mean?'

'I found him pinned to a door with a spear through him.'

Hallos coughed in surprise and Mace turned to Tara. Incredibly, she nodded.

'I see,' Hallos said carefully. 'Then he's extremely lucky to still be alive, isn't he? We'll keep him here until he wakes. Why don't you stay with him?'

Crys didn't acknowledge the words; he sat on the edge of the table and took Ash's hand in both of his, pressing kisses to each knuckle. Hallos gestured for Mace and Tara to precede him through into the next room; then he closed the door after him with a click.

Mace rested a hip against the wall. 'That's it,' he muttered, 'we've all gone mad. All of us.'

'If only, sir,' Tara said quietly. 'It's true what he said. Ash was . . . clearly, definitely dead. I know a corpse when I see one pinned to a door by a spear, and he was. His face was ruined. Barely recognisable. Crys . . . brought him back. Because he loves him, as you've probably worked out.'

'Crys what?' Mace asked, dismissing the second part of her statement because under normal circumstances he'd have to execute them both for their actions and he couldn't afford to. *Funny how necessity breeds contempt for the rule of law. And let's fucking face it, who are they hurting? And why am I even thinking about this now?* He focused on Tara again, noting Hallos's brimming curiosity. The physician's eyes were alight.

'Brought him back. I know how this sounds, but it's true. There are about three hundred witnesses, Rankers from the West and Palace, plus Wolves. We all saw him do it.'

Hallos pursed his lips and blew air. 'General Koridam tells me you assisted him in Last Bastion, which means you inhaled rather a lot of smoke. That can affect a person's comprehension of events.' He put a hand on her forehead. 'Tell me, have you hit your head recently?'

Tara slapped his hand away. 'I know what I saw, and it wasn't influenced by smoke inhalation. Look at him.' She beckoned and opened the door a crack. 'At Crys. Look at him.'

They crowded behind her, peering over her head. 'What are we looking for?' Mace murmured.

Tara shut the door again. 'He doesn't have a single injury,' she said in a low voice. 'When he healed Ash, when the silver light rose, it covered him too. He healed himself.'

'Silver light?' Mace asked, nonplussed. He wondered if he was the one who'd hit his head.

'Preposterous,' Hallos said, but Mace could see the fascination gleaming in his face. He realised he had absolutely no idea what to say next. Officer training had never included dealing with things like this.

He was spared having to think about it when the door slammed open again and Colonel Edris and Dalli burst in.

Dalli hurried to his side and winced when she saw the extent of his injuries, her face sliding over his skin with worried intensity. She settled for putting her filthy hand on a small patch of unbroken skin on his shoulder.

Edris saluted. 'General Koridam, I am glad to find you in . . . health,' he faltered. 'We still hold the South Gate, General, and we still hold the breach, though barely. And—'

'Mace, love, we found your father,' Dalli interrupted. 'I'm

so sorry, but he's gone. Fallen.' Her hand tightened on him as Mace's vision contracted down to a narrow tunnel of light with her face at the end.

'No.'

Dalli was ashen, but her voice was steady. 'He was crushed when the wall came down. It's likely to have been very quick.'

Mace's mouth was open. 'That can't be right,' he whispered. 'My father was the greatest soldier in Rilpor; he wouldn't just . . . he wouldn't just die under a pile of stone. That's not how men like him die.'

'It's him, love,' Dalli said softly. 'It's him.'

Mace turned at a noise and saw Hallos with his hand over his eyes, shoulders shaking. 'Hallos,' he tried, crossing the room. He put his hand on Hallos's back. 'It might not be—'

'Forgive me, lad,' Hallos said, his eyes wet. 'You've more cause to grieve than me. It's just . . . I've known that man for forty years. To think he died under a wall is . . . it's just wrong.'

'It might not be him,' Mace tried again, but Hallos's expression silenced him. He clenched his fists as a wave of new pain surged through him, obliterating the petty sting of his burns. 'Take me to him. And Tara? Bring Crys. In chains if needs be. I'll believe anything you like if he can repeat the miracle.'

The pain only grew as they made the walk from the hospital to the north barracks in Second Circle. His father had been laid out in the colonel's quarters there, and torches and candles burnt with a clean bright light, illuminating the desk on which lay Durdil Koridam, Commander of the Ranks.

He was very, very dead, his chest plate caved in and merged

with the flesh beneath so they couldn't remove it without tearing him further, but his face was strangely untouched. Someone – *probably Dalli,* Mace thought numbly, *it's the sort of thing she'd do* – had washed his face and hair, cleaned the blood and dirt from it and his hands, and he lay staring up at the flickers of light and shadow bouncing among the eaves with an expression of comical surprise, as though someone had burst in on him having a shit.

The room began to spin and Mace pressed his forehead to the table, fingers holding tight to the wood, the room echoing to his harsh breaths. The last days and weeks and months and all the deaths, all the losses, all the pains and aches and fatigue and the will to keep going, keep marching, keep fighting, all rose into one maelstrom of emotion that teetered over his head like a thundercloud and threatened to unleash everything in a single great deluge and Mace knew he'd never stand it, he wouldn't be able to cope, and he was going to drown just as he'd nearly drowned in the tunnels—

He caught a whiff of old sweat and then small hands and arms wrapped around him and Dalli's head pressed against his back and his burns yammered their hurt and the thundercloud grumbled, roiled and sullenly, reluctantly, retreated. Mace reached back and pulled Dalli around to his unburnt side and she clung there, silent and filthy and sweaty and there, right there where he needed her, and together they stared at the corpse of his father and the pain came again. Tears came too and there was no shame in them, not for Durdil.

'Tailorson,' he said softly, and Crys stepped to his side. His blue eye blazed with alien intelligence, the brown reflecting Mace's hurt back at him. 'Will you try?'

'We will,' Crys said, and Mace was dully surprised to see

tears on the man's face. Crys placed a hand on Durdil's forehead, the other wedged as far as it would go down under the breastplate. He closed his eyes and the room fell silent, men and women holding their breath. Crys was shaking with effort, cords standing out in his neck, vein throbbing in his temple.

Nothing happened.

Crys slumped, shaking. 'I'm sorry,' he muttered.

'Try again,' Mace said and heard the danger in his voice. Dalli squeezed him; he ignored her. 'Try again.'

Crys did, eyes closed, trembling and straining. There was a pop of silver light from his hands, like a flint striking steel that made them all jump, and then nothing. Crys slid on to his knees, his rasping breath echoing in the room. 'He's gone, sir. We – I – can't. He's gone.'

Mace stared down at him and felt nothing but a yawning, empty chasm within. 'Get him out of here,' he snarled and Tara reached down, helped Crys up and led him out.

'Forty years I was friends with that man,' Hallos murmured, reaching out to tweak the blanket straight. 'Treated more wounds of his than I care to remember. He was always going to be a soldier, and I was always going to be the man to heal him. Rotated through the Ranks together for a quarter of a century before he settled here and was made Commander.'

He put his hand on Mace's shoulder and Mace's breath hitched. 'I will miss him every day of my life until I see him again in the Light. But one thing I know about him, and about you: you're no fool and he didn't raise you to be one. Don't blame Tailorson, and don't blame yourself. Men die; soldiers die. Even Commanders of the Ranks die.'

'Sir,' Edris said from behind, 'the office of Commander is yours, sir. I know you will perform as well as he did.'

Mace remained silent, so Hallos turned him from the table. 'Do you have the will?'

No.

Yes.

I don't know . . .

'We have the will,' Dalli said for him and her voice was the strength he needed. 'Between us we'll see this war ended. For Durdil. For all of us.'

'I'll make him proud,' Mace whispered and Hallos's expression hardened. He grabbed him by both shoulders, unmindful of the burns or Mace's grunt of pain.

'You did that every single day of your life, you idiot,' he said roughly. 'Just concentrate on winning the war.' He let go and straightened Mace's jacket for him. 'Commander.'

RILLIRIN

'What do you think's happening now?'

'Men are fighting and dying,' Gilda said as they trudged south, their pace agonisingly slow. 'Gods are being invoked, pleas for mercy ignored. All the things that usually happen in wars, and none of which we can influence.' She coughed and took Rillirin's arm to steady herself.

'How does us running away help them?' Rillirin asked, more to take Gilda's mind off the pain than anything.

Gilda laughed, the sound breathy and weak. She'd aged a decade in the days since Rillirin had found her, since she'd had to tell her that both Cam and Sarilla were dead. Husband and daughter-by-marriage both. Gone.

Rillirin wondered if she'd aged too, on learning that Dom was . . . *a Darksoul, a betrayer, everything we've been taught to hate* . . . was ill and even more plagued with visions than before.

'We're not running away. We're taking word of the siege

213

to the South Rank – who I hope will sort out my arm – and then to Krike.'

Rillirin's eyebrows rose. 'Krike? What can Krike do for us?'

'I had a lot of time to think when I was Lanta's . . . guest, and this morning I felt the truth of Dom's words come alive in the world. Did you feel it, feel something wake?'

Rillirin shook her head, taking a little more of Gilda's weight. They'd need to stop again soon. 'I don't know what you're talking about. I spent all morning trying to work out if I felt pregnant.'

'I remembered all the knowings Dom had before he left us and what they might mean. It's Crys,' Gilda said and Rillirin frowned. 'The godlight Dom said lived inside him. It's woken now and the Krikites, well, they worship the Fox God even over the Dancer. If they felt the awakening too, they'll fight with us. I'm sure of it. You want to know what an old priestess and a fledgling warrior carrying a babe can do in this war? I'll tell you: we can bring Crys, Dom, Lim and all the others an army of Krikites dedicated to Crys and his cause, and together we can wipe the stain of the Red Gods from Gilgoras.'

Rillirin's mouth opened at the vehemence in Gilda's tone. 'So you're saying Crys is . . . what are you saying Crys is?'

Gilda's smile was slightly bemused as she wiped at the sweat on her forehead. 'I'm saying I believe – and I think Dom believed, or at least suspected – that Crys is the Fox God Himself. The Great Trickster.'

Rillirin screwed her face up and started to giggle, then laugh. 'Crys?' she gasped. 'Crys is a god?'

Gilda smiled and then stumbled, and Rillirin's laughter dried up. 'Remember,' Gilda croaked, 'He's called the Trickster for a reason. There are tales of His shape-changing, His many disguises to defeat Gilgoras's enemies. Why not disguise Himself as a mortal man?'

'Bloody good disguise,' Rillirin quipped, shaking her head.

They skirted a boggy stretch of ground, grimacing as mud sucked at their boots. 'The ways of gods are beyond our understanding. But Dom's knowings all point to it.'

Gilda's voice was hoarse with fever and infection, and Rillirin wondered if it was her sickness speaking, if the poor woman was hallucinating. It wasn't her faith in the gods that made her doubt, it was that the Fox God would choose someone like Crys to be His mortal disguise. She giggled again, unable to help herself.

Rillirin's hand went to her belly, as it did every few minutes, it seemed. Something else she struggled to believe was that she was carrying a child, Dom's child. After the abuses in Eagle Height and the abortions they'd forced upon her there, she hadn't thought she'd be able to. And yet she was filled with warm certainty, a joyous knowledge. And dread.

If I'm the herald that Dom foretold, surely I should be there with him, not here, despite Gilda's protestations. If he saw me, he wouldn't give me up to Lanta. He wouldn't.

She urged Gilda a little further, the old woman stumbling more frequently as her strength failed.

Is the child what I herald? Herald of the end, he called me, but how is that possible? The child is a beginning, not an end. Unless . . . what is it that I will birth – a monstrosity, a plague? Will its beginning be our ending?

The herald will bring death to love. And love to death.

The words echoed in her head, words she'd tried to dismiss and yet which always came back to haunt her. She coughed harshly and swallowed as a thick swell of nausea rose in her throat. Her hand dropped from her belly. Would Rillirin be destined to love an evil creature borne of fearful passion and a black-canker heart? Had Dom even then been falling, lost, his seed infected with rot?

What exactly was it that was growing inside her?

'Gilda?' she said when she couldn't bear the churning of her thoughts any more. Her voice was small. 'What if it's . . . bad?'

'I've borne a child myself and delivered hundreds,' Gilda comforted her, though she didn't look as though she could do much more than stumble along, let alone help a labouring woman. 'I won't let anything happen to you.'

Rillirin hesitated. 'Not the birth. The . . . the child. If Dom is what you say, if he's fallen, then the babe might be . . .' She couldn't finish the sentence, in case speaking it aloud made it true. Gilda stopped; she reached out and tucked a strand of russet hair behind Rillirin's ear. She was pale and clammy, her eyes too bright, but the love in them shone through.

'Dom was still true to himself and the gods when you lay together. Whatever has happened to him since, it was not there at that moment. It was just you, and him, and love. Don't fret on the babe. All babes are innocent; it is this world that moulds us, not the circumstances of our conception. Many a babe conceived in hate or haste has been raised with love. This one was conceived in neither; she'll be fine.'

'She?' Rillirin asked.

Gilda shrugged. 'Or he. Impossible to say.'

Rillirin walked on through the lush grass at the side of the straight road leading to the forts. Was Gilda telling the truth? Dom was being visited by the Dark Lady in his dreams weeks before that night. He was already tainted.

What if She'd been there, inside him, when they made love? Had his love even been his, or just put there by Her?

Gilda couldn't know for sure that all would be well. No one would know until the thing was born.

Baby, she reminded herself viciously. *It's a baby, not a thing. Think about it like that and it's got no hope. It's up to me; I have to love it enough for everyone, love it into being good.*

Though she was afraid, the thought strengthened her. She had a purpose now, other than just survival. She had meaning. She'd fought with the Wolves because they'd taken her in, protected her, because she owed them a blood debt.

She'd fight now, with everything she had and everything she was, to love the child in her belly and ensure it was raised in the Light. Raised to love, not death.

'I will fight for you,' she whispered. 'I will always fight for you.'

CORVUS

Beltane, evening, day forty-two of the siege
Mireces encampment, outside Rilporin, Wheat Lands

'You understand the risk you take,' Corvus said. The Godblind stood before him devoid of collar or shackles, washed and shaved and wearing a fresh blue shirt. He slumped under the weight of the armour. Still, he almost looked human again, if you didn't consider his gauntness, or the flicker of madness dancing in his eyes.

Excitement and anxiety swirled sickly in Corvus's stomach. If the Godblind won, victory was assured and treachery avoided. If he lost, though . . .

'I understand, Sire. Rivil killed my wife; I am prepared to test that truth against whatever excuse or justification he can find. Gods willing, I will kill him and clear your path to the throne. If not . . .' He shrugged, appearing supremely unconcerned.

'We all have to die sometime?' Corvus said, but the flippancy was forced.

'Yes, Sire. And on what better day to do it than today?

Beltane,' he added, when Corvus didn't speak. 'The Dancer's festival of life, one of Her most sacred days which we will now mark with blood? I thought it fitting.'

Corvus waved away the comment. 'And Galtas? You said he was part of her murder.'

The Godblind's nostrils flared. 'He raped her, yes, but it was Rivil who did the killing, Rivil whose blood must answer for hers. The day may come when I kill Galtas too, but it isn't today.'

Corvus folded his arms. 'Our purpose is far greater than your pathetic vengeance, Wolf. We are here for a higher purpose. We serve that above all else.'

Dom rubbed his hands over his face. 'What do you think I'm doing? I speak the truth as shown me by the Dark Lady. Rivil plans treachery. He wants you all dead and he'll risk his chance at taking the throne to see it happen. But if I kill him today, victory will be yours. We both get what we want.'

'Valan can kill Rivil. Fuck it, I can kill the little shit myself.'

The Godblind's eyes shadowed and his neck stretched long in that way he had when it wasn't his words he was speaking. 'I have seen your victory; I have seen the Dark Lady stand in the middle of Rilporin itself. I have seen all bow to you. My destiny does not affect yours; if I die here tonight, the outcome remains the same. Let me have this, I beg you. The last lingering pain from my past. With that gone, there is nothing tying me to my old life.'

Corvus drummed his fingers on his upper arm and stared at the Godblind, then at Lanta. 'Well?'

She was serene, confident. 'If the Godblind wins, we win the war. If the Godblind loses, you kill Rivil and we still win the war.'

'We risk much.'

Lanta smiled. 'We always have, Sire. It is in our nature to

do so. We are Mireces, not Rilporians; we understand the nature of risk.'

Corvus swore, glaring at Dom. 'Fuck this up, and I'll kill you myself.'

The man bowed, his smile feral. 'I won't.'

'I will fetch Skerris,' Lanta said. 'We should know in advance if he will be a problem, and he will not lie to me.'

The enormous general nearly brought the tent down when he squeezed in through the flaps and saluted.

'General, thank you for coming,' Corvus said. 'I would know where your loyalty lies.'

'With the gods, Your Majesty,' Skerris said without even the breath of hesitation. 'Always with Them. They are my guiding light.'

'And the Prince Rivil?'

'Rivil will be my king, gods willing. If the gods do not will, then They have Their reasons.'

'If Rivil were to die?' Lanta asked.

Skerris examined her for a long moment, his piggy eyes shrewd in the sweaty flab of his face. 'My loyalty is to the gods and then to my prince. If I were to suspect treachery—'

'If he fell in Hoth-Nagarre?' Lanta broke in.

Skerris's eyebrows shot up his head. He sucked the end of his moustache into his mouth and chewed thoughtfully, pudgy hands squeezing the wide leather of his belt. He spat. 'Hoth-Nagarre is rarely invoked and never lightly. If the prince challenged someone, he would—'

'The prince is the one being challenged,' Lanta said and Skerris's eyebrows vanished into his hairline once more.

Skerris stared up at the tent roof, and then around at Lanta, Corvus and the Godblind. Carefully, wincing, he lowered himself to one knee. 'I serve the gods. My desire is to see my prince rule; if that is not meant to be, I will do as They command me, and I will serve who They raise up in his stead.'

And there it is. Don't fuck this up, Godblind.

'Thank you, General. In Lord Morellis's absence, will you act as the prince's adviser through the ritual?'

'I will, Sire. May I know the identity of his adversary?'

Corvus flicked his fingers at the Godblind. Skerris turned to look at him, and instead of laughing, as Corvus expected, he sucked the end of his moustache into his mouth again with a worried slurp. 'I see,' he said. 'By your leave, I will make my prince ready.' And without waiting for permission, he hurried from the tent.

Corvus exchanged a bemused look with Lanta. 'Looks like you've got the fat man scared,' he said to the Godblind.

Dom bared his teeth. 'So he should be.'

DOM

Beltane, night, day forty-two of the siege
Mireces encampment, outside Rilporin, Wheat Lands

'Prince Rivil Evendoom, last of your House, I invoke the rite of Hoth-Nagarre, a battle to the death in which the Gods of Blood Themselves will weigh our truths. Step into the circle and be judged.'

The chainmail was heavier than Dom remembered, but comforting too, a favourite coat long abandoned and put back on. The sword was his own, taken from him when he'd surrendered, and so was the dagger. Other old friends reunited. The wound in his shoulder and the swollen tear in his cheek throbbed, but they would not slow him. All would be as the Lady willed.

'My feet are on the Path,' he murmured. The Dark Lady breathed on the back of his neck and even Gosfath was here, crouched on the other side of the torn veil, His presence thick with curiosity, pressing down on Dom's head like the beat of a heavy summer sun.

'Whose side will you be on, my love?' he asked the goddess

222

whose presence lingered like a whiff of rot on the sweet breath of an infant. The Mireces were used to him talking to himself by now; no one paid his words any mind as Rivil shrugged his armour to check it moved freely and then drew his sword.

'Two of my children are about to fight to the death. You'll just have to wait and see, Calestar,' the Dark Lady purred. 'Just you wait and see.'

Not the answer he'd been expecting and Dom felt a flicker of disquiet. His was the right and he knew it. She knew it. Didn't She?

Dom pushed away the unease, intent now on his prey. On his last battle.

There were only two outcomes, and both of them suited Dom: Rivil died and Dom had his vengeance; or Dom died and he could rest in the lap of his Bloody Mother forever. Cracked lips stretched in a smile and he turned his face up to the setting sun, let the dying light brush against his eyelids and cheeks. Maybe the last light he'd ever see.

'Let's get this fucking farce over with,' Rivil snarled at him, settling the shield on his arm. 'There's a war on, remember, and your wife was fair game to any of the true faith. I have nothing to apologise for. My feet are on the Path and my faith is strong. The gods will see all I have done for Them. They will judge fairly.'

Dom didn't have a shield. He was weighed down by mail and helmet already and wasn't sure he could stand the extra bulk. Two days of rest and food were nowhere near enough to restore his strength.

He closed his eyes and inhaled deeply through his nose. Scents of crushed grass and smoke and death, the taint of shit and rot. The air was still, the breeze dying with the noise of the crowd and men stilling, waiting for the violence to begin. The irony was that Dom could barely remember Hazel's face any more. The compulsion to kill Rivil was the final dying kick of a drowning man. It was the last thing from his old life, from the time before the gods, before Her. There was nothing else.

There's Rillirin.

The thought prompted a spike of pain behind his eye. It didn't matter; she didn't matter.

She's carrying my child.

Doesn't matter. It doesn't.

He'd made the challenge and there was no backing out. Corvus nodded encouragement when Dom met his eyes, and the Blessed One was praying, Skerris at her side intoning the words with her. They were praying for truth, not for him, and Dom felt another, bigger flicker of doubt.

'The gods are watching,' Lanta shouted. 'Let them judge. Begin!'

Dom leapt. His feet barely touched the grass as he closed the six strides between them. Rivil snapped up his sword, but Dom's weight was behind his overhead blow and he forced Rivil to take a step back. The clash of blades hung copper-bright in the silence.

As Rivil recovered, Dom's blade swept down and around, screeching off his breastplate. Without pause, he reversed direction, a vicious upsweeping backhand arcing towards Rivil's left armpit and the gap in the armour there. Rivil twisted his torso sideways out of reach and punched Dom in the face with his sword hand. Dom's blow slid wild and his momentum faltered.

Eyes watering, nose throbbing and his lungs already heaving, he took a step back and surrendered to instinct. Sensing rather than seeing the attack, he blocked two-handed above his head, Rivil's strike so powerful that it battered his own sword down almost to his helmet. Rivil hammered another blow at his head, and another. And another. And another.

Dom gave ground under each attack, slipping away from the force of the blow towards the ring of Mireces at his back, the sunset smearing in his eyes. He backed, and backed again, until the men behind started clattering blades on shields and he knew he was out of space.

Rivil was red, grunting with each smashing blow, all force and fury and burgeoning embarrassment. *Not killed me yet, eh? You're supposed to be the king and you can't even defeat a madman who's been beaten, tortured and starved for weeks. Now that's just humiliating.*

Dom huffed a laugh despite his wobbling legs, his burning shoulders, and as the next blow arced towards him, he angled his sword, planted his feet and parried, driving upwards from the thighs. Rivil's blade screeched along his and off the edge, plummeting towards Dom's right leg. Dom skipped forward, brought his right foot up and stamped it heel-first through the outside of Rivil's right knee.

The joint came apart with a crunching pop like breaking a chicken's neck, only louder, meatier. Rivil's sword thudded into the sod and he fell forwards with an agonised howl. Dom stepped through and pivoted, the movement driving his sword in a flat trajectory, red light gleaming along its edge in a long, unstoppable backhand at the kneeling Rivil's neck.

Rivil fell on to his face and Dom missed, blade hissing above his back. The prince twisted on to his side and flailed his sword, forcing Dom away. His vision swam as knowings chased the black dots in his eyes. The Dark Lady wasn't playing fair and he could hear Her laughter as the wind picked up, whipping clouds across the dying sun and making it even harder to see.

She wants me to lose?

The wind strengthened and torches failed, men crying out in fear, praying in loud voices. Hoth-Nagarre had never been fought quite this close to the gods before. *This is what it'll be like every day once we've won,* Dom thought muzzily. *Them so close, always so close.*

An image of Rillirin seared into his head, nearly blinding him, forcing him to step out of range and shake his head like a dog. He'd always known what would come should he fail, but now he began to see what would come if he won, and it was almost enough to make him drop his sword and throw himself on to Rivil's blade; a quick end no one could deny or prevent.

'No, you won't.' The words were a whisper in his head, the voice all around and inside him, pain pulsing low in warning. 'Think of the horrors that would await you if you displeased me.'

'I won't,' he panted. More cries of terror as one of the dead torches popped into life on its own. Men scrambled away from it and more voices were raised in prayer. Rivil was somehow on his feet again, weight on his left leg, using the shield as a crutch. Dom lunged, slid in beneath his guard and slashed at his stomach; again the heavy plate resisted. He leapt away, almost blocking Rivil's counter; the sword tip raked across the back of his forearm, slicing through the vambrace. He winced and jerked away, felt the blood begin to flow.

Circling slowly, seeking an opening and trying to slow the bird-fast thumping of his heart. Rivil bent and grabbed his knee, then slipped his hand into the top of his boot. Dom snapped his sword into guard, too late. Rivil threw the dagger and the slim blade thudded into Dom's thigh.

Dom screeched and his leg folded. He flailed at Rivil as

the man hobbled in and tried to drag himself to his feet, but Rivil struck out and disarmed him. Dom's sword spun away.

'Is that all you've got, Wolf?' Rivil asked, though he was panting. 'Is this what seven years of vengeance looks like? A starving madman kneeling in the grass before his rightful king, unable to defend himself. Unable to save his wife's memory, just like he couldn't save her life? Gosfath's balls, but you're pathetic. I'd hoped for more of a contest.'

A sob bubbled out of Dom's throat as he clutched his leg in both hands, blood soaking through the wool, pain making him dizzy. 'Please,' he mumbled, 'please.'

The Dark Lady laughed and Gosfath lapped up his pain like a cat.

Rivil limped closer. 'Please what?' he mocked, poking Dom in the shoulder with the tip of his sword. 'Please what?'

With one savage move, Dom ripped the dagger out of his own leg and drove it upwards, beneath the faulds that protected Rivil's waist and hips, and into his groin. It ripped through bladder and bowels and Rivil's scream was so powerful it burst the blood vessels in his eyes.

'Please just die,' Dom snarled, ripping the knife out and stabbing it back in as Rivil went over backwards. Stabbing over and over at thighs and lower belly and into the groin, sawing away gobbets of flesh, reaching inside to rip out handfuls of meat, slimy and warm and unidentifiable, hot blood pumping-spilling-jetting, on his hands, in his face, in his mouth. 'Die, die, you cunt. Fucking die!'

He forced a hand in through the mess, up into Rivil's body cavity, and tore out whatever didn't slip through his bloody fingers and threw the handful of innards into the prince's face, laughing madly.

Rivil was on his back, twitching and mewling, his hands

torn from trying to fend off the knife, a couple of fingers hanging by strings of flesh.

Dom bent over him and grabbed his face in a bloody hand. 'Judged,' he snarled. 'Judged and found wanting.'

Rivil was incapable of answering, life pumping out in a thick red flood, so Dom forced himself to stand, his dead wife's face before him for the last time. Men were staring at him with horror, with disgust and not a little fear. Dom cackled, blood on his teeth.

The circle shimmered and the Dark Lady appeared, and then Gosfath too, the god ignoring the onlookers, straddling Rivil and peering into his eyes, fascinated. Rivil's bubbling whimpers found new strength. Everyone in the circle fell to their faces in the dirt, horror, devotion and pure terror rising like steam. Dom groaned as he dropped to one knee, torn leg shaking.

'You have been found wanting, Rivil Evendoom, Prince of Rilpor,' the Dark Lady said as Gosfath grinned and ripped open the plate and chain as though it was eggshell. He reached in through the mess of Rivil's groin, his arm disappearing up to the elbow. Blood trickled from Rivil's mouth.

'Your faith was tempered with greed,' the Dark Lady continued and Dom giggled when he realised that the prince was, through some bloody magic, still alive and listening.

'You thought to use us instead of serving us. Your punishment was just. While you, my love,' She said, turning to Dom, 'you serve me well.'

She reached down and slid a hand over the wound in his thigh and Dom gritted his teeth against the pain, groaning as pale fire, so familiar from his time in the Waystation, licked down Her arm and into the wound, cauterising it. He smelt his flesh burn and groaned again. 'There is still much to do, my love. I must have you well to do it.'

Her eyes were golden and black, human and goddess and dead. Mostly they were pools beckoning him in, promising him lusts and agonies he would delight in. She put Her head on one side and studied him, while Her palms ran warm and gentle over his arms and more fire burnt in the hole in his shoulder and then his cheek. He could see it, burning below his eye. She pulled him to his feet, took his hands and placed them around Her waist, and leant in towards him.

'Despite everything, despite even this, I know there is something you hold back from me. That there is a secret you have somehow managed to guard through all our little . . . intimacies. I let you live because I want to know what it is.'

Dom smiled into those flat, dead, beautiful eyes and pressed a soft kiss to the tip of Her nose. 'There are no more secrets. I am a still pool and you can see all the way down through my depths. I have nothing left to hide and nowhere to hide it that you can't reach.' His red hands tightened on Her waist. 'I am nothing but what you make me.'

'Your whore carries your babe inside her.'

'She is nothing, and I do not know what the child may become. I care not unless you tell me to care.'

'You are my voice and eyes and will in this world, Calestar,' She said. Fires burnt in the pupils of Her eyes and Her teeth were pointed when She bared them at him. 'And I know you still lie. I will find your last secret, and I will rip it from you.'

'There's nothing to find,' he began, but the words ratcheted up into a scream as She wrenched at Dom's face and *pushed*. His knees buckled as She ripped open the godspace in his mind, searching for what She thought he still kept hidden. The night filled with screaming – not just his as Holy Gosfath

229

began to feed – and the scent of lightning; the torches blazed up and into searing bright life and Dom's nostrils filled with the smells of blood and sex and triumph.

Weeping, hands clawing at his head, seeking to soothe pain like he'd never known, pain that rippled from his skull down his spine and into every limb, Dom pressed his face to Her thighs and drooled, unable to breathe or think. Dimly, he was aware of blood leaking from his nose, his right ear. His thoughts were slow and his limbs heavy, a weight dragging him down into the depths of agony. *There is nothing left. There's nothing, my love. Nothing.*

'Dark Lady, beautiful goddess of death and power, your presence honours us. We glory in your beauty, your strength.' Lanta's voice was ragged around the edges, trembling with fear, but she approached her gods bent from the waist, hands out in supplication. Skerris trailed a few steps behind. 'We serve your holy purpose, shed blood in your name and that of your brother, Holy Gosfath. We exult in you.'

Dom felt Her shift, turning slightly to examine Her subjects ringed around Her.

'I welcome you, Blessed One. You have done well, you and my brother's high priest Gull, who yet lives and worships in the pit of vipers that is Rilporin.' Lanta preened just a little.

'King Corvus,' the Dark Lady called and Corvus stood, pale and hesitant, rightly afraid. 'Take men to the King Gate in the eastern wall. It will be open. Go now and kill for me.'

'At once, Lady,' Corvus said as he backed away, grabbed Valan and Fost and vanished out of the torchlight. Hundreds streamed after him, their relief palpable that they would be facing mere mortals in a fight to the death instead of their gods here in Gilgoras.

The Dark Lady caressed the back of Dom's head, soothing

the splintering pain just a little, then stood him up and turned him to face the remaining men. Gosfath came to stand on Her other side, His mouth and chin bloody, chunks of flesh beneath His black talons.

'Want,' He rumbled.

'Soon, my love,' She soothed, reaching out to take His hand and lick blood from it. She patted Dom's shoulder. 'See what I give you, Calestar? See the power you command? They kneel to me and to Gosfath, yes, but it is you at my side also. You they bow to.'

'I . . .' Dom tried, his voice thick, his thoughts sluggish. Whatever She'd done to him, something inside him had broken, something he didn't think was going to mend. 'I don't want them kneeling to me. I just want you.'

Again he saw Rillirin, those great grey eyes watching him, always watching. He couldn't read her expression, but it looked sad.

'Don't think about her,' the Dark Lady murmured. 'You have me now. You have all this.' She kissed him, flooding him with lust and need and rage and want and desperation and fear, and more lust, and more, until he moaned into Her mouth and pulled Her hard against him, ignoring Lanta hovering close by and Gosfath watching through veiled eyes. Ignoring the jealousy. Ignoring the shattered parts of himself and the woman who would make him a father.

His goddess wound Her arms around him and the world fell away and there was nothing but Her and him and they were wedded, to each other and to darkness, mouth to mouth and soul to bloody soul.

King of the fucking world.

CRYS

He'd tried, gods know he'd tried, but it seemed the thing inside wasn't to be bribed or bargained with. Durdil had died and he wasn't coming back. He'd seen how his failure had broken Mace's final hope, and once out of the room he'd shrugged off Tara's supporting hand and fled back to Ash. His lover had slept through the night and all day, peaceful but deep, and Crys had sat with him, willing him to wake. It was Beltane, the holiest of days. The fire festival. If anything could wake him, it was this day. And he would wake. He had to.

But now they wanted to take him away again.

'I'm not going anywhere until he wakes up.'

'You are an officer, Tailorson. You have a duty. He is more than safe in the care of this hospital, and I need to be at the palace soon.'

'I can't.' And it was true. He couldn't. He didn't phys-

232

ically have the will to stand up from the cot and walk away. It had nearly killed him to leave Ash just long enough to visit Durdil's body; he couldn't do it again. Ash was pale and quiet, deeply asleep, not fevered, not in any danger. He just wouldn't wake up, and Crys needed him to. Needed it as he'd never needed anything before in his entire life.

'Trickster's cock, man,' Renik hissed and Crys twitched, 'he's asleep and breathing easy. He has no life-threatening injuries – if you and the overly curious physician are to be believed, he has no injuries at all. He's just sleeping. Therefore, you're going to damn well do your part in the defence of this city even if I have to drag you to the wall and throw you at the enemy myself. Get up.'

It was a good rant, an excellent rant, and if Crys had delivered it himself the men it was aimed at would already be vibrating at attention. It washed over Crys like smoke.

Renik gripped his shoulder and forced him to meet his eyes. His were suspicious and worried in equal measure. 'There are a lot of rumours flying around about you, Tailorson. One of them is most unseemly. Major . . . it cannot stand.'

'But it's true,' Crys said, his voice steady. He found he didn't care what anyone thought; he didn't care that what he was about to admit was tantamount to courting a death sentence because of some idiotic and ancient law. 'This one, anyway. Ash and I are heart-bound.' Renik's mouth fell open. 'And Mace knows. He hasn't arrested me.'

'Be that as it may,' he spluttered, 'I *will* arrest you for dereliction of duty if you do not get off your arse. Durdil is dead and Mace's grief has eaten up his capacity for mercy. Yarrow is dead. At this rate we'll be promoting Dorcas into his command and I worked with him years ago. He was an arsehole then and he's an arsehole now. So you're going to say your farewells and then you're going to report to the south wall which is your command and you're going to godsdamn fucking command it. Am I clear?'

Everything Renik was saying made sense. Renik was prepared to pretend he hadn't heard Crys's confession, and in a way that was worse than being punished for it. It was a dismissal of who they were and the oath they'd sworn to each other. He looked helplessly at Ash, at the small furrow between his eyebrows.

'Major Tailorson, we've all lost someone we love in this war. This is the safest place in the city,' Renik said, gently now. 'So allow me to let you in on a not-so-secret secret.'

That got Crys's attention and his hand closed tighter on Ash's.

'We are *losing this war*. Do you hear me? We are losing. And whatever it is you do to inspire the soldiers under your command, we need you to do it. We've all seen their fanaticism around you – I've felt it myself, to be honest – and we need it. There's talk of surrender. What do you think will happen to the patients in the hospitals if that happens? The Mireces'll slaughter them. Meaning this man will die. If you want to stop that happening, you have got to get your arse on the wall.'

'We're losing?' The voice was little more than a croak, but it was his.

Crys spun to Ash's cot so fast he over-balanced. 'Ash? Ash, thank the gods. Hallos! Hallos, he's awake.'

Ash was as grey as his name, but he was breathing and talking and alive. His eyes were wells of confusion and Renik's words were lost in them, as Crys was lost in them. He brought Ash's hand up to his lips, kissed it and then pressed it to his cheek. 'You came back,' he whispered.

Ash managed a smile and a frown at the same time. 'I went somewhere?' he asked.

'It doesn't matter now,' Crys said as Hallos moved Renik aside. He edged Crys away, too, and the majors gave him space to check Ash's pulse, pupils and reactions, moving briskly but gently.

'There you go,' Renik said quietly. 'He lives and is awake. Your time in this hospital is done.'

'Give me a minute with him, Renik, please,' Crys said without looking at him. 'Please. I'll do anything you want after that, but . . . please.'

Renik was silent for a while. 'Never pegged you as one,' he said eventually. 'Crooked.'

It didn't sting the way he'd thought it would. 'Nor did I,' he said instead of taking offence, 'but I guess none of us can help who we fall in love with. That's why it's called falling.'

'And the other rumour? About you bringing him back from the dead?'

Crys shrugged. 'Horseshit,' he said. 'Didn't work on Durdil, did it? Battle fatigue, clouds men's minds.'

Renik wasn't convinced and Crys moved hurriedly to Ash when Hallos called him.

He brushed Ash's hair back from his face. The Wolf was sitting up, legs dangling over the edge of the cot, swaying like a reed in the breeze, but upright at least. 'Exhaustion and concussion, no injuries,' Hallos said, peering at Crys with the same expression as Renik. 'A good meal and I can discharge him.'

The words were distant. 'What do you remember?' Crys asked, because Ash was shaking his head in denial.

'That's not right. I was going to make my way to the south wall, was taking the long route to stretch my legs, and I met a . . . Personal. We were walking together and . . . we

235

fought, I can't remember why.' His face drained of blood so fast that Hallos put a steadying hand on his shoulder. 'And he killed me.'

Crys's heart was thudding and Ash's words were a bucket of cold water in the face of his denial. What he'd said to Renik, what he was telling himself, was a lie. Something inside him slithered against his skin, powerful, alien, an unsubtle reminder of its presence. He shuddered and put a hand on Ash's bare back, comforting them both with the contact.

Hallos was stroking his beard. 'Nonsense. You were knocked unconscious and covered in your enemy's blood. You, Major, panicked, thinking he was dead. When he woke, your exhausted witnesses assumed you'd brought him back to life. Which is clearly ridiculous. You couldn't bring Durdil back, therefore you didn't bring Ash back.' He sounded as if he was lecturing apprentice healers. He sounded as if he was trying to convince them all.

'You're just confused, man,' he said to Ash, not unkindly.

'It was Galtas who killed me,' Ash gasped. 'Galtas was in the city and I recognised him from your descriptions. I hurt him, cleaved his knee before he . . . before he . . .' Ash's hand came up to the thick purple scar. 'He took my face off.'

His eyes filled with tears. 'I remember it happening. I remember what it felt like. He stabbed me in the back and the pain . . . and then he ripped my face off.' He paused to pant, Hallos's fingers on his pulse even as he muttered protestations.

'I was gone, Crys. I was dead. I was in the Light. And then you—' Ash broke off, choking, and Crys's heart broke a little as he shifted away from him, not so much fear as bone-deep confusion. 'How did you . . .'

Crys wanted to hush him, but the thing inside stretched again, filling his limbs and tongue with tingling until he couldn't speak, couldn't deny it.

'You brought me back,' Ash whispered. Hallos bent close, Renik pressed against Crys's back to better see the archer. 'I felt you in the Light. You came and got me. Didn't you?' Crys nodded, a convulsive jerk of the head. 'Then you are, you must be . . . Him.'

'I don't know,' Crys whispered.

'You're Him.' Crys even heard the capital letter adorning the pronoun. 'You're the Fox God.'

There was a moment of stunned silence. 'That's what the men are saying, too,' Renik breathed. 'But how?'

'Splitsoul,' Ash whispered, as though he couldn't stop himself. 'Trickster.'

'Godlight,' Crys added for him and Ash's hands closed convulsively on his.

'That's right. That's what Dom called you, didn't he, after his knowing? God's eyes, godlight, something like that.'

'I think we all need to calm down,' Hallos said, sounding shaken. 'I am a man of science, and—'

'Then explain to me how I'm alive?' Ash demanded, gesturing to the new scars on his face, back and chest. Hallos closed his mouth. He couldn't.

Why me? Crys screamed at the thing moving through him.

Why not? it replied. *It must be someone.*

Are you . . . Him?

He felt it smile. *No. We are Him. Split. One part human, one part . . . other. Together, we have such things to do. Such things.*

What do I call you? he asked, feeling stupid, aware that Ash and Hallos were watching him.

We are not separate, Crys. I am you and you are me. We must still be tempered, but even now we are one. No longer a splitsoul, but a single being, each bringing different strengths, different perspectives, to what is to come.

'Will I survive it?' Crys asked aloud.

That is not a question we should ask ourselves. It serves no purpose. Live well, fight hard, love harder. That is all any of us can do.

'Will you survive what?' Ash asked. 'Who are you talking to?'

'Sweet Dancer, Major. Your eyes are glowing,' Hallos said. He gripped Crys's arm. 'Let me just get a lantern, I'd like to examine—'

'Hallos. Feed him, water him, keep an eye on him. I need to get to the breach.' Crys ignored Ash's protests and Renik's reminder he should be on the southern wall. He leant in and kissed Ash's lips, unmindful of witnesses. 'Don't be scared of me, love. Please. I don't understand what's happening, but you're the only anchor I have in this world.'

Ash cupped his chin and smiled, wan and worried. 'I could never fear you,' he whispered. 'Heart-bound.'

Crys felt a loosening in his chest, and a corresponding movement as something else slid into the space. 'You remembered.'

'Always. Fox God.'

It looked like the Afterworld, the hell that was the Red Gods' paradise. Lit only by intermittent moonlight and the orange rags and flickers of torches, shadows leaping like animals at men, men struggling like drunks with each other, the breach was horror made flesh.

Crys felt like he'd left his heart in the hospital and his sanity somewhere else. The questions in his head were too big to even contemplate answering, and the . . . voice, which spoke with his voice, had fallen silent. Silent, but not still. He could feel it again, stretching and moving inside him, like a fish under a skin of water, pressing upwards but not quite breaking the surface.

Was it really what it said it was? How was it even possible? Crys's religious history was hazy, but even he'd heard tales of the Trickster wearing a mortal's flesh. The thought pulled him up short, wobbling in the darkness, his temples throbbing. *Do I even exist? Am I just a cloak, a disguise for Him? Who am I?*

It didn't answer.

Men had cleared a path through the rubble so that troops could move along the base of First Circle's wall, and someone had tried laying planks over the debris to aid the ascent, but it had little effect. The only way to the top was by scrambling and hoping you didn't break a leg. So Crys scrambled, his breath whistling in his throat, his limbs tingling with the same energy he'd felt when he first saw Ash dead in the doorway.

The top of the collapse, where the rubble had settled into something almost level, was a seething, writhing mass of men, fighting with swords, knives, axes and fists. Knees and elbows, feet and teeth. Blood splatted and pattered, sweat slid, men cursed and shrieked, stumbled and fell, snapped ankles and tore knees on the uneven ground. And fought. Endlessly fought through the stink of smashed stone and shit, smoke and rot.

He saw clearly despite the dim and flickering light, picking out blue shirts and even East Rank insignia, mixed together for this all-out assault. Mace was in the thick of it close to the slump of Second Tower, Dorcas and Vaunt flanking him, so Crys picked his way north towards the remains of Last Bastion, letting the oh-so-familiar movements of battle preparation distract him from the roiling inside his head and body. The thing was a cool and reassuring presence, but it did nothing to convince him he'd live through the night.

He spotted an abandoned spear and sheathed his sword in preference for it, more than happy to stab advancing Mireces before they could get close enough to stab him. Soon enough a knot of Palace Rankers formed around him, the beginnings of a ragged line, peppered with gaps where the terrain was too unstable to find a decent footing.

'All right, this is how it goes,' Crys said, relaxing into command and pushing all else away. 'Those with spears at the fore. Those with anything else, find a gap in the line and stand behind it – if any get through, it'll be there. They pass our line, they're yours to kill. Make sure you do. Last thing we want is to be surrounded.'

'There's thousands of them, sir,' a lad squeaked, his spear tip wobbling about all over the place.

'But he's the Fox God,' a voice from further down, shrouded in darkness, said.

Crys ignored them both. 'Listen up. We're going to hold this breach and hold it all night. There's enough of us because there has to be, it's as simple as that. We're going to kill five of them for every one of us who goes to the Light, and when dawn breaks we're going to be standing behind a second wall, this one built of heathens' corpses. It's going to be so high the enemy won't be able to reach us over its own dead.'

He grinned and the boy looked more scared of him than the Mireces. Scared and awed. 'And do you know what else we're going to do?' The boy shook his head and a few others did too, so Crys raised his voice. 'We're going to provide cover so that people behind us can start piling rock in such a way we have another wall of sorts, and we're going to lay planks behind it to stand on, and we're going to get a stinger in the ruins of Last Bastion to work in tandem with the catapult in Second Tower and keep their fucking heads down. Because this is how we beat them.'

240

'But we'll be on the wrong side of the wall, sir!'

Crys winked. 'Not for long,' he promised. 'We hold until it's built, and then we hop over it and have a nice rest while reinforcements do some fighting. How's that sound?'

'Good, sir!' the boy said, his teeth showing with sudden hope.

The thing inside stirred.

'Arrows,' Crys shouted and grabbed the shield leaning against his leg and flung it overhead. The other spearmen did likewise, but the boy was still staring at Crys with worshipful eyes and an arrow took him in the throat and tumbled him down the rubble in a tangle of arms and legs. *Poor bastard.*

'Learn from that,' Crys shouted when Second Tower sent a return flight of arrows into the night. 'Watch the enemy, not me. We're silhouetted up here by our own torches, so be aware for the hum of arrows heading your way. All right, here they come.'

The Mireces charged in the wake of the volley, hoping to find most of the defenders wounded or dead. They splashed against Crys's line, which held and then forced them back. One slipped by Crys's spear while he engaged a second and lunged past him. Crys let him go, hoping the men behind would do as he'd ordered. He didn't get stabbed, so he guessed they had.

The line to his left started to buckle. 'Hold,' he roared, 'Hold the high ground or we die.' Still they dropped back a step, so Crys turned to the men either side of him. 'Hold this position.' Apparently they saw something in his face or his eyes, because they nodded hurriedly and straightened, stepping in slightly to cover the gap made by his departure, waiting for the next attack.

Crys faded out of the line and moved between it and the second row armed with close-quarter weapons. They nodded or saluted and he nodded back, picking his way through the rubble as fast as he dared to the other end of the line. It was slipping because it was loose, the last man with no cover to his left to anchor him, just yawning darkness where Mireces could slip around his side and come at him from all angles. He was doing his best, but he was looking for support that wasn't there. Crys slid into place.

'All right? Major Tailorson here to lend a hand. You are?'

'Brock,' the man said, his relief tangible. 'Are you Him?'

'I'm Crys. Listen, Brock, we're going to stiffen this line, because we're a few steps behind now and that's not good for anyone. Come on, push forward.' Together, they fought back into the line and then Crys put his back to Brock and faced outward. 'I can't see you, soldier,' he called back, 'so don't you fucking leave me, all right? Hold your position.'

'Holding, sir,' Brock said, his tone steadier now. Crys knew if the man fell or fucked up, his back would be exposed to attack, but Brock needed an anchor for the line and so Crys was it. The thing inside rumbled its approval and its certainty that he wouldn't die here tonight, and that was enough for him. *Betting my life on the shadow inside me. What could possibly go wrong?*

In the seconds between the short, vicious battles he fought, he called for reports on the line and each one confirmed it was holding. The Mireces had slowed their attack, pausing at the bottom of the hill to reassess.

'They'll be up with spears next,' Crys shouted as he turned back into the line. 'They know they can't pass us with short weapons, so you'll be fencing away with polearms soon enough. Stay tight, wound if you can't kill, give them openings through to the second line of defence if you must.'

'But we haven't got spears,' one of those in the second rank shouted back.

'Then it's a good job you won't be facing as many attackers as we are,' Crys said and got a laugh and a round of boos from the front rank. 'Arrows,' he bellowed, though he hadn't heard anything this time, just knew, and those that still had shields readied them while the rest, Crys included, crouched low and hoped. Long seconds, and then impact. Screams, one vile expletive Crys decided to memorise for future use, and then a stream of jeers directed down the slope.

Crys stood and squinted along the breach. 'Vaunt! Major Vaunt!' He waved. 'Form up, will you, we could use some support this end.'

He watched as Vaunt picked his way towards him, eyes wide as he strained to see. 'Tailorson?'

'That's me, now where's my back-up?' Crys asked. Vaunt was in a half-crouch and Crys bent forward. 'You wounded or have you just done your back in?'

'Arrows,' Vaunt hissed.

Crys straightened. 'You can hear them coming,' he said. 'Don't worry about it. Look, we need to complete a line here, stand firm and not let them past us. We throw a bunch of lit torches down there and they won't be able to see us, but we'll see them.'

'Anyone can see your bloody eyes glowing,' Vaunt muttered as he straightened with an air of extreme reluctance. 'Bloody off-putting.'

'My eyes are no one's concern but mine. Look, we form a line here and hold them off, get men behind us shifting this rubble and building fortifications. Fuck it, get civilians doing it, it's about time they helped out.' He gripped Vaunt's arm. 'A wall on top of the breach. Anything to slow them down, Major, but no one can start work if we haven't got a line to hold. There's a hundred strides between me and Mace and I've seen men slipping through that gap. There's Mireces in the city, Vaunt. We have to form a line.'

'I've got a Hundred down there picking them off,' Vaunt said, waving a hand.

'Oh. Good. Let's hope they don't send more than that then, eh?' Vaunt's lip curled but he had no response. 'Come on, man, help me out here,' Crys said, 'I'm going to be dead soon if you don't. We've got a fragile line, but this lot are close to shitting their linens. It'd mean a lot if they had some support from their mates. Their commanding officers.'

Vaunt groaned and rubbed the back of his neck. 'All right, fine. You know this is mostly suicide, don't you?'

Crys shrugged and smiled. 'We all die sometime. Let it be for something good, eh?'

'Doesn't look like I've got a choice, does it?' Vaunt said, but then he brightened. 'Maybe they'll write songs about us once we're dead.'

'I'd prefer it if they wrote songs we were alive to hear, but whatever gets you standing at my side, Major, I'll count as a win.' He cocked his head. 'Arrows,' he yelled. This time his men didn't hesitate, though Vaunt did.

'I don't—'

Crys dragged him on to the shattered stone. Seconds later they heard the splintering impact of arrows breaking all around them, Vaunt yelping as one ricocheted and laid open his right arse cheek. 'Fuck the fucking gods, that hurts,' he bellowed when Crys let him up.

Crys found himself laughing, then apologising for laughing. He helped Vaunt to stand, canted over to one side to take the pressure off his new wound. 'All right, you stay here and anchor the line, you're not going to be moving at speed with that . . .

injury. I'll be back soon with more men and we'll fill this breach with soldiers. Just hold, you hear me?' He stared into Vaunt's eyes and could almost see a tiny glint of yellow that might have been his own, reflected in Vaunt's. 'Hold.'

'Yes, sir,' Vaunt said and practically saluted him.

'I'll find some linen,' Crys called back over his shoulder as he turned, 'though how you bandage an arse, I do not know.' Vaunt advised him to do something unmentionable to himself, and Crys grinned and jogged away over the breach, picking his way among the fallen slabs of stone to Mace's position. It was easier if he didn't really think about anything, and the thing seemed content to let him.

'General, we're going to—' Colonel Dorcas squawked and thrust a pike at him; Crys slipped it and jerked it out of his hands.

'Major Tailorson of the West, or maybe Palace, I don't really know,' Crys said hurriedly. He frowned. 'Didn't you see me coming?'

'What do you want?' Mace snarled and Crys knew he was a long way from being forgiven for Durdil still being dead. *Lim and now Mace hate me. Perfect.*

'Sir, we're forming a line to hold the breach. Kill those who come up in front of us, get civilians if possible building fortifications behind us. A wall within the breach. Then we can fall back over it – probably quite literally – and defend from relative safety. The line only extends halfway so far and I've seen Raiders slipping between it and your position. Vaunt's anchoring my end. I need men – these men – to fill the breach and stand firm.'

Mace squinted across the breach. 'A line? Where?'

Crys turned and pointed to the line of men he could plainly see. 'There, sir, right there.' Part of his brain was asking why he was the only one able to see them, but it was such a tiny question in the sea of mysteries he let it be. The thing inside stretched, self-satisfied and gleeful.

Are you coming out? he asked it as Mace conferred with Dorcas.

There is no 'you' and 'I', remember? There's only us. And we're doing beautifully.

'I say.' Dorcas tapped him on the arm while Mace spoke to a runner. 'Did you know your eyes are glowing? Bright yellow, like an animal's. Really quite remarkable.'

'Down,' Crys roared instead of answering him, throwing himself on top of Mace, one flailing hand catching Dorcas and pulling him off-balance. Mace hit hard, and Crys hit Mace even harder, the two of them practically bouncing on the slope as the lone arrow arced overhead and clattered among the stones.

Crys eeled down the other side of the breach looking for the archer. There were so many corpses down here that it wouldn't be too hard for an enterprising assassin to conceal himself among them. And if the others really were as blind as they seemed . . .

There was a twitch of movement and Crys pulled his knife, rose on to fingers and toes, and launched himself at the not-corpse. Twang of a bowstring and an arrow whipping past so close the tail feathers burnt his ear, and he was on him, thrashing through the rubble, vambrace jammed against his windpipe, knife hand clutched in the Mireces' straining fist.

The thing inside filled him, full to bursting with clarity, with energy and sight and hearing, all his senses exploding into life, the shock of it nearly his undoing. He saw the Raider's face clear as a bright spring morning, saw the hate twisting his mouth and the desperation in his eyes. Crys leant harder on his forearm, pressing the man's neck into the stone, cutting off his air. He twisted his right hand free and stabbed into the armpit, three short, fast blows that stole his strength. The man fell still and Crys opened his throat to finish him, then crouched on top of him and stared at the slope of stone, saw the hundreds of Mireces and Easterners climbing stealthily, slowly, inch by inch, up the rubble. Protected by the dark.

Not from us, you're not.

He turned his back on them and stared up. Mace and Dorcas were calling for him. 'Finish that godsdamn front,' he roared at them, heard Mace repeat the order and the scuffle of boots picking their way towards Vaunt and the shaky line of flesh and steel that was all that stood between the enemy and the city.

Crys looked again across the slope, chose his target and began to move, placing his feet with the surety of a mountain goat, his vision clear in the night. He couldn't get them all, but he could pick off enough to slow the advance.

Rippling with energy, the Fox God slid among the enemy and began to kill.

THE BLESSED ONE

Beltane, night, day forty-two of the siege
Mireces encampment, outside Rilporin, Wheat Lands

Lanta paced the tent in a swirl of blue skirts, Dom unconscious and yet raving on her own cot, arms flailing, legs
twitching as though he'd been poisoned.

'Shut up!' she shrieked when she could bear it no longer.
The physician, Barra, leapt in the air, and then leant hurriedly
back over his charge. Lanta had insisted he tend the Godblind,
though there appeared little that could be done for him.

She was here, in our world, Her feet in Gilgoras once more.
Her glory blinding. And Holy Gosfath, our Red Father. She
was here and She spoke to me and it was sweet. So sweet.

It had been more than Lanta could have possibly imagined,
more than she had dared to dream. *And it was the Godblind*
who stood at Their side.

Yes. And now it is the Godblind who lies there shattered,
a broken prophet, a slave. It is the Lady's will and my feet
are on the Path.

'How is he?' she snapped when another interminable hour

248

had crawled by and the ravings had lessened to breathy mutterings.

Barra flinched. 'He lives, Blessed One. The blood has stopped leaking from his ear now, and he sleeps peacefully. His other wounds are treated.' He pointed a trembling finger at the slit in the man's trousers, where Rivil's knife had entered his thigh, then the face. Wounds the Dark Lady Herself had burnt shut, black and scabby now, but sealed.

'Then disturb him no further. Get out.' Barra snatched up his things, sketched a bow and ran for the exit. Lanta watched him go with a curl to her lip.

Fatigue clawed at her. The gods' visit had drained her, the endlessness of the siege and the interminable screaming of the wounded a constant grate against her nerves. She longed for sleep, but her people needed her – and the Godblind had her fucking bed.

'Godblind, wake up.' She slapped his face. 'What have you seen? Tell me everything.'

As her hand came back for another slap he awoke, his gaze bloodshot and sunken and burning with mania. 'She was here, wasn't She, Blessed One? Wasn't She here?'

Lanta's mouth curved. 'She was, Godblind. You stood by Her side and She granted you much, pain and pleasure both. She stood in Gilgoras with Her Brother-Lover and stamped Her claim once more upon its fields and forests.'

He seized her hand, his own weak and palsied, clammy. Lanta grimaced but didn't pull away. 'She was here, and She is here too.' He put his free hand on Lanta's chest and then his own. 'Always.' He moaned, his right eyelid flickering.

'What did you see?' she asked again.

'The hidden thing wakes,' he said. 'The hidden thing makes itself known. It moves, and it begins to guide its allies.'

'What is it?'

The Godblind pouted. 'She's not the only god moving in Gilgoras,' he said. He pushed himself up on to one elbow, facing Lanta, and she leant back from the brush of his sour breath. 'The Fox God enters the great game, hidden in a man, but beginning to emerge.' He circled a finger in the air. 'Kill Him, and none will ever stand before you.'

'And do you know this man? Who is he? How can we recognise him?' Lanta demanded, excitement buzzing through her fingertips. She stroked his cheek, unmindful of his old sweat now, the lingering taint of blood and the beginnings of rot.

The Godblind giggled, crazed and fever-bright. 'You met him once, when you sacrificed his prince to the Red Gods.' He tapped his cheeks below his eyes. 'One blue. One brown. Splitsoul. Godlight. The hope of all children of Light.'

Lanta looked away from those maddening brown pools, vortexes into a world of torment she could not begin to imagine. She remembered the man. The gallant captain. *So gallant he knelt and watched it happen, did nothing. Still, I must find him. I will.*

'Where is he now? Right now?' she asked. The Godblind mewled and shrank back from her, palms pressed to either side of his head. 'Hush, I know. But this is your purpose. It is who and what you are. A tool left unused rusts. We must keep you sharp. Seek him.'

'You give me no chance to rust, honoured,' he mumbled in a dying show of futile defiance. The pupil of his right eye was blown wide. *The better to see into the realm of the gods?*

'Where is the Fox God?'

His breath hitched and warbled, fingers curling into claws as he rolled on to his side, drawing his knees up to his chest. 'Rilporin,' he said after a pause. 'He's on the breach, on the curtain wall.'

Lanta slapped her fist into her palm and rose to her feet, stalking the tent. 'Of course. And if we'd known this earlier, we could have told Corvus before he left for the city. He would've made it a priority to find and kill him. The East Rank is on the breach. They can kill him. Can't they?'

The man moaned again, head rolling on the blanket, denying her. 'Please don't,' he whispered, jagged. 'Please no more. Let me rest. Rust.'

'Tell me whether the East Rank can kill the Fox God, and then you can sleep,' she said, her tone softer than any Mireces had ever heard it.

'They will fail; even now He slaughters them, a thief of life stalking the black. Take the city, as you have already planned to do, despite the losses He and the defenders will inflict.' The Godblind paused, coughed, his skin grey and his eyes sunken. 'He'll be in the city somewhere, fighting, doing something . . . tricksy. Take Him and win.'

Lanta nodded and wiped her palms on her skirts. 'Take the city,' she murmured. She left him on her bed and exited the tent, staring at the orange-lit city across the stinking camp. The Fox God had clothed Himself in mortal flesh to aid the Rilporians and the whore Rillirin was carrying the Godblind's child. A child that could mend or end the world and all their hopes.

The war was being fought on more fronts than any common warrior could hope to comprehend. Its planes and edges stretched even Lanta's limits. The future was changing faster than they could blink, written like sunlight on shattered water, shifting, twisting, there and then gone. What purpose to a babe not even born? How could clothing Himself as a man accomplish a god's desires?

Lanta knelt in the grass outside her tent and drew her knife. Pulling back her sleeve she slashed through the thick, myriad lines of old scars to the red meat, let the blood flow, let the tears spring to her eyes.

'Dark Lady, beautiful goddess of death and glory, accept this small token as proof of my just devotion and my obedience.' She cut again. 'Holy Gosfath, God of Blood, I honour and worship you. Victory draws nearer. Our enemies' deepest secrets are laid bare before us by your hands, and all will be used to your advantage. Soon, my gods, soon we will have crushed the unbelievers and taken their fairest city. The grip of the Gods of Light will weaken, their followers wither. Red Gods, with my blood, my flesh, my breath, my soul, I honour you.'

There was a whisper of a smile on the cool night breeze, the teasing of fingertips across the back of her neck. Lanta shivered. Lanta hoped.

Lanta believed.

TARA

Tara stretched and groaned. Even her eyelids ached. The restrictions of bandages made themselves felt as she tried to squeeze the stiffness out of her limbs. The injuries from Blood Pass and Yew Cove were healing well, but she had more than enough new ones, including a clean slice to her inner thigh that chafed with every step until she wanted to scream.

She rolled on to her side and managed to sit upright on the edge of the bed, her head hanging, trying to work out if the nausea was pain or hunger. *Need to eat, girl. Get some energy in you or you're going to drop.*

She checked the expensive sand-clock, and it confirmed she'd woken just before she needed to, the lesson drilled into her over endless night watches in the West Rank forts. Don't be late. Tara groaned her way to her feet and into her linens and filthy breast band, stained with old sweat and older blood. Funny how you couldn't find decent women's underwear in the palace. The hair on one side of her head had been singed to the scalp, so she didn't think it was worth brushing out the rest of it.

Someone had left a tray of pork stew and greens outside the door, along with a heel of bread, some cheese and a pitcher of goat's milk. A smile cracked her face and she took it all back inside, thanking her mysterious benefactor in the instant before she tore into the food. *A Beltane feast, and the closest I'll get to a celebration tonight.*

The stew was cold and thick with a rime of grease, which she smeared on to the bread with a spoon and licked from her fingers. Yet another groan made its way from her throat, this one of ecstasy as her taste buds woke up and began clamouring for more.

Tara didn't stop until she could feel her belly begin to press against her belt. She looked at the shattered remains with intense regret, but knew she'd only throw up if she ate any more. Instead, she stuffed the rest of the cheese into a pouch on her belt, swigged the last of the milk, struggled into her armour and made her way out of her quarters. She was due at North One half an hour before her troops to get the handover from the officer on duty, so she moved quietly through the corridors and left them sleeping just a little longer.

The palace was silent as she made her way towards the main exit and the gate into Fourth Circle, her boot heels clicking softly on the marble and her stomach gurgling its pleasure at the meal. She patted it, grinning, wishing every pleasure in life was so easily satisfied, and then paused at the sound of voices. Not unusual, but there was a secretive timbre she didn't like, one that put her hackles up on instinct. Tara faded into the shadows between two giant marble columns.

Torchlight and many footsteps, sibilant mutterings and the unmistakeably round tones of the nobility. Tara frowned. They weren't heading for the war room for the day's debrief. She peeked out as the party passed and managed to identify Lorca, Silais and half a dozen others. With them were dozens of servants carrying boxes and richly dressed women and children.

Tara bit her tongue, looked towards the exit and her post, and then in the direction the group had disappeared. 'Mace is going to kill me,' she muttered, and crept after them. She was pretty sure she knew where they were going, but there was no time for her to summon guards. She'd have to do this herself.

The group exited into a small courtyard and Tara followed them out, the nobles at the front so intent on their destination that they didn't notice her, and the servants blinded by the loads they struggled beneath. It was no big feat to slip into the shadows and get in front of them. Get between them and the barred gate that led into the tunnel and down, all the way under the Circle walls to East Tower. To the King Gate, the bridge, and a way out of the city. The royal family's not-so-secret escape route.

'Of course, my lord, everything proceeds as planned. Your guards await you below East Tower, a full complement, and the war council has been told you are delayed by an hour; by the time they realise you're not coming, you'll be long gone.'

Tara's eyes narrowed. *Well, this has been well thought out, hasn't it, you fucking cowards?*

'And it will be safe, will it, Chamberlain?' Lorca asked. His eyes darted around the courtyard, stared straight at Tara and didn't see her. Most people don't see what's in front of them when they're nervous, and this man was very, very nervous.

'Absolutely safe, my lord. East Tower is manned by some of the city's finest. Once you are through the gate they will have no choice but to ensure your safe escape. It would be dishonourable to do otherwise. We—' The chamberlain's voice choked off in a squeak of alarm and he threw his hands up in front of him. 'No, no, don't hurt me!'

Tara hadn't even drawn her sword as she stalked forward. She grabbed him by his fur collar, jerked him close so his face was a hair's breadth from hers. His breath stank. The nobles and their servants and families had drawn back in squeaking, protesting alarm, huddling together.

'What is happening here?' Tara demanded. 'Commander Koridam gave explicit orders that no one was to exit the city.'

The man processed the register of her voice and straightened up, lowering his hands and assuming a supercilious air that made Tara want to punch his nose into the back of his head. Her patience died a little death. 'Young woman, I have no idea who you think you are, but you are impeding me in my duty. Lord Lorca—'

'My name is Major Tara Carter of the West Rank, you snivelling little weasel, and the King Gate stays shut. Commander's orders.'

'Commander Koridam is dead—'

'Commander Mace Koridam's orders,' Tara snarled.

Lorca forced his way out of the protection of his servants and gave her a condescending smile. Tara's patience rolled in its grave. 'Rastoth died mad and with his only heir hundreds of miles away in Listre. It is my duty to inform Tresh he is now our monarch. Thusly, I am leaving this city and—'

Tara let go of the chamberlain's sticky collar and wiped her hand on her trousers before balling it into a fist, stepping past him and burying it in Lorca's gut. The man doubled over with a most satisfying wheeze. The nobles, including Lorca's own heir, drew back into a tighter huddle.

'There is no "thusly", Lord Lorca. It is extremely simple; the gate stays shut.'

'He's locking us up here to use us as hostages when Rivil wins,' Lorca wheezed. 'Just like his father did.'

'Why would Rivil want you?' Tara asked, genuinely confused. 'Unless you are to be the first sacrifices to the Red Gods.'

Lorca blanched even further but forced himself erect. He shook a finger in her face. 'He will do anything to save his own hide, much like Durdil would've if a fucking wall hadn't fallen on him. Strange, is it not, that Rastoth was wounded with only Durdil Koridam as witness? That when he died, Durdil was present yet again? And now Mace steps from his father's shadow and takes on a position he is not entitled to? Conspiracy, I tell you. Conspiracy and villainy, and I will have no part in it. I will not bow to the arbitrary whims of a jumped-up soldier from the west, and I will not stay here to be bartered away in return for the lives of the peasant stock. Now step aside, woman.'

It was the 'woman' that did it. It always was, especially when it was sneered at her with the intimation that possession of a fine and perky pair of tits automatically reduced any associated brain function to the overriding imperative of finding a husband.

Tara drew her sword. The chamberlain goggled and tugged at his oily hair, scampering back to burrow among the women and children, adding his own voice to their strident cries for help. Tara needed to shut them up, but more than that, she needed to ensure the city remained sealed.

'No one leaves the city, not you, not anyone. We fight.'

She was stepping in front of the tunnel entrance when movement dragged at the corner of her eye. Tara ducked, and the arrow vanished into the night over her head.

'Run, milords, go now, before the Mireces murder us all in our beds!' They moved in a many-legged, bellowing mass of nobles and servants, slipping past Tara as she dived for cover and vanishing into the tunnel.

'The fuck are you?' Tara grunted as she sped for the palace door. It was locked. 'Shit.'

Tara held her breath and jerked her arm out of the doorway's paltry cover. The man loosed and she was running as soon as the arrow hummed past. He was in the tunnel himself, loosing through the gate to force her back, when the light from a palace window struck his face. The second of recognition nearly killed her. He grinned and loosed a final time before vanishing into the dark. The arrow slammed into the chainmail covering her belly.

She staggered back a step, ripping at the shaft. It came out with a grating noise and she threw it away, sucking in air and feeling for blood. A dribble, no more. A scratch.

Tara tightened her grip on her sword and wished she walked around with a great heavy shield all the time. 'I'm going to kill you, Galtas fucking Morellis,' she shouted. The blackness of the tunnel was almost complete and she crept in and flattened herself against the wall, holding her breath, mouth open slightly to better her hearing.

She could hear the scuffling of boots and the drag of boxes, and a click and shuffle she couldn't identify, but nothing else. No taunting or shouted obscenities, which would've been really useful. No blazing torch held in his hand to show her where he hid, which would've been even better. Tara slid her sword back into its sheath and pulled a dagger. In this darkness, any fighting she did would be up close and personal. Unless she was skewered through the throat by an arrow she didn't see coming. There was the dull orange of a torch up ahead, brightening slowly as she moved; everything else was shrouded in utter dark. *Fuck it.* Tara broke into a run, speeding along the curve of the passageway, thinking only of catching up with the torch-bearer.

The end of the tunnel led up and into a small courtyard at the base of East Tower, with the door out of the city nestled into the curtain wall. The chamberlain was already at the heavy iron-banded door, while Lorca and Silais remonstrated in loud voices with the captain in charge of East Tower, ordering the man to stand aside. Confused faces peered down from the tower itself.

''Ware!' Tara yelled and the captain debating with Lorca jerked his head in her direction. 'Don't open that door,' she screeched.

'Must get out, must get out,' Chamberlain was panting, his hands flapping at the lock, key skittering over the iron.

'You there, stop this minute,' the captain shouted, plainly relieved that a superior officer was taking charge. He pushed Lorca out of his way and shoved through the crowd of servants. 'Keep that door closed,' he echoed and soldiers began clattering down the stairwell inside East Tower, yelling, while others on the allure called out a warning of their own.

The nobles' hired guards squared up to the advancing Rankers and Tara tried to think of some way to calm the situation. Nothing sprang to mind. 'Gate stays shut,' she yelled again, 'Commander's orders.'

The captain barged through the press, tripping over boxes, heaving servants out of his path. Then he drew his sword. 'Stand away from the door or die,' he bellowed. 'Stand away!'

'Fuck,' Tara swore as the nobles' guards drew steel.

Tara was quartering the courtyard – *where is that cock-weasel, he's got to be here somewhere* – when Galtas limped out of the tunnel behind her, bow in hand and arrow clamped to the stock with his finger, other hand wielding a crutch for his splinted leg.

She turned as she heard him and realised she must've run straight past the clever little bastard, and then he clubbed his crutch into her face. Tara distinctly heard the breaking of her nose and hit the stone like a stunned salmon. Galtas hobbled past, avoiding her clutching fingers, and began loosing arrows at the East Tower defenders.

'The gate,' he roared, 'quickly.'

'Don't,' Tara bubbled, trying desperately to work out which way was up through the spinning in her head. The square was in uproar, servants and nobles screeching, soldiers running for Galtas, and Tara was contemplating puking up her entire meal when the chamberlain gave a great heave and dragged open the heavy wooden door. Night air and the sound of the river flooded in, followed an instant later by armed men.

Mireces.

Tara gaped. Some quick-thinking Tower soldiers were shoving at the door, pressing against the tide of flesh straining to get in. Others formed up against those Raiders already inside, and Tara saw at least one vanish back into the tower and race for the warning bell at the top.

The nobles' guards took one look at the advancing Mireces and decided they weren't being paid enough to die. As one, they surged off north, into the tanneries and the maze of alleys and stalls, losing themselves in the dark and the stench.

Tara staggered to her feet spitting blood as the Mireces cut their way through servants, nobles and soldiers alike, the leader clapping Galtas on the arm when they met in the centre of the carnage as though it had all been planned.

It has been fucking planned, twat. Why else would that little shit be in the city?

'King Corvus,' Galtas said. 'You lead the forces yourself?'

'The Dark Lady has returned through the veil and into the world, Her Brother with Her. I have seen Them with my own eyes. What is there to fear now our gods walk the world?' He indicated the splinted leg. 'You are hurt?'

'It slows me but will not kill me. Not yet anyway.'

'Get back to camp. We'll be moving fast and I can't wait for you.' Galtas nodded and vanished through the gate that was guarded now only by the dead and the dying.

There was nothing Tara could do against numbers such as these, though her fingers twitched with the urge to kill as many as she could. But there weren't enough Rankers to hold the gate closed, and though the bell was ringing from the top of the tower, reinforcements from North or South Two wouldn't reach them in time.

She eased sideways, slid into the tunnel and began to run back the way she'd come. *It's bloody Corvus himself. I need soldiers. I need lots of soldiers.*

The tunnel was longer than it had been before, she was sure of it. Longer, and darker, and more treacherous underfoot, or maybe it was the blow to her face that was confusing her, or the horror of the breach, or Lorca's spilling intestines as a Mireces opened him up, or Galtas's cool, amused smile. Or all of it.

She ran on through the endless black of the tunnel, stumbling and bleeding, her breath harsh in her throat, until eventually there was the faintest lightening of the inky dark ahead and she put on a last, desperate burst of speed, hands outstretched for the gate, and threw herself at it.

It flung her back on to her arse, shuddering. Locked.

'No!' Tara scrambled to her feet, clawing at the gate, rattling it in its frame. 'Help!' she screeched. 'Let me out! Let me the fuck out right fucking now! Breach! Breach, you bastards!'

She could hear them running behind her now, gaining on her, and her with nowhere to go but into death. She pressed her back to the gate and drew sword and dagger, bubbling blood at them. 'Come on then, cunts. Come on, you miserable heathen bastards, I'll fucking kill the lot of you, starting with King C—'

The gate shifted and hands grabbed her by the shoulders and dragged her through, spun her on to the cobbles and lunged back for the gate. Renik.

'Run,' he growled as he fumbled with the lock. 'Fucking run. I'll make sure they come to you at the palace, so gather any soldiers you can and make your stand there.' He thumbed the latch on the gate, the latch Tara could easily have opened from inside if she hadn't been blinded by panic. Renik wedged a heavy stick between the bars and the frame, trying to force it closed because the chamberlain had taken the keys, then gripped a long spear and took up position. He spared her a single final glance. 'I fucking said run.'

'I'm sorry, I'm sorry,' Tara babbled, knowing she was leaving him to die. 'Dancer's grace.' Renik nodded once and Tara left him there, sprinting along the side of the palace towards the northern entrance and anyone who might be in there who could help.

CORVUS

Corvus pushed his way to the front of the crowd squeezed tight at the tunnel exit. The gate was shut and a man in armour stood on the other side, a long spear in his hands that he was using to poke away at the men crowding the gate. It stabbed for Corvus and he slipped sideways, let it slide past him into someone else – *the Lady's will* – and then grabbed the haft in both hands. The man stiffened and yanked back on the spear, and Corvus resisted a second and then let go.

The man stumbled back three steps and Corvus slid his hand outside the bars of the gate and fiddled with the lock. It clicked open, but there was a bar, no a stick, jammed sideways between lock and frame. Corvus pulled the gate tighter shut, slid the stick out as the man lunged again, too late. There was a soft squeal of hinges, and it swung open.

'Quiet.'

Mireces spilt out of the tunnel into Fifth Circle, into the

263

very fucking heart of Rilporin, a small blue tide of righteous, silent fury. The soldier killed three before several weapons pressed against him. Valan pulled the spear from his hands, though he held on long enough that a blade had to part the skin of his neck in warning.

Corvus held up a hand and the weapons retreated. 'I am King Corvus of the Mireces. You?'

The man hesitated, clearly torn between spitting at them and lengthening his life by a few more breaths. 'Major Artem Renik of His Majesty's Palace Rank. You can go no further, Sire.' He drew a sword and a dagger and stood in front of Corvus, relaxed, coiled, and no doubt deadly.

'On the contrary,' Corvus said, flicking his fingers so that his men peeled away, blocking the roads to either side of the palace and cutting off Renik's retreat, 'I will go wherever I choose and the gods decree. Right now I want to go into the palace to find your Commander of the Ranks and kill him. Stand aside and be granted a quick death.'

'I cannot allow you into the palace. Return through the tunnel and be granted the chance to see the dawn,' Renik replied, his voice calm.

Corvus tutted. So keen to die for their country, their false gods. His legs were heavy from the swim across the Gil to reach the King Gate and then the charge along the tunnel, his clothing sodden and his chainmail beginning to chafe. None of it would stop him. The gods walked at his side. Mireces were still moving into position when Renik erupted and cut hard and low for Corvus's knee, on his axe side.

Unexpected and very nearly effective, but Corvus danced sideways out of range. He slammed his elbow into a wall, caught a glint that was the knife coming up fast, under his sword arm, and twisted, pulling his shoulder back and away from danger, into the wall again, letting the momentum fling his axe hand forward. And the bastard's sword was there, intercepting and flicking it away before a heavy boot slammed down on his foot with a sickening crunch.

Corvus grunted and the world split into colours and scents and the breath of wind and the stir of breath on his face. Everything slowed, torches swirling and smearing as the pain lanced up as far as his knee and Corvus saw his own death in Renik's eyes. Inevitable. Unstoppable despite the promises of the Dark Lady Herself.

The sword arced upwards again and Corvus blocked with sword and hand axe. He squinted into Renik's face. No triumph, no trickery, nothing to give away the fact that his knife was unaccounted for and hot in Corvus's shoulder, stabbing deep into the flesh.

Corvus's breath came out in a yelp that jolted him from the vision of his impending death and back into the real world. He was herded against the wall, his men waiting patiently, Renik a whirling mass of armour and edged steel blocking his every attack, stamping on his feet, squeezing him against the stone.

The city itself was fighting him, allying against its conquerors. Renik knew this city, he knew how to fight in these narrow streets, while Corvus's shoulders and elbows and the back of his skull were raw from impacts with the wall as he moved instinctively into space that wasn't there. And Renik pressed, and pressed, and pressed again, and now there was a flicker in his eyes, an acknowledgment that he too saw Corvus's death looming at his shoulder.

'Take him,' Corvus roared and saw Renik's face fall, saw a glimmer of betrayal in his eyes. *Didn't expect that, did you? You wanted an honourable death while buying your friends time to mount a counter-attack. But this is war, not the fencing yard.*

But Renik surprised him again, fleeing as the others charged in, jumping backwards and giving Corvus room to chase him. So Corvus pressed, harrying him until his men crowded past, eager at the kill. Only Renik wasn't quite ready to be killed, kept retreating, back to a little alcove in the wall of the palace with a door set in it. There was a handle in the wall and Renik grabbed it and pulled. Valan lunged for him, expecting him to vanish through an opening, but instead there was a thunk from deep inside the palace, the single deep toll of a bell, and the handle came off in Renik's hand. He threw it and it hit a Mireces in the face.

'What did you do?' Corvus asked, stilling his men, curious and impressed despite himself.

'Locked the door,' Renik said. 'Can't be opened from this side. Only way you're getting in now is through the main gates around the other side. Sorry.' He grinned, not looking at all sorry, and Corvus felt a surge of admiration.

'You'd have made a fine Raider, Major Renik,' he said, and Renik laughed.

'Not in this life, and not in death either,' he replied, and readied himself in the alcove, his back and flanks protected by stone and wood. He exhaled, soft and slow through his nostrils. His shoulders dropped, fingers flexed on knife and sword hilt, and then he raised his knife hand and beckoned. 'Come on then, you fuckers. Let's dance.'

His voice echoed like the clattering of steel down the street. *Come on then, you fuckers*. Corvus bit the tip of his tongue and found himself smiling, dipped his head in a salute, and then watched as his men lunged forward, crowding the alcove, crowding each other, hurling blades and curses, jostling to be the one to bring him down.

Renik held out for longer than Corvus expected, attacking only as far as his flanks were protected, but still far enough to kill four. Seconds stretched into what felt like days and Corvus watched the backs of his men, the frenzied pumping of their sword arms, knowing it was inevitable but still a little voice in him wanting Renik to live. To win. To beat them all, despite the odds. What a fucking song that would be.

And then he went down, and he didn't scream, and he didn't beg. He just died, as all men must and a damn sight finer than many.

The men stepped back, panting and smeared with blood, theirs and Renik's. Corvus peered into the alcove and grunted, grunted again as Valan secured a wad of linen over the hole in his shoulder. 'Let's find a way into the palace. We need to find this fucking Commander of theirs and kill or capture him. Right now I don't care which. This ends – tonight.'

They turned right and trotted down the northern side of the palace, weapons bright and ready. Distantly, more bells began to clang. The city knew they were coming.

TARA

Is it actually possible to cough up a lung?

Tara clung to the door she'd burst through and coughed, her inability to get enough air lending a dazed and hysterical edge to her thoughts. She coughed some more, each spasm sending shards of pain through her nose, and swore again to never set foot in a burning building.

'Help,' she croaked, and was ignored.

'You all watched it happen. You were there. I *felt* it happen. Crys is the Fox God. He is – has to be – our priority now. More even than the defence of the city.' Ash was squared up to Lim, Dalli trying vainly to separate them.

'Even if he is—' Lim began and even from here Tara could see the cold fury, the refusal to accept, in his haggard face.

Ash ripped at his chainmail, dragged it over his head and pulled off his jerkin and shirt. 'I don't have one single bruise, let alone a cut. No strained muscles, no torn flesh. Look at this.' He spun and Tara saw another scar, the same fresh-healed

268

purple as the one on his face. 'Galtas stabbed me in the back and then took my fucking face off with a knife. I felt it happen and then I died. I died and Crys brought me back. The Red Gods are back, and now the Fox God walks the earth. We have to protect him. He's gone to the breach and I—'

'*Why you?*' Lim roared the words so loudly that everyone in the room stilled and Tara found she was holding her breath, the urge to cough smothered by sheer animal instinct.

'What makes you so special?' Lim continued in a more normal tone. 'Why not any of our dead in the Valley? My father, for instance? Why not anyone in Watchtown, any of the *thousands* of our people who died there? The children, Ash, the fucking children.'

Tara's throat tightened.

'Chief, I don't think it's that—' Ash tried, his tone pleading now.

'What about the tunnels?' Lim went on, relentless, and they could all see it coming, inevitable as sunrise, implacable as death. His voice dropped to a timbre that made Tara want to run and hide. 'What about my wife?'

'I don't think he knows how to use it,' Ash tried, patting the air. 'It wasn't on purpose, it just . . . happened. I don't understand any of this, but I do know that if he could, he'd have saved her. He'd have saved all of them. And he'd have saved Durdil too. I know—'

'You know ever such a lot, don't you, Ash?' Lim's hand was near his knife now despite Dalli's desperate attempt to herd him away.

This is either the best or the worst time to step in. Thank the gods I'm wearing armour.

'Mireces in Fifth Circle,' she yelled and all eyes turned on her. 'King Gate's open and Corvus himself is leading an army straight here. Don't know numbers, but I can't imagine he'd

set foot in the city without a sizeable force to back him up.'
She looked at Ash. 'Galtas Morellis let them in.'

No one moved. 'Come on,' she tried, forcing her voice a
bit louder. 'We've got the chance to take Corvus himself and
end this war. These are the Mireces – this is the man who
burnt your city, slaughtered your people. Fucking move!'

'This isn't over,' Lim snarled up at Ash as the taller man
struggled back into his shirt and jerkin.

Ash poked Lim hard in the chest and Dalli's mouth popped
open. She took a careful step back. 'I love you, Lim, you're
a brother to me, but Crys isn't responsible for any of this.
He didn't kill Sarilla and if you want revenge, take it out
on the men who did. The ones who are outside right now.
Dom saw all this coming, he could have warned—'

'Did he see the Mireces coming?' Tara bellowed as loud
as she could, cutting them off. 'We have godsdamn fucking
incoming, so save the sodding theology for later.'

She'd regained their attention and lowered her voice, her
lungs aching, wanting to cough. 'Major Renik is standing
alone against them. He told me he'd send them here. Chances
are extremely good that he died doing that, and I for one
have no intention of disrespecting his sacrifice by not doing
all I can to kill every last shitting bastard out there. Now,
they must be nearly at the main entrance, so shut up and
follow me. Right. Now.'

Ash got his chainmail back on and moved towards her,
Dalli a step behind. The Wolves looked between her and
Lim and then one by one they moved to her side. Lim's lips
peeled back from his teeth.

'Chief Lim?' Tara said. 'I suggest an ambush in or near
the war room; I imagine that's where they'll expect Mace
to be. Your thoughts?'

Lim stared at her in silence and Tara's palms prickled

with sweat under his dead gaze. 'Lead on,' he said in the end, but his tone promised that they, too, would be having words when this was all done. Tara decided not to worry about it. She was fairly convinced she wouldn't live to be shouted at.

Ash was next to her as they crept through the guest wing towards the public rooms and the servants' passages that riddled the palace. She glanced at him, at the thick, jagged line on his face almost obliterating an older scar. Glanced away. Glanced back.

'Eyes front,' he snapped, blushing, and Tara complied with a red flush of her own, quartering the corridors.

I saw it myself; I saw him come back. Crys is who Ash says he is. Crys is the . . . the . . . She couldn't even finish the thought. It all made sense until she put Crys in the picture but then she just wanted to laugh. And this wasn't the time for laughter.

The servants' corridors were mostly empty if you didn't count the blood smeared over the walls and the echoing of their soft footfalls. They found a gaggle of cooks and sent them towards a smaller exit with orders to be swift and silent. Others were no more than tangles of meat heaped against the walls.

'They're already in,' Tara whispered. 'Element of surprise is gone. We'll have to improvise.'

They haunted the corridors and public rooms, listened at doors to private chambers and found them empty, and finally reached the war room. She could hear strident voices inside and put a finger to her lips, rose on to her toes and crept forward.

The voice rose into a hysterical shout. 'I tell you, I am a captain, just a captain. I have no idea where the Commander is! He doesn't come here; no one does. He fights on the wall. No! I've told you—'

Tara burst through the door in time to see the man Galtas had called King Corvus stab a Palace Rank officer in the throat. The captain fell choking, vainly trying to stem the bleeding, and Tara yelled and launched herself at his attacker with no thought whatsoever.

The war room was small and more Mireces were crowded in the doorway that led out into a wider space, some sort of function hall. 'On me,' she yelled and Wolves spilt through the door at her back. Corvus spat a curse and retreated through into the hall, forming up with his men.

'We follow through there, we'll be coming at them a few at a time,' Tara began, before Lim pushed past her, screaming, sword raised. He charged the door.

'No!' Dalli screamed and ran after him, and then they were all moving, pelting after the pair and squeezing through the door like a bunch of bloody amateurs.

'Fucking shit.' Tara ran with them, and somehow they made it through the door without all being killed. The hall was huge and marble and chilly, banked fires and tall iron candlesticks breaking up the darkness.

She cleared the door, but there wasn't time to line up or form a wedge. Corvus was backing rapidly into space. To either side his warriors formed a line and then each end advanced, curving around so that they could come at the Wolves from three sides. If they got to the door and cut them off, it was all over.

No way she was going for the centre of the half-circle and Corvus; too easy to be surrounded. Instead she lunged for the man on the end of the line, a Mireces with a neck as big as her head and an axe the size of the end of the world. She ducked the first swing, helping the axe over her head with a parry of her sword, then cracked the hilt into the bastard's face.

He reversed the swing and she danced backwards to avoid the blow, slipped and her left knee slammed into the marble with a sickening crack. The axe whistled down and smashed chips from the floor. He hefted it again and Tara stabbed at him, trying to force her numb leg to move, skating sideways across the floor on her arse.

The Raider took a lumbering step and she shuffled further back, then rolled to her left to avoid another blow from the axe. She jumped up, left leg shuddering with pain, and stabbed at him again, raking a line down the outside of his thigh. He bellowed like a castrated bull and batted the sword away.

Tara let the shove carry her and her blade in a circle and this time as she faced him, she rammed the tip up beneath his chainmail, gouging through his other thigh and ripping open his groin as the wind from the axe flittered across her face and stirred the scant hair poking from her helmet.

The Raider's squeal was nasal and blubbering and the axe clattered against the marble as he grabbed at the wound, blood spurting between his fingers. Tara rammed the sword through his neck and he toppled like a felled tree, choking on steel.

Wolves were engaging the curved ends of the line, securing the door but vulnerable to flank attacks from those in the centre, breaking ranks only long enough to disrupt the Wolves' rhythm before scurrying back to protect Corvus.

There were too many of them, hundreds too many. They needed to split the line if they were to have any hope of surviving.

Lim had clearly come to the same decision. He lunged past her with a howling war cry that made her shiver. Corvus ran to meet him, ignoring the warning yells of his bodyguards. He caught Lim's sword squealing on his own and skipped out of range before the Wolf could thrust past his guard. They circled and clashed again, and again, Corvus's seconds lunging to their king's defence, Lim's friends running to his.

The line broke, dissolved into a melee as Tara felt a warning tingle down her spine. She threw herself flat, knee cracking the marble again, flipped over and scythed a man's legs from beneath him with her foot. He fell, helmet clonking off the ground, and Tara managed an awkward kick to his ribs that scooted them in opposite directions on the slick floor.

Someone fell over her, their knee sending white lights through her head as it connected with her broken nose. Over her own roar of pain, she heard a jubilant cheer from deeper into the hall. She twisted just in time to see Lim over-balance, one hand pressed against his neck, his sword arm falling to his side. A corresponding screech of denial went up from the Wolves. Corvus glanced around the room and then kicked Lim over on to his back. The Wolf's hand came away from his neck and blood fountained in the gloom as he fell.

A single stroke from Corvus's sword parted Lim's head from his body.

'Oh, shit,' Tara bubbled and got to her feet, spitting blood and checking her surroundings. The Wolves charged again in a shrieking onslaught, apparently intending to die on Mireces blades in order to accompany their chief into death.

The fighting reached a pitch of savagery Tara had never seen, not even when they'd sounded the all-out at the Blood Pass Valley and slaughtered the Mireces army to the last man. The Wolves were spending their lives like copper knights, with thoughtless, reckless abandon, trying to reach Lim's corpse deep in a tight knot of Mireces.

'We need to pull back.' She spoke without thinking, quiet,

no one close enough to hear, and then louder. 'We need to pull back.'

For all their earlier shouting, Ash had almost reached Lim; Dalli, Isbet and a score of others at his back. Tara gave them a chance to recover their chief's corpse, but only one. As soon as Ash was forced back a step, she gave the order. 'Fall back! Fall back!' The Wolves closest to her looked in her direction, and the Mireces let out another bellow of triumph and surged forwards, pushing against the line, hacking madly.

'Fall back,' she yelled again, and then Dalli was shouting it too and Ash was screaming wordless rage as he was pushed away from Lim's body. 'Controlled retreat,' Tara added, knowing there was no such bloody thing but needing to sound like she was in charge.

In step and in time, the Wolves began to move backwards, losing fewer than Tara thought possible amid the storm of steel. She stayed behind them with a few others, picking off those who tried to slip around to the rear, until her back pressed against the plaster next to the door.

'Down!' bellowed a new voice and Tara spun to the doorway to see a squad of Palace Rankers armed with long-bows.

'Down!' Tara echoed and most of the Wolves complied. The flight of arrows thrummed overhead and cut down the first rank of Mireces, then the second. The attack faltered and warriors began throwing themselves through the doorway as more and more arrows cut the air above them.

'Who're you?' Tara gasped as she made it to the lieutenant's side. 'Weaverson? *Roger?*'

The young man grinned despite the situation. 'Hello, Major. Fifth Circle gate guard reporting for duty. Heard the commotion and then some palace servants came to fetch us, said you'd sent them out in a hurry.'

Of course. Gate guards carry bows. Sweet Dancer, thank you.

'I'll have you promoted for this, Lieutenant,' she said. 'All right, cover us. We need to pull back and then trap them in Fifth Circle somehow, send for as many reinforcements as we can and then take him.' She pointed. 'Mireces king. Corvus himself. See?'

Weaverson's eyes were wide but he nodded. 'Got it. Get into the tunnel and lock the gate behind you – no point us all being trapped in here with them. Once you're safe we'll break for the gatehouse, barricade ourselves in. They'll either go for the tunnel or the gatehouse; they can't know about the guardsman's exit. We hold them at whichever exit they attempt and they'll be fish in a big barrel.'

Tara eyed the doorway. All the Wolves who were coming were through; the Mireces were out of bowshot to either side of the door, shouting threats but keeping out of sight. She tapped Ash and Dalli. 'Pass the word. Let's go.'

GALTAS

'Skerris! Good man, still alive. Listen, Corvus is in. He's going for Mace at the palace. We should be able to force a— What?'

Skerris handed Galtas the distance-viewer and pointed. 'Might not be able to make him out, but I'm almost certain that's Mace up by Second Tower. His presence rallies the defenders; they're holding the breach.'

Galtas felt his stomach drop into his feet, but then a surge of excitement had him grabbing Skerris's shoulder. He leant close, wincing at the agony spiking through his knee. 'This could be perfect,' he hissed. 'Corvus gets trapped in the palace, executed or killed in the fighting, and Rivil has an uncontested claim to the throne and all of Rilpor. He— What now?'

He'd been short-tempered enough as the siege progressed, but the hours it'd taken Galtas to limp around the outside of the city, expecting at any moment to feel an arrow between the shoulders, had drained him of the last of his patience. Now Skerris looked like a partially deflated waterskin. 'What?' Galtas repeated.

'Milord, you've been gone for weeks. Much has happened.' Skerris paused to roar more orders at an exhausted Fifty and their lieutenant. The men stood up – slow, laboured – and made their equally laboured way out of sight. Galtas had no doubt they'd sit down again as soon as they could.

'The Godblind who the Blessed One told us of arrived. He challenged the prince to single combat in the rite of Hoth-Nagarre, a fight witnessed and judged by the gods Themselves. It is a fight to the death and once a man has been challenged, he may not refuse the trial.'

Galtas's hand came up to stroke his restored eye patch, the familiar, soothing gesture the only indication of his sudden unease. 'Yes, all right, a duel. What of it?'

'Lord . . . the gods saw fit to pass judgement. The Godblind triumphed; Rivil is dead.'

Galtas stumbled back a step, his splinted leg sliding in the mud. He would have fallen if Skerris's huge paw hadn't darted out and steadied him. 'What shittery is this?' He forced a laugh. 'Rivil cannot be dead, and certainly not because of some heathen prophet.'

'I'm afraid he is, milord. The gods Themselves witnessed it. The gods Themselves . . . were present.' Even in the flickering torchlight Galtas could see how he'd lost colour. He found he didn't want to know what Skerris meant. 'Corvus is our only hope now if we are to restore the faith to Rilpor and all Gilgoras. He is the king we must follow.'

Corvus as king? Rivil is supposed to king! I'm supposed to be his First Adviser, Commander of his Ranks, heir to his throne until he has a child. The faith was a distant fucking second to that.

And yet . . . he said the gods passed this sentence.

'Of course, the faith is all,' Galtas muttered piously. He had no wish to anger gods who had determined Rivil should die. 'Though this is a fucking setback. And the Godblind killed him? Why? Tell me, damn you!'

Skerris let him go. 'He accused the prince – and you, milord – of raping his wife and then killing her and his unborn child. Her name was Hazel. In the western woods, about seven years ago, I think. Does it sound familiar?'

He knows it does. Rivil clearly admitted it or there'd be no reason for the duel. Godsdamnit, he waited seven years to get his revenge? No wonder he went bastard mad.

Galtas nodded slowly. 'I know what you're referring to, yes.' He spat, trying hard to hide how shaken he was. 'Ironic, no, that he ends up being a kind of ally and still manages to fuck up all our plans?'

Skerris licked his teeth and inspected Galtas through piggy eyes. 'Not really, if I'm going to be honest, milord. While I am a good son of the Red Gods, I still don't want Mireces running my country. Rivil was a king I could get behind. Corvus . . . less so. Irony's the last thing I'm feeling right now and I know many in the Rank are beginning to question just why we're still fighting.'

Probably time for that backup plan, Galtas thought, *though being crippled doesn't help me execute it.* 'The nobles I spoke with in the city said that Rastoth's distant cousin Tresh is next in line. He's in exile in Highcrop in Listre, but perhaps it is time to sound him out. It might be good to have a backup – we don't know what might happen to Corvus, after all.'

Skerris pursed his lips and rubbed at the sweat in the folds of his neck. 'Not sure what good that'll do us now, Galtas,' he said, dropping the man's title for the first time. Galtas noticed it; he saw as well the corresponding decrease in deference. It did more than Skerris's words to convince him just how far his star had fallen when Rivil did. 'Tresh can lay claim to the throne if he wants, but any army he raises will be facing us. Despite the rumblings of dissent in the Rank, we're here to restore the faith, not to elevate just one man. If Tresh wishes to convert, or indeed already walks the Dark Path, then excellent. Otherwise, we go with Corvus. There is no one else.'

There's me, Galtas thought, but didn't say it.

'Corvus is cut off in Fifth Circle,' he snapped instead, 'and the officers he was hoping to capture are leading the defence of the breach on the other fucking side of the city. We're likely to lose him too if word reaches Mace that Corvus is in there.'

Skerris squinted into the pre-dawn gloom at the torch-lit breach. 'All right. Then we take Mace and take the breach.'

'Oh, aye, we just take Mace, do we?' Galtas grunted. 'How fucking exactly?'

'Men and artillery and blood and steel, the same as always. Your friend Crys Tailorson is up there too, by the way,' he added, as though dangling a mouse for a hungry cat. 'Rivil boasted that the East Rank would meet the Mireces in the centre of the city. Perhaps we should do just that. Storm the breach and then press on, no stopping, surge through the city and cut down everyone we come across. Rivil wanted us to preserve as much of his city as possible; I don't see we have that problem any more. Unless you have a pressing desire to do otherwise?'

'Rivil wanted a city to rule, it's true. Perhaps Corvus doesn't deserve one.' Galtas's stomach rolled with sudden acid, sudden anger. 'Well, it looks like we're out of other options, doesn't it? Very well, I agree. We take Mace, take this wall, and then we join up with Corvus. I've little doubt he'll head for the temple district at some point – we can meet him there.' He squinted at Skerris. 'You're a general, I know that. But you still take orders. You will take them from me from now on, not from the Mireces. Yes?'

Skerris adjusted his belt over his massive gut with thoughtful deliberation. 'As long as your orders put the faith and victory first, we won't have a problem. Milord.'

Galtas nodded and turned to inspect the assault on the breach. Despite his words and promises, he'd no intention of seeing Corvus on the throne. Not now. Not ever.

A high vantage point, a bow and quiver, and Galtas would do his patriotic duty and prevent a Mireces ruling Rilpor. As for who would eventually take the throne, well, Galtas was a war hero and the confidant of kings. There were worse choices.

CORVUS

Fifth moon, dawn, day forty-three of the siege
Guardsman's entrance, Fifth Circle, Rilporin,
Wheat Lands

Rivil won't be pleased I've fired his palace, Corvus thought. *Oh, wait.* He grinned and rolled his shoulders, his nerves settling as his confidence grew. They were in, and they were alive, and no one was currently trying to kill them.

The Wolves had fled. Outnumbered and outfought, they'd retreated to the tunnel to First Circle with Fost in pursuit, then barricaded the gate and run back to the East Tower with their tails between their legs. They'd left a fair amount of dead behind them, though, their own and Corvus's. *The Lady's will.*

Corvus's guide, an East Ranker, was adamant. 'Guardsman's entrance into Fourth Circle. Nobility aren't fighters; they'll die easy. Gold, jewels, coin. Food, water. It's all in Fourth. Ain't nothing here in Fifth but a trap, but get into Fourth and we've got options.'

'I would've thought it'd all be in the palace? The gold?'

Valan grunted, stretching his back. He turned from the Ranker to check the approach behind him, check Corvus was still there, still safe. Corvus met his eyes and winked.

'What's your name again?' he asked.

'Runt, they call me,' the Ranker said. 'And the treasury is in the palace, aye, but it'd take a week to break in there even if you hadn't just set it on fire. Nobles though, well, they just leave their coin lyin' around in heaps. Take a few of 'em hostage, the rest'll be clamouring to surrender. Once one Circle falls, the others'll follow soon enough.'

'You know a lot for a lowly Ranker,' Corvus put in, though in truth he didn't much care. Controlling the coin and food might bring the city to its knees, but Corvus wanted blood and conversion, sacrifice and vengeance. He wanted to make Rilpor bleed for a thousand years of apostasy, a thousand years of contempt. Enough food for his army and enough coin to quiet the East Rank, and he'd be happy. This wasn't about land or riches, no matter what the enemy or even his allies thought. This was justice and the gods' glory.

'I keep my ear to the ground, Yer Majesty,' Runt said, sniffing. 'It ain't difficult.'

'So we get into Fourth Circle and we've free rein?' Valan checked.

Runt sniffed again. 'Nah. Circles're divided into districts, so there's walls and big fancy gates splitting them into sections, like spokes on a wheel. No one tell you any of this? Rivil just sent you in blind, did he? Cunt. Anyway, district gates're more for show than security, made to be pretty, not functional, at least in Fourth. They'll only be guarded by the City Watch and a few swings with a ram would bring 'em down, I reckon. If they're even locked. Nobles're arrogant. Some of those gates probably haven't been closed in years. You won't have too much trouble getting through, I shouldn't think.'

'All right,' Corvus said and waved them on. 'Get this gate open. We came for Mace and we haven't got him, so we go with the backup plan. House to house in the noble quarter. Kill everyone – men, women, children, servants, dogs. Everyone. Blood for the gods, to wash the Dancer's stain from the stone. Then burn it. Fear and despair will win us this city, and with Fifth and Fourth both alight, their seat of power is lost.'

Valan's eyes were gleaming in the dawn light and Corvus punched his fist into his palm. 'Then the temple district. Stupid bastards've put all their holy places together, makes it easier for us to rededicate them to the Red Gods. Take the temple district and the one next to it, the one with the gate into the killing field,' he snapped his fingers.

'Merchant quarter,' Runt supplied.

'Right, take the temple and merchant quarters and fortify. That's our base. We launch assaults from there until Skerris takes the breach, then we go all out and meet him in the middle of whatever's left. Our feet are on the Path.'

'Our feet are on the Path,' Valan echoed, his teeth gleaming white in the gloom of the gateway. He slapped Runt on the back. 'Let's fucking do this.'

The battering ram was made of the posts from the royal bed lashed together. Corvus didn't hold out much hope for it, but if the gates were as weak as Runt insisted, it might be enough.

They were bloody and bruised, filled with rage and religion, and they could smell riches. If Runt was right, no one was expecting them to come through here. It should give them more than enough time to make an impression on Rilporin's noblest families.

Corvus grimaced as the ram team ran at the gate and bounced off it, the oak rattling in its frame. But half a dozen solid blows later and the gate was splintering, twisting and squealing on its hinges even as the ram started to come apart. The team backed out of the way and set to work fixing it while others finished smashing the gate with axes.

The advance party went through, weapons ready and shields up. They slid out of sight and Corvus held up a clenched fist for silence. They waited, tense, for screams and the clash of weapons, but there was nothing.

Runt looked back at the king. 'Whoever was on duty either died of fright or scarpered to raise the alarm. Wonder which it could be?' His grin was evil and unconcerned.

'I suspect the latter,' Corvus said, his tone sour. Runt's nonchalance was starting to piss him off. 'Let's go. Fost and his lot will have to catch us up. That' – he pointed to the fierce glow of the burning palace and the sparks drifting on the dawn breeze – 'is going to tell everyone exactly where we are. So let's not be where they think us.'

Valan got into position in front of Corvus and led him through the gate. Fourth Circle was quiet, seeming deserted, and they paused to take in the spectacle of wide-open streets and enormous stone buildings, each one a home for just a single family. The longhouse in Eagle Height could have fitted inside any one of them three times over.

'Squads of fifty,' Corvus hissed and the order was passed. 'Take a house each, keep it quiet if you can, move fast. Blood and fire.'

'Blood and fire,' the Mireces echoed, savage grins splitting their faces as they peeled off down the streets, climbing broad stairs to ornate front doors or wide windows full of expensive, but so very fragile, glass.

The first sounds came – windows shattering, axes in doors

– the first shouts, the first screams. 'Looks like we've woken the neighbours.' Corvus laughed. 'Come on.'

The sun was a finger's width over the horizon, not that you could see either through the black smoke of the burning palace. In the end, Fourth Circle had defeated them through its sheer size, and as the time passed Corvus had decided that making for the temple district was more important than killing rich folk. They'd taken the gate into the cloth district of Third Circle and fought a brief and one-sided battle against the shopkeepers and stall-holders who lived there.

Now they jogged along the street with shields on their backs, weapons in one hand and lit torches in the other. Many of the district's goods were stored in long, low warehouses, and as the Mireces passed each one, they threw torches through doors and windows. The crackle of flame and heat pressed against their backs as they advanced.

They were approaching the gate into Second Circle when the clash of arms erupted and Corvus skidded to a halt behind Valan's out-flung arm. 'Wolves and Rankers,' a Mireces gasped, legging it back around the bend towards them. 'Good few hundred, looks like.'

'Shit,' Corvus said. By not pursuing the Wolves out of Fifth, he'd given them time to regroup and find backup. Now they had to fight them all over again. 'The Lady's will. Kill them.' The man bobbed his head and vanished back around the corner. The noise of battle increased. The thousand he'd brought into the city numbered far fewer now, but he still had more than half, surely enough. He grabbed Runt. 'You. Another gate into Second?'

Runt shook his head and wiped soot from streaming eyes. 'Next gate to Second is on the King's Way. It'll be fully fortified and heavily guarded. It's here or nowhere, Sire.'

Corvus chewed his lip and then nodded. 'Valan, we break through here. All of us, full assault, no reserve.' Valan blew out his cheeks but didn't argue, passing the word fast and low.

'Let's go. Runt, with me. We need your knowledge of this fucking rabbit warren.'

'As you say.' Runt shrugged and pulled his sword. They broke into a jog, and then into a run, and then they swept around the corner and into the fight.

MACE

*Fifth moon, morning, day forty-three of the siege
Gatehouse, western wall, Rilporin, Wheat Lands*

*Second Last is lost, towers and all. Double First will be theirs
by dusk. The palace is burning and the nobles' quarter has
been sacked.*

The wall's lost. Two Circles are lost. But is the war lost?

As he hunkered down with his back to the gatehouse
stones, Mace suspected it just might be. There were no reinforcements. Durdil and Yarrow were dead. Dorcas – poor
bastard – had lost his other eye and was raving in a hospital
bed somewhere. He had no idea where Renik, Tara or the
Wolves were – just had to hope they were alive and safe –
and Mireces were loose in the city and digging in. Colonel
Edris was in the hospital, his leg missing from the knee
down, and not expected to last the day.

Vaunt was still with him, reeling on his feet with fatigue,
concussed and bleeding, and Crys was . . . Crys was fright-
ening the living shit out of Mace. He'd seen Crys fight before,
skirmishes, brawls and all-out battles, but he'd never seen

anything like this. He moved with a grace that shouldn't even be possible, sliding out of range of weapons, edged steel missing by a hair's breadth, seeming to hear attacks before they occurred. And the eyes . . .

The enemy fell at his feet like wheat, the men around him made monsters or heroes simply by his presence. Mace knew he was one of them, moving to a will other than his own. Crys hadn't saved Mace's father, but he'd almost singlehandedly held the breach through the long hours of the night and into the dawn, soldiers dying as though just to garner his approval. That had to count for something.

If Mace put away his grief and his rage, it did mean something. It meant everything. *It means he's who they're saying he is.*

Archers were holding the rubble wall perched on top of the breach, and everyone else was poisoning First Circle's wells and setting fire to the grain stores, filling the tower rooms and stairwells with rubble, piling furniture and rock against the doors to hold them closed, doing everything possible to prevent the Mireces having an easy way into the city. Down the scree of the breach or not at all, those were the options.

Mace fished a filthy square of linen from inside his breastplate and used it to dab at the burst blisters on the side of his face and down his neck. The pain was unrelenting, maddening, gnawing at his bones and brain until it was hard to concentrate. And gods, he was so shitting thirsty.

A rope appeared from above, snaking on to the flagstones in front of him. Mace stared at it, uncomprehending, and seconds later Crys slid down it and landed with a soft thump.

'Gatehouse is sealed and the catapult is disabled, Commander. I've left a candle stub burning in a pool of pitch and soaked the engine itself. Hour or so and the whole lot will go up. Not sure how much damage it'll do, but better it be destroyed than it ends up in enemy hands.'

Mace nodded dumbly. 'The Mireces are to our south, in the temple district.' He gestured and Crys followed his finger to see the new blooms of smoke darkening the sky.

'They're burning the temples?' he asked, his voice hollow. 'The temples?'

Mace's shrug barely rattled his pauldrons, he was so tired. 'Looks like it. Better those than the housing districts. Better the temples than a lot of places.'

Crys's lips were white but he gave a jerky nod of the head. 'Orders, sir?'

'First Circle is lost.' It didn't sound any better coming from his scratchy throat than it did in his head. 'We retreat, prop Second Circle's gates and start the defence all over again.'

The words tasted bitter, and he coughed into his hand. So thirsty. Crys saluted and stepped sideways. 'Where are you going?' Mace demanded. 'We need all hands to secure Second Circle.'

'If we're abandoning First Circle, we need to make sure the siege engines are disabled or destroyed in every tower, not just the gatehouse. Don't want them turning our own artillery on us.' He pointed. 'I'll nip up through First Bastion – they haven't quite closed it off yet – and make my way around. Could use some help, you've got anyone to spare.'

Mace closed his mouth and dabbed at the blisters again. *I should've thought of that. Father would've thought of that; he'd have ordered it done by now. He always could see the bigger picture.*

He waved Crys away. 'You find 'em, you can have 'em,' he said. 'Dancer's grace, Major, especially if you're going south.'

Crys grinned and, Mace would swear, winked. 'Don't you worry about me, Commander. Get safe in Second Circle and I'll see you in there in time for supper. Oi, Weaverson!' he called and the young lieutenant limped in his direction. 'We're surrendering First Circle, so we need to disable the engines in the towers.'

Mace saw Weaverson's face drain of blood. He didn't blame him one bit.

'Get a decent bunch of lads and head north, all right? North One and Two are yours, East Tower if you can make it, then get your arses into Second Circle and have a breather. You see any of ours on your travels, you send them inwards too.'

The youth brightened and Mace nearly smiled; the northern wall had seen precious little action throughout the siege. Not only were the towers in good repair, but no enemies had been spotted moving in that direction since the wall had collapsed. Chances were good they'd be unhindered and alive by the end of the exercise. More than could be said for Crys.

The pair separated and loped off in opposite directions. Mace supposed he should get up. *Father wouldn't be sitting here while everyone else did the work.* Durdil's dead face swam into his vision and Mace felt another flare of pain, from inside this time. *How did you keep going, Da? How did you never let anyone see your despair? Did you despair?*

'Incoming!' The shout was high and full of fear and it sent a message to Mace's legs that his brain hadn't been able to. He was up and running away from the gatehouse, out into the killing field, spinning to look up in the direction of the call. A rock tumbled through the sky, sailing over the breach and smashing into shrapnel on the flagstones a hundred strides from Mace. Men screeched as splintered stone cut into them in a deadly hail.

'Treb?' he bellowed, adrenaline narrowing his focus down to the threat and suppressing his grief in a surge of clarity.

'Treb,' came the confirmation. 'They're bringing her up to the wall for a better angle. She'll be loosing into Second Circle soon enough.'

'Bastards,' Mace muttered, staring along the wall. There was nothing they could do. The wall was falling; the catapults were shattered, burning or being destroyed. They had nothing to send back at it. 'Enemy on the breach?' Mace called up, focusing on a problem he might be able to solve.

There was a pause long enough for him to begin picking his way through the rubble in preparation to begin the climb. 'Couple hundred!' came the yell, strident and panicked.

Mace stared without seeing as he ran the numbers, soldiers poised for his order. Those were their mates up there, brothers in arms, family. Every single one of them wanted Mace to give a particular order. And every single one was terrified that he actually would.

'Can you hold?' he roared, fingers tight on the hilt of his sword. *If they say no . . . if they say no we're going to have to go up there.*

'Shit . . . yes, Commander. Yes, we can hold. How long?'

'As long as you can give us,' Mace shouted, 'but for fuck's sake give us some warning before you pull back.'

'Understood.'

Vaunt was at his side. 'The more men we send them, the longer they'll hold, sir.'

'The more men we send them, the more men we lose,' Mace countered, and though the words cut him he met Vaunt's gaze as he spoke. 'They're not coming down alive and they know it, Major. I'm sorry.'

'Permission to—'

'Denied.'

He gazed to his left, all the way down to First Bastion where Crys had disappeared and the wide sweeping left-hand curve of the city. The merchant quarter was around that bend. Merchant quarter sat next to the temple district, and he knew the Mireces were in there, working their way closer, burning and killing as they came.

Godsdamn enemy is everywhere now, tightening the noose. I've got the ideas and the plans, I just don't have the numbers any more.

'Vaunt, check the gate out of the merchant quarter is still locked. Then bar and prop it from this side. They make it through there and we'll be fighting on two fronts, so station a Fifty outside that gate with orders to send a runner as soon as they assault it. That'll be our signal to pull back into Second Circle, so make sure he's fast and loud.'

'Yes, sir.' Vaunt didn't move. 'And the Fifty on the gate?'

Vaunt was asking all the difficult questions today. 'If they can, they pull back and we cover their retreat with bows from Second Circle's wall. If not, they make sure they're not taken alive. I can't imagine the Mireces will have anything good in mind for prisoners.' He grabbed Vaunt's shoulder. 'Make sure they know.'

'Sir, how do we win this? I mean, once we lose the wall, we lose our way out.'

Mace spat, or tried to; his mouth was dry as bone. 'War of attrition,' he said. 'You weren't at the Blood Pass Valley, but the plan's the same. Kill them all. If they haven't the numbers to overwhelm us, we survive the day. And the next day. And the next. Whoever has the biggest army at the end wins.'

He gestured to the breach. 'That's why I can't reinforce those men. That's why I can't send anyone with Major Tailorson on his suicide mission. That's why I'm praying Carter and the Wolves are alive and make it back to us. We preserve numbers, we put weapons in the hands of the populace, and we kill those who stand against us.'

Vaunt licked cracked lips with a pale tongue. His throat clicked as he swallowed. 'I'll lead the men on the district gate.'

'Denied, Major. I need you with me.'

Vaunt sucked in a deep breath and then looked Mace square in the eye. 'It wasn't a suggestion, sir. You risk your life every day. Well, it appears I've learnt from the best. I'll bring them back, sir. You just hold the Second Circle gate on the King's Way; I swear we'll be coming through it.'

Mace blinked and then saluted Vaunt. 'I understand why my father had such respect for you, Major. Fight hard; run fast.'

'You know it, sir.' Vaunt dashed away, calling to the men lined up at the base of the breach. He gestured south, and Mace's heart swelled when the men snapped to attention, every one of them stepping forward to volunteer.

'These men,' Mace muttered to himself as they double-timed it past him, unashamed of the sting in his eyes. 'These fucking men. And women,' he added as Tara's cocksure, angry face flashed across his inner eye.

'Incoming!'

It was a different voice from the breach, startling Mace from his reverie, and he felt another little piece of his soul splinter away. He hadn't even known the first soldier's name, and he didn't know this one's. Didn't know his face or his family. Knew only that he'd called out a warning and Mace had left him to fight alone.

He ducked into the shelter of the wall and gave himself a mental shake. 'Get a fucking grip, Koridam. Time to make the old man proud.'

Threescore men made it down alive from the breach defences into the killing field, a wave of East Rankers and Mireces only strides behind. Second Circle's archers took most of them, but then the defenders turned at bay and fighting erupted again.

Mace wasn't willing to sacrifice those threescore men, no matter what he'd said to Vaunt. Without conscious thought or decision, he bolted out of the King's Way gate into the killing field and intercepted an Easterner with a spear, the weapon passing him so close it tore a hole in the leg of his trousers. Mace's shield broke the fucker's face and sent him over backwards, and then a small flood of his own hard-faced, grim-eyed West Rankers flowed around him and into the attackers.

West is best. The old adage had been disproved time and again over the last days as Palace Rankers, Personal Guards and even some of the City Watch did things that would earn them a commendation in any other conflict and now passed unremarked. Still, it was a comfort to see men he'd known and trained with for years surge around him like water round a boulder and take it to the enemy, in line and in step, parting to let the fleeing defenders through and then snapping shields together, an impenetrable wall.

The stingers positioned in the King's Way gate loosed, pinning men to the debris and scattering others like spilt salt. They all knew their orders; they all knew where they needed to get to if they were to stay alive, and with the fleeing defenders clear of the field and through the gate, Mace's line began shuffling backwards, in line and in step again, men behind guiding them, archers loosing from the walls, the stingers being wheeled inside for later use.

'Wait!'

Mace glanced left and then roared, 'Stand! Left flank friendlies. Stand!'

The shield wall stopped again and the enemy pressed forward, howling, some running to meet Vaunt and his sprinting Fifty – or what was left of them. More Mireces behind Vaunt – *they've broken through the district gate, we have to move* – and Mace ordered his end of the line to advance, pushing the enemy back and opening a path behind them straight to the gate for Vaunt and his men.

'Come on!' he bellowed, ducking a sword and thrusting back, catching the man a slicing cut through his scalp that sheeted blood into his eyes, blinding him. Mace knew better than to step from the line to end him, though every nerve in his body screamed at him to do so – one less man to face, one less threat.

Vaunt was fucking slowing, letting his men pass him, herding them to safety. 'Move your fucking arse, soldier!' Mace screamed. Instead, Vaunt stopped to help a man with an arrow in his guts, slinging his arm over his shoulder and dragging him forwards.

Mace lunged forward to help, but the shields to either side restrained him. 'Let me through,' he yelled, but they didn't.

'Fucking run!' came a shout from further along the line. 'We can't hold!'

'Going to kill you myself, Vaunt!' Mace added, though the labouring major needed no encouragement. His face was red with strain, the man in his grip grey but still conscious, mouth a straight line of agony as the arrow jolted in his guts with every limping stride. 'Thanks,' he panted as he passed behind Mace.

'Pull back,' Mace ordered and the line shrank from two deep to four, shortening and retreating at the same time until the rear ranks could slip through the gate to safety, those in the front line defending with increasing desperation.

Mace paused to cover the men flanking him as they ducked inside, and then a fist in his collar yanked him backwards with a strength he couldn't combat. He twisted in his captor's hands and saw Hallos, the burly physician wrestling him backwards. His free hand held a short club with a lump of iron on one end; Mace could see hair and blood caked into the metal.

'We need you,' Hallos growled. 'Alive.'

A dozen of his soldiers were still outside and they halted, an unbroken line of battered steel and weary flesh, winning the defenders enough time to slam the gates.

'Rilpor!' one yelled and the others took up the cry, stiffening the line and offering themselves to the enemy to ensure that others survived.

'No! Let me go,' Mace shouted, struggling, but Vaunt added his strength to Hallos's and Mace's view of his men was cut off just as the Mireces crashed into them. The line wavered, buckled and broke, overwhelmed by a sea of blue. A heartbeat later, the gate slammed shut, sealing them outside, sealing their fates.

'*No!*'

CRYS

Whose bloody stupid idea was this anyway?

Oh. Yeah. Mine.

The guard wall was chill against his cheek as, breath by breath, Crys lifted his head to see down into the temple district below. The wall was a mess of broken weaponry and scattered bodies. The Mireces had forced the tower doors, swarming inside and killing their way up to the allure and then along it as the multiple breaches destroyed the defenders' cohesion. Scores of the dead wore Mireces blue, but most were Palace, South and West Rank.

The catapult in South One had been intact and unguarded, so Crys had sawn through the rope connecting the throwing arm to the winch, then done the same trick with the candle and the pitch as he'd left in the gatehouse, wrestling some barrels into position as well. By the time the tower went up, he'd be long gone.

Parts of the long, wide temple district below were on fire,

like much of the city. The grand temple though, where the royal family went to worship, stood serene and intact beneath him and Crys felt a stab of worry. That's where they'd perform their sacrifices, washing the Light from the stone with blood. And Blood.

The thing inside snarled at that, and Crys felt a compulsion to throw himself off the wall and defend the temple. An urge he didn't think was his. *No. Patience.* He could feel the voice's resentment, but it held its peace and Crys focused on the men scurrying about below. No one was approaching either tower base, so he was probably safe for a while.

No, we're not. Behind.

Crys dived sideways without wasting time looking, and an arrow clattered off the stonework above his head.

'Captain Tailorson.' The voice sent tendrils of oily anger curling into Crys's gut, and he turned slowly, breath heavy and almost liquid in his chest.

'Major, actually,' he said. Galtas hawked and spat on to the allure. Dismissing the correction. 'Your missing eye the reason you can't shoot an arrow for shit?'

Galtas tossed the bow behind him. 'Just getting your attention,' he said. 'Didn't want you dying at someone else's hands, did I? Besides, your presence – your corpse, I should say – will be the perfect alibi.'

Crys shifted his feet and smiled. 'Treachery is like wine to you, isn't it? Sorry to let you down, though, but you're the one who's going to die.'

They drew steel at the same time, stalked each other along the allure, their only witnesses the dead.

'You sure?' Galtas asked with a wicked smile as he limped on a bandaged, splinted leg. He was slow. 'Your Wolf friend did.'

'Ash?' Crys laughed and the Trickster inside coiled in satisfaction. 'Ash isn't dead.'

Galtas frowned, clearly not believing him. He shrugged and his smile came back. 'Whatever you say. Your family is, though, I know that for a fact.'

His tone was so calm and casual that it took Crys a second, but when his brain caught up with his ears he stopped moving, stopped blinking, stopped breathing. 'What did you say?' he asked.

A broad grin smeared across Galtas's face. 'You know, considering Mara's had three children and one not that long ago – Wenna, your sister, right? Well, despite that, your Ma's surprisingly tight. You know, down there.' He gestured. 'Well, she was at the start.'

Crys swallowed puke and *felt* the yellow glow start in his eyes.

'Would not stop bloody screaming though. Mouth like a fucking fishwife. Had to take her tongue in the end, muffle some of the noise.' Galtas watched him intently and obviously saw what he wanted to in Crys's expression, because he nodded once. 'There it is,' he murmured, approving. He set his feet and waited.

Rage bubbled up in Crys's soul and spilt into every limb, tingling with ice and fire and overtaking the voice murmuring restraint. He screamed, one long bellowing cry as he ran at Galtas. 'Kill you,' he raged, spit frothing from his mouth. 'I'll fucking kill you.'

There was nothing of caution and little of finesse in Crys's attack. Blinded by tears and choking on fury, he threw himself at Galtas who, laughing, parried and thrust back, the blow screeching across Crys's chainmail. Crys pivoted on his right foot, out of the line of attack, and elbowed Galtas in the face with his sword arm. The man staggered, staggered again as his injured leg took his weight, his single eye glittering with sudden tears. He pulled a knife in his free hand, swept low and sliced it through Crys's thigh.

Crys howled and Galtas hopped back, fist on the guard wall to take the weight from his leg. Crys hobbled for Galtas and closed just fast enough to slam the knife out of Galtas's hand with his blade. His sword came back up to cut into the armpit, but the man stepped into his guard and grabbed his wrist even as Crys did the same. They strained, holding each other's swords at bay, both struggling on a wounded leg, panting into each other's faces.

'Fucking . . . bastard,' Crys grunted, and headbutted the taller man. Missed his nose, but the rim of his helmet split open Galtas's chin and rocked him back on to his bad leg. He stumbled, grip weakening for a second, and Crys managed to club him on the shoulder with the pommel of his sword.

Galtas dropped his head and rammed it into Crys's chest, breaking their mutual grip. The air blasted from Crys's lungs and in the second it took him to suck in more, Galtas disarmed him.

Crys leapt back again, his cut leg shaking and threatening to dump him on the stone. No weapons. He snatched the helmet from his head and used it to parry the next attack. All he could do now was defend.

No. Attack.

Crys ignored the voice. God or no, it clearly had no idea how to survive a fight like this.

Crys's heels came up against the low wall of a small redoubt built into the inside face of the wall. He threw himself into it and the skin came off his palms as he hit the ground and rolled, shoulder taking a battering from his armour, and then he came up facing Galtas again.

'Sword, spear, shield even . . .' he muttered, but the redoubt was distressingly empty of all but himself and a slumped figure cradling his own guts in his lap. 'Bollocks.'

Galtas lunged over the wall and Crys, roaring, battered the sword away with the helmet and then drove up, into Galtas's face, the crown of the helmet splintering a couple of teeth and knocking him backwards.

Crys scrambled over the low wall and on to Galtas, snarling like an animal. He knocked Galtas's sword hand away and got a grip on the helmet's rim with both hands. Straddling the prostrate figure, he smashed the helmet again into the man's face. And again: knocked the sword away with his elbow and hit him again. And again.

Hit him over and over, bash bash bash, until Galtas's face wasn't a face any more, was red and white and mush and splinters of bone and the twitching had stopped and Crys's arms were shaking with the effort.

And one more blow, because he could, because the bastard wasn't – could never be – dead enough for Crys.

Bash.

Crys was splattered in gore, the helmet dented and crusted with blood and hair and slimes of brain, and he threw it aside and forced himself to his feet. Chest heaving, he managed to spit on the corpse and stagger, groggy, for South Tower One.

Between him and it were three Mireces armed with bows and spears. Crys ran at them, nothing else for it. The archer loosed and on instinct Crys slapped the arrow out of the air. His hand spasmed in agony and as his arm came up again he saw the shaft had skewered the web between his thumb and forefinger.

He yelled in pain and ripped it free, using it to stab and gouge at the enemy. He knocked a spear aside as he barrelled into them, but they were three and he was one, and injured, and exhausted. A fist crashed into his jaw and he rocked back, punched in his turn and managed a glancing blow to the nearest spearman's cheek.

Something, spear butt maybe, drove into the back of his head and stole his strength and sight. He felt his knees, chest and then face smack the stone. And then he felt nothing.

Ash . . .

Crys couldn't quite tell if he or the thing inside opened his eyes and saw the world. He suspected both of them would react the same.

He was in the square outside the grand temple and there were bodies strewn across it like autumn leaves blown together, if leaves were bloody, torn and tangled. Some in Rank uniforms. Most in civilian dress. Men. Women. Children. Infants.

The sun's position told Crys he'd been out for a couple of hours, though whether that was long enough for anyone to miss him he didn't know. It wasn't like they could mount a rescue anyway, not here. There were Mireces everywhere, and trickles and dribbles of East Rankers were filing in from the merchant quarter, the killing field, the breach.

Mace has surrendered First Circle. Enemy'll be guarding the gates into Second, but enough can be here for . . . whatever this is.

That answers our question about a rescue then.

'Sire? Sire, he's awake.'

Crys grunted at the boot in his ribs, the pain triggering memories and hurts elsewhere. The rip in his hand was crusty with dried blood, the digits stiff and unresponsive. His leg was a sharp, throbbing, insistent hurt that pulsed in time with his accelerating heartbeat, and the back of his head felt as though someone was holding a burning coal against it.

A figure squatted in front of him, the sun behind him so Crys had to squint. 'Oh, it's you. Hello, Corvus. Killed any princes lately?'

The Mireces king put his head on one side. 'It's funny you should say that, though it wasn't my hand that did the killing, just like it wasn't with your beloved Janis.' He winked. 'But Rivil's dead.'

Despite everything, Crys felt an unexpected stab of pain. No matter what he'd done, Rivil had been his friend once, had favoured him and laughed with him, drunk and gambled with him. 'Who did it?' he asked.

'Our little friend and informant, the Godblind.'

'The god-what?' Crys's peripheral vision was attempting to count the numbers of the enemy, possible escape routes. Straight into the smoke-filled roads leading east was probably his best bet. He shifted, rolling on to his knees.

Cold metal pressed against the back of his neck. 'Easy,' a voice growled.

Corvus smiled. 'Don't worry, Valan. He won't hurt me, will you, Major?'

Crys managed a loose-lipped grin in return. 'Won't I? What makes you say that?'

Corvus stood, dark against the bright sky. 'Because for a start, neither I nor Valan will give you the chance, and second, because you've been promised to a friend of mine.'

Crys snorted. 'I can't imagine having anything in common with any friend of yours.'

'Oh, I'm sure you and Galtas will have a lot to catch up on. He's been most insistent – to the point of fucking boredom, if I'm honest – on two things: that we capture you alive, and that we give you to him. Seems there's some sort of blood feud between you.'

Corvus's words dried up as Crys began to laugh, choking

giggles halfway to being sobs jerking their way out of his throat. 'Galtas? Galtas is dead. I smashed his head in up there on the allure. I'd apologise but, you know, I'm not sorry.'

Corvus's pale eyes were unreadable. 'Did you now?' he said softly. 'Well, isn't it fortunate for us that we have other friends, like the Godblind, or Skerris and his Rank. Like the gods Themselves, here in Gilgoras.' He winked. 'I'm sure we can find someone to . . . deal with you as you deserve.'

'Deserve? I'm just a soldier, mate. Execute me and get it over with.'

'Sire, East Rank at the far gate, the one into the killing field,' a Raider called.

'They've taken the breach; the outer ring of the city is ours,' Corvus shouted. A cheer went up. He turned to Valan, who was busy tying Crys's hands behind him and threading a rope down and around his ankles so he couldn't stand. 'Second? How secure are we?'

'Good as we're getting, Sire,' Valan said, tugging the knots tight and then kneeing Crys in the shoulder so he toppled sideways. The side of his face slapped into the stone and he grunted as he felt his eyebrow open up.

'Safe to let them in?' Corvus asked the messenger.

'Aye, Sire. They've got prisoners, Sire.'

'Good. Open the gate.'

Crys waited in silence, his eye stinging with blood and dust, until shouts and curses heralded the arrival of the reinforcements and their prisoners. He rolled as far as his bonds would allow and lifted his head. The East Rank marched in, prisoners in their midst: soldiers, Personals, civilians.

Skerris and the Blessed One walked at their head. At her side stalked a man, ragged, blue-clad, skinny to the point of skeletal, but familiar. He turned a glazed, mad face in Crys's direction and Crys blinked. 'Dom?'

'Welcome, Blessed One, General. Skerris, I regret to inform you that it appears Lord Morellis is dead. Killed by his rival, in fact, Crys Tailorson, who we have captured . . .' Dom jerked and his head swung, ponderous and slow, in Crys's direction. 'What?' Corvus demanded.

'The captain of Rivil's honour guard?' the Blessed One interrupted. 'You're sure it's him?'

Corvus nodded and pointed. Crys pulled at the ropes binding his wrists, suddenly sure he didn't want to be under their scrutiny. Even Galtas would've been preferable to the animal expression on that woman's face.

'Sire, while you fought your way into the city, the Godblind provided some very interesting information about that man. You – go and make sure. If you're wrong . . .' She let the threat trail off.

Dom advanced on Crys, the Blessed One and Corvus following at a distance, the king curious, the woman cautiously delighted. Crys was overwhelmed with the sudden desire to run, struggling against the bonds. He squirmed backwards until he hit the wall of the temple, the skin peeling from his wrists in strips as he yanked and twisted against the ropes.

Dom dropped to hands and knees in front of him and crawled forward as silence fell over the square, scores of curious faces turned in their direction. Lanta, Skerris and Corvus came closer still, but Crys couldn't look away from Dom.

'Hello, Dom,' he managed. 'You look like shit. What's going on?'

'I'm the Godblind. I killed Rivil last night, and then the God of Blood came and ate what was left of him.'

Crys swallowed hard. 'Well,' he managed, 'how about that?'

Dom reached out and put his hand over Crys's mouth to quiet him. His eyes were brown wells of torment, right eyelid flickering, his gaunt face ablaze with need. He pulled the hand away and inspected it, licked the palm, and then pushed his face into Crys's and sniffed. Sniffed his mouth, his eyes, his hair, buried his face in the angle of Crys's neck, sniffed his chainmail, hands pawing at his clothes.

'The fuck is this?' Crys yelped, shifting backwards again. It was like being smelt by a dog that could tear your face off at any second. 'Dom? Dom, you crazy bastard, what are you doing? Get the fuck off me!'

Dom froze, his face a hair's breadth from Crys's, so close they could've kissed. A string of drool hung from his lip and then dropped on to Crys's chest. 'Splitsoul. God's eyes. Godlight.' He inhaled slowly, breathing Crys in, and then sat back on his haunches. 'Trickster.'

This is the beginning of our trial—

Shut the fuck up right now!

'Blessed One, Sire, he is the Trickster,' Dom said, his voice carrying across the square. 'He is the Fox God in mortal form. He is the godlight, leading his people into death – and back out of it.' He swivelled on his knees in the dust, looking up at Lanta's intent face; Corvus was frowning with confusion.

Dom reached out without looking and caressed the side of Crys's face, wiped his thumb through the blood from his cut eyebrow, and sucked it clean. 'Galtas is gone, but this one's fate remains unchanged. Kill him, and you win the war.'

TARA

Fifth moon, afternoon, day forty-three of the siege
Main hospital, Second Circle, Rilporin, Wheat Lands

'How can someone so small weigh so shitting much?' Tara groaned as she adjusted Dalli's weight over her shoulder. The other woman's hand knocked against her back with every wobbling, burning step, but the hospital was only strides away and healers were already running towards them with stretchers.

Hands reached for her. 'Easy,' Tara barked, 'gut wound.' They lifted her gently off Tara's shoulders and she half expected to be left with a string of intestines festooned around her neck, but the bandaging had held and, though Tara was wet with Dalli's blood and the Wolf was grey, she still breathed.

'How long?' a healer asked.

Tara glanced at the sun. 'I don't know. Hour or two?'

'Which, one or two?' he snapped.

'Did you see gut?' another asked. 'Was there a bulge?'

'Yes,' Tara said, bracing herself against a wall and

answering the one she could. 'Soaked the bandages in water and kept dousing them every time we stopped so the gut didn't harden.'

The healers exchanged a glance. 'Might be enough if we move fast.' They hoisted the stretcher and trotted for the hospital. Tara groaned and stretched the kinks out of her back before following them, breath whistling through her mouth and barely able to see through the swelling around her eyes.

She stopped at the hospital entrance and counted her warriors in. Walking, limping, slung over shoulders or on stretchers. Fewer than three hundred Wolves had made it this far. She put a hand on Ash's arm and stilled him and together they watched the rest file in, haunted.

'Talk to me,' she murmured when they were all inside.

Ash's face was expressionless. 'Lim was our chief. Despite his rashness after Sarilla was killed, his denial of Crys's . . . true nature, he was the best of us.'

Tara kept her face stoic. She'd seen a lot of good Wolves in the last months; her opinion and Ash's differed over Lim. But now wasn't the time for her famous lack of tact.

'And we had to leave him,' Ash went on, pushing sweat-lank curls out of his eyes. As his hand came away it touched the new scar, the dent in the jaw.

'He was dead,' Tara began.

Ash cocked his head. 'So was I,' he said quietly.

Tara scowled. 'Ash . . . they beheaded him. Crys couldn't heal that. No one could.'

'Suppose not.' His face was bleak.

She put her arm around his waist and squeezed. 'Let's go in, have a sit down, and then see how we can help.'

Ash had the ghost of a smile on his face. 'And for the love of the gods, get someone to fix that nose, woman. It's fucking hideous.'

Tara bit back a retort and gestured him inside, then turned and cast one final look up and down the road, lingering and suddenly reluctant to enter the hospital. Second Circle was locked tight, but Tara found she didn't trust anyone or anything these days.

Finally, she ducked in through the door and followed the corridor to the main room. Every bed was occupied, as were the spaces on the floor in between. Soldiers lay on stretchers on the floor; walking wounded queued up for treatment in a second, smaller room, while blood-curdling shrieks echoed from the operating room deep inside the hospital. Healers, apprentices, soldiers and civilians moved among the beds, administering water, changing bandages, feeding soup to the injured. Praying.

She found Mace sitting in a chair in the second treatment room, stripped to the waist, while a woman dabbed his burns and wrapped them. Tara spared a second to wonder where they'd even found fresh linen among all this horror. Then she noticed the embroidery around the hem and realised it was a lady's fine scarf. Seemed as though at least some of the nobles were prepared to help the war effort.

'Major Carter reporting for duty,' Tara croaked.

Mace looked up at her and his eyes widened. 'Bloody hell, Major, what happened to you?'

Tara touched a fingertip to her nose. 'You know, I don't even remember.' She tried to think, realised she was swaying gently, and put her hand on the wall again. 'Oh, yeah. It was Galtas. He was in the city. Gone now,' she mumbled as the room began to spin. 'Fucker.'

She was sitting on the floor, legs splayed in front of her and no idea how she'd got there. Mace crouched at her left, the woman to her right. 'Hello,' Tara said, knowing she was grinning stupidly and unable to stop.

'Hello,' the woman said, 'I'm Elissa Hardoc, Lady of Pine Lock. I think you could do with some food and water and a lie-down. What do you say?'

Tara pawed at her arm; then she patted her own face. 'Can you fix this?' she asked.

Elissa looked horrified. 'Me?'

'Tara.' She turned to look at Mace and he put one hand on the back of her head, grabbed her nose and wrenched it sideways. Elissa fell backwards, shrieking and flapping her hands, while Tara bellowed snot and blood and contemplated puking on him. After a long moment full of white lights and the peculiar almost-scent of pain, she dropped her head forward and let the blood run into her lap.

Now would be a really good time for hysterics, she thought, and gave it a moment's serious consideration.

'Lim died,' she said instead and Mace grunted, lowered himself to sitting.

'Gods. Lim. How?'

'Corvus. In the palace. We tried to hold them, sir, I swear, but there was just too many of them. We had to retreat, and then—'

'Corvus is in the city? Is that who's dug in in the temple district? Shit, if we can get him, this is over. How long ago?'

'Fought them in Fifth,' Tara mumbled. 'Fought them again in Third. Couldn't hold.'

Fresh tears ran, tears that had nothing to do with the pain in her face and everywhere else. 'Tried, sir. Can try again.'

Mace squeezed her leg. 'Not you. Take a breather, Major.' His voice was soft. 'Someone needs to attempt it, but the losses . . . How many more retreats before it becomes a rout? Or we run out of room to back into?'

'We blocked the tunnel to Fifth; they can't flank us, at least. They'll be coming from First Circle and nowhere else.'

'That's a mercy, I suppose,' Mace said, his tone dull with bone-deep weariness as Elissa patted at his burns again.

Tara swallowed a sticky mouthful of bloody mucus. 'About the losses, sir. Dalli's here. Gut wound. It's bad, sir.'

Mace lurched to his feet, reached down and hauled her up. Both of them rocked on their feet and fresh blood pattered on to the floor. Elissa made a noise, half concern, half disgust, and shoved a wad of material into Tara's hand. She clutched it on reflex.

'Where?'

'I didn't see where they took her, but I'd guess the operating—'

Mace was gone before she could finish the sentence. She watched him disappear, still naked from the waist up, his burns half treated, swathes of blistered, weeping red standing proud and raw.

'Lady Elissa,' Tara said, turning to the woman. 'Please take your bandages and your . . . whatever that is and follow the Commander. He'll be fussing over his future wife, but when he realises he's not allowed to help, he'll stay still. When he does, treat him. And don't take no for an answer. You're a noble lady; if he protests, remind him of that.'

Elissa's eyes were wide. 'He's to marry?' she breathed and her bottom lip wobbled. 'My dear, dear Ned fought today, you know,' and Tara could see her winding up for a story. 'He fell. Lord Hardoc of Pine Lock, he fell in First Bastion. A hero, they say, a true hero.'

Elissa sucked in a breath and dabbed at her eyes. 'I will honour his memory by doing all I can here,' she said before Tara could think up a platitude for a nobleman she'd never met but heard a couple of stories about. The woman gathered up the pot and the bandages, bobbed a curtsey as though Tara was the lady, and scurried after Mace.

'I . . . have no idea what's going on,' Tara mumbled, dabbing at her face with what was, she now realised, a silk stocking. 'Bloody hell.' She stuffed it into her sleeve and made for the table at the side, replete with pitchers of water and trays of bread and cooked meat. Her stomach warbled, reminding her she hadn't eaten that day, maybe, and she grabbed a jug and drank until she sloshed with every movement.

She'd taken her first bite of pork when Ash found her and she didn't like the look on his face one bit. 'What now?'

'Crys is missing. We need to find him.'

She blinked at him, and had another hard think about those hysterics as she chewed. 'How long and from where?'

'Apparently he went to disable the southern siege engines, stop them being used against us. He volunteered. This morning. No one's seen him since. He sent a spotty lieutenant to do the ones on the northern wall and he got back within an hour, but Crys has vanished.'

'He's going to be stuck on the wall with Mireces between him and us, isn't he?' Tara said. She stuffed more meat into her mouth, as much as she could manage without choking, and then shoved a few more slices under her vambrace for later.

'Probably. I'm sorry to put this on you, but there's no one else. The Wolves, we're done for a while, exhausted, and . . .' Ash trailed off and rubbed his face.

'They're not the only ones,' Tara mumbled and then patted his arm to take the sting out of her words. 'Gods, Mace is going to kill me. All right, let's go. He's too good an officer to lose, whatever else he may also be.'

'You're a good officer as well,' a voice said as she felt someone come into the room behind her. 'Lieutenant Weaverson. The spotty one,' he added and gave Ash a stare. 'With so many senior officers dead, I'd have to report it if you took matters into your own hands and went off without informing the Commander.'

Ash rounded on him, but Tara recognised the look in Weaverson's eye. 'Hello again, Roger,' she said. 'The antics in the palace whet your appetite, did they? Want to come with?'

Weaverson grinned. 'Lead on, Major,' he said. 'Six eyes are better than four, and Major Tailorson always treated me well. Least I can do now is watch his back.'

'And his front,' Tara muttered. 'If we die because of him, I swear I'll come back and haunt the bastard, Fox God or no.'

'Fox God?' Weaverson asked and then chuckled. 'Oh yes, the eyes.'

Tara and Ash exchanged a glance; clearly the rumour hadn't reached every corner of the city just yet. 'That's right,' she mumbled. 'The eyes.'

CRYS

The woman Lanta had taken seven of the captives so far and killed them, sacrificed them, *butchered* them while Crys waited bound on his knees in the centre of the square.

He'd thrown up as the first was killed even though he'd seen worse by now, so much worse. The woman died howling and writhing, bent backwards over a barrel and carved open. It was messy and fast, nothing like the sacrifice of Prince Janis that still gave him nightmares. As though Lanta was just warming up for the grand event.

Us.

The ground beneath the barrel was a red slurry of blood and piss and dust pooling on the stone, the sky fractured with screams as the crowd of prisoners shrank and the pile of corpses grew. Mireces were picking through the confiscated armour and weapons, while others checked the belts and hands of the dead for money pouches and rings. Scavengers. *Raiders.*

Lanta's blue dress had darkened to purple and black in

315

great sodden swathes, the cloth clotting about her legs as she chanted obscene prayers and slaughtered helpless men and women, even children, cutting hard and deep, opening the victims from sternum to groin while General fat fucking Skerris helped hold them down.

Dom watched, face bright with blazing exaltation, cackling at the screams. It was almost as bad as what Lanta herself was doing to the victims, seeing Dom so changed, so other. Almost.

What they're doing to them, what they did to Janis . . . will it be that bad? Crys had tried to avoid asking the question, telling himself he didn't want to know, but the screams were like rusty blades against his skin, pricking, scratching away at his will, his courage. The bones of himself.

The thing inside – he still couldn't bring himself to name it – shifted and stretched, sliding beneath his skin, an odd unknowable comfort.

Worse.

Crys blew out his cheeks and clenched his arse before he shat himself. *Fucking idiot. Never,* never *ask questions like that.*

His attention was snagged again by Lanta gesturing with a bloody hand at the prisoners. Bound hands were awkwardly raised to press fingertips to hearts and lips mumbled broken, desperate prayers as the Mireces moved among them, choosing.

'Convert or die, soldier,' Lanta said as they dragged the man, young Captain Lark of Crys's south wall command, towards the barrel. 'Embrace the Dark Lady and Gosfath, God of Blood, or suffer the torments of agony and death, the slow leaching of your life into the earth.'

She gestured and Lark's eyes rolled in their sockets as he strained to see the other bodies. Not all of them were dead yet, piled on top of one another, bleeding on to, into each other. Tangled in limbs and blood and the poison of opened bowels, suffocating under dead flesh.

'I am a child of Light,' Lark shouted into the woman's face. He aimed a gob of spit at her, missed.

'So be it,' Lanta said, unemotional.

'Dancer's grace!' Crys found himself shouting, before Valan kicked him between the shoulder blades and sent him face first on to the stone.

Lanta raised hand and knife and invoked her filthy gods, then slit the screaming man wide open, a great gaping red-lipped smile bulging with guts, a mouth teeming with frogspawn. The sweating Mireces lifted him off the barrel and tossed him on to the pile, intestines spilling out after him in a long, dragging mess across the stone. One of the men skidded in them as he passed, then kicked Lark right in the hole the knife had made in him. The strike ruptured something and blood gouted, flooded, flowed. Lark stopped screaming, then stopped breathing. A quicker death than some of the others.

It'll be me soon.

Us.

Me or us is still fucking me!

He didn't get a response to that. Crys pressed his eyes closed and inhaled through flared nostrils as Valan dragged him roughly back up on to his knees. 'Hey, Skerris,' he shouted to distract himself. 'Whatever happened to the North Rank? Why didn't they come?'

Skerris wiped sweat out of the folds of his chin. 'Sent them a commission of new blankets soaked in poison and left to dry. When they went to bed, blankets touched their skin and body heat and the braziers released poison vapour. None of 'em ever woke up. Five thousand men, gone.' He snapped his fingers.

'That's . . .' Crys trailed off.

'Inspired,' Lanta cut in. She beckoned with a bloody hand. 'Come, little fox. It's time.'

Crys grinned at her, bravado the only thing between him and soiling his linens. 'While it's a lovely offer, and you're a pretty woman in a terrifying touch-me-and-I'll-carve-you-open sort of way, I'm just not interested. Sorry. So if you could just untie me—'

Valan's fist crashed into his jaw.

If the last weeks had taught him anything, it was that the sound of a man screaming was enough to haunt the dreams of anyone listening. Trickster knew he'd made enough men scream on the long, bloody march from the Blood Pass Valley.

So now, though there was no one but enemies and prisoners to hear, he tried everything he could to hold them in. Even so, they roared and hiccupped and bellowed their way out of his throat, and every one of them tore a little splinter of Crys away and replaced it with something else.

No barrel for him to lie over, belly reaching for the sky, oh no. Lanta's ingenuity knew no bounds, and they'd nailed rings into the grand temple's oak door frame and stretched him by the wrists and ankles in its open maw. Stretched him so tight that the pain in his joints was almost worse than what was being done to him.

No, it really isn't.

Behind him through the open door yawned the peace of the temple, the quiet slap of water in the godpool, heard but unseen, its breath cool on Crys's naked skin. In front stood the Mireces and the East Rank, as many who could crowd into the square as possible to witness the death of a god.

Really not feeling too godlike at the moment, though at least they left me my linens. Be a fucking disappointment to all concerned otherwise.

Lanta stood in her bloodstained gown, her knife and hammer loose in her hands, watching with a small smile. She took no part in his torture.

'Why?' Crys gasped as Dom paused to catch his breath.

'I am the instrument of the gods,' Dom said, sucking at a split knuckle, cut on Crys's tooth. 'As are we all.'

'I'm not,' Crys grunted. 'I'm not an instrument.' He pushed his head forwards and did his best to glare at the calestar. The Godblind. 'I'm the musician.'

Dom clapped. 'I thought it would take you longer to accept,' he said, 'and yet here you are, proclaiming yourself divine before us all. Should I kneel?'

Crys spat bloody phlegm at him. 'I thought you only knelt to Blood these days? I thought the Dom we all knew and loved was a husk, dead inside. Of all the names people have given you, Darksoul shames you the most. That one's a stain you won't ever wash clean.'

Dom's mouth twisted and he picked up a chisel and hammer. Crys's head filled with the image of Janis, upside down, bollocks nailed to his arsehole. He put every ounce of strength he had into snapping his thighs together. They trembled, didn't move so much as a hair's breadth, and sweat popped out on his brow, leaked down his spine and into the filthy waistband of his linens.

Dear fucking gods, please don't, please. Hey, Foxy, you in here? You said worse but you didn't mean this, did you? Trickster? Tell me he's not going near my bollocks. Please?

No answer. 'Look, Dom, I'm sorry, listen, I'm sure we can come to some sort of arrangement, just, you know, man to man. It's a bit much . . .'

Dom looked at the hammer and then into Crys's face. 'Oh,' he said, and grinned. Then he chuckled, waving it about. 'Oh my, is that what you think?' He set the chisel against the inside of Crys's right leg. 'We've a long way to go before that, Fox God,' he said and, with a single blow, he drove the chisel underneath Crys's kneecap and popped it out of place.

Crys screeched, for the first time his voice moving up a register into the realm of screams. Pain exploded beneath his kneecap, fire racing into his toes and up into his groin, his belly. Nausea surged up his throat as he made out his kneecap sitting on the side of his leg.

This is our test, our trial. This is our forging, two souls into one. Together, we'll be unstoppable. If we live.

The voice in Crys's head had really helped, right up until those last three words. He let out a sound, half-laugh, half-sob, and Dom leant in close.

'Who are you talking to in there? Your brush-tailed friend?' He jammed stiffened fingers up under Crys's ribcage and lifted until Crys was howling. 'Come out, come out, little fox, or I start taking pieces that won't grow back.'

Crys made himself smile, though from the look on Dom's face it wasn't pretty. 'Did the Dark Lady teach you all this, too?' he asked. 'To take pleasure in others' pain? What do you think Rillirin will think when she learns what it is you've become? You—'

The words blended into a screech at the blinding, burning, searing pain in his hand. Dom held up a pair of slender tongs, a bloody fingernail clenched in their teeth. Crys roared, bobbing on a sea of hurt.

Funny how we tell the men in our command to be stoic when faced with pain, Crys thought in a not very funny way at all, revising his earlier opinion. *Why do we do that? What possible good would it do me to stop screaming? I like screaming. It reminds me I'm still alive.*

'Rillirin, yes,' Dom said, and for a second Crys saw sadness in his face. 'She's carrying my babe, you know. Conceived at the West Rank forts, back when I believed in happy endings. Back when they might even have been possible, if not for the choices we all made. Pity. Once they have the child, they won't need her.'

'You think Corvus will kill his sister?' Crys managed as the thing inside rumbled interest, pressed forwards.

'The Blessed One will, of that there is no doubt.' Dom gave a small shake of the head, but forestalled further conversation with a knife, flensing strips of skin from Crys's arms and chest until he bucked and roared and blood dripped from his toes on to the stone below.

'Getting tired?' Crys croaked through a raw throat when Dom paused to flex his hands and roll his shoulders. The Godblind casually punched him in the balls and Crys's world contracted, his eyes bulged and he didn't scream, but only because he couldn't breathe.

Endless seconds until he forced away the nausea, his body straining against the ropes. 'Wondered,' he gasped, 'wondered how long it'd take . . . before you . . . felt me up.' He puckered split lips and kissed the air.

Dom disappeared behind him and Crys chanced a glance at his audience again: Corvus's cool amusement, Lanta's white-knuckled intensity, the jeering laughter of the warriors.

Dom's finger poked into the ragged slice in the side of Crys's thigh, eliciting another roar, and then his forearm came around his throat and began to squeeze. Crys gladly gave himself up to darkness.

More time had passed; he didn't know how much. Everything hurt. Everything *hurt*. And despite his jabbering pleas to the thing inside to come the fuck out and kill everyone in the square, himself included if necessary, something else gathered close, a brooding darkness at the edges of his vision, a sound like madness beneath his bellows and screams.

'Time to wake up, Fox God.'

'What?'

Dom leant in close and pressed a kiss to Crys's cut eyebrow, tender, almost loving. 'Time to wake up.'

'What are you doing, Godblind?' Lanta demanded, moving swiftly to Dom's side and yanking at his arm.

'I brought Him,' Dom said, glancing at Lanta but pointing to Crys. 'He comes and so does She.' He looked back at Crys. 'Time to wake up, Fox God. Time to meet your new mistress.'

'Wake up,' Dom repeated, and then clutched at his head. 'My love, my love,' he called, 'He's here. I found Him. I found the Trickster for you.'

The sky darkened and a cold wind blew, a sudden howling gale that swept around the temples, whistling down the roads, stirring the hair and clothes of the sacrificed.

Crys boiled with sudden heat, sudden fury as something, *Someone*, shimmered into being between Dom and Lanta and they fell to their knees before it.

All around the square, soldiers and Mireces knelt and pressed their faces to the stone. Even the prisoners were felled by the appearance. She was the most beautiful, the most terrifying woman Crys had ever laid eyes upon. Lanta was an angry, petulant child in comparison.

An uncomfortable lust rose in Crys when She swept Her gaze across him. He felt his mouth dry under that flat, reptilian regard. She approached, flashes of thigh and belly through Her dark, smoky robe, until She stopped close enough that Crys could smell Her. Taste Her on the wind. Musk and madness.

She extended a finger and pressed it to his chest, the nail

sliding easily through the skin into the flesh beneath, blood dribbling. Cold and heat chased each other through his body and Crys was horrifyingly aware of his burgeoning erection.

Ash, I love Ash. Think about Ash.

She chuckled, as though She knew exactly what was going on in his head. 'The Trickster in a mortal's flesh.' She leant in so close Her breath tickled his face. 'Those eyes.' Her tongue darted out impossibly far, impossibly fast, and tasted his blue iris. Crys jerked and blinked, the thing inside growing angrier.

Now's the time, Fox God. Now is really the fucking time.

The Dark Lady turned Her attention on Dom. 'You have done well, my love,' She said.

Crys watched, sickened, as Dom stood and stroked Her cheek. 'I live only to serve you,' he said. 'This is my gift to you, my love. One of your greatest enemies, bound and helpless and at your mercy.'

This time when She looked at him, there was such hunger in Her eyes that Crys writhed with the animal instinct to flee. 'Then let us pull the little fox free,' She said, licking Her lips and reaching for the ropes binding Crys, 'and have some fun.'

Shouts erupted from the eastern end of the district, and moments later from the western. 'Attack,' came the call, 'full attack on the gates!'

The Dark Lady snarled Her frustration and snapped the ropes holding Crys, dragged him free and clutched him to Her chest like a doll.

Finally, finally, the thing inside Crys began to move.

DOM

The earth was salted with blood and the sky wept and men died and Dom had his love by his side. It was beautiful. It was perfect.

The Fox God was struggling to escape, but the Dark Lady was enraptured with Her new toy. The possible futures shifted and aligned into new patterns in Dom's head as the assault on the gates drew more and more men from the square. Patterns if the Mireces won, patterns if they lost, patterns if the Fox God died, patterns if He lived . . . all flowing and sliding over each other like plates of ice on a winter pond.

The images stole his vision and he flailed for the Dark Lady, for the heat of Her skin and the fire of Her touch. 'It's all changing,' he gasped, one hand on Her, one on the Fox God, 'everything's changing second by second, death by death. The future hanging from the tip of a sword. I can't see. I can't . . . I can't see.'

His voice crept up into a terrified squeak and She was there, soothing him, cupping the back of his skull in one hand, the other holding the Fox God by the throat. 'Hush, little calestar,' She murmured. 'Hush. Your work is nearly done.'

'Are you there?' he asked, gripping Her forearm. 'Can you help me?'

He heard Her chuckle, the sound like maggots in his head. 'I can, yes,' She said. 'The question is whether I will.'

She shoved him away and Dom was bereft, weeping, blind with visions. He heard the Fox God cry out in terror and pain shivered through his head, his right eye.

'Time to wake up, Fox God!' he screamed, the force of it clearing his sight. Crys was on his knees, the Dark Lady's hands pressed either side of his skull, squeezing.

'No,' Crys said with the voice of a god, even though the pain in his skull must be monstrous, 'it's time for you to wake up. Calestar.'

The words silenced the whirling chaos in Dom's head, and the blue eye of the Fox God burnt into him as he met its gaze, scouring him clean as everything fell away but the shining silver light and the warmth, the joy and the utter love. For the first time in months, for the first time in years, nothing ate away at the edges of him and he was still. Just still.

I forgive you, He said, the words echoing clear in the godspace in Dom's head, *and I love you. I am awake, and I waken you in turn. You know what you need to do.*

Dom breathed in the scent of flowers, the tang of lightning. The storm raging inside shivered and fell away. 'Stop, my love. Stop.'

The Dark Lady held the Fox God's jaw open, Her other hand forcing between His teeth and down His throat to pull Him from His fleshy host. The man surrounding the godseed writhed and choked, hands pulling at Her wrists, helpless.

Dom could see his throat swelling, veins standing proud in his temples.

'Stop,' Dom said again.

The murderous glare She turned in Dom's direction nearly buckled his knees, but he forced himself on.

'I've done everything you've ever wanted. You know I love you? You know, don't you? I've killed for you, hurt people for you, given you every secret I hold and given them gladly. For you. To you.'

The Dark Lady was impatient, but She allowed Dom to slide his arm around Her waist, holding the Fox God a little looser, allowing Him to breathe. 'I know,' She murmured. 'But now is not the time to demand a reward.'

Dom smiled. 'You know I could never demand anything from you, my love,' he said, voice cracking. 'I only ask you to forgive me. I do love you, more than you will ever know, but everything else was a lie.'

A frown marred the Dark Lady's perfect features as Dom tightened his grip on Her waist, pulled the dagger from his belt and stabbed Her in the heart.

There was nothing in Dom's world except Her. Beautiful, terrible, mocking, clever Her. Arrogant Her, who couldn't conceive that there might be anything left in him She hadn't seen. One tiny silver shining shimmer of Light in a sea of Blood. A light Dom had thought guttered long ago, but which had sparked in the Fox God's presence, its brightness hidden in His reflected godlight.

Even so, it shouldn't have worked. It was impossible. You couldn't kill a goddess with a knife. And yet . . . as Her hands fell slack in disbelief, the Fox God surged off his knees and kissed Her on the mouth, swallowing Her scream. *Drinking* Her.

Silver light and black light billowed upwards in a vortex that blinded Dom and pierced the clouds. The silver light surrounded the black in a shining net and drew it back down. Down into the Fox God.

The Trickster broke the kiss and fell back, choking, retching and racked with pain. Black lines ran from His mouth up to His eyes, down His bulging throat. Black lines chased by silver as the essences fought for control of the flesh.

There was another sheeting, discordant blare of black light, so bright She was outlined by it, and Her second scream, unconstrained by the Fox God's mouth this time, burst Dom's eardrums and blasted from their feet every child of the Dark Path within hearing.

And pain, oh gods the pain, as every pulse of the raw energy that made Her divine, that She'd stolen from the Dancer so long ago and claimed and twisted and warped for Herself, arced from Her through the knife and into him.

They collapsed together to their knees, the Dark Lady keening and Dom convulsing with black lightning. He could feel blood running from his eardrums, could smell scorched flesh as his hand, melted to the knife hilt, blackened into a claw. His vision smeared as his eyes boiled in his head.

'But . . . but you love me,' She said, Her voice small, disbelieving and, slowly, scared. Her fear cracked his heart into pieces. Her eyes were gold and filling with black blood, streaking down Her cheeks like lines of ink. It ran from the corners of Her mouth, obscuring Her words, pumped steadily from around the blade, hissing like snakes as it fell to melt the stone beneath Her and stain his arm.

Her pain crashed in waves of emotion so strong it knocked weapons from hands, burst eardrums, ruptured hearts. Scores died and hundreds more were driven past the edge of madness and still She lived. Suffered at his hand, Her pain his torment, Her fear his eternity.

Oh, my love, forgive me. Forgive me, please. I love you I love you I love you.

Dom was pain personified, pain perfected, pain distilled into its purest essence. A gibbering, writhing wreck of a man. Her eyes were entirely black now, and he couldn't see past the blood to the expression they held. And still he loved Her. He always would.

The Fox God wrapped Dom in His arms and pulled, breaking Dom's fingers to free him, and then wrestled him away, the black lightning flickering over Him without harm.

'*No!*' The loss was so profound that, despite the agony, Dom struggled to reach for his love. To take it back, to apologise, to tell Her again that he loved Her. To ask to go with.

The Fox God cradled him against His chest and murmured words he had no ears to hear, while a great sucking, howling vacuum rushed around them with the noise of a million screaming sacrifices.

At its centre the Dark Lady.

At its centre pain and avarice and a lust vaster than the world. She arched Her spine, hands even now trying to cup the blood and press it back inside. Her mouth opened impossibly wide and every one of Her teeth curved backwards like a snake's. She screamed like the death of innocents, like *She* was innocent, a scream that shattered Dom's heart into a million weeping pieces and which he echoed with every fibre of his being.

And then She burst.

THE BLESSED ONE

Fifth moon, afternoon, day forty-three of the siege
Grand temple square, First Circle, Rilporin, Wheat Lands

Lanta wept. She knelt on the stone, dragging the black stains of the Dark Lady's blood on to her arms and face, and she wept with all the broken-soul intensity of a bereaved parent, a lost child, a betrayed lover. Her goddess, her guiding light, her beautiful Bloody Mother . . .

The Dark Lady had been here in the real world that was Her divine right, terrible and beautiful and powerful and . . . screaming. Bleeding. Dying.

Time had passed. She didn't know how much, but the sun stood still in the sky, looking down with infinite sorrow on the dead, the dying and the deranged. Corvus was there, on his knees by a pool of puke, hands clawing at his hair, his cheeks, fingernails cutting bloody runnels in his skin. Lanta's grief swelled again.

What had happened? *How* had it happened? Lanta still had the after-images of the . . . the vanishing seared into her eyes, the fluttering black flags of lightning arcing crazily across the square, ripping the life from those they touched but not enough, nowhere near enough to restore Her to life, before a final blast and She was gone.

Gone.

There was no lore, no history to explain what she'd witnessed. It was impossible, and yet it had happened, and Lanta knew exactly who was to blame for it. And yet . . .

And yet she lay on the stone and she wept.

At either end of the district was the sound of slaughter. Not battle, not the clash of weapons and the roars of the fighters, but slaughter. Not even pleas for mercy. The Mireces and East Rankers were being murdered where they lay in their grief. It meant nothing.

The Fox God and the Godblind slumped nearby, dazed, and Lanta knew that they should be punished, tormented over days and weeks and months for their crimes. And though she knew it, for the first time in her life, she hadn't the will to see it done.

'Mother,' she sobbed, holding hands black with divine blood to her lips and eyelids, smearing it across her cheeks and down her chin in looping swirls. 'Mother, come back. Come back, I beg you.'

There was no response, nothing but the howling void of loss and the black rot of hysteria creeping in around the edges of her mind. It would be so easy to just give in, the way she could see hundreds of the faithful doing, tearing at themselves and each other with fingers, with knives and arrow heads, carving themselves open in the hopes their blood might summon Her back. Even Corvus, rocking on his knees with a knife slashing at his forearm, stuttering, roaring howls tearing out of his throat. Many cut and cut and cut too deep, arterial blood red against blue sky and white stone and black loss.

'No.' It was a whisper, mumbled through lips stiff with grief. 'No, I don't believe it. I don't believe She's gone.' Lanta glanced again at the Godblind, sobbing with uncontrollable loss in the Fox God's arms.

'No,' she said louder and Corvus looked up. '*No!* I do not accept it!'

She traced whorls down her throat and across her collar-bones with the black blood, tore off her sleeves and continued the patterns down her arms, acting on pure instinct, a lifetime of devotion. She pulled up her skirts and traced patterns on her legs and over her belly, down under her linens.

'Dark Lady, beautiful goddess of fear and death, I offer you this body, that you might live again. God of Blood, of war and mutilation, I offer myself as your consort, that your Sister-Lover might live again. Red Gods, I worship you. Dark Lady, beautiful goddess of fear and death, I offer you this body, that you might live again . . .'

Lanta lay on her back in the blood, ignoring the chaos, and she summoned her will to conquer the madness and fear, and she searched. Somewhere far away, wounded and in pain, feeling abandoned, the Dark Lady might be hiding. Not dead, just . . . gone. Yearning for Her children. Perhaps even afraid.

Figures shuffled towards her, Corvus, Skerris and Valan, war chiefs and officers, Raiders and soldiers, their voices torn with weeping, halting along with hers. None of them touched the black blood. Behind them, the Godblind mouthed the words as well while at the edges of the plaza, the enemy slunk, scenting blood.

Lanta closed her eyes; they were irrelevant. She had one task and one only and she would see it done, no matter the cost.

The voices around her cracked and then swelled, adding

power to her power, and Lanta felt her soul tug free of its moorings and tumble through Rilpor, through Gilgoras, and past the tattered veil.

There. Just about. Not the loving embrace, but the hungry one. *It's a start. A good start. From Him to Her, perhaps.*

'Holy Gosfath, God of Blood, lover of war and death, come to me. Use me to guide you into the world, to walk where your Sister-Lover so briefly did. Come for vengeance, Holy One, come for justice. Blood and more blood shall be yours. Theirs and ours, if you will it.'

She raised her arms to the sky, back arching with need and strain. 'Holy Gosfath, I summon you to war,' she shrieked. 'Wreak bloody fucking destruction on them all!'

The clouds that had presaged the Dark Lady's arrival darkened again, roiling above the plain. Thunder muttered. Lanta lay still, arms up, sacred blood soaking through her gown, warm and sticky against her back and arse and thighs, like the leavings of a messy lover. Tears trickled from her eyes and her heart and soul bled, but still she strained, beckoning, coercing, her will a guiding light that could not be denied as her acolytes continued the prayer around her and the Wolves crept closer, swords bright with faithful blood.

Pain seared Lanta's skull and she screamed, offered the hurt to Him if only He would come.

All this and more, Lord. My body to restore Her, my will bent to your desire. More sacrifices than you have ever seen before and your Sister-Lover in your arms again. Come to me, Red Father, come and kill!

The clouds were black and blotted out the afternoon sun, and in their roiling a shape formed, crimson as sunset and bleak as disease. Shouts of alarm from the attackers told her they saw Him too and now she opened her eyes and looked in awe and wonder on what she had done.

As tall as the sky, with mountain goat horns curling from His head and black talons tipping each finger, Gosfath, God of Blood, bulled through the tatters of the veil and into Gilgoras. He came roaring His pain and loss and world-breaking rage. All across the sky within reach of His voice, birds fell dead.

Lanta felt a manic giggle swell in her chest as she climbed to her feet. The faithful around her rose as well, turning to face the god and the Wolves ranged in front of Him, their horrified gazes snared by His presence.

Gosfath's strength is in His impulses. He is the jealous one, reminding us that the world is cruel and senseless and death is arbitrary. He can rape the whole world if only it will bring Her back to me.

I care not.

'Welcome, Lord,' she shouted, a hard wind whipping her hair and gown behind her. It whined through the streets and buildings of the temple district, stinking of rot and whispering through the Dancer's sanctuaries as silent as plague.

'Your Sister-Lover, our Bloody Mother, the Dark Lady Herself, is dead. Murdered! Will you take vengeance on those who dared to raise a hand to Her? Will you spill their blood as they spilt Hers?'

Lanta was drunk on power and insane with grief, the blood of a goddess fizzing on her skin and warm as lust upon her tongue. She revelled in Gosfath's slow, calculating regard. She smelt of His Sister and knew a flicker of delicious fear. His appetite was well known. The love of a god. How blessed she would be to die in such a way.

'Lord, Father, he is here, both of them are here! The ones you seek, the killers. See?' She flung her hand towards the Godblind and the Fox God, and Gosfath bared white fangs and stepped into the city, crushing walls and buildings beneath His feet, shrinking to twice man-height as He came.

His shadow blasted the life from everything it touched and left disease and rot strewn in its wake. He pushed through buildings and walls, smashing stone from His path as He neared, scattering allies and enemies alike with great sweeps of His hands. He came for vengeance, and it would be terrible.

Every Mireces and East Ranker stiffened and howled as the god's bloodlust infected them. Lanta felt it herself, an almost overwhelming urge to pick up a knife and kill. Kill everyone, everything that stood between her and her gods. She resisted, barely, and only because Gosfath needed her, His presence anchoring her to her duty.

The men around her felt no such restraint. Roars of pure fury burst from throats, dragging the attention of the Wolves away from the god, and battle erupted across the square, the true believers squandering their lives with no thought of defence, their only desire to take as many of the enemy screaming into death with them.

They would not stop. They could not. They would have red fucking slaughter and the city would drown in it.

From the corner of her eye, Lanta saw the Fox God climb to His feet, dragging the Godblind up and pushing him gently away. She smiled. Her own power was great, but the power of the Trickster would do even more to open a channel for the Dark Lady's return, if they could but harvest it.

'Yes,' she called, 'yes, Father. Him,' she pointed. 'Kill Him, the Fox God, and then kill them all. I will deal with the Godblind cunt.'

Lanta held back her hair as the wind howled and Gosfath smashed through the last wall between Him and the Fox God. So close Lanta could feel the electricity playing across

His skin, the waves of His divine fury, divine need. Her own needs rose to match His, bloodlust and fucklust like nothing she'd ever felt before, so hard and hot she nearly buckled.

The Fox God stepped forward in the wide square.

Lanta licked godblood from her palm, felt it ricochet through her limbs and pulse in her ears and heart and womb; then she raised her hands palms up to the sky and threw back her head. 'Blood rises!'

DOM

The wind tasted of sulphur and rot, black and cold against the sweat on his face, the thing that used to be his hand.

The stone rocked beneath his feet, blasted, cracked and as desolate as time. Black light burnt in his eyes, obscuring his surroundings, and black wind howled in his ears, smothering all sound.

His body was heavy, rooting him to earth, and yet weightless, straining into the sky. He didn't know if he stood or floated, didn't know if he breathed. If he lived.

There had been something inside him once, but now it was gone. He thought it might have been his soul, but such words and concepts didn't exist any more. Empty, he understood. Pain, he knew that too. There wasn't anything else.

He couldn't remember his name, or where or why he was. Just pain and emptiness and the blackness, in his eyes, in his ears. In him. The wind blew, and the black light burnt,

336

and he existed at its core, in its very heart, a spinning fragment of consciousness in a vortex of madness.

His mouth was open now, the rotten tempest howling past his lips and teeth and down his throat, poisoning him with its taint. Straining to fill the emptiness and failing. Too much emptiness, so much he could drown in it with just a little effort. Just a step.

'Why?'

Hands on him, pawing, slapping, shaking. He felt them rain against him, distant as hope, heard the slide of a knife drawn from leather.

'*How could you?*'

Sobbing now, the sound skating into his ears on the back of the wind, the sobs sliding into his throat, oily. Another's pain for him to choke on, to swallow down into his bones, corrupting. The sharp bright sting of parting flesh high on his cheek; he blinked, embracing the pain, welcoming it as the slightest anchor of mind to flesh.

'You loved Her.'

A flicker within now, something other than pain. Something so huge it surely couldn't all be contained within, not unless his insides were as vast as the night sky. A frown creased his face, the edges of his awareness lightening further. He came back to the earth and himself, knowledge of feet on stone, the weight of his body dragging and the slow throbbing agony in his left hand, dead and wrong.

He blinked again and then he saw. A woman stood before him, coal-coloured loops and swirls decorating her skin in sigils of power, runes of magic and summoning. Dark magic, black power, and the bright lunacy of loss burning in her face.

'You loved Her,' she repeated, her tone broken and uncomprehending, and the vast emptiness within roared its denial and its lust for obliteration.

She raised her knife and though he wanted to open his arms to welcome the blade, he reached out instead and seized her throat, squeezing, shaking, slamming her to the ground before she could give him back his name and everything that surely must go with it. The knife skittered from her grip.

Gods fought behind her and he turned away. He couldn't look back; the gods' presence threatened to remind him of something that would tear him apart and he refused to acknowledge it. Not now. Not ever.

Legs unsteady beneath him, he staggered from the square, leaving the madness of battle, taking the emptiness of loss. Behind him, broken and alone, the woman sobbed.

CRYS

Gosfath was tall and muscular and bright red. He was unarmed, if you didn't count the horns and the talons, and he was naked but for a short kilt, the slabs of His face carved from cruelty and a terrible lust. Crys was pretty sure his own weapons would be more than useless against Him, despite the lack of armour.

His memory of what had happened with the Dark Lady was vague, hazy, but one thing was certain: he wasn't going to be kissing the God of Blood.

Throw them away. The weapons, get rid of them. They're not going to do us any good.

Crys ignored the voice and launched a flurry of attacks with the knife and metal poker he'd taken from the torture table, roaring as his relocated kneecap crunched and popped. He swung the iron rod hard into Gosfath's upraised forearm, waiting for the greenwood crack of splintering bone. The poker bounced off the arm with a sound like a tuning fork, numbing Crys's hand, already slippery with blood. It slid from his grasp.

Happy now?

And the knife. Just do it. What use is it going to be anyway?

Dom stabbed Her; I can stab Him. Stands to reason.

He didn't wait for an answer, throwing himself up and forward, blade aiming for the baleful eye. Gosfath caught him around the throat with one hand, talons puncturing into the back of his neck. Crys slashed at the arm, at the chest he could just reach, at the face. It was like trying to score granite, the blade making no impression.

Well, that's just not fair.

He's the Lord of War, what did you expect?

Gosfath's mouth opened wide, so wide, His pointed black tongue flicking towards Crys's face. Crys swung again, a wild, desperate slash that sliced through the tongue's tip and sprayed him with black blood.

Gosfath roared so loud it was a physical pressure, and then Crys was slamming into the stone and Gosfath had both hands pressed to His mouth. His eyes flared brighter and His roar was a heady mix of rage and pain.

Well done. That's exactly what we were trying to avoid.

What, hurting Him? Crys asked as he scrambled backwards, searching for another weapon and feeling the hot leak of blood between his shoulders.

No. Pissing Him off, the voice said and Crys looked back just in time to take a palm the size of his ribcage straight in the face. There was a moment of bleary confusion as he flew through the air, limbs flailing, before impact with the temple wall sent a series of cracks through his neck and back.

Crys screamed as agony filled him, there and then gone just as fast, replaced with a long, awful moment of absolute absence when he couldn't feel anything at all, and then a steady, dull ache deep in his bones accompanied with a blinding flare of silver light. He gritted his teeth and lifted his arm, waiting for the pain, but there was nothing. He could move. The Trickster emanated a profound smugness entirely at odds with their predicament.

Gosfath was strutting before him like a triumphant bully, and Crys was more than happy to let Him prance as he checked escape routes again.

The god's rage bounced from Crys's skin like dull hammer blows, but it seemed to penetrate the Mireces and East Rankers, driving them into an even deeper frenzy, barely human now, all bloody teeth and wild eyes and clawing fingers and bright, sharp weapons. All across the square were fierce battles and indiscriminate slaughter, as the defenders who'd stormed the gates found themselves beset by madmen spending their lives without restraint.

The Dark Lady's death and Gosfath's presence – His pissed-off presence, we might add – enflames Their followers. Her loss fills them with agony; His rage directs that agony into violence. They won't stop until every Rilporian is dead.

Let's distract Him, then. Crys pushed himself upright, cast away the knife and raised his fists. Gosfath laughed, clapping His hands at the delicious joke. Crys didn't much blame Him.

Well? Throwing away the weapons was your idea. What now?

Now we use our other gifts.

We don't have any— He yelped as his feet began to move and he ran straight at Gosfath, his body not entirely under his control any more. He was screaming, and as he dashed across the square, silver light burnt all around him. Coming from his skin, from *inside* his skin. Radiant.

Gosfath's laughter dried up, His eyes narrowed and He set His feet to accept the attack. Again Crys leapt for His head, again Gosfath reached for Him, but as the silver light touched His red skin, the god howled and snatched His hand away. Crys smashed into Him and they went down together, Gosfath's roars becoming squeals as the light burnt wherever it touched.

'Ha!' Crys screamed in His face, punching anything within reach, knees pumping against the stone-hard stomach. He lunged and sank his teeth into Gosfath's cheek and, though not even a knife could cut Him, they sank through the skin into the flesh below. As though his teeth were . . . different. A predator's. Hot blood washed into Crys's mouth, bitter as gall, and Gosfath bucked and squealed again, tried to throw him off.

Crys's fingers were hooked into claws and tearing at Gosfath's throat and chest as he shook his head from side to side, doing his best to bite the god's face off. His light was growing brighter and he was getting stronger, he was sure of it, but then Gosfath gave a mighty heave and tore his face from between Crys's jaws, grabbed him by the shoulders and hurled him away.

Crys twisted in the air and landed on his hands and toes, spitting blood and astonishingly unhurt. 'I'm winning,' he gasped, and then the poison in Gosfath's blood reached his brain and he collapsed, thrashing on the stone, writhing as fire burnt inside his veins and froth bubbled in his mouth, as his heart was held in a steel gauntlet and squeezed and his skin became too small, too tight, too hot.

Head jolting and already weakened from absorbing the Dark Lady's tainted divinity, he only saw in flashes as Gosfath rolled to His feet, face healed, burns from the light healed, and grew in size until He stood as tall as the southern towers which were His sudden focus. Around them, the fighting reached a new pitch of intensity. Citizens were hurled from the walls or beaten to death against the stone, Rankers fighting a desperate holding action and still being pushed back, Mireces soaked in blood howling madness in their faces.

The Afterworld come to Gilgoras. Muscles bunching beneath His skin, Gosfath grasped South Tower One in both arms and began to pull, clearly planning on crushing everyone in the square and not just Crys.

Crys managed a stuttering wail of pain as the thing inside went to work against the poison. *We are Trickster,* it said. *And it is in our nature to deceive. Watch.*

The tower began to rock and move and Gosfath was bellowing rage and joy at the imminent destruction of His foe, talons scoring deep into the stone of the tower. Crys's spasms lessened to twitches and he managed to roll on to his belly, force himself up to his knees, but there was no way he was getting further than that. That tower was coming down on top of him and there was nothing he could do about it. He doubted if even the presence inside could heal him once he was a red smear on the stone.

We need to get out of . . . Crys began, but the thought faltered as a sudden bloom of yellow seared his eyes. The whump of explosion came a heartbeat later, and Crys had a vivid image of the candle he'd left in a pool of pitch beneath South One's catapult, fire barrels stacked high all around with small holes hammered into their bases. That really was a lot of pitch, he realised belatedly. A whole lake of it, slowly filling the platform.

The explosion blew the tower to pieces and took Gosfath with it, hurling Him backwards, over the walls of both First and Second Circles, to smash down somewhere in Third. Debris rained across a quarter of the city, shrapnel whining overhead, people screaming as they faced the twin foes of enemy weapons and falling stone.

Crys rocked backwards and reached his feet, staggered as the world spun around him and vanished in plumes of dust and smoke, and then found a semblance of balance. He gazed around in bewildered triumph, shaking his head to stop the ringing in his ears. 'Is He dead?'

What do you think?

'Then I need to find Him. End this. Somehow.'

Not a fucking chance. That brought Crys to a halt. *We need to go. Right now.*

'Why?' Crys asked, looking for the shortest route through the chaos to Third Circle.

Because now we've really *pissed Him off.*

Gosfath brought His fists down on the tall, elegant spires of the goldsmiths' guildhouse deep in Third Circle's jewellery district, smashing them flat, before kicking holes in the wall through into Fourth Circle, a monstrous child destroying a mud castle for no other reason than that He could.

Thousands were dying: soldiers, civilians, children of Light and children of Blood. Gosfath made no distinction, lost in an orgy of violence and braying His challenge to the sky.

This is the worst idea I've had in a long history of bad ideas. The fact that it went against the express advice of the voice made it even worse.

Crys ducked through the chaos of battle, sliding through diminishing gaps, rolling past swords and axes, a judicious elbow or foot here and there to trip a Mireces and provide the defenders with a chance.

'Run,' he shouted as he passed a knot of hard-pressed Westies and Wolves, 'get everyone out now! Go!'

Some turned in recognition but Crys was already past

them, no time to do anything more to help. *Please get out. Please.*

'Fox God!' He heard the shout behind him, heard it taken up by more and more voices, behind and ahead now, to either side. 'Fox God!'

It looked as though Gosfath was planning on wading through the whole city and slaughtering every inhabitant He found. He threw chunks of stone at buildings and walls, heaving them high into the air to fall in arbitrary, deadly arcs throughout the city.

Stop. Stop, you can't do anything. We can't do anything. We can stop Him!

We can't. But the Lady clothed in sunlight can. Stop, or be caught up in Her retribution.

That did it. Crys skidded to a halt, hands on his knees as he panted for breath. Gosfath was knee-deep in buildings and walls, plumes and pleats of fire springing up in His wake. He flung back His head and brayed another challenge. The sky muttered a response and lightning fizzed, then struck, arcing into the ground right next to Him. Gosfath staggered and brayed again, the sound lost in the thunderclap, and raised a bloody, talon-tipped fist at the clouds.

More lightning. More strikes shaking the earth around Him, destroying even more structures, starting even more fires. Killing even more people.

'Is this it?' Crys demanded. 'She destroys everything to stop Him? People are dying!'

The man-god-goat went to one knee and then rose up again, hurling masonry at the sky and bellowing. He was wild with rage and hate, leaping into the air and clawing at nothing, trampling shops and homes every time He landed, the impacts shivering through the city and toppling buildings as far away as the outskirts.

The god paused, glaring into the sky and all around the devastation, and then He retreated back the way He'd come and Crys knew, somehow just knew, He was going for the hospital in Second.

'No, no we have to lure Him away. He'll kill all the patients!'

Watch. And Crys found he couldn't move.

Three great spitting bolts of lightning struck Gosfath in the chest one after the other after the other. He screeched and shook His head, groggy, hurting, one hand pressed to the blasted, blackened ruin of His ribs, and as the sky built again, rumble upon rumble with threat, He vanished, tore back through the veil and into the Afterworld to escape the Dancer's wrath. His departure was marked with a thunder-clap so strong it felled the remaining buildings in the vicinity and blew smoke and flame out in a horizontal plume, a great wheel of orange blackness crouched above the city.

More thunder muttered but there were no gods this time, no lightning. Instead rain fell, icy and bleak, in great grey sheets that cut off everything more than ten paces distant. Crys stared at the space where the god had been, open-mouthed, dazed, shuddering with cold and shock and just barely holding on to the contents of his stomach and his arse. There was a prolonged moment of frozen, drenching silence, and then the wailing began, rising and falling against the roar of the storm.

'He's still not dead, is He?'

He has fled back through the veil. He has failed.

'Failed? Look at this, look! He's destroyed the city, killed thousands.'

We still live.

'We still live? Who cares if we still live? And if She controls lightning, She could've done that earlier,' Crys added. 'Before

I was nearly flattened by a building. Before all these people were killed. She could've just done that to the Mireces villages years ago, in fact, wiped them all out. No worshippers, no gods, isn't that how it works?'

The voice was uncharacteristically silent about what Crys felt was an important theological point. 'Couldn't She?' he insisted.

It's not that simple. We are gods; we see things – events here on Gilgoras – differently. And besides, such intervention is draining, only used when all else has failed.

'When I've failed, you mean. Thanks, that really helps. So is it over? Who won?' The clash of arms rose once more to overtake the screams of the shocked and the injured. 'More fighting?' Crys asked dully. 'Haven't they had enough? I fucking have.'

He began picking his way back through the blasted city, every muscle aching, bare feet bruised and torn and the storm washing blood in sheets from his naked, shivering skin. It took him a few minutes to realise the silver light was back, but this time it was spreading out across the city, flowing like slow water down streets and through doorways.

'What are you – what are we doing now?' he asked, suddenly weary beyond all measure, as if the light was sucking away his strength.

Healing people. As many as we can.

'Good. If the Mireces insist on fighting, we'll need everyone to get clear of this graveyard.'

We heal the Mireces too.

Crys halted, staring at an arm, fingers delicately curled as though beckoning him, sticking out from beneath a collapsed building. He was surrounded with corpses, most still clutching weapons, some still locked together in eternal struggle. At the end of the street three Rankers fought to escape two ravening Mireces.

'We're doing what?' he croaked.

Everyone is welcome in the Light. So everyone is welcome to be healed.

Crys turned in a circle. 'Look at this!' he screamed. 'Look what they've done, them and their foul gods. You cannot. We cannot.' He clapped both hands to his head. 'I. Will. *Not.*'

He fought to reel in the silver light, to draw it back into his body, constrain it. It pulsed and flowed, ebbed in and back out, as Crys trembled and sweated and forced his will against the other's.

We are one, Fox God and man. We do this because it is right. You – Crys Tailorson the mortal – were chosen because you understand right and wrong. Let their bodies heal.

No. They're still fighting us. We need every advantage.

You gave them the grace on the battlefield. This is no different.

'This is completely different,' he bellowed aloud. 'The battle's not over! The city is in ruins; our defences are gone. The only advantage you could give us over them is health. *Do you want us to lose?*' He roared the last words, hurling them at the other like a spear. There was no reply.

Crys didn't feel the impact as his knees hit the stone, didn't hear the clash of battle behind him or smell the opened-bowel stink of the body next to him, axe clutched tight in dead fingers. He closed his eyes and wept, knowing he was saving men just so that they could destroy more lives and spread their poison across Rilpor. Aiding the enemy. Collusion. Betrayal.

Justice. Good. Right.

'Fox God?'

It was so easy to ignore the voice, to ignore everything as the silver light shone across the city and blazed through

Crys's eyelids. To wait for it to fade. To pretend it wasn't him betraying his people.

'Fox God?'

But then Crys recognised the speaker and his eyes snapped open and there he was, kneeling opposite, confusion creasing his face, saying, 'Can you tell me what's happening?'

The light winked out as Crys slammed both his palms into Dom's chest and sent him over on to his back, head cracking from the stone hard enough to split scalp. Anger boiled in his veins as he snatched up the axe and hacked at the blackened arm. He expected it to shatter it looked so withered and dry, like a stick of charcoal. It didn't though, and the inside of it was red and meaty, thick viscous blood splattering as the axe rose and fell, rose and fell, Dom screaming with every impact until it was done.

Crys leant in close and spat in his face. 'That's for torturing me, you sick fuck.'

He sat back, picked up the severed limb and hurled it as far as he could to be lost with the other severed limbs amid the blood-washed, scream-stained streets.

'And we're not healing it, either.'

RILLIRIN

Fifth moon, eighteenth year of the reign of King Rastoth
Guest quarters, Fort One, South Rank forts, Western Plain

The fire in the hearth was a cheerful orange, a warm flag
of humanity and defiance after the cold camps of their
journey. Rillirin took an obscene amount of pleasure from
its heat despite how warm the last days had been. Besides,
Gilda needed it.

The wound from Dom's knife – *don't think about that*
– was angry and full of thick yellow pus, the flesh swollen
red and hard to the touch. *Corrupted. Dealt by a Darksoul,
a traitor.*

Don't think about it!

The last few days of their trek to the forts had been a
feverish nightmare for Gilda and a helpless torment for
Rillirin as she did all she could to halt the spread of infection
and tried not to rail against Dom and his betrayal. As she
attempted to reconcile that night in the forts when he'd eased
her fears and shown her his soul, when they'd created a life,
with the monster he'd become.

'Nearly done now,' she muttered, forcing her mind back to the present. Gilda lay on her bed, her face turned away, but Rillirin could see the cords of muscle in her throat, the tension in the old shoulders despite the opium the Rank's healer had given her. Rillirin sat on the other side of the bed, holding Gilda's good hand and trying not to gag as the man cut away the rotten flesh and then cleaned and stitched the wound, pulling the lips of skin tight together. He poulticed it and bandaged it with crisp fresh linen, and then left them with a promise to return in the morning.

Rillirin sat in silence as Gilda drifted on the edges of unconsciousness, occasionally dabbing the sweat from the priestess's face. The healer had muttered about amputation if the infection could not be stemmed, and all Rillirin could think in her selfishness was how would Gilda deliver her babe with only one arm?

How much credence had General Hadir and his staff given to their tale, with Gilda feverish and having to work hard not to ramble, while Rillirin's very voice betrayed her, loaded down with mountain harshness, the accent narrowing eyes and generating scorn and suspicion?

For hours they'd been in his office, the same questions over and over from different angles, searching out inconsistencies, separating fact from emotion. They'd agreed beforehand not to mention Dom, neither his betrayal nor his knowings. They knew instinctively that their task would be hard enough without mentioning calestars and prophecies and Fox Gods in mortal guise.

'He believed us, of course he did. He had to. We gave him the most up-to-date information he's received since the siege began. The only bloody information he's received. He'll reinforce. He can't do otherwise. He can't.'

Gilda stirred at her voice and Rillirin watched with dismay

as the pain intruded upon her consciousness and she woke.

'Do you think you can manage some more stew?' Rillirin asked when it was clear Gilda wouldn't drift back into sleep.

Gilda licked her lips and grimaced, scowling at Rillirin. 'I feel sick to my stomach but yes, I'll eat. Unlike most of the idiot men I've treated over the years, I take my healer's advice seriously and understand the need to keep up my strength.'

Rillirin brought her a bowl and spoon and then sat at the small table with a third helping for herself. The irritation in Gilda's tone was new and Rillirin felt an old, instinctive urge to hunch her shoulders and fade into the shadows. She didn't, swallowing the old habits as best she could along with the food.

She put her hand to her belly, swollen with food and nothing else – not yet – and smiled to herself. *Little warrior. Nothing's going to stop you, is it? As tough as your Da* . . . but that led to thoughts she didn't want to contemplate. Not here and now, anyway. *As tough as me, then. And loved. So loved.*

'What do you think they'll do?' she asked when she'd finished eating and licked her spoon clean.

Gilda's mouth twitched. 'Congratulations,' she said sourly, easing herself back against the wall and draping the blanket over her legs as Rillirin took the empty bowl from her, 'you managed to wait until after the meal to begin your interrogation again.'

Rillirin raised her chin. 'It's a valid question.'

Gilda snorted. 'And one you've asked me four times already, which means you know that I don't know. We've given them all the information we can, and my time as Lanta's pet at least ensured I was privy to some of their plans, so Hadir understands the urgency. Hopefully it will be enough, and my authority as high priestess should count for something. It's clear to us that they must reinforce

Rilporin, but we don't know the situation here. Krike has always been belligerent; if they get wind of the invasion, they may stage one of their own just to see how much of the Western Plain they can claim while our backs are turned.'

'We . . .' Rillirin trailed off.

'What? Speak up, girl.'

Rillirin stood tall in the face of Gilda's impatience. 'I was going to say, if Hadir – *when* Hadir – decides to go to Rilporin, we'll push on to Krike.'

Gilda glowered at her. 'Why would we go to Krike?'

Rillirin opened her mouth and then closed it again, confused. 'What?' She said eventually. 'Going to Krike was your idea. On the way here you said we'd go there and convince them to fight for Crys, tell them who he really is.'

The scorn in Gilda's face made her blush.

'I was half out of my head with fever, lass. Of course we can't go to Krike. No one would believe us. Krike's only an ally if we offer them something in return for aid. Telling them their god walks the earth won't do it – we can't prove it. It was a fever-dream, Rillirin. I can't believe you've been pinning your hopes on it all this time.'

Rillirin blew out her cheeks and folded her arms. 'Fine, so I'm not very good at this. I still feel we should be doing something.'

'We've only just stopped doing lots and lots of somethings,' Gilda pointed out, before heaving a sigh and closing her eyes. When she opened them again, her expression was softer. 'We'll talk to Hadir again tomorrow. That really is all we can do. Come on, get into bed. Us old folk need our rest, and so do you pregnant ones. And ignore an old woman's short temper,' she added. 'Talk of amputation makes me . . . unsettled.'

Rillirin hauled off her boots, stripped down to her linens and eased into the bed next to Gilda, swamped with relief.

She kissed Gilda's cheek and then blew out the candle. 'No one's taking your arm,' she promised.

'Healer, are you?' Gilda said, and then huffed a breath. 'I'm sure you're right. And despite my protestations to the contrary, I've never been the best of patients.'

'I'm astonished,' Rillirin muttered, was rewarded with a grudging chuckle in the dark. She grinned and closed her eyes.

'The worry never goes away, you know,' Gilda said after a long silence. 'Nor the grief – for Cam, for Sarilla and, aye, for Dom too, though a part of me will always have hope of his redemption, no matter what the rest of me thinks. I have to, lass, have to believe he can be saved. Because if he can't . . . But spring is here and there are thick walls between us and the enemy and a healer to fix my arm. The Dancer teaches us to take what pleasures we can, when we can. Let's do that, at least for now.'

She yawned and her voice grew softer, distant with dreams. 'The trials will start again soon enough. That's the only certainty in this world.'

Rillirin lay with her hands on her belly, staring at the flickers of light from the fire dancing orange on the ceiling as Gilda's breathing deepened and she began to snore.

'I don't think we'll get much sleep with that racket,' she whispered to the babe and smiled. 'But she's right, though. We'll win this war, and by the time you're born, it will just be an evil memory. Nothing for you to worry about, little Wolf. You'll be born into peace and plenty, with Grandma Gilda and Uncle Lim and your Da and me all around you, loving you. I promise.'

A wondering smile crossed Rillirin's face in the dark and her hands stroked the skin of her stomach. 'Little Wolf. You'll be absolutely perfect. And nothing will ever hurt you.'

CORVUS

Fifth moon, night, day forty-three of the siege
Grand temple square, First Circle, Rilporin, Wheat Lands

The need to kill every enemy of the faith rose up in Corvus like a storm, every other instinct and emotion drowning beneath its red darkness. It didn't matter what happened afterwards, whether he was ever crowned king of this shit-stinking hovel of a country or even if he survived. There was a hole carved into his heart by the Dark Lady's destruction and Corvus had one imperative, one single, all-consuming purpose: to fill that hole to overflowing with the blood of these fucking savages.

He'd charged after the Wolves and Rankers, howling a wordless war cry, sword cleaving Rilporians' arms, hacking into faces and chests and elbows, stabbing guts and thighs. He waded through them like a man through wheat. Corvus was filled with the loss of a god and the rage of another. Unstoppable. Unkillable. He knew no fear, knew nothing but the need to kill. And kill he would, until all the world was gore.

355

And the Godblind. The traitorous shit who'd managed to fool them all was here somewhere; Corvus had seen him, seen him take a knife to the Dark Lady – he screamed at the memory – and kill Her. Amid the utter shock that had followed his actions and the arrival of Holy Gosfath, he'd disappeared, but that wouldn't save him. Corvus was going to find him and he was going to give him a death that would last for years, utter destruction of mind, spirit and body, so that all he knew, all he was, was pain.

It wouldn't be enough, nothing he could devise would ever be enough, but Corvus pledged to do it anyway, to find new depths of depravity, to invent new torments, and use every one of them on the deicide.

He sliced a man across the eyes and sent him reeling, shrieking, back into the melee.

Gosfath had travelled back through the veil to marshal His strength for the fight to come, for the search for His Sister-Lover. Corvus suppressed the voice that whispered Gosfath had fled, abandoned them as the Dark Lady had, left them spiritual orphans in a hostile land.

No, never. His bloodlust flows in my veins, in all of us. It is His presence that sustains us now. His love. He gives us strength and demands that we use it to annihilate this city and all within it. We must not fail Him as we failed Her.

Neither Corvus nor Skerris nor the Blessed One had issued any orders, but the Mireces and Easterners moved as one, harrying the defenders and pushing them back, shoving them through the streets, herding them like so much dumb, lowing beef through gates and districts, and then from First Circle into Second, and then Second into Third.

Dusk came while he killed and the growing darkness didn't matter, the madness gnawing at the ragged tatters of his soul didn't matter. What mattered was the fight, was the blood spilt in Her name. Sacred blood and heathen blood, the Blessed One had said back in Eagle Height all those months ago, they would spill it all if it would bring the Red Gods back to Gilgoras. Now they were spilling it to bring back the Dark Lady, to atone for what had been done to Her. To call Her from beyond death and back into their hearts. Tears rolled down his face as he killed.

There were Mireces around him now, and Valan of course, still alive, still protecting his king despite the agony racking his heart. The men and women ahead of him were civilians, and they were running, running and screaming, some armed with scavenged weapons, others with sticks or kitchen knives. Most carried bundles, as though sacks of precious things would save their lives. Others carried children, more precious and just as useless.

Corvus hadn't spoken a word he could remember in hours, but his throat was raw from screaming and his sword heavier than a mountain, his legs like lead and his chest labouring to breathe the smoky night air. The roaring in his head and heart compelled him after the runners but he paused, leant his sword against a wall and flexed stiff fingers as he breathed, as he tried to think.

His heartbeat pounded out the imperative: *kill, kill, kill.* The God of Blood's need, lacking the Dark Lady's meticulous planning. They were killing blind, hoping. The sacrifices in the temple were structured, ritualised. This slaughter had none of that.

'Valan,' he croaked. 'Where are we?'

His second came to a twitching halt at his side, eyes locked on the fleeing Rilporians, sword arm flailing gently. 'Third Circle I think, Sire. Or Fourth. Does it matter? Kill them.'

Corvus turned, looking for landmarks. He pointed with his chin. 'That's the palace? Then that puts us in Third.

Further than I realised and a good place to organise. We need to hold here, bring up reinforcements. I want every single Rilporian trapped in Fifth by this time tomorrow. Drive them in, kill if necessary, but I want as many alive as we can manage.'

A frown cracked the dried blood on Valan's brow and sent flakes tumbling on the breeze. 'Not kill them?'

Corvus grabbed his shoulder and squeezed. 'Not yet. We hold here, wait for others to reinforce us, then start sending out runners with the order.' He looked up at the house on his left, mostly intact. 'See if there's water or ale in there, any food. We'll be fighting through the night. We'll be fighting until this is done. We've already got them on the run; we can't give them a chance to regroup.'

Valan finally tore his eyes from the fleeing citizens and met Corvus's. 'Your will, Sire,' he said, and something in his face told Corvus he knew what his king was planning and approved. One final mass sacrifice: if that wasn't enough to draw the Dark Lady back, nothing was.

First and Second Circles were aflame. Smoke swirled through the streets, catching in throats and blurring eyes, constricting lungs and drizzling ash on to tongues. Soot insinuated itself into every wrinkle and fold of skin and cloth, dulling the shine on weapons and armour, brightening the feverish zeal in the eyes of the righteous.

The silver light that the Dark Lady must have sent as a last gift before She vanished, the light that had healed them all, hadn't reappeared; new injuries sustained in the intervening hours behaved as normal – bleeding, slowing, killing. Their numbers were thinning, but they had enough to see this last great assault bring them victory, though every step he took felt like defeat without Her presence in his soul.

Corvus paused to wipe black snot from his upper lip and spit phlegm on to the stone. He hacked out a cough as the wind blew hot and foul down the street. The city was backlit in orange, the pursuers outlined by flame, and the fleeing soldiery had finally organised. They knew they were being driven now, and they knew the city better than the Mireces ever would. Progress had halted completely in some areas as fierce fighting broke out or ambushes felled a squad of his men, and at least two Mireces bands had been forced back into fires they themselves had set, caught between flame and steel.

Small bands of Rilporians had wriggled past his flanks and fled into the burning city, twisting and turning through streets and alleys to throw off any pursuit. Corvus had ordered them hunted down, every last one. None would escape, none be allowed the succour of an easy death in the flames. They were destined for sacrifice, for an act of devotion so monumental that gods Themselves would weep for joy – and return to honour Their worshippers. Gilgoras would know the touch of its true gods once again: the scabbed slices in Corvus's arms promised it; the hole in his heart demanded it.

He would reduce Rilporin to a blackened skeleton knee-deep in blood. With the Blessed One at his side, Corvus would kill the world if that was what it took.

MACE

The war didn't make sense any more.

One minute he'd been standing over Dalli listening to healers explain how unlikely it was that she'd survive, and the next the entire city had begun screaming at once, so much so that he'd left her there and sprinted outside. And witnessed the impossible.

A god.

It could be nothing else. Gosfath, God of Blood, towered over the city and then moved through it, leaving carnage in His wake. Men who'd fought for weeks without hesitation or visible fear had thrown down their weapons and fled, screaming, as Gosfath tore through the city. Mace neither blamed nor condemned them; it'd taken all he had not to piss his linens.

Hundreds, thousands, had died while more fled, tearing open the gates they were supposed to be guarding and running heedless through the streets among the fleeing citizenry, the raining stone, their only thought to get as far away as they could. And then the Mireces, at first knocked to their knees by what he'd later learnt was Dom's execution of the Dark Lady – and he wouldn't have believed that if he hadn't seen another god with his own eyes – were tearing holes through the fleeing Rilporians and raining bloody fucking murder on every man, woman and child they could find.

But the ravaging Mireces hadn't frightened him half so much as Dalli had when she came out of the hospital with her guts safely back in her body and nothing to show for it but shadows beneath her eyes and a thick purple scar jagging across her belly, visible through the tatters of her shirt and the ragged edges of her chainmail.

Even the realisation that his own burns and wounds had healed themselves couldn't dilute the primal terror that clawed into his throat as hundreds of wounded soldiers rose from their beds, put on their armour and fell upon the advancing Mireces. The mysterious healing – and Mace recalled the strange silver light that had bled across the city – had only gone so far: Edris's leg hadn't grown back and Dorcas still only had one eye, though it had mended enough to give him a little vision.

But pulled from the brink of death by divine intervention wasn't an impenetrable shield against the Mireces' fresh assault. They'd hammered into his soldiers and hacked them open, as though affronted they'd had the balls to stand against them a second time, and the bone-deep exhaustion of near death slowed their reflexes. Some of them lived; the rest gave their second chance at life to ensure others survived. Mace hadn't wasted their deaths; he'd dragged Dalli away even as the pair of them roared orders for formations that went unheard in the screaming, clanging fury.

There had been no stopping the Mireces' advance, no

reasoning with the mad or defending against the suicidal. Once the Ranks broke and fled they couldn't stop, and it had taken hours, the coming of night, the starting of the fires and the realisation there was nowhere left to flee to that finally restored order to his soldiers and the Wolves.

And now they were here, the remains of his army, the remnants of the Wolves and thousands of hysterical civilians with screaming children and sacks of useless wealth. They'd fled with coin and jewels when they should have brought food, water and bandages, medicines, poultices. Some had brought their animals with them, not just dogs but the goats and yearling pigs they hadn't slaughtered for food yet.

Mace and those of his officers who were alive huddled in the remains of Fourth Circle, the district shattered and smoking. They'd propped the gates as best they could and manned the gatehouses and other sections of the wall with those archers who had shafts left.

The little intel he had indicated that First and Second Circles were burning and the Mireces and East Rankers occupied Third, almost but not quite surrounding them. Fourth was smoky but not burning, while plumes of black lit by whirling sparks still rose from the palace in Fifth. They were trapped between fire and the enemy and they had nowhere to run and not enough soldiers to defend the Rilporians crowded in with them.

Running out of options, running out of soldiers, running out of space. How the fuck did it get so bad so fast?

The ambushes and traps they'd laid as they fled through the districts had slowed the enemy's advance and given them a small lead, and for reasons Mace wasn't sure he wanted to learn the Mireces had stopped their outright slaughter and concentrated on herding together as many survivors as possible, pressing them into smaller and ever smaller spaces until even the spacious Fourth Circle was blanketed in people. Herding them like cattle to a slaughterhouse. Mace pushed away the image.

'Count?' he whispered and then smothered a cough in the crook of his elbow. Gods, he was thirsty, had been for what felt like days now.

'Almost impossible to tell,' Vaunt said. 'Couple of thousand Rankers in here with us, at least three times that in civilians, if not more, and a few hundred Wolves. No idea how many soldiers have fallen since the Dark Lady was destroyed and the Fox God defeated Gosfath, but there're scanty reports that a thousand or so may have escaped into the northern side of the city, or at least taken refuge somewhere safe. It may be they'll reinforce us when we make our stand, or try and flank the Mireces to give us a way out. With luck, the Trickster leads them.'

'Make our stand? We're on the run, man. Even if he is the Trickster, he can't rally dead men.' *Can he?* 'I don't want suppositions and hope, I want facts.'

Vaunt dipped his head. 'All right. Same estimated numbers in here with us, but the thousand we think might've escaped are all dead, along with all the others we've lost count and sight of. Anyone not in here with us can be assumed lost. We have no idea where the Fox God is and He's probably the only one who can help us, because there are no reinforcements and there's no way of making a stand because we're fucked and can't get the civilians out of danger or even out of the bastard way to let us die in lines as we've trained.'

He spat something black and glistening on to the flagstones, and then wiped his mouth. 'That make you feel better?'

'Steady on.' Edris cast a glare in Vaunt's direction. Mace knew he should reprimand the major, didn't bother.

'Why are we getting the civilians out of the way again?' Dalli asked. 'I'm a civilian, all us Wolves are. We still fight. Why aren't this lot fighting?'

'No weapons, no idea what they're doing,' Vaunt said shortly.

Dalli nodded. 'Uh-huh. Take a lot of skill to throw a rock at a man's head, does it?' She waved a hand to cut off Vaunt as he bristled. 'Get the archers off the wall and send these people up there. Arm them with rocks, stones, rubble, boiling water. Send them up there with heavy cooking pots if you have to. They can throw the fucking pigs for all I care, but get our archers down here where they can wield blade or spear alongside us and get the civilians on the walls out of immediate danger where they can actually do some good. They're scared because they don't have any control. They're a second fucking army and they outnumber us and the Mireces put together. Use them.'

Mace knew she was right. They all did. 'Do it, Major. We need all the help we can get and if they can take the pressure off us for a while, the rest of us might actually come up with a plan that'll see us live through the night.'

The faces around him were grim and he probably shouldn't have said that last bit, but someone needed to articulate exactly how deep was the shit they were in.

'Actually,' Colonel Edris interrupted in a low voice, 'Dorcas and I have an alternative position to present.' The man was grey with blood loss and exhaustion but his face was firm. Dorcas crouched by his side, head turning in exaggerated movements so his remaining eye could see everyone.

'Abandon the city,' Edris said and Mace wheezed as though he'd been punched in the chest. 'It's on its knees, it's burning, it's broken; let them have it.'

'We can't abandon Rilporin,' Mace spluttered. 'Not when

we've spent so many lives defending it. What were all the deaths for if we just give up on it now?' Anger was growing like a weed, strangling his weariness, his doubt. 'We can still win this!'

'Can we? I had this very conversation with your father a few weeks ago,' a voice said and Hallos appeared out of the darkness, bloody to the elbows and haggard as a corpse. 'Do you know what he told me when I said we should evacuate the king and the nobles prior to this siege beginning? He said Rilpor isn't to be found in stone houses and golden crowns or noble titles. Rilpor is its people, its faith, its way of life. We save them, not a pile of shattered stone.'

Hallos put a fingertip on Mace's chest. 'That's where Rilpor is. It's in Edris and Dorcas here. It's in Vaunt and Weaverson, Dalli and Tailorson and Carter, wherever they are and regardless of whether they still live. It's in the people huddled here hoping you'll protect them. It's even in me. We are Rilpor, not these walls and houses. And if we're to save Rilpor, perhaps we should let Rilporin go.'

'And then what?' Mace asked, spreading his hands and swallowing the bitterness of what tasted like defeat. 'We just keep running, abandon the country to the Mireces, flee as every other town and village falls to the Red Gods? Save our own skins at the expense of everyone else's? There are walls here to protect us; out there is nothing but leagues of farmland.'

'There are walls here,' Dalli said softly and he could see she was with the others. 'Walls for us to die behind. These bastards won't stop; we all know they won't stop. At least out there we can form a line between the people and the Mireces, give them a chance to run.'

'And not just them,' Edris said, as patient as if he was answering a green recruit's questions. 'You need to go too, sir. Find new allies to bolster our strength so that we can wipe them and their religion from Gilgoras. This is the battle, sir; it's not the war. Not if we can get you out.'

'Fuck 'em up,' Vaunt snarled before Mace could respond. 'Come back here with a new army and fuck 'em right the fuck up. That's a plan I can get behind.'

It wasn't as though Mace hadn't thought it himself, not for him personally to run, of course – that would never happen – but for the army to pull back to a new position of strength. But they'd just been thoughts, speculation in his darker moments. He'd been convinced there was still a way out, a way through to victory. Now all his officers, and Dalli, and even the bloody physician, were in agreement that the only hope of victory lay in retreat.

He looked at their grimy, bloody, sweaty faces one by one and he knew the decision had already been made, and that it wasn't one he could stand against. If he countermanded it, they'd stay and fight and die for him without hesitation. And he'd be haunted by their deaths until it was his turn to die.

'King Gate?' he asked, refusing to let his shoulders slump in defeat.

'North Gate and the ships,' Dalli said. They all looked at each other.

'Split our forces, take half the non-combatants each?' Edris suggested. 'A double break out means they're fighting to contain us on two fronts, gives us a greater chance.'

'I think that's our best option,' Mace said. 'Vaunt, Dorcas, take the tunnel to the King Gate with Palace and half of South. Edris, you're with me and the West. We'll take the Wolves too and go for the north harbour and the ships.'

'What's our staging location?' Vaunt asked. 'Listran border?'

Mace thought for a moment. 'No. Head due south, straight into the forest. Get out of sight before dawn. We'll take the ships downriver until we're out of sight of the city, then set them adrift and make our way to you. I want them thinking we're fleeing to Listre.'

Vaunt's smile was feral. 'When really?'

'When really we'll be looping wide and then making all speed for the South Rank forts. Three thousand rested, unbloodied soldiers in those forts. They'll have a point to prove, and we'll have a score to settle.'

Mace stood a little straighter, feeling a flicker of hope. *Not a retreat, just falling back to a position of strength.*

'All right, give the order. Arm as many civilians as you can with whatever you can scavenge; as soon as the Mireces see we're gone, they'll be forcing their way in through the gate and over that breach, so we'll need a rearguard. I want volunteers only for that duty; you all know why.'

Grim glances were exchanged and Mace swallowed, his throat thick and dry at the thought. 'Get the non-combatants moving now. Let's use the darkness for as long as we can. Dancer's grace.'

The others saluted and left him and Mace stared up at the gatehouse, black against the blackness. 'Where the fuck are you, Major Carter?' he muttered. 'And where the hell is the Fox God?'

DOM

Fifth moon, night, day forty-three of the siege
Jewellery district, Third Circle, Rilporin, Wheat Lands

Something was missing. His body was distant and blunted, and something was missing. Something that had been with him for what felt like forever.

Her.

She wasn't there any more and the godspace was a shrivelled womb empty of life. Dom shivered, aching with the intensity of Her absence. *My love, why have you abandoned me? Am I not your good son, your loving son? Where are you, my love? I need you.*

'Everything else was a lie.'

The words were quiet, innocuous, floating on a smoky breeze. But they were familiar, too. From before. A frown creased Dom's brow, and deepened when he heard noises that sounded like distant battle. Screams, thin and high.

'Everything else was a lie. That's what you said. After you'd tortured me.'

Pain, from his heart into his head. *Torture?* The memory

of the last days was lost beneath an impenetrable shroud, all of it tainted and stained by the awful absence of the Dark Lady.

'Godblind. That's what Lanta called you, isn't it? Come on then, Godblind, open your eyes. I know you're awake. Time to face your truth, and the consequences of your actions.'

Dom looked and roof beams swam into view, almost lost in shadow, light from a single candle barely illuminating the shape at his side. 'Who?' he managed.

'Crys Tailorson. Or maybe you know me as the Fox God, the Trickster. I know I once knew you as a friend. I'm the one you betrayed to Lanta and Corvus, the one you took knife and pliers and branding iron and fists to. Remember? Do you remember that, Godblind, my torture and the delight you took in it? Or are you honestly expecting me to believe that was a lie as well?'

'Splitsoul?' Dom muttered.

Crys raised an eyebrow. 'Not any more. Though you're still a Darksoul.' Face in shadow, his mismatched eyes flared yellow as he grabbed Dom by the shoulders and wrenched him upright. Dom screeched as pain flared in his left arm all the way up to his neck. He wriggled away until his shoulders cracked into a wall.

Crys dragged the candle closer and pulled up his ragged shirt, exposing lines and welts, brandings and great slicing cuts all over his belly and chest, down into the waistband of his too-short trousers, decorating his shoulders and forearms and probably other places Dom couldn't see. But they weren't red or purple, not fresh, plump lips silenced with stitches. Dom frowned and looked closer despite himself; then he gasped, skin going cold.

Every wound on Crys's body was healed, and each one

had healed silver, like lines of precious metal seamed into his body, a miner's fortune. Like sunlight on ribbons of water. The scales of a fish.

'Remember giving me these?' Crys hissed. 'What about taking away these?' and he shoved his hand in Dom's face; three of the nailbeds were exposed and hardened, the flesh cauterised and silvery, winking in the candlelight. 'Remember torturing me on behalf of Lanta, on behalf of the Red Gods? Do you? *Do you?*'

Dom's mouth tasted of blood as he stared at the silver scars decorating Crys's skin. 'I'm sorry,' he whispered.

Crys slapped him across the face. 'Not good enough. Not ever going to be good enough. Why did you do it?'

My love? My love, what's happening? What's he saying?

There was no answer, and Dom's fear grew like the emptiness inside. *She's abandoned me. I let Her down, stumbled from the Path somehow and my hand slipped from Hers.*

My hand . . .

The sense of wrongness in his body found its source, the pain its origin. Dom held his breath and raised his left arm in front of his face, squinting in the yellow light. It didn't end in a hand and fingers. It ended halfway past his elbow in a swathe of white and red linen. Dom's left arm . . . ended.

'Where's . . . where's my hand?' he asked, knowing it was stupid. 'What happened to my hand? Where's my fucking hand?'

'I cut it off.' Crys laughed, his features ugly with triumph, and ice and heat chased each other through Dom's body, his stomach rolling slowly. Images rose and fell in the mist of his memory, disjointed, tangled with sounds and scents that didn't belong.

Nothing makes sense. My love, I can't think without you, I can't live. Please come back. I don't understand any of this. Why did he hurt me? Why is he saying I hurt him? Those memories aren't real.

Are they?

He remembered the touch of the Dark Lady in his soul, Her voice in his head and he reached blindly, straining. There was nothing there. 'Why?' he asked eventually.

Crys lifted his shirt again in answer, growling when Dom rolled his head against the wall in wordless denial.

'I don't understand. I just did what She asked of me, what I had to.' He met Crys's eyes, bewildered. 'It wasn't my fault.'

An axe appeared in Crys's hand, a big double-headed axe, and Crys laid one of the blades against Dom's other arm. 'It's not your fault?' he hissed. 'It's not your fault?' he repeated, louder now. 'You will fucking well take responsibility for your actions or I will make you pay in ways you couldn't imagine.'

'But I can't . . . What do you want me to say?'

'I want you to admit everything you've done. Remember,' Crys ordered, and Dom did, in a painful rush that scoured away the tatters of his dignity.

Shame constricted his throat, breath whistling, shame that crept dead fingers over his skin, shame that tore. 'I told them how to get in, when and where to breach the defences. I tried to kill Gilda; I did kill captives. Friends, war-kin. I told them about Rillirin; I told them about you.'

Each word was a knife, cutting away pieces of the man he'd always thought himself to be. Always fought to be.

'I remember hurting you now,' he stuttered. 'I remember telling the Blessed One that if we could get the Fox God out of you, we'd – they'd – win the war.'

'But why you?' Crys whispered, and the anger bled into sadness. 'We were friends. Why was it you who hurt me?'

Dom looked at the split and swollen knuckles on his right

hand, knuckles he'd skinned against Crys's face and ribs and humiliation flooded him, so hard and sudden that he gagged. 'I'm sorry,' he whispered again.

The fury reignited in a blink, whitening Crys's lips, tightening the muscles around his eyes. 'You're sorry. You're sorry? Do you have *any* idea how inadequate that is? *Thousands* of men, women and children are dead. Thousands. The city is overrun, the Mireces control the outer Circles, the Ranks are in retreat. They're killing everyone they can find. Because of you.'

Crys slammed the axe into the wood above Dom's head, making him cower. 'Time to wake up, *Darksoul*,' he snarled. 'Time to face it all. To remember why I cut off your arm.'

The words were splinters beneath the skin, barbs in Dom's flesh, tugging, tearing him a little wider until he broke open and the awful truth, the memory that he'd fought to bury beneath all the rest, surged back.

She's not here, my love, my Bloody Mother. She'll never be here again.

I killed Her.

His heart gave one great lurch and then started pounding so hard his vision greyed at the edges. A thin, high keening broke from him and he slid on to his side and curled up tight, racked with pain, with the knowledge that She was gone from the world because of him. All the other deaths, all the betrayals, were as nothing.

'No,' he pleaded. 'No, tell me I didn't. Please, tell me I didn't kill Her. Not my love.' It hurt to breathe, hurt to look at the angry delight in Crys, the dark justice.

He could feel the vortex swirling back, the black madness. He reached for it, blind. 'She was . . . everything, my whole world.' Dom seized Crys's hand. 'Kill me. Please, however you like, as slowly as you like but please, please kill me. Please.'

Crys blinked and then changed, subtly. Power rose in him as he ran fingers over the stump of Dom's arm, ignoring his pleading. 'You have caused great evil, Dom Calestar. Godblind and Darksoul are fates we did not foresee, and we regret them. But your task is not yet complete.'

Dom stared at the Fox God from the ruins of his pain and cold sweat bathed his back. 'No more,' he begged. 'Please, Lord. Please, I can do no more. It's too much. Let me die.'

'Be healed,' the Fox God said and silver light rose from his skin and snaked down Dom's arm and beneath the bandages. Dom sobbed as the splintered bone and flaps of meat and skin that was all that was left of his sword arm healed into a useless, misshapen lump, as all his hurts and wounds closed and faded, filling him with exhaustion and crystalline memories with edges sharp enough to cut.

His path, which had been so muddied and hard to find within the mists and confusions laid by the Dark Lady, lay straight and clear again before his feet, to an outcome he couldn't yet see but which filled him with dread. To either side yawned the chasm of Her loss, beckoning him in. A need so deep it didn't have a name.

Dom stood at the edge for a long time, looking down while the Fox God waited, silver as moonlight, hard as steel. Then he turned, weary as the end of the world, and took his place behind his Lord. There was no mercy and no forgiveness, not for the likes of him. But there was a task to do, and Dom would see it done.

Perhaps then he could rest. Perhaps then They'd let him die.

TARA

'West is best!' Tara bellowed as she sprinted up the King's
Way towards the closing gate into Fourth Circle. 'Friendlies.
Don't close the fucking gate!'

Tara and her companions put on a last desperate spurt of
speed as arrows whickered past them from behind. They
were still twenty strides out when the gate slammed shut,
trapping them in Third with the enemy. 'Mother . . . fucker,'
she panted. 'Roger?'

The lieutenant didn't even pause, dashing past the closed
gate and dodging into an alley so narrow Tara barked her
elbow against the stone as she followed him in, Ash labouring
behind.

The air in Third was thick with smoke, and Tara's lungs
pumped for air. Despite herself, her legs were slowing and
Roger was a mere shadow ahead. She tried to force her legs
faster, but they simply wouldn't respond, and less than a
minute later Roger burst out of the end of the alley. A second

after that he was punched off his feet by a flight of arrows, vanishing out of sight.

Tara skidded to a halt, Ash crashing into her back and sending them both on to the hard-packed dirt and rotting vegetable scraps. Then Ash's hand found her face and tapped twice, and then twice again – *don't move*.

Arrows clattered overhead, loosed blind into the alley, and Tara just closed her eyes and tried to suck air into her lungs, bruised with effort, crushed by Ash's weight. After what felt like an hour, he slid slowly to the side and then up the wall, keeping to the darkest shadow. Tara waited some more, in case his movement triggered a challenge, and then rose next to him.

'Roger,' she whispered, but she didn't go to look. Mireces in front, Mireces behind. What were their choices?

A soft grating had them both whirling away from the wall, weapons rasping into hands. Yellow eyes and a feral grin met their disbelieving stares. 'You coming in?' Crys breathed and they piled through the door in such haste they nearly went down again in a tangle of limbs. Crys slid shut the door and held a finger to his lips, a finger that was batted away and replaced with Ash's mouth for such a length of time that Tara felt herself begin to blush.

She turned her back on them and saw another figure huddled against the far wall, a man she vaguely recognised. He was so gaunt and haggard she couldn't put a name to his face, and he had no weapons, so she ignored him and crept to a broken shutter on the opposite side of the room and peeked out. The street looked empty.

A hand tapped her shoulder and Crys gave her a swift hug. 'How are you?' he asked. His eyes were still glowing and Tara felt her stomach cramp with awe.

'Well, Lord,' she said, ducking her head, feeling faintly ridiculous – this was Crys! – and yet unable to do otherwise.

The corner of Crys's mouth twitched. 'None of that shit,' he said. 'You remember Dom.'

Tara blinked and squinted at the hunched figure again. Then she let out a low, breathy whistle. 'Wow. Right, let's get back to the others.'

'None of us are going back to the Rank,' Crys said as Ash hugged Dom. 'Me and the calestar and Ash are going south for reinforcements. You can't come.'

'We are?' Ash asked, surprised.

'I can't?' Tara said. Her eyebrows rose. 'We've been looking for you for hours. We came out here, risked our lives and lost men, to find you and get you back to the Rank safely. Now you're telling me you're not only deserting, but that I'm not allowed to desert with you?'

'I need you here, and it's not going to be easy.'

'Defences never are,' Tara said shortly, folding her arms.

'The city's lost. The defenders will be dead, surrendered or fled by dawn. But I need you here, afterwards. I need you to do something for me.'

Tara blinked rapidly, her eyes sore. 'Is this a fellow officer giving me an order, or . . .'

'Not the officer,' Crys said softly. 'The other one.'

Shit.

He handed her a bundle of cloth, and when she shook it out she coughed a laugh. 'A gown? I have two questions for you. One: have you ever seen me in skirts? The answer's no. And two: how do I fight in a dress?'

Crys's face was solemn; the other occupants of the room listened intently. 'The Mireces know there are female Wolves, but they don't know about you or your training, your ability to plan. Skerris might, but he's never met you; you have no face for him to recognise. There are going to be hostages when this is over, and more than that . . .'

Tara looked at the dress again and licked sweat from her upper lip. 'You want me to kill Corvus.'

'Yes. And the Blessed One.'

Infiltrate the Mireces and kill the two most well-guarded and important figures in their army. Cut the head off the snake – or try to.

'You're the god; you do it.'

She was shocked she'd said it aloud, but Crys smiled. His eyes – the Fox God's eyes – were full of faith. She was the only one who could do this. He had His reasons and He'd chosen her. She appreciated His belief, but even so, she couldn't stop her hands from crushing the gown.

'What about those hostages?'

Crys blinked. 'What about them?'

'If I'm going in, I may as well do everything I can before they take me down, because I think we both know I don't get out of this pretty. So I'll free any hostages they have – as you said, there're bound to have some – before I ghost Corvus and the woman. Their deaths should give the rest the distraction they need to get out.'

'I don't think this is a good idea,' Ash murmured. 'One woman, alone in that nest of vipers . . .'

Tara's face twisted with sudden rage that she knew was a thin veneer over gut-loosening terror, but even so Ash took a shocked pace backwards.

'Fuck you, Bowman. Don't preach to me about the dangers of being a woman in the Mireces' world, because you have zero idea how it feels to be a woman in a Rank, surrounded by men who want to fuck you, not because you're pretty, but just because they haven't seen tits in a year and they think what they want is more important than what I want. That they have the right to take what they like, and my only right is to give it to them. I know exactly what I'm going

377

to be up against and I know exactly what it is I might have to do.'

Tara sucked in a deep breath, shocked at herself but thrumming with energy. 'I understand the risks and accept the likely outcome. I choose what happens to me, and when I can't choose, I fight. Right now, I choose to accept this task because my friend and fellow officer – and Lord – asks me to.'

Ash looked stricken, and Tara poked him in the chest before he could speak again and undermine her courage any further. 'And don't ever underestimate me because of my gender, Wolf. Women have got more strength than you'd know what to do with. If this is how we fight these bastards, then this is how we fight.'

'I'm a Wolf,' he protested weakly, 'I've been taught by women and knocked on my arse by women all my life. I'd never think you incapable. I just don't think you should be alone.'

'Like He said, I'm the only one they won't suspect, so I'm the only choice.'

Crys nodded his head once and Tara gathered the gown and backed away across the room, slipped through the door into the long kitchen and pressed her back against it. Nausea sloshed in her gut. *What have I done? What the living fuck have I just agreed to?*

'Gods alive,' she heard Ash mutter. 'The woman's a fucking menace.'

Crys laughed, low, and Tara felt a little strength return to her legs. A flicker of a smile creased her face as she began to unbuckle her armour.

'That she is, love,' Crys – or the Fox God – said. 'That she is.' He laughed again. 'If anyone can do it, she can. Corvus is fucked. Best of all he doesn't even know it.'

MACE

Hundreds were dead, hundreds more captured or fleeing in all directions, cut off from the rest of the group and the Rankers doing their damnedest to save them. The Mireces ambush had slammed into the side of the crowd like a wolf into deer, scattering some, panicking the rest. The defenders had cut down the wedge of enemy, and now Mace was in line with a hundred or so others, falling back step by step, fending off the next wave, conserving strength. Only killing when there was no other choice, too shitting tired for more.

The civilians who'd scattered raced down alleys and across plazas, lunging into cheap houses and low warehouses, pounding down smoky streets with more Mireces in pursuit, chased, cornered, beaten on to their knees and roped like cattle. A few made it into buildings without anyone noticing. Mace offered a swift prayer that they'd survive, somehow be safe when there was no one left in the city to protect them.

Once we've abandoned them.

Beyond the thousands of screaming, shoving, hysterical citizens yawned the North Gate and, beyond that, the harbour and the ships. Freedom. The heavy scent of old meat and stale blood rose from the warehouses nearby, clinging to nostrils and the backs of throats.

A score of massive, burly men and women emerged from the nearest abattoir armed with hooks and cleavers, flensing knives and heavy hatchets, carrying crates or stools as makeshift shields. They stepped up next to Mace's men, a trickle of support while the boiling mass of humanity behind forced its way through the gate, squeezing, falling, trampling. Screaming.

Most of the butchers dwarfed most of the soldiers, and Mace found a tired smirk creasing his face as the Mireces hesitated at the sight of them. The timing was perfect.

From above came a volley of arrows, and then another and another. Dalli had unblocked the entrance to North Tower One and got archers on the allure. The Mireces scattered.

'All right, lads, pause here. Give those behind some room,' Mace panted. He knew the dangers of space opening between the line and the fleeing citizenry, knew too the worse danger of crowding already panicked men and women. Too many had died in Yew Cove under the feet of their brothers; Mace didn't intend for the same to happen here.

'They'll be coming,' a Personal Guard muttered next to him. 'They want us alive for some evil purpose, so they'll be coming. Can't afford to let this many escape, arrows or not. There's no getting out, not for us.'

'That's enough, soldier,' Mace said quietly. 'We all know they'll be coming. Don't go scaring your mates now. We have a duty here to protect these people; let's see them safe, eh? And then concentrate on our own way out.'

The Personal grunted, but he dipped his head in acknowledgment and kept further opinions to himself.

'Fall back,' he heard and chanced a glance over his shoulder; the crowd had thinned, even calmed a little, and Mace drew in a breath to order the line to pull back when the Mireces howled out of the darkness again. They'd got shields – some Rank-made, most just bits of scavenged crate – and they threw them up as protection against the volley and piled into the line.

Fucking hundreds of them, hacking madly to split Mace's line from the mass of non-combatants, peel them apart to scoop out the tender flesh of the unarmed, freshly screaming populace.

'Hold!' Mace roared, his voice breaking, his arm slow to counter, feet scuffing on the stone and tripping on the blood channels that ran down the edges of the road as he shuffled backwards. 'Hold.'

But they weren't holding. Not his soldiers, not the butchers or the slaughterhouse men. The assault was all out and overwhelming; whoever was leading these Mireces had pulled in every available body and, once again, they spent their lives like copper knights.

The Personal who'd foretold their deaths went to one knee next to him. When Mace extended his hand to pull the man up, an axe flashed through the air between them; Mace snatched away and the Personal was hacked in the chest plate, knocked on to his back, and dragged away out of the melee. Not dead, dear gods, not yet dead.

'For Rilpor!'

The shout echoed through the slaughter district and Mace recognised the voice as his own. His men stiffened the line, echoing his cry and bringing the Mireces attack to a grinding, shuddering halt, men straining chest to chest, snarling and biting at each other, weapons locked or flailing.

'For Koridam!' Mace heard next and his eyes stung with

tears at the honour they did his father even as he dropped the spear and pulled a knife, better for close quarters, and pumped it into a belly four, five, six times. The man fell and more rushed to take his place and Mace waited to be over-whelmed.

'Mace!' men roared all around him. 'Mace! Mace! Mace!' and the constriction in his throat wound tighter. He half flourished his knife in acknowledgment and then hacked it into a Mireces' neck, wrenched it free and kicked the man over on to his back, hoping to trip the next to face him.

'Front rank! Rotate!' the order came and Mace stepped to his left and then back two paces without thinking about it, the movement instinctive after thousands of hours of drill, a score of battles. Not all of the front rank obeyed, and Mace had time to wonder who'd ordered the rotate when hands grabbed him from behind and pulled him backwards, and that's when he understood.

For the second time in this siege, others were dying so he might live. While half of Mace's front rank obeyed the order, the rest simply moved to the side to allow others to step up next to them in the line.

Mace glanced back, sick with fear and hope, and the gate was almost clear. Close enough. 'Break for the gate,' he yelled, throwing off the restraining hands and putting all he had into the command. 'All ranks, to the gate, *at the fucking double!*'

He turned and pounded ahead of them, men clattering along. They fell in swathes, no longer attempting to delay the enemy, just to outrun them. For a second crystalline with hope, Mace thought they would make it.

And then the Mireces brought them to bay.

'Dancer's grace,' they shouted and Mace saw dozens of his men tap their fingertips to their hearts. He copied the gesture as he slid through the gap, and just before the gate was hauled closed, with his men on the inside, he saw them turn their backs on the Mireces and pair up, Ranker against Ranker, and before the Mireces could disarm them, they drove their blades into each others' chests and throats.

No souls for the Red Gods. No bodies for the Blessed One. Suicide over sacrifice.

And a sacrifice Mace would never forget. A gesture that broke him, as nothing else these long months had managed to do.

There were no words. He joined the others in piling barrels and rubbish and unstepped masts against the gate, and then they fled for the harbour, the ships, and the dubious safety of the river.

It was standing room only on the ships. Five men and women could stand in the space occupied by one prone casualty. If they couldn't stand and no one was able to hold them up, they were left on the dock with empty prayers ringing hollow in their ears.

Their faces would haunt him until he died.

We've lost the last dregs of our humanity. We've reached the level of the Mireces themselves, as savage as our enemies, as uncaring of our fallen as those we sought to defeat. We're monsters, every one of us.

The sun was lightening the sky and Mace stood at the stern of the rearmost ship and watched the black and orange and rubble of Rilporin fade with distance. His arm was wrapped tight around Dalli, and the short Wolf's hands were hastily bandaged; she'd burnt them raw sliding down a rope from the northern wall in the last seconds before the Mireces cleared the gate and charged towards the dock and the departing ships.

The early sun blushed the eastern tower pink and turned the river into a ribbon of molten gold leading to safety.

Somewhere on deck, quietly at first but with slow-growing vigour, someone began to sing. Cracked and broken over the weeping and the weary creak of oars the voices rose until the song jumped from ship to ship and Mace's heart was lifted, heavy and broken though it was, borne up on a shivering, delicate hope and a flickering ember of promise. *Retribution,* it breathed. *Vengeance.*

'It shouldn't be this way,' Dalli whispered.

'But it is,' he murmured, 'at least for now. But the next time I see that city, it'll be over the corpses of our enemies. This isn't over. Not by a long way.'

He stared at the city. 'I swear it.'

The sun rose on a shattered landscape, on the graveyard of all they were, the pyre of all their hopes.

It shouldn't be this way. And yet they sang.

EPILOGUE

TARA

Fifth moon, first year of the reign of King Corvus
Grand temple square, First Circle, Rilporin, Wheat Lands

The square was filled to capacity – Raiders, Easterners and as many slaves as could fit thronged outside the grand temple. It was a charnel pit now, the Light washed away in sacrificial blood, and Tara couldn't look into its gaping, stinking maw. She followed Valan – her master, her *owner* these last ten days – through the crowd and then paused at the edge as he moved to stand beside Corvus and the Blessed One.

'Rilporin is ours,' Corvus suddenly shouted, and the crowd fell into rapturous silence. 'Ours, though it has cost us more than we ever knew to pay. And though we all grieve, there is much still to do. Know now that all is not lost. While many of our enemies fled to Listre, the bulk of this city's inhabitants and its defenders now belong to us, prevented from fleeing through the King Gate like the cowards they are by our brave allies in the East Rank. They will serve us as slaves and consorts until our own can be brought down from the mountains. The rewards of holy war.'

Tara glanced around; either Corvus's calculations were wildly inaccurate or he couldn't count. From what she could see, only about a third of Rilporin's citizens remained, though the captured Rankers weren't present. She hadn't seen them once since Valan had bought her, had no idea where they were being held. She was unwilling to risk taking out Corvus and Lanta until she knew whether or not she could free them.

Soon, she promised them in the silence of her skull. *Trust me and stay alive. I'm coming.*

The Blessed One held up her arms. 'Our next steps are decided. The East Rank will be sent to the main towns and cities of Rilpor to bring them under our control. Their first act will be to secure a tithe of food and goods suitable to our status as their overlords.'

Tara grunted in reluctant agreement, the sound lost among the rustle of approval. Sending Rankers was less contentious than a band of ravening Mireces descending on the towns. The Rankers would initiate martial law and enforce it ruthlessly, but without unnecessary bloodshed.

'The rest of us will remain in Rilporin, to see it restored and its walls rebuilt against the threat of further assault. And we of the true faith, who have walked the Dark Path in gladness and in glory all our lives, have another task: to practise the blood magic of faith and search for our Bloody Mother.'

What?

Lanta indicated the stains on her arms and face, the black swirls that, if the rumours were true, were the Dark Lady's very blood decorating her flesh. 'My faith told me to do this, my connection to the gods and Their realm, my understanding of Their needs all guided me. I am guided still. I have not moved from this square and newly dedicated temple since I begged our Red Father to come for vengeance. Even when He stalked this damned place I did not move. I have lain here and I have searched – my soul, the world, the veil and past it, the Waystation. I have been to the limits of the Afterworld itself,' she said and there was a ripple of awe.

'And do you know what I have learnt?' Lanta suddenly screeched. 'Our Bloody Mother is not gone. Not forever.'

Tara gaped. *Not gone? What the fuck do you mean, not gone?*

'I can bring Her back.'

For one long, clanging second, the square was silent, awestruck, and then it erupted, a seething mass of joy and denial.

Tara stood immobile against the jostling of the mob. *Is this what you really sent me here for, Fox God? Killing a king and a lunatic priestess I can handle. Preventing the goddess of death from returning may be outside my skill set.*

A manic giggle threatened and she swallowed it down as Lanta gestured the audience was over and Valan pulled at her arm, led her back through the jubilant and despairing crowd to the house he'd taken for his own.

Tara's fingers were clumsy as she unbuckled his sword belt and vambraces, pulled his chainmail over his head and laid it on a table.

'Softly done,' he said. 'You dressed your husband for battle?'

Tara blinked, belatedly remembered her cover story. 'Many times, honoured, so that he would remember me when he fought.' She paused. 'Honoured, how can the Blessed One bring back your goddess? How is such a thing possible?'

Valan swilled wine around his mouth and then sat at the window, and she thought he wasn't going to answer. He rarely did.

'We need the king's sister,' he said eventually and Tara's head snapped up. She stared at his profile, unblinking. 'Corvus's sister Rillirin is pregnant. The Blessed One believes the child will be the vessel that returns the Dark Lady to us, divine essence clothed in mortal flesh. And so we will bring her here, and the Blessed One will do what is necessary to restore our goddess to us.'

Not if I can slaughter the bitch first, she won't.

'Rillirin,' Tara managed. 'That's a pretty name. I expect she will be glad to see her brother again.'

Valan grunted and drank more wine. 'Somehow, I doubt that.'

ACKNOWLEDGMENTS

Writing *Darksoul* has been a bigger challenge than I expected. Coming off the high of *Godblind* being published and excited for the awesomeness that awaits in Book 3, I found I wasn't entirely sure how to make *Darksoul* a worthy middle book with a story of its own.

So huge thanks go to Harry Illingworth, my superstar agent, and Natasha Bardon, my UK editor extraordinaire, for taking the rambling, incoherent mess that was the early version of *Darksoul*, and helping me turn it into something of which I'm very proud. I learnt a hell of a lot and I think between us we've done a fantastic job. I hope you agree.

Thanks also to Jack Renninson and Jaime Frost at Harper Voyager for generally putting up with my nonsense, to Dom Forbes for another epic cover and Richenda Todd for excellent copy editing (merlons not crenels; you learn something every day), Cameron McClure at Donald Maass, everyone at Louisa Pritchard Associates and the Marsh Agency, and of course to my foreign publishers – Skyhorse in the US, Bragelonne in France, Blanvalet in Germany, Luitingh-Sijthoff in the Netherlands, DOBROVSKY Publishing in the Czech

Republic and Papierowy Ksiezyc/Caput Mundi Books in Poland.

Eternal thanks as ever go to my supportive and very proud family, close and extended, for alternately holding my hand and clipping me around the ear to get *Darksoul* over the finish line. I was a bit of a mess for parts of this, so I'm grateful that you put up with me and cheered me on.

To Mark, the best husband, friend and partner in crime I could wish for, your endless support means more than you know. You were epically patient while listening to my many rants, tantrums, sulks and meltdowns, and somehow always managed to make me laugh and realise that, as difficult as some of this process has been, it's still my dream job. Thanks for keeping me focused and for coming to so many events and conventions with me. Having you there made it more special and less terrifying.

My first year as a published author has been a sensory overload in many ways, but lots of people have stood out as beacons of . . . I was going to say sanity, but that's clearly not the case, so let me just thank them.

My fellow 2017 debutantes, for wearing the same delighted but bewildered expression I spent most of last year wearing and for the breathless, excited conversations about reviews, books sales and conventions.

The Fantasy Five – Mike Evans, Kareem Mahfouz, Laura Hughes, JP Ashman and Sadir Samir. You lot took a very nervous young author and made her incredibly welcome, and have been a brilliant champion of *Godblind* ever since, so thank you. Bang-average!

Mike actually gets a second mention here, for dropping everything to beta-read the second-to-last version of *Darksoul* and offer invaluable advice when I was contemplating a nervous breakdown. I have no idea how he juggled that along with his job, his family and planning his wedding. Something superhuman was going on. Thanks, Sarge.

As ever, the lovelies that are Jen Williams, Edward Cox, Mark de Jager and Stuart Turton for support and chats and beers – all fabulous authors, all with books worth buying.

And to everyone who read *Godblind* and enjoyed it, who took the time to review or recommend it, thank you. It means more than you could know. I hope *Darksoul* lives up to your expectations.